ALSO BY CAROLINE BISHOP

The Lost Chapter

CAROLINE BISHOP

The Other Daughter

PUBLISHED BY SIMON & SCHUSTER
New York   London   Toronto   Sydney   New Delhi

**SIMON &
SCHUSTER
CANADA**

Simon & Schuster Canada
A Division of Simon & Schuster, Inc.
166 King Street East, Suite 300
Toronto, Ontario M5A 1J3

Permission to quote excerpt from *Superwoman* by Shirley Conran, published 1975, granted by the author.
Permission to quote excerpt on p. 125 granted by Cressrelles.
Permission to use *Daily Mirror* article on p. 285 granted by Mirrorpix.

This Simon & Schuster Canada edition January 2023

For information about special discounts for bulk purchases, please contact Simon & Schuster Special Sales at 1-800-268-3216 or CustomerService@simonandschuster.ca.

Library and Archives Canada Cataloguing in Publication

Title: The other daughter / Caroline Bishop.
Names: Bishop, Caroline H. (Helen), author.
Description: Simon & Schuster Canada edition.
Identifiers: Canadiana (print) 20220249253 | Canadiana (ebook) 2022024930X | ISBN 9781982196936 (softcover) | ISBN 9781982196943 (ebook)
Classification: LCC PR6102.I84 O84 2023 | DDC 823/.92—dc23

Manufactured in the United States of America

10 9 8 7 6 5 4 3 2

ISBN 978-1-9821-9693-6
ISBN 978-1-9821-9694-3 (ebook)

For my family

The Other Daughter

OCTOBER 2014

London, UK

I became a different person only because I walked around a corner I hadn't intended to.

Until that moment, I hadn't ever considered doing what we did that day, and neither had Dad. It was a spontaneous decision, a spur-of-the-moment thing, simply because the van happened to be parked there, around the corner next to the card shop.

'I forgot – I told Patrick I'd pick up a birthday card for his nephew.' I tugged Dad's arm away from the entrance to the tube, just steps from the museum where we'd spent the afternoon. 'I think there's a place nearby. I'll only be a minute.'

He frowned. A fine drizzle was settling on his glasses. My feet burned from inching past Aztec artefacts, the cafe's cake selection hadn't been up to scratch; we were definitely done for the day, but the shop wasn't far. Two minutes, grab something colourful with a number five on it, then back to the tube. Dad would get the train to Chichester, I'd go home to Peckham, and we'd both get through another Saturday night, another twenty-four hours in this strange new life without Mum.

Dad rolled his eyes. 'Go on then, Jessie, be quick.'

Countless times I've wondered if I would have ever found out if not for turning the corner that day. If I'd bought a card somewhere else, the day before, like I'd said I would. If Patrick had been more organised and done it himself. If the van hadn't been on that particular street on that particular day.

It's perfectly likely I'd have gone my whole life never knowing.

Maybe Patrick and I would still be married. Maybe I'd be head of department at St Mary's Comprehensive. Maybe we'd have a baby on the way. There'd still be that hole in my life, yes. But it would be *my* life, at least. My life.

Instead we took a left turn and saw the van. And that's the moment, right there. That's the moment I became someone else.

PART ONE

You may agree with women's lib
But what would be your view
If you came home to your liberated wife
And she gave you the washing to do?
Would you change places with your wife
And do her daily chores?
She has to do them all her life
Cleaning windows, clothes and floors.
'A man works harder than his mate'
Oh surely that's not true!
Each works in their appointed way
With certain things to do.
So let us say each works as hard
As he or she is able
One earns the money to pay for the food
The other sets the table.

A Man's Nightmare, by J. L. Hale of Haydock,
Merseyside, printed in the *Liverpool Echo*, 1976

FEBRUARY 1976

London, UK

Sylvia

'Feminism,' Roger said, each syllable thick with scepticism. 'Been done to death, hasn't it?'

Sylvia had been prepared for the snort of derision from Clive, the amused smiles from the other men around the room, Valerie's unfathomable gaze. But she'd also been prepared to stand her ground. She would not be cowed on this one; she would look her commissioning editor in the eye until he gave her a good enough reason to turn her story down. If only she didn't feel so damn nauseous. She really didn't have the stomach for a fight today.

'Hardly,' she said. 'And certainly very little about Switzerland. They're barely getting started with sexual equality. I mean, it's only five years since women got the vote at national level. They were the last democratic country in the Western world to get there.'

'Liechtenstein,' Clive said.

'Excuse me?'

'Liechtenstein still doesn't have women's suffrage. So Switzerland wasn't the last country in the Western world.'

'That's a tiny principality, it's hardly the same thing.'

She saw Clive mutter something to Ellis and they both laughed. She turned her gaze back to Roger. The less she looked at Clive's overstuffed face, the better.

Roger lit another cigarette and took a long drag. His shirt was crumpled, tie askew. Broken capillaries sprawled over his nose. In front of him on his desk, his usual mug – its British Press Awards logo fading and chipped after too many washes – was releasing pungent wafts of coffee mixed with whisky, only exacerbating Sylvia's queasiness.

'You've found someone to interview?' he asked.

Sylvia looked down at her notes. 'Yes, a woman named Evelyne Buchs. She's part of a campaign group out in Lausanne, in the French-speaking part. They're very active. She's already agreed to talk to me.' She'd come across the woman's name when she was scouring the paper's cuttings library for a spark of an idea, something to finally make Roger give her a damn break. Tucked away in the World News section of an edition from the previous summer had been a small article about an event in Geneva for International Women's Year 1975, and Sylvia's attention had been caught by the passionate words of one of the attendees, a young radical Swiss feminist called Evelyne Buchs.

Roger blew a long plume of smoke up to the ceiling where it joined the cloud that was a permanent fixture in this room. He shook his head. 'I don't know, Tallis. There could be a decent story in it, but I'm not sure the budget will stretch to sending you out there.'

She swallowed down a knee-jerk reaction. *Was he joking?* It was common knowledge that the paper wasn't short of a bob or two. Max had only recently come back from the Winter Olympics in Innsbruck. Marnie had spent a week in Italy last October following around Elio Fiorucci for a profile piece in the fashion pages, coming back with a new calf's skin handbag and a tan. And she knew the rumours about how much they'd offered veteran war reporter Ellis to poach him from Reuters last year. They could damn well afford a return flight to Switzerland and some meagre expenses.

'I think it's a good idea,' Max said. Her head flicked in his direction and he gave her an encouraging smile, though she caught a hint of mischief in his eyes as he continued. 'You know, comparing the situation of Swiss women with what's happened over here in recent years. Are British women really better off with this whole *liberation* thing?'

'That wasn't exactly the angle I was going for,' she said, careful to keep her voice even. 'I want to explore why Swiss women still haven't achieved the same legal rights as us on abortion, on maternity leave, on discrimination and equal pay, why their society is holding back and what they're doing to change it.' If she could only stop the waves of sickness washing over her, she'd be arguing this a lot better.

'But isn't this all a bit . . . *political* for the women's pages?' Clive waved his hand in the air as if brushing it all away. Sylvia saw, with some satisfaction, that his jowls wobbled as he did so. 'I mean, sex tips and clothes and . . . *menstruation*,' he almost whispered the word, 'that's what our female readers want to hear about, not all this vulgar bra-waving. We're not the bloody *Guardian*.'

'How do you know what women want, Clive, have you grown breasts?' Valerie said, and the room descended into titters. Sylvia threw her a grateful glance, but the columnist didn't return it. She knew better than to presume anything Valerie said came from a place of female solidarity – any support she offered was likely only a by-product of self-interest. 'However, much as I fail to agree with my esteemed colleague,' Valerie continued, her eyebrows firing disdain at Clive, 'I do think Sylvia's such a little whizz with her regulars and so marvellous at helping the whole team that I'm not sure we can spare her for a foreign trip.'

Little whizz? 'I can handle this on top, no problem.' She kept her eyes on Roger, willing him to listen to her. She could see him wavering. He knew it was a good idea. He *knew* it.

'I'll think about it,' he said.

'But—'

Roger held up his hand. 'I said I'll think about it. Now,

Max, did you get anything juicy out of that gay ice dancer in Innsbruck?'

The sickness dogged her all day. It made her head spin when she stood up from her desk. It sat in a dull ache in her stomach as she walked down Fleet Street, the air thick with the metallic tang of exhaust fumes. It made her legs shake as she negotiated the raised walkways of the Barbican, her heels echoing off the concrete walls. She wished she could go back to last night and refuse Jim's suggestion that they try that new restaurant in Clapham Junction. It occurred to her now that she was likely to see that prawn cocktail again.

'Tea, dear? You look like you need it,' Marjorie said.

Sylvia accepted and sunk into the dusty pink velvet of the armchair. The window from the fifth-floor flat looked out over the site where the Barbican Arts Centre was due to emerge, years late and over budget, if the construction workers, so keen on striking, ever finished the job. Ellis was writing a longform piece about that right now – the sort of meaty news feature she could only dream of. Of course, she had done much of the legwork – interviewing contractors, researching background material – but she wouldn't get a joint byline, not with the famous Ellis Barker, who wouldn't deign to share the glory with an underling like her.

'Marjorie makes the best cuppa.' Victor had crepe-paper skin and oversized ears, but the eyes he fixed on her were surely as bright as they had been half a century ago.

'Here you go, dear.' Marjorie handed her an elegant china

mug with a portrait of the Queen on it and sat down on the sofa next to her husband. Sylvia flipped open her notepad, fished a pen out of her bag and smiled at the two of them. Fifty years together and they looked like they were made that way. Like owners and their dogs, she thought, an unwelcome image of Jim's mother and her Jack Russell popping into her mind; after a while, they begin to resemble each other.

'So, how did you two meet?'

After so many months of writing the 'golden oldies' weekly feature, she had a good idea how the conversation would go. She knew what kept couples together for half a century – not blind devotion, not butterflies in the stomach, but compromise, patience, humour and a stoic tolerance of even the most unlovable of little habits – but something always cropped up that surprised her. There'd been the couple who'd recreated their first date on the same day every year for the past fifty; the man who said he once joked he'd only marry a left-handed woman – and then met his left-handed wife-to-be the very next day; and the 89-year-old who told her the key to not arguing was to stuff your mouth with marshmallows so you physically couldn't speak. Sylvia had already decided to present Jim with a bag of marshmallows on their wedding day, just to kick things off in the right direction.

However, although she didn't dislike writing the feature, it wasn't exactly why she became a journalist. It wasn't why she'd suffered through tutorials with Dirty Dan, Oxford's lecherous lecturer, or why she'd turned a blind eye to her student paper's 'prettiest undergraduate' competitions so that the editor, a belligerent third year from Eton, wouldn't refuse to publish her work.

Give it time, she'd told herself, when she started interviewing the wrinklies. *Give it more time*, Jim had said a few months down the line, when the political magazine he worked for gave him his first cover feature and she was still drinking tea with Marjories. *Fucking bad luck*, Max said when her feature ideas got rebuffed by Roger again and again.

After more than eighteen months in her role as junior features writer, Roger was yet to commission a story she'd pitched. It might have begun to make her think she wasn't good enough. But she had a first from Oxford and a portfolio of student writing that had won her a place on a graduate trainee scheme with a female acceptance rate of just 5 per cent. No, she knew she was good enough. The problem was something else – and she knew exactly what.

'You've been hired primarily to write *women's interest* stories, Tallis,' Roger had said after a few months, when she enquired, as politely as possible, why he always rejected her ideas. 'Any other junior would give their right arm to cover Ladies' Day at Ascot or the Chelsea ruddy Flower Show, but you're always pushing for something else. Don't be so bloody *serious*.'

Sylvia thought he'd missed the point on purpose. She didn't have a problem writing for the women's pages, but it was archaic to assume this meant covering only fashion, flowers and celebrities. She admired Valerie for having moved the conversation on in her decade-long tenure as

11

the so-called 'Queen' of the paper, writing in her witty, biting way about once-taboo subjects including infidelity, sexual satisfaction and domestic sluttery. But Sylvia didn't want to write about any of that, either. She wanted to write about the big political and social issues that impacted women's lives. Issues she, as a woman, was interested in. With her Switzerland idea she'd thought she had a good chance – yes it was *serious*, but what could be more female-focused than a feature about women's rights? And yet still it didn't look like Roger was going to budge. Well, neither would she – she wasn't going to stop pitching features that actually mattered.

'When's your own big day, dear?' Marjorie asked when the interview came to an end, nodding to Sylvia's hand.

'Oh, next year some time.' Sylvia twisted her ring around her finger. 'We haven't fixed a date yet.' She'd be happy with a registry office and a Marks & Spencer dress, but Jim wouldn't hear of it. *You only get married once; it's got to be a big bash.* At least that meant he'd help organise the silly thing.

'Well, we wish you all the luck in the world,' Marjorie said. She patted Victor's knee. 'You're going to need it.'

'Thank you,' she smiled. 'Can I use your bathroom before I go?'

The toilet lid had an avocado-green shagpile cover; the loo roll was hidden under the voluminous skirt of a plastic doll. Sylvia peed, wiped, stood up. The smell of air freshener was cloying. She washed her hands and steadied herself against the sink as another wave of nausea hit her, sweat beading on her forehead. *Oh God, no.* She lifted the toilet lid again and promptly threw up.

It had to be last night's prawns. She hurried back to the office, stopping only in the chemist to get some paracetamol. It took her a few minutes to find the right section. Shampoos. Deodorants. Sanitary products. Her mind paused, discarding a thought as lightly as it landed in her head.

'Roger wants to see you,' Max said, when she got back to her desk. His eyes were bloodshot after what she imagined was the usual three-hour lunch break in the pub. *Just a few sharpeners,* he always said. The sort of social boozing that worked tongues loose, ensuring stories were told, career-enhancing friendships were made and gossip was shared.

She knocked on the door of Roger's glass-walled office and he beckoned her in.

'Tallis. You look peaky.'

'I'm fine.' His office was airless. With no windows and the heating ramped up to combat the February chill, the air felt stagnant and smelt stale, a bilious blend of body odour, fags and vegetable soup that made her want to run to the toilet again. The same thought she'd had in the chemist popped into her head again, more vocal this time, insisting its presence, like Max with a shorthand notebook and a sensational headline ready to go.

Roger gestured to the chair in front of his desk. It was just about the only surface not covered with paper. It spilled out of box files stacked in dense rows along the floor-to-ceiling shelves behind his desk, it lay in piles on the industrial-grey carpet, ostensibly propping up the glass walls, and it smothered his desk: rival papers, opened envelopes, an overflowing in-tray of letters and board-meeting minutes neatly typed by Janice. She wondered if he ever read them.

'I've thought about it,' he said.

'I'm sorry?' Her head was full of Marjorie and weddings and avocado-green toilet lid covers and how many days it had been since—

'Your pitch. Five years on from women's suffrage in Switzerland.'

Her head cleared and she focused fully on her commissioning editor.

'June, you said the first vote was?' he continued.

'Yes. They were granted suffrage in February 1971, and first voted in a referendum in June.' She picked her fingernails behind her back. Was he going to . . . ?

'I know you want this, Tallis. And I know you've paid your dues around here. So I'm commissioning you. Go off to Switzerland and bring me back a damn good piece, okay? We'll run it before June.'

Sylvia couldn't help her eyebrows from shooting up. '*Really?*' Her head felt woozy, but she wasn't sure if it was the shock or the nausea. 'Thank you, thank you so much,' she managed.

'When can you get out there?'

She mentally ran through her diary and discarded

anything she found. 'Next week? There's a rally in Bern I'd like to go to on 6th March.'

A smile twitched at his mouth. 'Good. Ask Janice to book you a flight to Geneva. Expense the hotel. And make sure you get all your regulars done before you go. Oh, and I'm not throwing in a photographer so borrow the office camera and get some shots yourself, okay?'

'Right, yes. Absolutely.'

'And Tallis?'

'Yes?'

'Take a decent coat. Bloody freezing country.'

JUNE 2016

Montreux, Switzerland

JESS

I smooth down the wrinkles on my shirt and run my fingers through my tangled hair. The back of my neck is slick with sweat. It's probably only 25 degrees, but the sun feels even stronger after the grey, humid day I left behind in London. It's just a few hours since I was there, but already it's as though I've stepped into another life. Back home, right now, commuters are dodging puddles whilst running for the tube, heading home on a crammed Northern Line train that smells of cheap burgers and wet dog and armpits. But after only a short plane journey, an hour's train ride and a ridiculously expensive taxi up a steep hill from the station, I'm standing on a doorstop in Montreux in the blazing sun, looking out over a vast lake fringed by hazy mountains and dotted with sailboats, as if the tube and puddles don't exist at all.

I watch the taxi drive off down the hill and rummage in my handbag for a pocket mirror. I dust off the crumbs and give it a rub until I can see a square of my face in it. Dark smudges under my eyes. A spot brewing on my chin. Nose red from the heat. I look older, wearier, than I did when I picked up this little carved mirror from a Thai market stall on my honeymoon five years ago. Hardly surprising. I lick my finger and rub the mascara from under my eyes. There's little else I can do about my appearance right now. I ring the doorbell.

'You made it! *Bienvenue.* Welcome, Jessica.' The woman sticks out her hand. 'I'm Julia.' I see glossy dark hair and olive skin. She's wearing a vivid pink cardigan – *in this heat?* – over a cream camisole, with black cropped trousers. I smell her perfume when I step forward to shake her hand, my sticky palms meeting her cool skin. 'We're so pleased to have you here.' Her accent is lyrical, singsong, and makes me smile back.

'I'm glad to be here,' I say. 'Please call me Jess.'

I wheel my suitcase along the tiled floor of a corridor and into the main room, a large open-plan kitchen-living-room that's probably bigger than my entire flat in Peckham. I take in two plush, cream sofas, a capacious Bosch fridge with one of those ice-maker thingies I've always coveted, and a painting on the wall that's the sort of abstract stuff Patrick likes to mock: two swirls of red and a blue dot. Bet it cost a fortune. To the right, sliding glass doors lead out onto a terrace with a table and chairs beneath the shade of a tree. Beyond, I can see houses dotting the slope for half a mile down to the lakeshore, where a ferry is just sliding into port, a white V dissolving in the water behind it. On the far side of the lake, mountaintops are etched against the sky.

I've never even owned a place with a garden, let alone a view like this.

In Peckham, the bedroom looks out over a patchwork quilt of small gardens belonging to the neighbours, while the living room faces the road and the row of Georgian houses the other side, unaffected by the Second World War bombs that took out our side of the street, later replaced with solid but uninspiring apartment blocks.

'Better to live in the ugly house rather than have to look at it,' Patrick had said when he'd convinced me that third-floor flat should become our first home together. I wonder if my tenant now thinks the same. I wonder if Patrick's found himself a nicer place.

I take a step forward, drawn to the scene. 'Wow. That's amazing.'

Julia laughs. 'Go out if you want to.'

I step through the door onto the terrace and Julia joins me. We stand there for a moment, both gazing at the view. Down below, the sun glints off the water and I hear a bass rhythm coming from a tourist ferry – some kind of party boat, perhaps. I can't think of anything to say and it strikes me that this is like an awkward first date. Something about her poise, the confidence oozing from her, makes me feel I'm likely to say the wrong thing.

'Is this your first time in Switzerland?' she asks, and I feel relief that the silence is broken.

I nod. 'Is all of it this pretty?'

She laughs. 'Yes, I suppose it is.' She proffers a packet of cigarettes and I notice her nails are beautifully manicured. 'Do you smoke?'

I smile and take one in answer. I think how disapproving Patrick was about it, and how I actually managed to give up for a time, back when we were *trying* – that awful word. But in the last few months I've needed it more than ever.

'We only smoke out here. And I'd prefer you not to do it when the kids are around, okay?'

I nod again. 'I want to give up anyway.'

Julia smiles. 'Don't we all?' She slides into one of the wooden chairs and invites me to do the same. 'You'll meet Léa and Luca soon. Michel has taken them to the zoo, but they should be back in about half an hour.' She looks at her watch. 'And you'll have tomorrow to settle in – I'm not expecting you to start immediately. But from Monday we will both be at work so they're all yours.' She inhales on her cigarette and I notice, with an unexpected sense of satisfaction, tiny lines appear around her mouth.

'I've prepared rough lesson plans,' I say. 'But of course I'll adapt to what you want us to do and what suits them best.'

Julia waves the smoke away from our faces. 'The main thing is to get them speaking more. I want them to go back to school in the fall with a higher level of English than they have now. How you achieve that is up to you.'

19

'Right. I'll do my best.'

'You don't have to do formal lessons. You will have a budget and you can take them out, explore, do things. There's a lot nearby for kids. I've put some tourist brochures in your room. And of course you don't know the area, so it's a chance for you to get to know it too and have fun. It's summer, *n'est-ce pas?*'

Excitement flickers inside me, a long-dormant feeling unfurling like a leaf in spring. I think how reluctant I was when Maggie first touted the idea of me doing this. My god-mother was usually right about most things, but I had serious doubts about this particular suggestion. Did I really want to take a job looking after someone else's children? It felt like rubbing my face in it. But I was a teacher, I already spent my life around kids, so surely I could cope with a couple more? And I needed to do something with my semi-enforced sab-batical from St Mary's instead of sitting in Maggie's garden drinking endless cups of tea. Plus, the money was good.

But, really, it wasn't any of that. It was Switzerland. The place I'd imagined in my head for the past two years, ever since those tests threw up so many questions; the place I now felt compelled to be, in the hope that it might provide me with some answers.

'I'm still not sure why you need me, though,' I say. 'I mean, your English seems fantastic.'

'Thank you,' Julia says, and I can tell she's pleased. 'But we're not native English speakers and we don't speak it at home. The kids learn it at school, but I thought employing a native teacher over the summer holidays would give them the . . .'

'Upper hand?'

'Exactly. We want them to get a good start in life. English is so important.'

I think of my basic French, which never got past '*Où est la gare*' and '*Je voudrais un café s'il vous plaît*'.

A tune echoes in the back of my mind: Mum, at her laptop, humming a French song to herself, and I feel the familiar ache.

A key turns in the lock and I hear a gabble of voices in French chatter their way down the corridor and into the living room.

'*Elle est arrivée, elle est arrivée!*' The girl is a miniature version of her mother. Dark hair in a long plait down her back. Deep brown eyes. Skinny. Picture-pretty.

'*En anglais*,' Julia says.

'Hello,' the girl says to me. 'My name is Léa.' I say hello back and suppress the thought that always comes to me when I meet someone else's kids: if I'd had a daughter, would she have looked like me?

'And this is our son, Luca.' Julia nods to a little boy who comes up to stand shyly behind Léa.

'How do you do, Luca?' I say, and he giggles and turns away from me, burrowing his face into the legs of a tall man who enters the room after the children. They exchange a few words in French before the man steps round his son and onto the terrace to shake my hand. 'Don't worry about him, he's always shy with new people. I'm Michel. *Bienvenue*. Good to meet you.'

'And you.' He looks a bit older than Julia and yet he has the same poised, unflustered demeanour. Quite a feat after spending a day at the zoo with two under sevens.

'I'm glad you made it. Was the flight okay? I heard there were some delays on the trains today.'

'Fine, thanks. I didn't have any problems. Doesn't transport here always run on time?'

'That's a myth,' Michel says. He bends down to kiss Julia, putting his left hand on her shoulder. She reaches up and squeezes his hand and I see their wedding rings – matching gold bands. My ring finger got so used to being occupied that sometimes I think I'm still wearing it, the way amputees get phantom pains after they no longer have the limb.

'How would you know, you never take the train! He drives to work, while *I* get the train.' Julia rolls her eyes. 'But it's true, they are late sometimes.'

Their ease with each other is so familiar. That was Patrick and me, once, before everything.

'Shall we open a bottle?' Julia flashes Michel a smile. He nods, then squeezes himself through the kids who are still staring at me from the terrace doors.

'You like animals?' Léa asks in precise but heavily accented English.

'Very much.'

Léa claps her hands. 'We go to the zoo again with you?'

I look at Julia and she nods. 'Absolutely,' I say. 'You can show me your favourite animals.'

'What's your favourite animal, Léa?' Julia says.

'*Les éléphants.*'

'Ah, me too,' I say, and she beams back.

'*Éléphant, éléphant,*' she chants as she runs away from us into the living room, Luca chasing after her.

'They are a bit excited today,' Julia says. 'First day of the holidays. Eight weeks off. They will calm down.'

'No problem.' I think of Nicky in Year 9 at St Mary's who set fire to the boys' toilets on the final day of term before Easter. 'They seem great.'

Michel returns to the terrace with a bottle and three glasses. 'To welcome you.' He smiles. 'This is local. A Chasselas from Lavaux, just over there.' He pours the wine with one hand and gestures to our right with the other. In the distance I see vines strung in orderly terraces along the hillside.

I didn't know Switzerland had vineyards.

Excitement flickers again, sputtering into life like a creaky old banger. Not for the wine, but for the prospect of discovering so many more things I didn't know about this place. I have eight weeks to do things that are new. Eight weeks away from the flat that held me prisoner with memories, away from the job that failed to distract me from myself, away from the hollowness of so many endings.

Maggie *was* right about this. I need to be here. I need a temporary respite from everything back home in a brand-new country – and of course it had to be *this* country.

23

FEBRUARY 1976

London, UK

Sylvia

After a reluctant Saturday afternoon in the office, Sylvia squeezed herself onto a packed tube carriage. Over the shoulder of a fellow passenger, so close she could see dandruff speckling his dark coat, her eye caught a story on the front page of *The Times*:

STARS LINE UP FOR LAST NIGHT AT OLD VIC

After nearly 13 years, the National Theatre Company takes its final bow at the Old Vic tonight in view of its move to . . .

The doors opened at Embankment and Sylvia was propelled out of the tube and up into the cold, early evening air. She took the steps up to Hungerford Bridge and there it was on the other side: the Denys Lasdun building, which was to be Maggie's new workplace, its Brutalist towers an unapologetic presence on the South Bank. She walked across the bridge, down Waterloo Road and into The Cut, breathing in the buzz of a city supercharged by Saturday night fever.

London always filled her with such excitement. It was a living, breathing, capricious thing, with all the unpredictability of an errant teen, and she adored the sense of possibility it offered. It flooded her body like a drug, one she'd badly needed after growing up in the Home Counties, where the only possibilities were a Saturday job as a waitress in a cafe followed by a warm white wine in the George & Dragon, thanks to a landlord who turned a blind eye to minors.

But tonight her excitement about her new commission and her best friend's final show as an usher at the Old Vic was dampened by her still-lurching stomach and a nagging voice in her head telling her: *this isn't food poisoning, and you know it.*

The foyer of the Old Vic was packed. Smoke curled up to the ceiling, enveloping the chandelier in a haze, and the room hummed with an energy born of the collective antici-pation of hundreds of people. As she weaved her way through the crowd, she was impressed to spot the great actress Sybil Thorndike, still turning heads at ninety-three, while the Chancellor, Denis Healey, stood at the bar talking to another besuited man Sylvia didn't recognise. She caught Jim's eye and waved, and the news was out of her almost as soon as she'd reached him.

'Switzerland?' Jim leant forward as though he hadn't heard her properly.

'Isn't it exciting?'

'It's bloody brilliant, Syl. Roger finally caved to your genius. But what are you writing about, the origins of fondue?'

She slapped him lightly on the arm and smiled. 'As if.' She took a drag on her cigarette and blew it out slowly, savouring the moment of revelation. 'Women's rights, five years on from national suffrage.'

It wasn't often she rendered Jim speechless. She put her head back and blew out smoke to the ceiling. 'Your face is a picture.'

He laughed. 'I never thought Roger would go for that. Well done, Syl, I'm impressed.' He held out his glass. 'To my fabulous fiancée.'

She clinked her gin and tonic against his. 'Thanks, Jim.' She knew he meant it.

Thank God Jim wasn't one of those men who thought his wife's place was firmly in the kitchen. Sylvia didn't know how her friend Gilly put up with that. Nor Polly, Oxford-educated but treated like a fashion accessory by Alan, who only seemed proud of her if she wore designer clothes and kept herself in full make-up at all times. Each to their own, Sylvia supposed. She was pretty certain her friends were happy with their husbands, but she never would have chosen such a man herself.

Jim – wonderful Jim – had supported her career ambitions right from those early days working together on the student paper. Of course, back then it was partly because he wanted to get into her knickers. Most of the men she met at Oxford had seemed to want that; not, she knew, because she was any more attractive than anyone else, but simply because men far outnumbered women and they would take whatever they could get. That was surely why, in her first week at St Hilda's, they'd been subjected to a lecture by the college chaplain about *showing restraint.*

She'd wondered at the time if the male freshers had received the same advice.

But unlike the other boys, Jim hadn't felt the need to bring her down a peg or two simply because she was a woman with the cheek to show ambition. He'd liked her. He'd liked her writing. And it was both of those facts that eventually enabled him to get into her knickers.

She recalled lying in his college bed on a Sunday morning, breath visible in the frigid air, plotting their futures in parallel: they'd both move to London, apply for internships, trainee schemes and junior reporter positions, work hard, get promoted. Everything they wanted was in sync until the issue of children came up. So many heated conversations hashed out under the covers, or picnicking in Christ Church Meadow, or drinking in the Eagle and Child, as she gradually brought broody Jim round to her way of thinking. They'd have children, but only when she was ready: when her career was at a suitable point, when they could afford childcare so she could go back to work. Because she knew, with utter certainty, that if she had a baby too early, her much dreamed about career would diverge from that twin track and go down a different path entirely.

A flash of colour and a familiar hairstyle brought Sylvia out of her thoughts. She stuck out her hand and grabbed Maggie's arm, pulling her towards them. 'There you are!'

'You made it!' Maggie kissed them both and clapped her hands.

'Wouldn't have missed it for the world. You okay? Not too emotional?' Sylvia could practically see her flatmate's nervous energy emanating off her. She seemed heightened somehow, as did everything in the room – the laughter shriller than normal, the colours more vivid, the clothes extra glamorous for this special gala performance.

'A bit. But just wait 'til curtain down and I'll be bawling.'

'I'm sure everyone will. It's the end of an era.'

'And the start of something,' Jim said.

Maggie's eyes shone, and pride rushed through Sylvia. Years of ushering and studying part time at St Martin's and it was all about to pay off. One last show here, and then later in the year, Maggie would be starting the job she'd wanted for so long. Her future was finally on track; a messy, creative, fulfilling future surrounded by paint pots and fabric and set designs at that new concrete behemoth on the South Bank.

The bell rang loud and shrill. 'I have to go. I'm meant to

be in there.' Maggie jerked her head towards the doors of the auditorium. 'Enjoy. And don't wait up – I'm going to the after-show.'

Sylvia watched her sidle through the throng and then the crowds in the foyer began pushing past her and Jim – *terribly sorry, do excuse me* – shimmying shoulder to shoulder up the stairs, past the ushers tearing tickets and towards the auditorium.

Sylvia knocked back her drink, took a last drag on her cigarette and followed the hordes into the darkened theatre. When the house lights went down and Peggy Ashcroft stepped onto the stage, a trickle of sweat rolled down the back of Sylvia's neck. What had she done? What had she done to her own future?

JUNE 2016

Montreux, Switzerland

JESS

I'm having my doubts already. I'd thought fifteen years of teaching literature to kids who would rather look at their phones than listen to me meant I could handle any child just fine, but of course they're far harder to control when they're out of the confines of a classroom.

'Luca!' Léa runs after her brother, who's just charged down the ramparts, and I trot after the pair of them.

'Shall we see the dungeons?' I say. We've done the fancy-dress workshop and the face painting. Please let the dungeons entertain them for a while longer.

'What is duggons?' Léa's face is smudged with brown streaks the face painters thought depicted a dirty peasant. I wonder what immaculate Julia would think of her daughter looking like this after only one day in my care.

'The place where they keep the bad people.'

'Can we put Luca there?'

'I'm afraid not.' I shake my head, though some part of me agrees with the suggestion. He didn't seem too crazy back at the house under his parents' gaze. But today he's manic, running everywhere, whining, crying, chattering non-stop. Maybe he's testing me, or maybe he's just excited to be out, away from parents and pre-school and routine.

His behaviour looks all the worse next to Léa, who's clearly seven going on twenty-seven. I liked her immensely from the moment she took my hand this morning and announced she was taking me to Montreux town centre to show me around, but could I drive? I said I would, and that we should take Luca too, and she reluctantly agreed in a manner that suggested she had a choice in the matter, but would do me a favour this time.

It's chilly beneath the vaulted stone ceiling of Chillon Castle's underground prison. I read from my guidebook and find the name Byron carved into a pillar, supposedly put there by the poet himself when he visited the castle two hundred years ago. Léa pretends to be interested, nodding solemnly as I read. Luca's momentarily cowed into silence by the imposing room, until his sister whispers something to him and then he's crying. I don't need to speak French to know she's threatening to leave him here. It's clear we're all castled out.

We walk back over the drawbridge and wander down the lakeshore a little way to sit on the wall and eat our picnic.

Cheese and gherkin sandwiches, apples, and a fizzy drink called Rivella that Léa says is her favourite. The castle sticks out into the lake next to us. Whichever medieval bigwig built it certainly knew how to pick a spot: in front of us, the lake is flat calm, and the mountains on the other side meld shade upon shade like some perfect watercolour painting. I understand now why ladies in the nineteenth century came to Switzerland to cure their ailments. Not because of anything miraculous in the water – though it does look clean enough to drink – but because of this: the heady fragrance of the flowers decorating the promenade's verges, the ducks bobbing on the tranquil lake, the solid bulk of the Alps a constant, comforting backdrop. It's like I've stepped out of reality and into a picture book by a Swiss Enid Blyton. It's summer, I have Michel's credit card, Julia's car and free rein to explore, my only task being to gently impart some of my own language onto two already semi-bilingual children.

It's just what I need right now. My cure.

If only that's all it was.

Fear swells in my chest and I fix my eyes on the reflections in the water until it dissipates. It's only my first day on the job and yet I'm already thinking about what's ahead, about what I might find out if I let myself. I exhale a long, shaky breath. I don't need to do anything straight away. I don't need to do anything about it at all, if that's what I want. It's entirely possible that, when it comes down to it, I simply won't have the guts.

'Where do you live?' Léa says. She's finished her sandwich and is munching on a packet of paprika crisps.

'London. The capital of England.'

'Where the Queen lives?'

'Yes. Well, it's a big city, but yes.' I wonder if the Queen has ever been to Peckham.

'It is nice?'

I nod. 'It's busy. Exciting. Wonderful.' How else to describe the city that's been so much a part of my life to a seven-year-old Swiss who has never been?

'How old are you?'

'Thirty-nine.'

'You have children?'

I shake my head. It's not a loaded question coming from her, so I don't mind. Unlike the countless people who have asked me that, or a version of that, in recent years. A harmless enough question on the face of it, but one that's usually dripping with subtext: *Why not? What's wrong with you? Don't you want them?*

Sometimes I'm tempted just to tell them the truth. *Yes*, I want to say. *I want children so much it's like a physical pain, but after five years of trying and several failed rounds of IVF, my husband and I have separated, so my chances are slim, don't you think?*

But it's against social etiquette to say things like that, to make people feel awkward even though they were the one probing for gossip, so I just smile and brush it off. *Oh you know, perhaps one day . . .*

'You have a husband?' Léa asks.

'Nope.' An easier response than 'sort of'.

'Why?'

I look out into the lake. There's a question. 'Because life doesn't always turn out the way you want it to,' I say.

Léa continues eating her crisps and I think she's got bored of questioning me. She kicks her feet against the wall. '*Maman* says you can do whatever you want if you work hard,' she says after a minute, and I'm impressed by her sentence structure.

I finish my Rivella and look at her. 'If I had a daughter, I would say exactly the same to her.' *Even if it's not true.*

A wail turns both our heads to Luca. He's dropped his sandwich in the lake. A duck makes a beeline and starts pecking at it. A gherkin slice detaches and bobs about on the surface.

'*Arrête, arrête!*' Léa shouts, fingers in her ears, but Luca cries even harder.

I get off the wall and go to comfort Luca with the remaining bit of my own sandwich, but he continues to look at the duck and cry.

'Life doesn't always do the way you want,' Léa says to her brother with a glint in her eye, and I raise my eyebrows, pleased but also perturbed that I've taught her such a phrase.

'*Turn out* the way you want.' She may as well get it right.

I pick Luca off the wall. 'Come on, let's go home.'

I let us into the house and Léa runs to the living room and throws open the terrace door. '*Salut*, Maria!' she yells as she dashes past the kitchen.

Maria calls something after them in French and I pick out the word *glace*. I hear '*Oui!*' from the garden and the sound of splashing water. They're already in the paddling pool.

'*S'il te plaît!*' Maria calls back, her pleading for politeness falling on deaf ears. She pulls a tub of chocolate ice cream out of the freezer and gestures towards me. 'You want?'

'No, thank you. *Merci,*' I say. Given Maria is from Spain, maybe I should have said *gracias*. Not that I'd get any further in Spanish than in French, so I'm forced to demonstrate that fact by conversing in English to a Spaniard who has never visited England and yet still manages to speak my language far, far better than I could ever speak hers. If I'd grown up here, I could be like Julia and Michel, speaking two or three languages as though it was the most natural thing in the world. Instead I grew up in a country that doesn't promote language learning and expects the rest of the world to compensate for that. Out here, I'm quickly realising just how embarrassing that is.

I deliver ice cream to the kids, making a mental note to clean up the inevitable mess before Julia gets home, then I return to the kitchen where Maria is chopping vegetables for the evening meal. I offer to help but she won't hear of it. I'm the teacher and nanny, she's the cleaner and occasional cook, and our roles don't overlap. I can just hear Patrick taking the piss out of this whole set-up, and me, for being part of it. The thought makes me smile and I long to pick up the phone and tell him about it, though I know I shouldn't. Despite what he did, he's still the person I want to tell everything to.

Maria finishes chopping and washes her hands, wiping them on the apron pulled taut over her ample belly. She's short and round and all soft edges, reminding me of Erika. I only vaguely remember what my nanny looked like but I do recall her essence – the rounded wholesomeness of her, her scent of home cooking and perfume, her exotic foreignness. Was she Danish? I can't remember. But I know I adored her, that I only tolerated seeing her leave at the end of the day because it meant I got my parents back for a few short hours before another day started.

'What are you cooking?'

'A tagine, with chicken,' Maria says.

'Do you always cook for them?'

She shrugs. 'No. Only sometimes. They busy people. Work and work. Julia ask me to prepare dinner if she know they not home until late.'

There are more than two million foreigners in Switzerland, I read on my phone last night whilst lying in the double bed of the guest room between cotton sheets with a thread count that would make my bank balance weep. That's a quarter of the whole population. I wonder how it feels to make a life in a country that's not your own; to arrive for a job and then stay for a lifetime. Do you always feel as foreign as I do now?

'Why did you come here, Maria, if you don't mind my asking?' I pinch a carrot from the chopping board.

Maria smiles. 'Is better here. I make more money. There was no work for us in Toledo, and a friend who live here offered Filipe a job.'

'Filipe is your husband?'

She nods. 'He is concierge for two apartment blocks in Montreux.' She gets a tin of tomatoes out of the cupboard and selects two small jars from the rack above the hob. The heady spice of paprika catches in my throat as she shakes it into the hot pan. 'And you? Why you come to be teacher here?'

'I've taught in England for years,' I say. I bite into the carrot, forcing nonchalance. 'But I just wanted a change.'

Maria raises her eyebrows. 'But this is only for the summer. What happens after?'

'I don't know yet.' I think of John Peacock calling me into his office, the humiliation of standing in front of the head-master and being unable to stop the tears running down my face, his visible awkwardness as he addressed the concerns of my colleagues over my mental well-being, and the complaint of a student – Sally Brightman, daughter of a governor, of course – after that awful incident when I'd nearly slapped her in front of the whole class. I never would have done it, I'd told myself afterwards, but I knew it was too close for comfort. I never used to let them rile me like that. But then lots of things in my life weren't as they used to be, and it seemed Patrick's actions had finally broken something in me.

'Look, I don't want to pry into your personal life, but it's clear you're going through a tough time, and I don't like to see my staff burn out,' Peacock had said. 'It's nearly exam season, term's just about over. Would it be useful for you to have a sabbatical next year? Have a breather, sort things out? You can start right now; I can find cover for your final classes this term. I'll hold your job open for a year. You're a long-serving member of staff and we don't want to lose you. What do you say?'

I knew it wasn't really a question.

Maggie picked me up a week later and took me back to her place in Bath. I'd called her first because I knew she was the most able to pick up the pieces of my broken life and attempt to put me back together again. My fairy godmother. If only she could wave a wand and make everything all right. I can picture her now, probably pottering about the garden, pruning flowers, forgetting next to which bush she'd left the cup of Earl Grey she made herself half an hour ago, her mind already on her next theatre job. The cat will be stalking birds in the flowerbeds, or, if it's too hot and he can't be bothered, he'll be flaked out on the cool soil, a slight movement in his tail his only response should Maggie call his name.

The thought comforts me. A familiar scene, carried out repeatedly for years, unchanged by whatever else is happening in the world. The Middle East in turmoil, Europe voting in populist leaders, my life turned on its head . . . but Maggie will still be deadheading the dahlias. That's why I went to her after Peacock shepherded me away from the school, and not to Dad, caught up in his own web of denial and grief, who refused to talk to me about everything that had happened to our family.

Maggie's constancy, her intrinsic optimism, her quiet support was what I needed. But her pragmatic side wouldn't let me wallow for long.

'It's been long enough and this can't go on, it's destroying you,' she said. 'Go and find out what you need to know.'

She'd got on the internet one evening, searched for teaching jobs in Switzerland, and by the time I'd cooked us dinner she'd found me three to apply for. She'd tucked into the lasagne and looked at me. '*Well?*'

Could I go? I didn't know, but I knew I had to do *something*. A huge question mark had hung over me for nearly two years, infecting every aspect of my life, destroying my marriage and damaging my career, until there I was, licking my wounds at Maggie's – and I wouldn't find the answers I needed there. But then there was Dad, my kind, loving father, who'd begged me to leave it be, and I couldn't bear to hurt him any more than he had been already.

'He doesn't want me to do this. He thinks I'm ... I don't know, overreacting or something.'

'No, he doesn't. He's simply pretending it hasn't happened because he doesn't know how to deal with it,' Maggie said. 'He'll be okay. I'll talk to him.'

'And Mum?' I'd asked more quietly. That was at the heart of it. Would she have wanted me to go there, to try and find out what happened?

'Darling girl, what about *you*?' Maggie had said. 'If you're going to sort yourself out, you need to deal with what's churning around in your head. And I think your mum would want you to do whatever it took to be okay again.'

Tears pricked the back of my eyes. 'You think so?'

'She just wanted you to be happy, darling – and so does

your dad, even though he's not very good at saying so out loud.' She smiled, her face creasing into the crow's feet begot from years of laughter and joyful times, many of them with her best friend, whom I knew she missed almost as much as I did.

Julia and Michel arrive together at around eight o'clock. Maria's gone. The kids are dry and sitting in front of an animation in English that I'd loaded onto my iPad back home, the paddling pool now free of chocolate ice cream. I'm sitting on the terrace reading my guidebook.

I look up when the door opens and nerves flicker in my chest. It's weird being employed in a household. Like I have to wear my work face at all times. No sitting in your pyjamas picking your cuticles in front of the telly. No reading all evening and ignoring the people you live with. Patrick hated both of those habits.

Michel peers into the oven at the tagine that's been cooking for a good couple of hours now. 'That smells so good! *Bonsoir,* Jess. All okay?'

I nod and close my book. Julia greets me and then goes over to the kids, but they barely look up from *Frozen.* She rolls her eyes. 'You finish this and then no more.'

Léa nods without taking her eyes off the screen.

'Sorry, should I not . . .?' I say.

Julia waggles her head and makes a little pouty gesture with her mouth. 'It's okay. I don't normally let them watch much television, but I'll make an exception for English programmes. Part of their learning.' She gives me a tight smile. 'Anyway, tell me what you've done today.'

I recount our trip to the castle, the face painting and Byron and the picnic by the lake.

'Excellent. And what have you learned today?' Julia says to the kids.

'Duck!'

'Dungeons.'

Julia laughs. 'It's a start.' She slips into a chair and lets out a little sigh. She looks tired; there's a tinge of red rimming her big brown eyes, and strands of her glossy hair have slipped out of the neat chignon she put it in that morning. For some reason it pleases me to know she doesn't sail through her working day untouched.

'Long day?' I say.

'Always.' She slips into a chair. 'We have this big event on in a couple of months and there's so much to do.'

I did ask her what she does but, as with most jobs that aren't the kind that pop up on a school careers advice questionnaire, I haven't really understood it exactly. Something to do with sport and sponsorship and event planning. One of those jobs that, when you're a kid and you're considering what on earth you might do with your life, it never occurs to you to choose because you've never heard of it. It's always fascinated me, as someone who made an unimaginative career choice, how people end up in such obscure professions.

'But you don't have to do all of it yourself.' Michel sits

down next to her. 'She does far more for her boss than she should,' he says to me and Julia shakes her head.

'It's my job.'

He puts his hand on hers and gives it a gentle shake. 'Yes, but you let yourself get taken advantage of sometimes.'

Julia smiles and rolls her eyes at me. 'He thinks he knows everything.'

But despite their gentle chiding of each other, I can see the affection between them and I feel a hard knot in my throat at the sheer *perfection* of this whole family. The stable, mutually supportive marriage, the two beautiful children, the successful careers, the lovely home . . . *I* was meant to have this by now. But instead it's like a hand came out of nowhere and slapped my life off its axis. I ache to go back to before. I want the comfort of marriage, the certainty of my parents' love, the stability of St Mary's, the prospect of a family of my own. But I don't have any of that now.

I don't even know who I am anymore.

That night, when everyone else is asleep, I pull out the folder from my suitcase and put it on the bed in front of me. My accumulated research from the past two years. It's not much because I haven't had a lot to go on. The tests posed the question, but didn't give any hints to the answer. The hospital in Lausanne was little help, claiming there was no paper trail, though I've always wondered if they were just covering their own backs. All I had was a potential name – Brigitte Mela. That's all they could give me. The internet threw up very little of use, and of course I couldn't ask Mum.

Grief slugs me in the gut as it always does when I think of her. Sometimes, even after four years, I fully expect her to walk in the door like nothing has changed. Her personality, her essence, remains woven into my every day, even though she's not physically here anymore. But so much has happened since she's been gone, and I'm glad she wasn't here to see everything I've been through, that she didn't know the pain of receiving those test results. At least she was saved from that.

I sift through the papers in the folder, even though I've looked at them a hundred times. My eyes slide over the DNA clinic's letter, which I still find so hard to read, and printouts of emails from the hospital.

Please accept our sincere sympathy for your situation . . .

And then the newspaper article, the feature that Mum wrote after she came here in 1976. I pick it up and look at the photos: Evelyne Buchs standing in front of the Swiss parliament building holding a homemade banner demanding equality for women.

I've spent ages staring at that photo, hoping Evelyne can tell me something about what happened back then; hoping I can glean some information that would help. She's the reason Mum was here in 1976, so maybe she knows something. She might even still be here. But so far I've found nothing about her online, and my scouring of the British Library only turned up a brief mention of her in a book about feminism in Europe. It seems she didn't have much of an impact on the world beyond Switzerland, but I know how much Mum admired her when they met back then, because it's evident in this article, which I downloaded from the newspaper's online archive after much scouring of past issues. When I finally found it, I was overwhelmed to see it, to read the words Mum wrote about these women fighting for rights I know I take for granted, to see what she saw through the photos she took herself.

Mum was here. And while she was, something happened that changed the entire course of my life. Perhaps, if I can summon the courage, the next eight weeks will help me finally figure out what that was.

MARCH 1976

Lausanne, Switzerland

SYLVIA

Was Paris really the last time she was abroad? Sylvia recalled her student year at the Sorbonne with a rush of nostalgia for those walks by the Seine, coffee in smoky cafes, wine-fuelled dinners in the Marais, lectures on Sartre and Camus and Molière. It was only three years ago but seemed like an age, although she remembered the feeling it gave her so well – a voracious desire to devour everything she saw, to lap up every new experience, to revel in the sense of freedom being abroad gave her. Sylvia hadn't realised until now, walking through customs in Geneva, how badly she'd needed that again.

The train swept her along the length of Lake Geneva until the guard announced their arrival at Lausanne station in three languages. She stepped off the train and walked through a fug of cigarette smoke spiralling up to the high ceiling of the station concourse. She took a cab up the steep hill to the Hôtel de la Paix, a grand old building offering a glorious view of the lake far below. Not that she could see it from her room, of course, a pokey cube whose only window faced onto a building on a side street. Janice had warned her. *Budget's limited, love, this is the best you get.* Like hell it was. But Sylvia was abroad, on a foreign commission – the room could be in a shed for all she cared.

She unpacked and squeezed into the bathroom. She brushed her hair, applied a slick of lipstick and assessed herself in the mirror. She was wearing a beige trouser suit Maggie had helped her pick out when she'd started her job, with a pin brooch her parents gave her on graduation from Oxford, and platform shoes she'd scrubbed clean. She smoothed her clothes and her hand came to a rest on her stomach. Another image pushed into her mind: visiting her friend Gilly last month; her youngest child at her hip, bloodshot eyes and sick-stained clothes.

God, put the kettle on, won't you, while I change his nappy?

She blinked and blew out a shaky breath. She wouldn't think about that now.

'I apologise for the mess.' Evelyne Buchs swept a pile of papers from a battered old chair, gesturing for her to sit. 'Smoke?'

Sylvia took the proffered cigarette and leaned forward for her to light it. A collection of butts languished in an ashtray on a table, which was stacked with flyers and posters. A sign scrawled on the door had said '*Mouvement des Femmes Lausannoises*', both confirming its presence and suggesting its ephemeral state. It looked like a basement storeroom.

'We don't have a proper HQ,' Evelyne said in precise, measured French that seemed so different from the fast-flowing mumble Sylvia had learned to keep up with in Paris. 'But we use this tiny space as a drop-in centre for women interested in the movement.' She waved her hand around the room, sending a spray of ash to the floor. 'Oh, I'm very glad you're here. Any opportunity to get the word out; raise awareness of our situation.'

'I'm pleased to be here.' Sylvia felt her heart rate ease. She had always appreciated the slight nervousness she felt on going to interview a stranger – it kept her alert – but it had already dissipated in front of Evelyne's cluttered table and relaxed manner. The woman seemed about Sylvia's age, with a mass of unruly hair loosely tied back by a scarf. Her flared jeans and chunky red jumper made Sylvia feel ridiculously formal – and conformist – in her suit.

She took her notepad and pen out of her bag. 'I'm really keen to give a true picture of what's going on here within the Swiss feminist movement. How things have changed since women's suffrage in '71, and what's still to be achieved.'

'Oh, everything!' Evelyne said. 'That's in answer to the last part of your sentence, of course.' She sat back in her chair and took a drag on her cigarette. 'I mean, it was absolutely marvellous when women finally got the vote at federal level after so many bloody years of campaigning, but it was simply shameful it took so long, and it's not nearly enough. It means nothing as long as women are still controlled and restricted by rules made by men. What's needed now is a complete revolution, nothing less. We won't stop until we've dismantled the patriarchy and built a new society that doesn't marginalise women and exploit their bodies.'

'That's quite an aim,' Sylvia said.

'It certainly is, but there are plenty of us out there fighting for it.' Evelyne leaned forward, brushed a loose strand of hair behind her ear. 'However, it's slow progress. Part of the problem is that the country's system of direct democracy requires a referendum for constitutional change, but of course until '71 only men could vote in national referendums, so progressive policies regarding women's rights have been few and far between. I mean, that's why it took so bloody long to get the vote in the first place – only *men* could vote to give women the vote!' She shook her head and laughed. 'Of course, some men are more progressive than others. Here in the canton of Vaud, they granted women the vote back in '59 – we were the first in the country to get cantonal suffrage.'

'Meaning you could vote in cantonal elections and referendums but not national ones?'

'Precisely.' Evelyne leaned forward to flick ash into the ashtray and looked at Sylvia. 'I'm sorry, do you know much about the Swiss system? It *is* rather complicated.'

'It's a federal state, made up of different cantons, yes?'

She nodded. 'Each canton has its own political powers,

and can legislate on certain matters, while the federal government deals with nationwide issues. Attitudes can vary widely from canton to canton, so while several progressive cantons granted cantonal suffrage prior to 1971, a couple *still* haven't even now.'

'Still? You mean there are parts of Switzerland where women can now vote on national issues but not cantonal ones?'

'Hard to believe, but yes.' She laughed. 'So now you understand that things take time to change in Switzerland, which is frustrating because there's so much more to do – statutory maternity leave, more nurseries, equal access to education, pay equality, among other things.' She blew out a long trail of smoke to the ceiling. 'But it's about far more than legislation. Fundamentally, we need these basic rights so that we can take back control of our lives. We need easy and free access to contraception and the complete decriminalisation of abortion so we can control our own bodies, and we need to smash the system that casts women as unpaid workers in the home, raising children and doing the housework, all the while being controlled by their husbands. I mean, married women here must ask their husband's *permission* to have a job or a bank account, and even then all their money is under his control. Did you know that?'

Sylvia shook her head, her pen flying across the page. She hadn't known that, but it didn't surprise her – it was only last year that financial discrimination against women was outlawed back home. When she'd opened a bank account several years ago, the bank had required her father's signature as well as her own.

'So it's more than women's rights – it's women's *liberation*. Liberation from the male-dominated society that has been imposed upon us for centuries.' Evelyne sighed. 'But unfortunately,' she went on, Sylvia realising that questions were not going to be entirely necessary in this interview, 'with this dire economic climate, it's women who are bearing the brunt and it's undoing all the progress that's been made. Women are the first to lose their jobs and get sent back to the kitchen. Well, after foreigners of course.'

Sylvia raised her eyebrows.

'Foreigners are even less appreciated in Switzerland than women. So as a foreign woman, well, you've haven't much of a hope!' Evelyne laughed and stubbed out her cigarette. 'Come on, I've had enough of this place. Shall we go and get a drink?'

The air was frigid as they hurried through the cobbled streets, but the cold seemed to suit Lausanne so much better than London. Rather than bone-chillingly damp, it was dry and fresh and easily fended off with her Afghan coat and woolly hat. Nevertheless, Sylvia was glad to step into the warmth of Le Barbare, a little cafe perched on the old market steps that could have been there for centuries. It was late afternoon and the snug interior was already busy, mostly with young people, beers and cigarettes in hand. A hum of chatter and laughter was the only soundtrack, though in one corner

Sylvia saw a drum kit and assorted microphones, indicating live music had been and gone, but would likely come again.

Heads turned their way as they walked in. Sylvia unwound her scarf and shrugged off her coat as Evelyne greeted the woman behind the bar as though they knew each other well. She returned with two glasses of beer and slipped into a chair opposite Sylvia.

'This place is where we come to plot,' she said with a smile. 'The drinking establishment of Lausanne's young radical lefties. And don't they know it!'

'They?' Sylvia said.

'The fusty old conservatives, I mean. They succeeded in shutting it down a few years ago, complaining about drugs and homosexuals and "moral danger".' Evelyne shrugged. 'It was only a bit of weed, for God's sake. Sometimes it's as though the sixties never happened. That's part of the bloody problem in Switzerland – too many people stuck in the past.'

And she was off. Evelyne, Sylvia had realised already, wasn't the sort of person to need alcohol to talk – but it clearly wasn't going to slow her down, either. Sylvia's shorthand was pushed to its limits as she listened to Evelyne tell her how she joined the *Mouvement des Femmes Lausannoises* three years ago while she was still at university, inspired by the fellow students she met for whom traditional feminism wasn't enough, who were pursuing something more radical.

'We owe them a lot, those older feminists. They've fought for voting rights for years, but many of them still think a woman's place is at home keeping house and making babies.'

Sylvia heard how, last year, the MFL joined other militant groups to boycott a women's congress led by those traditional Swiss feminists after they refused to put abortion on the debate agenda, and how they created an anti-congress of fierce debates, controversial films and pieces of feminist theatre that gained more press attention than the real congress. She heard how the local authorities tried to shut down the printing of the MFL newsletter, and how they teamed up with other campaigners from around the country to interrupt a session of parliament to demonstrate in favour of abortion rights. Sylvia couldn't help but feel rather lucky. Britain wasn't perfect, by a long way, but at least things were moving in the right direction. She had the right to request a termination – *yes*, she reminded herself, *I do* – and, as of just last year, legal recourse should she face discrimination at work or unequal pay. But then her thoughts flickered to Clive, his sneers and his putdowns, and she considered Evelyne to be right – legislation was necessary, but something more fundamental was still needed, and not just in Switzerland. The women's lib movement may have made more progress in the UK, but it still hadn't achieved all its aims – far from it.

'I admire your determination, your passion, I really do.'

'Well, someone has to do it.' Evelyne drained her glass. 'And I'm not saying it's just us at the MFL; there are thousands of women across the country standing up for change.' She signalled to the waitress and gestured for more drinks. 'But some people don't understand – and that includes many women, too, especially the older ones. They think we're being too militant, too aggressive; that we're making a fuss unnecessarily and should simply pipe down and get back to our husbands and children where we belong. *Putain!* They're simply wrong. There's so much that should change, so much we should be making a fuss about.' She shook her head. 'I have a friend who is about to get married, and because her fiancé is French, she will lose her Swiss citizenship when she marries, unless she specifically asks to retain it. And yet if it was the other way around – a Swiss *man* marrying a foreigner – he'd automatically keep his nationality.'

Sylvia shook her head. 'Wow. That's—'

'I don't want *more* than what men have,' Evelyne went on. 'I simply want the freedom to live my life as I please, free from their control, their oppression. And if it can't happen for me then I want it for all the girls I teach every day, so they can grow up knowing they are as valued in society as the boys.'

'You're a teacher?'

'Primary. You didn't think this was the day job, did you?' She laughed, one eyebrow arched. '*Mon amie*, I'm a member of the MFL for love, not for money. For the love of myself, my girls, and even those *Hausfrauen* who think we're unfeminine hell-raisers. Because it's important. And if we end up achieving nothing, well, at least I can hold my head up high knowing I tried.' She paused and looked at her watch. 'Speaking of teaching, I must go. I have a pile of prep to do for next week. But listen, what are you doing later? I'm having some friends from the MFL over for food. Come too?' She scribbled her address on a bar mat. 'It's been great to meet you. Sorry if I rambled on a bit. Once you get me started, you know.'

Sylvia agreed to come and then Evelyne was off, a breezy '*À plus tard!*' as she rushed out the door. A gush of cold air hit Sylvia and then the door slammed shut.

JUNE 2016

Montreux, Switzerland

JESS

By Wednesday, I feel we've established something of a routine already. Thankfully, Michel deals with Luca when he wakes at 6.30am, while Julia showers and dashes around the flat knocking back coffee and shoving papers into her bag. She doesn't seem to eat breakfast and I wonder if she has anything at the office. Breakfast is the most important meal of the day, Maggie would say when she'd turn up in my room with scrambled eggs on a tray as though I was some kind of invalid. I suppose I was – mentally injured, if not physically.

Julia's out the door by the time I'm showered and contemplating breakfast. Léa, Luca and I sit munching bircher muesli as Michel gets dressed and then joins us at the table. Luca's already chattering away, wanting to know what we're doing that day, but Michel's taciturn before he's poured himself a coffee. This morning his hair's still wet from the shower and there's a tiny spot of blood on his jawline where he nicked the skin with his razor. I want to reach out and wipe it away, but of course, I don't. And then he's gone too, and I'm left with the kids, cast into the role of stay-at-home mum. I feel a strange mix of happiness and anguish. I used to think I'd be one of those for real. I think I'd have loved it.

The whole day stretches out in front of us to be filled with whatever activities we so desire, and I feel like a kid too, eager for Switzerland to entertain me. We've been to the castle, but there's still the zoo and the outdoor pool in Pully and the water park at Le Bouveret and the botanical gardens in Lausanne, and maybe I can even persuade the kids to go to the museum about Charlie Chaplin in Vevey. I've looked it all up in my guidebook and compiled a large to-do list. Not that this is about me, of course, but I'm sure there's educational value in all these things.

But this afternoon we have a prior engagement – tennis lessons for the pair of them in Lausanne, an eight-week course arranged by Julia to give me a couple of hours off each Wednesday afternoon. I deliver the kids to the sports centre just about on time, though it's a tricky operation involving hunting down Léa's lost sports shorts, calming Luca out of his latest tantrum, and negotiating a traffic jam on the motorway. I could stay and watch, I suppose, but I tell myself off for even thinking about it. This break from childcare is an opportunity I should seize. Now's the time. If I don't start now, I never will.

My stomach flips at the prospect.

I leave the car parked in a street near Mon Repos and walk across a short road bridge. Down below are the cobbled streets and red rooftops of Lausanne's city centre, and beyond, far down the hill, Lake Geneva and the mountains the other side, hazy in the afternoon heat. The cathedral's up a hill to my right, but I resist taking myself on a sightseeing tour. I have a purpose and I need to stick to it. So instead I search the map on my phone and follow the directions down some stone steps into a vast square with a bizarre mix of grandiose buildings and ugly concrete apartment blocks. I wonder if Mum walked here, if she saw this, if that restaurant was here when she was. I wish with all my heart I could ask her.

I find the university library inside the most imposing building in the square. There are a couple of desks with staff serving customers, and beyond that rows and rows of bookshelves. It's quiet, of course, apart from the turning of pages and the low words of the librarians. I hesitate in the foyer, then hear Maggie's voice in my head. *It's destroying you. Go and find out what you need to know.*

I take a breath and walk over to the desk. '*Est-ce que vous pouvez . . .*' I start to say to the young woman sitting behind it, the words I looked up in the dictionary yesterday.

She looks at me, cocks her head. 'Perhaps I can help you in English,' she says with the merest hint of an accent. A smile flutters about her mouth.

'Thanks. I'm looking for a book on feminism in Switzerland during the 1970s. Do you have anything?'

'Do you know a title or author?'

'No, I don't know of a specific book. I'm just looking to research the topic,' I say.

'We have a large local history section, with some texts that may cover the subject,' she says. She comes out from behind the desk. 'Let me show you.'

I follow her to a sweep of shelves towards the back. I can't remember the last time I went to a library and the thought makes me sad. I remember going with Mum to Greenwich Library as a child, choosing five books a time and wanting many more.

'Here. But they are mostly in French or German,' she says.

'Right.' Of course I'd known that, but I'd hoped there would be one or two in English at least. I don't know what to do now. The rows of books are daunting. There's no way I can get any information out of them without help, and I don't have anyone to help me. I suppose I could ask someone. Julia? Michel? No. That would be weird, and could spark too many questions I don't want to answer. Anyway, both of them seem far too busy to spend time wading through history books.

The woman − Emilie, her name badge says − gives me an apologetic smile and starts to move away, but I take the print-out of Mum's article out of my bag and hand it out to her. 'I'm looking for a woman mentioned in this article. I don't suppose you know the name Evelyne Buchs?'

She takes the paper from me and scans the headline, before shaking her head slowly. 'No, but I know this organisation was very active around here years ago.' She points at a name in the article – *Mouvement des Femmes Lausannoises*. 'Actually, I think some of their newsletters are in our archives. Do you want me to look?'

Fifteen minutes later I'm sitting at a desk with several papers laid out in front of me. My heart quickens as I read the header on each: *Mouvement des Femmes Lausannoises*; March 1975; August 1976; January 1977. I can't understand anything of the text, of course, but I'm drawn to the names – and the grainy black and white pictures. I squint at one particular photo and my stomach jolts when I look at the caption and see the familiar name – it's Evelyne, giving a speech in Vevey, which I recall driving past on the motorway to come here.

Where are you now? I want to ask the photo. *Why is there no trace of you online?*

Perhaps, it occurs to me, I might find something about her old friends instead. I take a notepad out of my bag and start to write down any other name mentioned in a picture caption or quote. Sonja Jeanneret, Marie Rochat, Monica Gerber, Nina Favre, Fabienne Aebischer . . .

When I've scoured all the newsletters available, I have a list of twenty names in front of me. I take out my phone and open a browser. I've known for quite some time that it's pretty easy to look up an address and telephone number in Switzerland's online phone book. It's even in English. Of course, I tried Brigitte Mela long ago, and then Evelyne Buchs, drawing a blank both times. But when I put in the names from the newsletters, much to my shock, I actually get results. Three Sonja Jeannerets, ten Marie Rochats . . . I start writing them all down but then glance at the time and see that I have just fifteen minutes to get back to the sports centre. I try to quell my frustration as I put the notepad back in my bag and stand up from the desk.

Now I have a hint of a way forward, I want to keep going. It's possible it will all lead to nothing. But it's also possible that one of them might just know something about Evelyne Buchs, or Brigitte Mela, or anything at all that might help me decipher the mystery of my life.

Luca's tired after tennis, so I put him down for a nap as soon as we get home. I set up Léa in the living room with some paper and coloured pencils and a book of animals to copy, getting her to draw her favourite ones and learn their names in English.

'Jess, what is this called?'

She's a pretty good artist, definitely advanced for her age. She's drawing eyes and tails and snouts with a studiousness that makes me smile. 'Guinea pig,' I say. 'Have you ever had one of those as a pet?'

Léa shakes her head. '*Maman* says we can't have pets.'

I think of Bruno, the tiny kitten Dad got for me when I was about Léa's age. A vague memory of an argument.

She doesn't have any siblings so at least let her have a cat.

Mum snapping back: *As long as I don't have to feed it, I've got enough on my plate.*

I was devastated when, years later, we found him dead under the buddleia in the garden. Mum consoled me, but I thought she was secretly pleased, since he had inevitably been left for her to feed most of the time.

'Well, she must have her reasons,' I say. *Killjoy*, I think.

Léa frowns and looks down at her drawing, and my heart swells with affection for her serious little face. I hope Julia likes the drawings. I hope she can get away from work early enough to see them tonight before Léa goes to bed; I can see how much it would mean to her.

It hits me in the stomach right then: a physical ache for a child of my own, a child like Léa, another being on this planet who shares my genes, who is physically connected to me. I don't need to be a psychologist to know that what's happened in recent years has only heightened my need for a child. Ever since the tests, I feel like I've been floating alone in this world, linked to nothing and no one.

Untethered.

It doesn't have to change a thing. We can just forget about it, Dad had said.

But as much as I wish he were right, I know deep down that I can't forget. What's done is done and it changes everything. Even so, I long to return to Léa's age, safe in the cocoon of family life with Dad and Mum and Bruno and nanny Erika.

Back before I knew it was all a lie.

MARCH 1976

Lausanne, Switzerland

SYLVIA

Rue Haldimand 8, like all the buildings on the street, was an elegant old dame: tall, slim, well kept, but fading. Sylvia pressed the intercom for 'Buchs', stepped inside, glanced at the minuscule lift and took the stairs. The door was ajar when she reached the fourth-floor flat, so she knocked and pushed it open. A warm, orange light and soft music drew her in.

'You're here! *Bienvenue!*' Evelyne appeared in the doorway. She kissed her on both cheeks and Sylvia pulled back after two, not expecting a third. 'It's three here, darling!' Evelyne laughed. She took Sylvia's coat and led her into the living room where several women were standing around a table with what looked like bedsheets spread out over it. One had a paint brush in her hand.

'*Les filles!* This is Sylvia; she's come to help us share our plight with the world!'

The women in turn came to greet her: Monique, Sophie, Nina, Sonja; names Sylvia knew she'd never remember.

'Any good with a paintbrush?' one of them said to Sylvia. Nina, was it? Her jet black hair parted in the middle and fell nearly to her waist, framing a serious face that lit up when she smiled.

'I suppose so. What are you doing?'

'Banners.' An older woman with red hair and a warm, round face smiled at her. 'We're prepping for the rally in Bern tomorrow.'

Reading upside down across the table Sylvia could make out, in wonky letters: '*Les enfants ou non, c'est nous qui décidons*'. 'Children or not, it's us who decide', she translated in her head. '*Tous égaux devant la loi*' said another, 'Everyone equal in the eyes of the law'.

'You're coming, right?' Evelyne said.

She nodded. That was the plan. Her chest prickled at the thought. A demonstration in the Swiss capital, just before International Women's Day, was exactly what she needed for her story. If she did it right, maybe she could offload the golden oldies column onto some other poor sod.

'We don't exactly have a ton of womanpower here.' Nina gestured to the table. 'So if you can write straight and spell, we'll have you.'

'She's a writer, she should be able to manage that,' Evelyne said.

Nina smiled at Sylvia sideways. 'Then you're in.'

She pulled up a chair and grabbed a paintbrush, tasked with writing 'Marriage is a work contract' in French across a metre-long banner, wondering, as she did so, what the women here thought of the single diamond on her left hand. Part of her agreed with the banner's sentiment – for some of her friends, that's certainly how marriage appeared – but she'd never thought it would be like that with Jim. Jim was different.

They worked for an hour or more, Evelyne refilling their glasses with a regularity Sylvia was more accustomed to seeing from Max and Ellis in El Vino's wine bar. She thought, briefly, that maybe she shouldn't be drinking so much, but then dismissed it with a coldness that surprised her. It didn't feel real, so perhaps it wasn't. By the time Evelyne emerged from the kitchen with a platter of raw meat and a pot of hot oil, she was feeling heady from booze and paint fumes. The *fondue bourguignonne* was a Lausanne speciality, they said, but to Sylvia it felt distinctly British; it reminded her of dinner parties her parents would throw when they wanted to impress someone. Her mother in the floor-length dress she pulled out twice a year, a long string of fake pearls and a precious dab of Chanel No. 5, serving up a platter of beef and an assortment of supermarket sauces decanted into individual ceramic pots.

'God, this must all seem like repeating ancient history to you,' Nina said. She skewered a piece of meat and placed the long fork in the broth.

'What do you mean?'

'All this.' She waved her hand towards the stack of flyers and banners they'd just prepared. 'Our struggle, when you've got so much already. I mean, abortion is perfectly legal, isn't it?'

'Not on demand – you need two doctors' permission, but essentially yes, since '67,' Sylvia said.

'Here it's more or less banned, unless you find a doctor with a liberal interpretation of the law, which is impossible in some parts of the country,' Nina said with a shake of her head. 'And though contraception is legal, it can be difficult and costly to get hold of, especially in conservative cantons that don't believe in family planning. So women are screwed either way.'

'You have paid maternity leave now too, right?' Sonja asked.

Sylvia nodded. 'Yes, a new employment protection law passed last year. But only women who've been in their job for two years will benefit – and it's not in force yet.' She stopped herself thinking any more about that – to consider if she would be eligible for maternity leave was to acknowledge a reality she was trying hard to suppress.

'And now you have *Madame* Thatcher – surely she's going to make things even better for women if she gets into power.'

'*La dame de fer!*' Nina laughed. 'Switzerland must seem like the most backwards place to you.'

Sylvia thought of turning up at Dirty Dan's door to find him in his bathrobe, coincidentally just out of the shower even though her tutorial times were fixed weeks in advance. She thought of Clive squeezing her waist in false bonhomie as he brushed past her in the office kitchen. And the way all the men in the newsroom talked to Marnie's substantial chest rather than her face.

'Not exactly,' she said. 'I'm grateful for the legislative progress that's been made back home. But there's still so much to do, and just like here, attitudes take longer to change. Feminists aren't exactly championed in the media.'

'We know all about that. Here we're either cast as old ladies in flat shoes or hysterical banshees,' Nina said.

'In the UK they think we're all hard-faced, bra-burning ball-crushers.' Sylvia smiled. 'And as for Thatcher, though it's wonderful we have a woman as leader of the opposition, she's hardly the ultimate feminist. I think she's out for herself, not for all women.'

'But she's a symbol, at least,' Monique said. 'Whatever she's actually like, she shows women that they can do it, they can get there. We need that here. I mean, it will probably come, now we can vote and stand for office, but there still aren't *any* women in the Federal Council.'

Sylvia nodded. The Swiss cabinet, she knew from her research.

'It might take years yet because women weren't in a position to get any experience of federal politics until we got the vote. And you can't change the world in five years.'

'Especially when society is against us right from the start.' Evelyne leaned forward. 'I mean, did you know that in many schools here, girls don't even have the same education path as boys? They're forced to take classes in needlework and knitting and homemaking, leaving them less time for maths and science. Girls are *literally* being brought up to be house-wives.' She took a swig of wine and Sylvia saw her eyes were slightly glazed.

'And that's why we're doing this,' Monique said. 'Maths not knitting – shall we put it on a banner?'

It was late when the door buzzed and no one else seemed to hear it. Someone had turned the speakers right up and David Bowie's *Suffragette City* flooded the room. Sonja and Monique were dancing around the room, and Sophie was smoking out of the open window, the winter chill seeping into the room. Nina had her camera out and was snapping photos of them all in silly poses.

It buzzed again and Sylvia gestured to the door. 'Wasn't that the bell?'

'Who the . . .?' Evelyne got up, cigarette and wine glass in hand, and pressed the intercom. Sylvia saw the smile on her face fall away as she opened the flat door and went out onto the landing, waiting for her visitor.

Footsteps and a low male voice on the stairs. Whispers in fraught, pained Swiss German. And then Evelyne re-appeared, a too bright smile on her face.

The man behind her was tall and broad, but with a youth-ful face that belied his imposing stature. The mass of dark hair that curled around his ears was so similar to Evelyne's own unruly mop that Sylvia knew immediately this was a relative.

'*Regardez qui vient d'arriver!*' Evelyne said. *Look who's here.*

'Hey, what are you doing here?' Sonja walked over and kissed the visitor, as did the others, before Evelyne grabbed his hand and dragged him over to her.

'Sylvia, this is my baby brother, Daniel. Spontaneous visit at . . . ooh, midnight.' She smiled, but there was something else behind it.

He shook Sylvia's hand and sat down in Evelyne's chair as she left them to fetch him a beer. Despite his youth he looked weary, eyes bloodshot.

'Have you come a long way?' Sylvia said.

'From Betten.' He said it as though she should know where that was, but she shook her head and he raised his eyebrows. 'In the Valais. Where Evelyne and I are from.' His French was curious: precise, singsong, clearly influenced by his native Swiss German.

'Right. Sorry, I just met Evelyne today. I'm here from London to write about the MFL.'

'Huh.' He smiled at her, but his expression made her uneasy.

'Are you a teacher too?' Her eyes flicked to the kitchen, but she could see Evelyne still rooting around in the fridge.

'Me? Oh no.' His brief laugh was loaded with bitterness. 'I'm a farmer. I only teach the farmhands how to milk a cow and mend a fence.'

Sylvia smiled. 'That must be interesting.'

'Fucking fascinating.' He sat back in his chair and looked towards the open window. Smoke hung in the air, illuminated by the street light outside the apartment block.

'I'm sorry, I thought . . . Well, I'm sure it's a tough life but it must be—'

'*Voilà!*' Evelyne appeared and held out a beer to Daniel. Sylvia excused herself and went to the toilet. Under the bright light of the bathroom she felt dizzy, tiredness and booze overcoming her. She felt a sudden need to see Jim, to wash Daniel's scowl out of her eyes. She patted water on her forehead and cheeks and dried her face on a towel before stepping out into the living room. It was time to go.

'Don't mind my brother, he's such a bore sometimes,' Evelyne whispered at the door.

'Oh, he was fine. No problem.'

'He's had a falling out with our father. *Again*. It happens a couple of times a year at least. He'll stay with me for a few days, then Mother will call and persuade him to go back, and he'll agree because he can't bear her to be upset, and then we'll be back to square one until the volcano starts bubbling up again.' Sylvia's eyes flicked over Evelyne's shoulder to Daniel, now smoking by the window, beer in hand. '*C'est la vie!* Anyway, at least I get to see him for a bit. Baby brother.' Evelyne looked over at him herself with a sad smile. 'He's pretty much the only family member I do see.'

'You don't see your parents?'

She shook her head. 'Dad basically disowned me when I decided to leave the farm and go to university. He wanted me to stay and work until I could be married off to some other farmer's son.' She rolled her eyes. 'Mum backed me, but doesn't like to admit it in front of him. So I don't see her either.'

'I'm so sorry.'

She shrugged. 'Anyway, enough of that.' She grabbed Sylvia's arm. 'Thank you so much for coming tonight and helping us out. I'll see you back here tomorrow, okay?'

JUNE 2016

Montreux, Switzerland

JESS

Over the course of the week following my library trip, I snatch moments whenever I can to call the many incarnations of the names on my list, hoping they speak enough English to point me in the right direction. There are several Fabienne Aebischers, but none of them have heard of the *Mouvement des Femmes Lausannoises*. Marie Rochat in Neuchâtel is too young, and Marie Rochat in Geneva speaks no English and hangs up on me after I've reeled off a few pre-prepared phrases in French and not understood her responses.

It's hardly watertight research, this.

But then I call a Nina Favre, listed as living in Lausanne, and I think it surprises her as much as me when I bring up the MFL and she says, 'Yes, yes I know it.'

With my heart pumping in overdrive, I ask if she would

be happy to meet with me, and suddenly I'm writing down her address and accepting an invitation to go round next Wednesday afternoon when the kids are at their next tennis lesson. It's a start, a step forward in my search, and I immediately message Maggie for reassurance.

Am I doing the right thing?

Her reply comes back almost instantly: *Yes, darling. Just go for it. And remember, I'm always here for you, whatever you find out.*

A second message arrives a moment later: *I'm taking your father to dinner next week and I'm going to sort him out, so don't worry.*

I smile, picturing the two of them together. Maggie's always been there for Dad, as much as she was for Mum, usually acting as mediator when their relationship blew a fuse, ushering them towards reconciliation like a mother hen shepherding her chicks. And she's always been there for me too, even more so since Mum died.

My surrogate daughter, she calls me.

I've never understood why Maggie didn't marry and have kids of her own, but she swears she prefers it that way. *I'm far too set in my ways to live with anyone.* I guess everyone's life is a bit of a mystery, not just mine.

I know it's going to feel a long wait until my visit to see Nina Favre next week, so I try to push thoughts of my search aside and focus on the job. I build some structure into my time with the children, making sure we have some sort of outing each day as well as a couple of hours of more formal learning at home. Léa and Luca are bright kids, and it pleases me to see them responding to my teaching, to hear them use words and phrases I've taught them. In those moments it reminds me that I was a good teacher. I *am* a good teacher, but like everything else good in my life, that feeling has eroded away in recent months. Each day I'm here, it bobs up to the surface when I'm alone with the kids, but sinks back down when I see Julia in her suit and lipstick, her laptop bag slung over her shoulder as she downs a coffee and heads for the door every morning. I never wanted a career like hers, and I've always felt that teaching children is one of the most valuable professions there is, so it's strange to feel so small when she wishes us a good day and rushes away to catch her train.

I wonder if she looks at me and feels big.

Perhaps, I think later, it's that feeling that makes me do it. It's the afternoon, and Léa and Luca are playing a word game I created, when I leave them and head down the hall to the toilet in the main bathroom. As I do, I pass Julia and Michel's bedroom door, which is open a crack, and the glimpse I get of the room inside stops me in my tracks.

My pulse quickens a notch.

I shouldn't. I don't know why I want to.

I glance back into the hallway, but no one's there. I can hear the kids in the lounge, arguing over something trivial. I push open the door, making a mental note of the size of the gap, so I can leave it just so.

The room is big, dominated by a king-size bed in the

middle. There's an armchair in one corner with a jacket draped over it, mirrored wardrobes down one side and a door to what I imagine is an en-suite bathroom on the opposite side. My gaze settles on an antique wooden dressing table covered in perfumes, make-up and hair products. Strands of Julia's dark hair are caught in a hairbrush. I pick up a perfume bottle and smell her familiar scent. I run my fingers over a necklace of delicate glass beads strung over the corner of the mirror and wonder if Michel bought it for her and why. An anniversary? A holiday gift? Just because?

I slide open the wardrobe door and see her clothes hanging on the rail. I flick through a few hangers. A silk dress. A linen skirt. Several blouses from shops I didn't think anyone actually bought stuff in. Hermès. Chanel. The labels remind me of that copycat Diane von Furstenburg dress from the seventies that Mum passed on to me a few years back. A classic style that she encouraged me to wear, but that I always felt wasn't quite right on me. I pick out a bright pink silk top and hold it up against myself in the mirrored door. The colour doesn't suit me at all. I look washed out. Not like Julia with her flawless olive skin and mahogany hair. I feel a sudden irrational urge to rip the shirt to shreds.

'Jess!'

My heart jumps into my mouth. *What am I doing?* I put the shirt back, look around quickly and judge that nothing is out of its place, and then hurry towards the door.

'Coming!' I call back and dash out of the room, making

sure to leave the door ajar as before. I know, without quite understanding why, that I'll go in there again some time.

Julia doesn't come home when she's meant to, so when the afternoon progresses to dinnertime and then bedtime for the kids, I offer to read Léa a story and tuck her in. She nods but doesn't smile back.

'That would be great, Jess, *merci,*' Michel says. He put Luca to bed an hour ago. It's the third night since I arrived that Julia's worked late. Léa's asked five times when she'll be home, and all Michel could do was shake his head.

'*Bientôt, chérie.*' Soon. It's a refrain I remember from my childhood. Such were my parents' jobs that rarely were they both at home in the evening, one of them inevitably caught up in a breaking story or a tight deadline or a source meeting that just couldn't wait. Part of me was always in awe of their stellar careers, the other part of me wished they'd just be home for dinner. But they did their best to take it in turns, at least.

Léa's bedroom is every little girl's fantasy. It has cream walls with hot pink and lime green painted wardrobes and a lampshade with cut-out stars that project a mini milky way onto the walls. A purple velvet chair sits in one corner between a crammed bookshelf and a small desk. Her bed has a fuchsia duvet cover and is lined along the far edge by a menagerie of stuffed toys.

'Who's this?' I say, stroking the plush fur of a large St Bernard.

'Barry.' Léa gets under the covers and pulls him into a hug.

'Are you okay? *Ça va chérie?*' I offer my badly accented French in an attempt to make her smile, and she does, briefly.

She nods and picks up a book, the first Harry Potter, one of several that Julia got in English for me to read to the children. She hands it to me. 'Please read.'

I settle next to her on the bed and she nestles into me. The clean, warm scent of her hair is comforting and I stroke it as I read. I wonder what Julia's doing now, what project is keeping her from this moment, and I feel a sudden flash of rage towards her, with her high-powered job and her wardrobe stuffed full of designer labels. Because I know that no bumper salary or career ambitions or taste for expensive clothes would keep me from having moments like these with my own child if I had one.

I give Léa a squeeze. It's lucky she's got me to read to her, I think, before my conscience slaps me down.

She's not yours. Don't get too attached. But I know it's already too late for that.

MARCH 1976

Lausanne/Bern, Switzerland

SYLVIA

She spent the night in bursts of restless sleep and wakeful-
ness, images of angry red slogans and steam rising from the
fondue pot and Daniel's bitter smile merging into some
strange triptych in her mind. The next morning she ditched
the suit for a pair of flared jeans, a turtle neck and a purple
bobble hat her mother had crocheted for her, and arrived
back at the flat at 9am when Evelyne and the girls – and
Daniel, she was surprised to see – were loading banners into
a battered old van.

'Right, everybody in!' Evelyne said.

'Wait!' Nina tugged her arm. 'This is an important day
in the life of the MFL. We need a photo. Here,' she thrust a
camera at Daniel. 'You take it.'

They lined up in front of the building, insisting that

Sylvia be included, and smiled as Daniel snapped a couple of shots, his expression impenetrable behind the camera.

There was a boisterous atmosphere in the van on the way, and when they arrived in the Swiss capital, Sylvia could tell they were all desperate to get out and march. They parked near the train station and Sylvia took her share of the equipment from the van, slung her bag over her shoulder and followed the others into Bern's Old Town. They'd passed the famed *Röstigraben* linguistic border somewhere near Fribourg, and here felt like another country entirely, even though they were only forty or so miles away from Lausanne. All the street signs were in German, and the architecture was darker and more austere than Lausanne's pastel shutters and wrought-iron balconies. Here, the centuries-old stone houses had tiny attic windows, umber roof tiles and gargoyles. Trolley buses rattled up and down worn cobbles, while on each side of the street covered walkways protected pedestrians from the light snow that was falling languorously from the grey sky. Sylvia adjusted her hat over her ears and looked up, feeling the snowflakes on her face with an unexpected sense of joy.

Soon, the street opened out into a large rectangular space lined with cafes. They turned right and reached another square dominated by the Swiss parliament, an imposing building with columns on its facade and a domed roof. On one side of the square, a small stage had been set up, decorated with banners. People were milling about, some holding signs, others just standing in small groups talking and laughing. There was a visceral hum in the air, a collective energy building up as everyone waited for something to happen.

Mon corps, mon choix! she read on one banner. 'My body, my choice!' *Avortement – oui!* said another. 'Abortion – yes!'

The words hit Sylvia like a punch in the stomach. The wine, the fondue, the music, the sights and sounds of a new country ... It had been all too easy to put aside what she knew, with increasing certainty, was happening to her. Seeing the signs here, she knew she was lucky to at least have some choice in the matter. But she wished someone could just tell her which choice was the right one.

Evelyne and her friends were greeted by another group of women and a round of three-kisses began, a ritual that could take some time, Sylvia felt. She found herself standing alone with Daniel.

'Evelyne must be pleased to have a brother who supports her in this.'

He looked at the ground when she spoke. 'It's no big deal.'

She stared at him, willing him to meet her eyes. Was he shy? Or just naturally surly?

'Oh, it is,' she said. She looked out over the crowds gathering in the square. 'It's a huge deal to have men supporting women because we'll never get true equality unless men agree it's important too.'

He didn't respond, and they stood in silence for a minute, Daniel scuffing his feet on the floor. She thought of Maggie's father, who never wanted her to go to art school and instead pulled strings with an acquaintance to get her a job as a bank clerk so she could *make some pocket money* and hopefully meet a respectable moneyed man to marry. But Maggie had only endured three months at the bank before quitting and spending her last month's salary on a ticket to Thailand where she passed another three months backpacking, drawing by day and partying by night. Sylvia remembered her friend arriving home with her hair in corn rows, a suitcase full of tie-dyed skirts and a portfolio of sketches and paintings that got her into art school later that year. But Sylvia knew how much it pained Maggie that her father still hadn't forgiven her.

'I just think everyone should be free to do whatever the hell they want in life,' Daniel said.

Sylvia turned, cocked her head. 'Are you free?' She said it as a reflex, and then immediately regretted saying it out loud. 'Forget it, it's none of my business.'

He finally turned to look at her and she saw something soften in his eyes, the hint of a smile at the corner of his mouth. 'Evelyne never was any good at keeping her mouth shut,' he said.

She received no more answer than that because at that moment a woman in a woolly hat and long coat started speaking on the stage, a microphone projecting her voice across the large space so it echoed off the parliament building's facade. Soon the square had taken on the charged atmosphere of a festival as people cheered at her speech, brandishing their placards and shouting rally chants in French and German.

Equality for women! Our bodies belong to us! Liberation means revolution!

Sylvia took her camera out of her bag and began snapping, slipping amongst the crowd until she'd soon lost Evelyne, Daniel and the others altogether.

Half an hour later, the opening speeches over, the demonstrators began to march out of the square and through the streets of Bern. Chanting and singing as they walked, the trail of people moved up the middle of a cobbled street named Marktgasse, past a stone fountain topped with a curious figure in red and gold. In the distance, Sylvia could see the pointed form of a clock tower; she assumed this was the medieval Zytglogge, displaying an astronomical clock she'd read dated from the sixteenth century. She was suddenly struck by the incongruity of a march for women's rights taking place amid streets built so long ago. How were they expected to bring change to the modern world when they had so much history to shrug off?

Stashing her camera in her bag, she began to talk to demonstrators – in English and French mostly, plus a mix of very basic German and sign language – about their motives, their hopes, the experiences that had brought them here. She spoke to university students demanding a different future to their mothers, women in their sixties reinvigorated by finally getting the vote, and single women demanding the right to live their lives as they wanted, not as expectation prescribed. There was Sarah, the young wife marching in defiance of her new husband, who had demanded she resign from the job she loved; Mathilde, who'd had an illegal abortion two years ago and nearly died; and Hanna, a striking 25-year-old who was placed in a reform school at the age of sixteen for having the temerity to fall in love with the wrong sort of boy.

'When I got out of that hell hole,' she told Sylvia, 'I vowed never to let anyone dictate my life again.'

She wrote down their words and photographed their passionate faces, seeing the determination and cautious hope in their eyes, the fire that had ignited from being told they must behave in a certain way simply because they were women.

'Take my picture,' Hanna said, grabbing Sylvia's arm. 'Put it in your newspaper and tell the world what we are fighting for.'

As Sylvia continued to walk, talk and photograph, she saw her feature taking shape; she knew whose stories she would highlight, whose words she would quote, which picture she hoped would turn out well enough to use. Powered by the crowd's energy and her own adrenaline, she felt hyper-alert, as though on a high from a drug she couldn't find anywhere else but here – and she understood in that moment that she loved it, this drug. She loved being right in the middle of something important, experiencing history in-the-making. She loved talking to these women leading such different lives to hers, and yet seeing herself reflected in their passion, in their basic need for freedom, for escape from society's constraints, for control over their own bodies. But most of all she loved being in a position to tell their story. This job was what made her happiest. It was what she was made to do. And she knew she just couldn't give it up.

JUNE 2016

Lausanne, Switzerland

Jess

On Wednesday, I drop the kids at the sports centre in Lausanne for their tennis lesson and drive on up the hill until I reach Sallaz. On the phone, Nina described this area as 'the Bronx', but it's far from that, just not as pretty as the old town centre or the manicured lakeside. Rows of fairly new but unimaginative apartment blocks sit on both sides of the main road. They are so identikit that I have trouble finding the right one, but after ten minutes of driving up and down I find block eighteen and park up on the road outside.

'*Bienvenue.* I do not know what I can tell you, but you are welcome.'

Nina Favre ushers me in. Probably in her late sixties, she's stylishly dressed in a cream shirt and navy trousers, a red scarf tied around her neck. Dark hair cut into a sleek bob skims her shoulders. Her smile is wide and there's a warmth in her face that makes me like her immediately.

I slip my shoes off at the apartment door and attempt to avoid the little yappy dog that barks in excitement.

'*Arrête, minou, arrête!*' Nina Favre flaps her hands at the dog and it trots over to a leopard-print basket in the corner and curls itself into a circle, nose on paws. 'Would you like a *café*?' she says. 'Or *du thé*. You are British, yes?'

I nod and accept the tea when it arrives, even though it's just a mug of already cooling water and a Lipton Yellow Label on the side. I made the mistake of ordering tea last week in a cafe in Montreux and it came like this. Maggie would be aghast.

'I do not speak of *Le Mouvement des Femmes Lausannoises* for many years,' Nina says once we're installed on the cream leather couch.

'You were part of it?'

She nods and a wide smile spreads across her face. '*Absolument*. It was a fantastic movement. With fantastic people.' She pauses. 'Fantastic *women*.'

It takes little prompting for her to go on, and even though she struggles for the English words at times, I get the idea, not least from her animated expression as she talks, that this was one of the best times of her life. Women coming together, newly enfranchised, to fight for further rights, to shout for revolution and demand they be heard. Salary equality, childcare provision, reproductive rights . . . all causes they championed through rallies across Switzerland, joining other women from around the country. For a time, Nina lived in an all-women commune, she tells me, and she once spent a night in a police cell for participating in an illegal protest outside a government building – there's a definite sense of pride in her face when she tells me that. Having read Mum's article, I knew something of Switzerland's history of women's rights before coming here, but until now, hearing Nina talk, I hadn't known quite how late some rights came to women here. It took until 2002 for the abortion law to be liberalised, she tells me, while statutory maternity pay was agreed two years later.

'Women in the canton of *Appenzell Rhodes-Intérieures*, they could not vote in cantonal elections until *mille neuf cent nonante et un*,' she says, adding slowly in careful English: 'Nineteen ninety-one.' She laughs at my shock. 'Yes, we fought a long battle. Now you understand!'

I take a sip of tea. 'I wanted to ask you about someone in the organisation. Did you know Evelyne Buchs?'

My heart leaps when Nina claps her hands. '*Oui, bien sûr.* Evelyne was so passionate about our cause. And she was a good friend.'

'Was?'

Nina nods. 'She died many years ago, after an illness.'

My stomach plunges and I'm embarrassed to feel my eyes prick with tears that I fight back. I didn't even know Evelyne, but I suddenly realise how much I wanted to meet her, not only because she might have known something about what happened to my mother in 1976, but to hear someone who knew and liked Mum speak of her once again.

I drain the teacup. It rattles as I put it back in the saucer. 'I'm sorry to hear that.'

Nina shrugs. '*C'est la vie.*'

'How about Brigitte Mela, does that name mean anything to you?'

Nina frowns. 'In the movement? No, I don't remember anyone by that name.'

My hopes sink, but I try not to show it. 'Were any men involved?' I change tack.

Nina smiles. 'We didn't allow men to be members of our group – the movement was *by* women, *for* women – but sometimes they would come to the demonstrations. Boyfriends and friends of the women, the younger ones. But not really the older ones, especially husbands. Married men, they do not prefer to encourage their wives.' She leans forward, conspiratorially. 'That is why I prefer a dog to a husband,' she says and lets out a peal of laughter.

I smile back at her and look down at the little yappy thing in the basket. Can't say I can see the appeal. 'I don't suppose you remember a British woman who came to visit Evelyne once, in 1976. She was a journalist.'

Nina thinks for a minute, as though trying to dig out a memory, and then shakes her head. 'Maybe, but … *non, désolée.* It was a long time ago.'

I take out the article and smooth out the creases, handing

it to her. 'The journalist who visited is my mother. This is what she wrote.'

Nina takes it from me, puts on a pair of reading glasses and studies the print-out. She gives a sharp intake of breath when she sees the photos. '*C'est moi!*' she says, pointing to a photo of a young woman in scruffy dungarees and an over-sized brown cardigan, long dark hair almost to her waist. I smile, unable to equate that figure with the elegant person I see in front of me now.

'*Oui*, I remember that day,' she says. 'We were in Bern for a demonstration. So many people. It was a very wonder-ful experience. And yes, perhaps I do remember a British woman, a writer. But I was so excited about the event, I'm sorry, I don't remember anything about her.'

I take the article and put it back in my bag, deflated. I don't know what else to ask her. Evelyne's gone. Nina doesn't really remember Mum. I don't know anyone else who spent time with them in Switzerland back then. Frustration curls into a knot in my chest. Perhaps she sees my expression because she pats my knee and disappears, before coming back a few minutes later with a photo album.

'I think in here there is something of Evelyne. You want to see?' She motions for me to move closer and opens the album – a bulky affair with tracing paper in between thick pages of black card. As she turns the pages, I see the dates – 1975 *Décembre*; 1976 *Mars* – and the pictures, most in black and white, some in faded colour, depicting people in flares and turtle neck knits, kids on long wooden skis.

'Here!' Nina points to a picture of a group of people lined up outside a building, which the handwritten note below the photo says is Rue Haldimand 8, Lausanne. 'This is Evelyne.'

And my breath sticks in my throat because standing right next to Evelyne is my mother.

'That's her,' I say.

'Your *maman*?' Nina looks at me and then back at the photo. 'She looks *sympa*. Very nice.'

'She was,' I say, fighting to keep my voice even. I stare at the photo, at this version of Mum that existed before I was born, and I wonder what was going on in her head that day. Was she excited about her trip? Did she like being in Switzerland? She's wearing a heavy Afghan coat and flared trousers, a purple bobble hat on her head, and she looks so young. It's strange to think that those were the hands that later held mine, that was the smile I knew so well, yet right then, at that point in time, she was completely unaware of everything that was to come later. Did she even know she was pregnant?

Nina cocks her head as she looks at the photo and I can almost see the memory coming to her. I wait, not wanting to disturb the flow.

'*En fait*,' she says eventually. 'I think I *do* remember a journalist visiting. And it was the same time as Evelyne's brother. Yes, that's right. They arrived on the same night, just before the demonstration. He must have taken this photo.'

'A brother?'

'Yes. A younger brother. I think he was here in Lausanne,

staying with Evelyne. A few weeks, a month, perhaps. After that, I don't know. I hear nothing of him since.'

It's a glimmer of hope. Evelyne may be gone, but perhaps this man might remember something, *anything*, that could help me hurdle the brick wall I'm facing.

'Do you remember his name?' I say.

Nina squeezes her eyes shut and purses her mouth while she thinks.

'Daniel,' she says finally, a note of triumph in her voice. 'Daniel Buchs.'

MARCH 1976

London, UK

SYLVIA

'Pregnant?'

'Yes.'

'*You?*'

She nodded.

'Fuck, Sylvia.'

'Yes, that must have been how it happened,' Sylvia said, even though she didn't think this was anything to make light of. Maggie, sitting next to her on the sofa in their tiny Clapham flat, was fiddling with the frayed end of her tunic like it was a string of worry beads, a gesture that provoked a flood of panic in Sylvia. Maggie rarely worried, her essential optimism was one of the things Sylvia admired most about her. She turned back to the television and the two of them watched – or, at least, stared at without seeing – as Columbo peered at some dirt on the carpet and then transferred his inscrutable gaze to a tall man with white hair and a dastardly air.

Maggie turned back to her. 'Seriously though, *how*?'

Sylvia shook her head. 'That's what I've been asking myself.'

At least, that's what she'd been asking herself when she dared think about it. She'd managed, fairly successfully, to keep the thing caged in some far corner of her mind throughout her trip to Switzerland, but on the plane home, and the long taxi ride back to Clapham, she'd been unable to keep it from wrestling its way forward. There'd been a young mother on the plane with a screaming toddler, of course. An apologetic smile on her face. Tears in her eyes when a businessman pointedly asked to move seats.

How? Well, she supposed it didn't matter now. But she still wanted to know. She remembered going to a family planning clinic in her first year of university and the lecture the doctor gave her when she requested a prescription; her refusal to cower with humiliation when he asked if she was married, even though the pill had been perfectly legal for unmarried women since 1967. She didn't care that the conservative media said it turned girls like her into promiscuous harlots. For her it was about freedom and control. It was a way to protect herself, to keep her life exactly as she wanted it, until she and Jim decided otherwise. A way to stop herself turning into Gilly, married at eighteen, with three children by the time she turned twenty-four.

How long had it been since Gilly's wedding? Nearly six

years, she supposed, the autumn of the year they finished school. Six whole years since they all lay sprawled on the grass outside the assembly hall the afternoon of their final A Level exams. Sylvia still recalled the sense of freedom that welled up in her chest back then. It returned to her every time she smelled cut grass and spring blossom in the air – or heard *Let It Be* on the radio, because it was the end of something for John, Paul, George and Ringo then too, back in 1970.

'I reckon you'll marry a lumberjack.'

'What?' Fiona had propped herself up on her elbow and squinted at Gilly.

'I think you're going to marry a lumberjack – or someone like that – and live in the woods.'

Fiona laughed. 'That's the future you have mapped out for me? Gee, thanks.' She punched Gilly lightly on the arm and lay back on the grass, staring up at the sky. 'It's scary, isn't it?'

'What, the prospect of marrying a lumberjack? I should say so,' Maggie said.

'No, silly! The future, I mean. What's going to happen next. We've got our whole lives ahead of us and no clue where we'll end up. I think it's scary.'

'It's exciting, more like,' Sylvia said. 'We can finally do anything we want.'

'You really think so?'

She shrugged. 'Well, you can try at least. Why not dream big?'

'It's all right for you,' Gilly said. 'You're clever. You're going to Oxford.'

'You're clever too,' she said, though lately she'd wondered if that were true. If Gilly were clever, why was her only plan to marry Brian and settle down in a semi-detached right here in Hertford? Didn't she want to get out? See what the rest of the world had to offer? Sylvia felt full to the brim with it: the urge to leave where she grew up and forge her own path.

'Well, we all know where *you'll* be, Gills,' Fiona said.

'His parents are meeting mine tonight. We're all going out to dinner to celebrate.' Gilly beamed. She hadn't stopped fiddling with her ring all afternoon.

'What are you going to wear?'

'I went shopping with Mum the other day and got this lovely green dress. It's sophisticated, you know. And it shows off my boobs.' She jiggled her breasts and the others giggled, even Maggie, though Sylvia caught all she needed to know about Maggie's opinion of Gilly's engagement from a briefly arched eyebrow and a loaded glance in her direction. They'd always been able to communicate silently – a sort of telepathy honed over ten years of sitting next to each other at school.

'Are you sure this is what you want?' Sylvia picked at a daisy and twirled it in her fingers. 'I mean, what's the rush?'

A flash of annoyance passed across Gilly's face. 'Of course it is. We've been together two whole years, why would we wait any longer?'

'Oh, I don't know, because there might be other more exciting—'

Maggie elbowed her arm. *Don't*, she mouthed. 'Well,

good for you, Gills. I love a wedding. All that cake and champagne.'

'And the dishy waiters.' Tracey was lying on the grass staring up at the sky. 'My sister said they're right goers, waiters at weddings. She worked at one once and said they had a bet going to see who could get off with a bridesmaid.' She rolled on her side and looked at Gilly. 'Can I be a bridesmaid?'

Fiona laughed. 'Slapper!'

'Just an opportunist,' Tracey grinned. 'Well, how about it, Gills?'

'Er, well, I'll have to see.' Gilly's voice was shrill. 'I know Brian's sisters have to be in the wedding party so I don't know how many more bridesmaids I can have.' She waved her hand. 'Anyway, back to the topic in hand.'

'What was that?' Fiona said.

'Our futures! Predicting where we'll all end up! I think we should write it down.' She fished around in her bag and pulled out a pen and a school textbook, tearing off the back to write on. 'Won't be needing that anymore,' she trilled. 'Right. So, Fiona: lumberjack.'

'Is that it? Is that *all* you predict for me?'

'Well, for the moment. How about Maggie – bank teller?'

'That's not a prediction, that's a fact!' Fiona laughed.

'That really stinks, that's what that is,' Tracey said.

Sylvia saw the expression on Maggie's face. She couldn't think of a worse job for her best friend, who'd always hated maths at school, but she knew Maggie wouldn't dare say no to her father's plans for her. 'That's just a stopgap until you figure out what you want to do, right Mags?'

Maggie blew her fringe off her forehead. 'Try telling that to Dad.'

'Okay, temporary bank teller. Just until you get married and have kids. I reckon you'll have three.'

'You're talking out of your backside, Gills,' Tracey said.

'Stop being such a spoilsport, it's just for fun, okay? I'm going to keep this and then one day in twenty years or something we'll meet up and laugh about what we said.' Gilly gave them all a pointed stare and wrote down 'three kids' in big letters next to Maggie's name. 'Right, how about Sylvia?'

'Prime minister!' Janine said.

'Astronaut!'

'Stop taking the piss,' Sylvia said. She'd always felt faintly embarrassed by her reputation at school. She couldn't help it if she did well in exams. She couldn't help being interested in things. But it had never been cool to be academic, so she'd apologised for herself, almost been pleased when she'd got a B instead of an A in a test, just so she could feel she fitted in with the other kids. But all that was behind her now, she realised. Today was the end of all that. She'd been released from the shackles of schoolyard social pressures and would be going to Oxford, where no one, she was sure, ever had to apologise for doing well.

'I know what.' Maggie put her arm around her and smiled. 'She's going to be a newspaper editor on Fleet Street.'

Sylvia snorted. 'Like that's possible,' she said. But as the smell of summer mingled with the thrill of the new, she thought, *yes, maybe I just will.*

That all seemed so long ago now. How cross she would have been with her future self if she'd known what would happen! She couldn't bear the thought she'd potentially squandered her opportunity for freedom so soon after escaping the limitations of childhood. She thought of the women she'd met in Switzerland, how much she admired their fight, and felt determination well up in her again. A baby simply wasn't part of her plan. It would ruin everything.

'What does Jim think?' Maggie said.

Sylvia shook her head, staring at Peter Falk as he cuffed the murderer. 'I haven't told him.'

Maggie's eyes narrowed. 'And when will you?'

'I don't know. When I've sorted out in my head what I want to do.'

'You're not considering . . . ?'

Sylvia looked at her. 'Maybe. At least, I'm going to look into it.'

She thought of Jim, cooing over her sister's kids whenever they visited; the delight in their faces when they saw him, since kids seemed to love Jim as much as he loved them. Yes, he'd agreed to wait until they were older, but she knew he'd never agree to a termination now it had happened. So if she decided she wanted to get rid of it, she couldn't ever tell him she'd been pregnant. She met Maggie's eyes and knew she didn't need to spell it out.

'I get it, Syl. God, I get it. But you can't do that to him.' Maggie took Sylvia's hand and held it in her lap, and Sylvia felt the roughness of her friend's skin, a badge of honour for the hours she'd spent in the art studios at Saint Martin's, creating the pieces that had won her a hard-earned art degree and her new job at the National Theatre. 'Can you?'

'I don't know, Mags.' But she didn't think she could do the alternative, either.

She made an appointment for the next morning and had her suspicions confirmed. Dr Greenham clearly expected a delighted response on delivering such *happy news*, but she sat mute, in shock despite having already known what he would say. Then he glanced at the single diamond on her finger and his face changed.

'When are you due to marry?' he asked.

'Next summer,' she said.

'Do it quickly and you're out of trouble.' He said it kindly, conspiratorially, as though she should be grateful. But instead she felt as though the walls of the office were closing in.

'What are my other options?' She held her head high as she said it, watching his smile drop and his eyes narrow. He handed her a piece of paper, telling her to read it and think very carefully. It's not an *option*, he said. It's a medical procedure only carried out if two doctors agree to it. It's not like having a tooth out. He glared at her over his spectacles and she bristled at being made to feel like a child in front of the headmaster.

When she left the surgery, she walked along the Thames at Blackfriars instead of going straight back to the office. She bought a takeaway Tetley from the corner cafe and leaned over the railings, staring at the grey, turgid water. The air was damp cold and she clutched the warm polystyrene cup with both hands. Something caught her eye and she turned her head to the right to see a squirrel running up the trunk of a tree. It stopped for a second, looked straight at her and then darted into the higher branches. Two children walking past with their mother saw it too. They stopped and pointed, the younger child delighted to spot the tiny creature. The woman smiled at Sylvia. 'You'll catch your death standing there,' she said.

When Sylvia was about that child's age – four, five? – her mother must have been twenty-nine or so. A mum for eight years already. No career, only two years as a secretary before she had married. She spent her days making house. Days dominated by washing cycles and groceries and rubbish collection dates and endless dusting. Sylvia always thought her mother was relatively happy. She certainly never complained – unless you made a mess of her tidy home, of course. But, growing up in the sixties, all Sylvia saw when she looked at her mother's life was a trap she didn't want to fall into herself.

These days, with Sylvia and her siblings grown and gone, her mum spent most of her time making clothes. Sewing dresses and shorts for the grandkids, crocheting hats and scarves for friends. They were beautiful, detailed, intricately patterned with carefully chosen colours. She was talented. Sylvia had once found a sketchbook filled with drawings, tucked under the guestroom bed. Women in elegant dresses, maxi skirts, tailored coats. Some pages had fabric swatches glued beside them, and she'd realised with a jolt that these were her mother's own designs. She'd taken the book downstairs and waved it triumphantly at her.

'These are brilliant, Mum – why haven't you ever shown me?'

Her mother had snatched the book away. 'Give me that! It's nothing. Just a hobby. Not for anyone's eyes.'

In that moment, Sylvia saw it. Just the tiniest hint of something she realised was regret. Regret over an aspiration she'd never had the opportunity, or confidence, to fulfil.

She spent the afternoon at Brent Cross interviewing shoppers for their opinions about the glossy new commercial centre. 'Are American-style malls the next big thing? Is this the new way to shop?' fashion editor Marnie had said when she'd packed Sylvia off to write a 'lively' piece for tomorrow's paper. Frankly, Sylvia didn't care an ounce, but she dutifully spent the morning talking to women picking out lingerie in John Lewis and mothers gossiping over coffee while their kids played on the giant wooden caterpillar designed to entertain the under sevens.

Yes, was the enthusiastic conclusion she wrote up afterwards.

Hold on to your purse strings! With everything under one roof, Brent Cross is a revolutionary new shopping experience that is likely to transform the way we buy – and how long we spend doing it. With restaurants and cafes, children's entertainment and a vast range of shops, this American-style mall is designed to entice us in and keep us there for as long as it can, much to the likely dismay of husbands all over London.

She bored herself, but Marnie seemed pleased.

Jim was waiting for her after work with a bunch of drooping tulips wrapped in cellophane. She laughed. 'What's that for?'

'I've missed you.' He swept her into an embrace and she hugged him back, the flowers squashed between them.

They walked along the river to Embankment and entered the musty confines of Gordon's Wine Bar. He went to order drinks and she sat down, smiled at a group of six around the table next to her, greeting cards opened and displayed on the wooden table top. She caught the writing on one: 'Congratulations on your engagement'. The girl showed off her ring, curled into her fiancé, beamed up at him.

The first time she came to this bar was within weeks of moving to London. Jim had arranged an internship at a political magazine, and she was applying for every junior reporter job and graduate trainee scheme going, hoping to get one before her money ran out and she'd be forced to temp, a prospect that scared her more than staying jobless, not least because the words of her French literature tutor rang loud in her ears: *Never tell anyone you can touch-type or you'll be forever pigeonholed as a secretary.* What little money they did have went towards rent on their respective flatshares two stops apart down the Northern Line: she with Maggie in Clapham, Jim with his uni friend David down the road in Balham, a set-up forged mainly to placate Jim's mother, for whom *living in sin* was simply an unacceptable state of affairs for her only son. This pokey old bar had seemed to epitomise everything they loved about being in London, so they'd cobbled together enough money for one glass each and had come here to toast their new lives.

Back then – what, only a year and a half or so? – everything had seemed new, fresh, exciting, hopeful. Their futures were a clean slate, waiting to be imprinted with success and money and respect and experience.

She still felt like that last week, she realised now. Just last week.

'So, this weekend.' Jim put a wine bucket on the table, an uncorked bottle nestled in the ice. 'We'll drive to Haversham Manor first, then it's a quick scoot up the M40 to Beckton Abbey. I wondered if we could go via Bellhampton too. I know we don't have an appointment, but it's on the way so we could have a quick peek in the grounds, just to see. I know you thought it would be too grand, but I wouldn't mind a look. You only get married once, after all.'

Sylvia nodded. Should she tell him now? Just blurt it out?

'And then we're booked in for a cuppa at Mum and Dad's after all that, around 5ish, okay?'

She could just say the words. But then it would be out there and she'd have no control over it anymore. Right now, nothing had to change. She and Jim were getting married next year. They'd have several years before they even tried to have a family and she'd continue to build up her career until a suitable point when she felt comfortable taking time out. Then perhaps she'd go freelance while the children were young, but she'd have enough contacts by then, and a good enough reputation, that she could do that without fear of losing what she'd built. That was the plan. That's what was meant to happen.

'Did you hear what I said?'

'Yes, sorry.' She felt like screaming. Everything was so easy for him, while she'd always felt like a general preparing a battle plan.

'You *are* looking forward to it, aren't you?'

She smiled at him. That open, happy, carefree face. She wanted to reach out and smooth his hair, watch his eyes crinkle at the corners as he smiled back. Would it have Jim's blond hair, his height? Or perhaps her darker skin that tanned easily in the sun, her brown eyes? She flicked the thought away. 'I am,' she said. 'Very much.'

JUNE 2016

Montreux, Switzerland

JESS

Julia isn't around on Saturday when Michel asks if I want to join him and the kids on a hike. I was planning to spend some time trying to track down Daniel Buchs; however, it seems silly to pass up the opportunity to explore the area with a local. But it's more than that, I have to admit. As I take my place in the passenger seat of his car, the kids in the back, I feel a little thrill to be stepping into Julia's shoes.

An hour into our walk, and halfway up what feels like a colossus of a mountain, I remember that the last time I walked up any significant hill was on a school trip to Snowdonia when I was twelve. And I wasn't very good at it then.

I'm slick with sweat. It soaks the back of my T-shirt, runs between my breasts, drips suncream into my eyes. Luckily, only the cows are witnessing my sorry state. Léa is far ahead, more or less skipping up the slope, Michel and Luca not long behind her.

I place one foot in front of the other, trying to keep as regular a rhythm as my straining lungs will allow. Big brown eyes look up as I pick my way over loose stones and dried cowpats. I hear the swish of their tails and the discordant, irregular chime of the bells around their necks, smell the rich pong of the countryside. The grass is speckled with wildflowers whose names I don't know, and I think of Maggie and her garden. She'd know. I pull out my phone and crouch down to take a picture of a bright pink flower to text to her, glad of the excuse for a momentary pause.

'*Ça va*, Jess?' Michel says when I finally reach the top where the three of them are sprawled on the grass near a giant metal cross. I nod, hands on hips, gulping greedy breaths until my pulse starts to slow.

'Wow,' I say when I can speak again. 'It's stunning up here.' The lake puddles below us, shadows sliding over its vast surface. I instantly don't care about the pain and the sweat. It's completely worth it.

'Yes, it's nice here,' Michel says, and my mouth drops open at his understatement.

'*Nice?* It's incredible. I've never seen anything like it.'

He laughs. 'There are a lot of good views in Switzerland. It's not even that high up here.'

Not that high? I look at the three of them. They've barely broken a sweat and I realise with dismay that what's been a Herculean task for me is simply a stroll in the park for them. 'Well,' I say, 'this isn't half bad for my first-ever hike.'

He looks at me, eyebrows raised. 'You have never hiked before?'

I feel my cheeks burn, but then it doesn't matter, they're red anyway. 'Er, no, not really. Not for a long time anyway.' I look down at the top-of-the-range leather hiking boots I bought especially for the trip, a little present to myself after my last payday at St Mary's. Maggie came with me to choose them and clapped her hands when she saw me. *You're all set now. Ready for Switzerland.* I'd sighed at myself in the shop mirror. *All the gear, no idea.*

'*Mon Dieu*, what do the British do at the weekend?' Michel says, and as I stand there looking at the sun searing the lake, I really can't fathom. What on earth *did* I do back home, before everything changed? Met friends for coffee on Lordship Lane. Marked Year 11 literature mocks. Sat in the park with a book and ready-mixed gin and tonic out of a can. Watched box sets with Patrick. Planned to hit the gym but never actually went.

'Hiking is what we do here. It's a national sport,' he adds and I nod.

It's another life, here. A life I could have had.

We picnic on bread, dried meat and cheese, and then pack up and walk on, downhill this time, in the direction of a wood cabin Michel tells me is some kind of restaurant. He's promised me a cup of tea and a slice of cake as a reward for my unprecedented exertions. Léa and Luca scamper on ahead, but Michel hangs back with me.

'Thanks for inviting me,' I say. 'This is wonderful.'

'You're welcome. It's nice to see Switzerland through a foreigner's eyes.'

His English is American-accented. 'You speak such good English. Did you study in the States?'

He smiles. '*Merci*. Yes, I did a business postgraduate degree there. Columbia. A long time ago now.'

'Was Julia out there with you?'

'No. She stayed here. She'd just got a great job and it didn't make sense for her to come so we were long distance for a while.'

I nod. I wonder where he met Julia and how long they've been together. I wonder what they love about each other, which of Julia's little habits Michel finds beguiling and which frustrate the hell out of him. I want to know everything about them; I want to know the steps they took to get here, to become this perfect family. Perhaps there's a secret I've not been privy to. Maybe if I knew, I could make it happen for me.

'And you? Where did you study?'

'Bristol. English degree. Very unoriginal.'

'You always wanted to be an English teacher?'

'Not really. I didn't know what else to do and I loved books, so ...' I realise how rubbish that sounds, but to his credit, he doesn't say so.

'Well, you're good at it.' He looks at me and my eyes

clearly show surprise. 'Léa's raving about you. The other day she took me through every animal name you taught her. It was a long list.' He laughs and I smile back, a thrill warming my insides at his praise.

'Well, duck-billed platypus is an essential piece of everyday vocabulary,' I say. I look ahead to where I can just see Léa and Luca. Luca's running ahead, as fast as his little legs can take him. Léa's bending down to look at something. I feel a surge of happiness to be here with them, included in this scene. Like I'm a member of their family rather than an employee.

But that's not what you are, I remind myself. I'm paid to be here with Michel, Léa and Luca; I'm not a friend or a relative. I'm not his wife, their mother, though I wonder if that's what it looks like to the people we pass and I try to suppress the guilty pleasure that provokes. How lucky Julia is to have all this and how ridiculous she's choosing to spend her day in the office instead. I know all too well that you only appreciate what you have when you don't have it anymore. Maybe Julia will realise that too, someday.

'What a shame Julia had to miss out on this,' I say.

'She won't mind. She's been here many times before. She has this big project going on right now, so we're not seeing her very much on Saturdays.' He looks ahead to the kids and I can't glean anything from his expression.

'When will that be over?'

'Soon. In the fall it's the world championships. It's all building up to that. Then she should be able to take a holiday.'

'That's good. She seems pretty dedicated to it right now.'

Michel smiles. 'Yes, she is.'

I'm willing him to elaborate, but he doesn't. Part of me wants him to criticise her, to agree with my unspoken judgement that she should be here with her family, not in the office, but I can sense he's far too loyal for that.

'Well, it's good she has you supporting h—' I'm cut off by a scream and then Léa's rushing towards us yelling something in French. I don't understand what she's saying, but I know it's something serious when Michel takes off at a sprint, leaving me to run after him, cursing my lack of fitness once again. When I catch up and see Luca, my stomach flips over because it doesn't look like he's moving. But then I hear him cry and relief courses through me. 'What happened?' I say.

Michel is cradling his son's head and I can see a gash on his forehead. Blood runs down his face and the sight shocks me far more than the grazed knees and elbows I got used to seeing in the school playground at St Mary's.

'*Il est tombé*,' Léa says, big shuddering sobs shaking her slight frame.

'He tripped and hit his head on a rock,' Michel explains. 'Jess, hand me the first-aid kit.' He gestures to his backpack, which he's flung on the ground. 'Front pocket.'

I unzip the bag and take out a small case with a cross on it and squat down next to Michel. 'What can I do?'

'There's a roll of sticking plaster in there, and some antiseptic cream.'

I fish them out and hand them over along with a wad of

tissues that Michel presses onto the wound, making Luca scream. I stroke his hair and try to calm him as Michel cuts a strip of plaster.

'I think he'll be fine, but we'll take him to the hospital, just to be sure.' He turns to Léa and says something to her in a soothing voice, but it doesn't stop her sobs. I kneel down next to her and she folds herself into my hug, her tears dampening my neck. 'It's okay. He's going to be fine.' I rub her back and feel her shudders subside. I draw back and wipe the tears from her cheeks, wanting to lift the distress from her pretty face.

'*Bon. On y va.* Let's go.' Michel picks up Luca.

I pack up his backpack and put it on myself, before taking Léa by the hand. The four of us go back the way we came, the quickest route to the car park, Luca in Michel's arms and Léa clinging to my hand. I give hers a squeeze and she looks up at me with a small smile that warms every cell in my body.

It's only when we pull into the car park at the hospital that I realise. My head spins as I take in what the sign says. The community hospital in Lausanne. Of course it would be here. My jaw starts to throb and I realise I'm clenching my teeth. I swallow, take a breath.

It's newer, quieter and smarter than any hospital I've known in the UK and the emergency room sees us so quickly that I think we must have accidentally queue-jumped. A young doctor examines Luca and decides he needs a few stitches. She addresses me and Michel equally, assuming we're both his parents, and something in me is pleased Michel seems to feel no need to set her straight.

But I'm fidgety; I can't concentrate.

I wonder if the person I spoke to on the phone is here somewhere, in an administration building perhaps, getting on with his day, drinking coffee, laughing with colleagues. His words come back to me.

Full investigation. Every effort has been made. Please accept our sympathy for these tragic circumstances.

I don't want the apology that was never offered. I don't care about sorry. What I *do* need is to know who – and why.

No paperwork. Nothing we can do.

I feel sick just thinking about it.

I want to take a look around, wander through the corridors. I want to know if I'll feel it, if I'll somehow know in which room my mother brought me into the world. But I can't think of an excuse to do it. And I can't explain it to Michel without the whole thing spilling out. So I sit next to him and Léa as the doctor stitches Luca's forehead and I wonder how on earth I arrived back here, nearly forty years later.

We're all quiet in the car on the way home. Léa's fallen asleep, Michel is silent and I gaze out of the window as we cross the long, high motorway bridge back to Montreux. When we get to the house, Michel carries Luca in first and I hear a gasp from Julia.

I'm surprised she's actually home from work.

There's a fraught exchange in French and then she takes Luca from Michel and goes over to the sofa. Michel sits beside them and Léa follows, squeezing herself against Julia, who puts an arm around both children and hugs them tight. I remain in the doorway and swallow down a hard lump of envy in my throat.

She has everything I want.

MARCH 1976

London, UK

Sylvia

The bar was already heaving when they arrived. Sylvia was sure many of the regulars had been there all afternoon. She wondered how they ever got any work done. But on the other hand, she knew that a stint in El Vino's or one of the other hack hangouts was a necessity. Over claret and cigars, journalists were creating firm friendships that would likely pay dividends later in their careers, keeping their ears to the ground for an opening on another paper, schmoozing with their seniors in the hope of gaining a regular column or a pay rise, and gossiping over the latest news in and out of Fleet Street: at the moment, it was the breakdown of Princess Margaret's marriage and Prime Minister Harold Wilson's shock resignation. Though she disliked the bar's owner for his ridiculous attitude towards women and supported those who were suing him over it, she begrudgingly went there anyway because to boycott it was only to shoot yourself in the foot. Pick your battles, she'd decided.

She inched her way through the sea of shirts, jackets and ties towards the tables in the back room where the owner deigned to allow women to sit. Marnie was already there with Janice and a couple of other women she didn't know.

'What can I get yer, love?' A waiter was clearing glasses as she sat down.

'A dry white wine, please,' she said, hating her own complicity. What bloody use was the new Sex Discrimination Act if she couldn't just go and order her drink at the bar like the men?

'I hear he's paying her ten thousand a year.' Marnie leant back in her seat and took a long drag on her cigarette.

'And a fair bit else besides – usually late at night bent over his desk,' Janice said, and the others laughed.

'Who are you talking about?' Sylvia asked. She slipped off her coat and lit a cigarette proffered by Marnie, whose cleavage heaved as she leaned forward. As usual, the fashion editor's eye-catching outfit made the most of her natural assets – her patterned wrap dress cut a deep V over her ample bosom, which seemed on the brink of spilling out altogether. Though Sylvia thought it crazy to wear clothes like that to work, she sort of admired her devil-may-care attitude in the face of the men's regular jibes. Marnie didn't even seem to mind they'd nicknamed her 'bouncy castle'. Of course, it had occurred to Sylvia that flaunting what she had gave her colleague certain advantages.

'Jean Yardley-Jones,' Marnie said. 'Columnist at the *Mirror*. Rumour has it she's going to take over from Elizabeth Franks at the *Express* next month.'

'Oh right. I've read her stuff, she's a good writer.'

'And good at blow jobs, apparently.' Janice cackled and the others joined in. Sylvia was weary of rumours like these, but she knew there was likely to be truth in it. She remembered Janice hinting as much about Valerie and Roger. An open secret – to all except their spouses, apparently. Was that why Valerie basically had free rein to interview whomever she liked?

'Valerie's furious because it wasn't offered to her.' Marnie lowered her voice and added with a smirk, 'Doesn't realise it's only Roger who thinks the sun shines out of her arse.'

With a glance to her right, Marnie got up, heading for the ladies, and to Sylvia's surprise Valerie sidled through the throng and sat down next to her, a glass of sherry in her hand.

'Shouldn't it be champagne?' Valerie nodded towards Sylvia's glass. 'I hear you've done rather well.'

Sylvia cocked her head. 'What do you mean?'

'Your piece on women's lib in Switzerland. Sam had less of a workout than he was expecting. I didn't hear him swear once.'

'He's subbed it?'

Valerie blew out smoke above Sylvia's head. 'Said it wasn't bad at all. Though of course you knew it was good, didn't you?'

Sylvia couldn't suppress a smile. She'd worked bloody hard on the feature, and yes, she knew it was good, but she'd still felt concerned that somehow it wouldn't make it past Roger's critical eye or sub-editor Sam's ruthless pencil. 'When's it going in, do you know?'

'Friday, I believe.'

Valerie's face was unreadable, as ever, and her lack of expression – bar a touch of something (amusement?) in her pale blue eyes – made Sylvia feel uneasy, as though there was a whirl of thoughts and judgements going on in the columnist's head that she, the underling, wasn't privy to. It made her respond in kind; to anyone else she'd admit she was ecstatic to hear her feature was subbed and approved by Roger and going to be published, but to Valerie she felt forced to adopt a disinterested, almost haughty air.

It was strange, feeling unable to talk with any frankness to Valerie, given she knew so much intimate detail about her life – or, at least, the version of her life she portrayed in her column. She knew Valerie thought she was dying when she started her periods at fourteen because her mother had never spoken about this rite of passage. She knew Valerie had one lover before marrying her husband and stopped herself getting pregnant with him in that pre-pill era by religiously counting days and feigning a headache on the most fertile ones. She knew Valerie had helped a friend leave her violent husband, and that she'd suffered from depression after the birth of her second child. She knew all this, yet she had never really had a conversation with the columnist that went beyond superficial chitchat. But today of all days she needed to know something – and boosted by Valerie's words about her feature, she felt she could summon the balls to ask.

'Valerie, can I ask you something?'

'Of course,' she said, a smile on her mouth that didn't reach her eyes.

'How have you managed it? Being such a successful journalist whilst bringing up two children?'

Valerie drained her glass and looked at her. 'Well,' she said. 'I insisted they pay me exceedingly well so I can employ a live-in nanny.'

'It's that simple?'

Valerie laughed. 'Darling, it's never simple. You know that already, or you wouldn't have made it to Fleet Street in the first place.' She leaned forward. 'You want my advice? Don't do it. Or at least, don't do it until you're a star writer with the freedom to do as you please and a pay packet that gives you considerably more clout than you have now. And believe you me, that's not as easy as I've made it look.' She paused, cocked her head. 'Max Harmer started the same time as you, yes?'

Sylvia nodded. 'Same week.'

'Well you must know he's on significantly more than you, and only for the mere fact of owning a pair of bollocks. So much for the Equal Pay Act.' Valerie stubbed her cigarette out in the ashtray, smoke spiralling into Sylvia's face. 'And even if you do manage to convince an editor to dip into his deep pockets, if you're at all serious about your career you won't want to step back from it, not even for a minute. No editor will reward you for buggering off to have a baby. And no ambitious young hack wants to miss out on a story because she has to tuck her kids into bed.' She narrowed her eyes, nodded to Sylvia's engagement ring. 'You're contemplating it?'

'Oh, no,' Sylvia said. She waved her hand in the air, as though the ring was nothing. 'We don't intend to have children just yet. My fiancé is entirely supportive of my career.'

Valerie nodded. 'Jim Millson, isn't it?'

Sylvia's surprise must have shown on her face because Valerie added, 'Oh I know most things about most people round here.' She drained her glass and put it down on the table. 'Supportive,' she repeated.

'Very. We've always wanted the same thing, and he sees no reason why I shouldn't aim high.'

Valerie raised her eyebrows. 'Well jolly good. Just make sure you don't do better than him, or it's curtains for your marriage. But then, you're a woman, and this is Fleet Street, so frankly the odds are stacked against you anyway. Oh!' She grabbed a passing arm. 'David darling – order me another sherry, there's a dear.' And with that she got up and left the table without a backwards glance.

Greenham looked at her over his glasses with a pointed expression of disapproval, but all Sylvia could focus on were his bushy eyebrows, alarmingly thick and black, which waggled when he talked. She felt an inappropriate desire to laugh. He questioned her at length, kept repeating the word *distress*.

Was the pregnancy really causing her mental *distress*? Did she feel too *distressed* to carry on? Had she thought of the *distress* that a termination would cause her?

Yes, she said. Yes, yes. But the thought of continuing the pregnancy was far worse. It lay heavy on her windpipe, twisted her intestines and throbbed in her head.

'It's not uncommon to have doubts about becoming a mother.' He attempted a coercive smile.

'I don't have doubts. I'm certain I don't want to be,' she said. She saw Jim's face again. How delighted he'd be.

He never has to know.

Greenham sighed. 'You're not a teenager. You're a young woman soon to be married. There's no physical reason why you shouldn't have this baby, and I find it very dubious that a bright young woman such as yourself would find this sufficiently distressing to warrant a termination.'

She wondered what he knew about *sufficiently distressing*. The photo on his desk showed a couple in their twenties holding a small baby. Perhaps his son or daughter and grandchild. The woman was smiling in delight at the tiny face peering up at her. The loving husband had a beatific gaze: the lion with his pride.

A picture of the perfect family, right there.

But she knew it was never as simple as that. The picture didn't show the sacrifices the woman had made: the physical difficulties of having a baby – difficulties that her sister, Susie, had delighted in telling her in intimate detail – or the personal and professional desires that got shoved under the

119

bed. It didn't show the endless days of nappies and bottles and puke until her loving husband came home and she could finally get some sleep – if she wasn't cooking him dinner or doing the washing.

'It doesn't have to be like that,' Maggie had said. Jim was a modern man. He could cook, change nappies, do a bottle. It was '76, not '56.

But, she realised, she didn't want to do any of that either. She simply didn't. And it occurred to her then that perhaps she actually didn't want children at all – not just now, but ever. Despite her career ambitions, despite her seemingly insatiable desire to see what the world could offer, she'd never entertained the possibility she could *choose* not to have children. She'd always assumed she would one day because that's what you did, because that's what society expected, because that's what Jim wanted, her parents wanted, because it was what so many of her friends were doing. But perhaps she simply didn't want them at all.

It surprised her to realise this, and with the realisation came relief.

'If you won't say yes then I'll find another doctor who will,' she said.

He sighed and signed the form.

It smelt cloying in the clinic, a mixture of air freshener and disinfectant. She gave her name to the receptionist, who directed her to the waiting room where she sat on one of the hard, plastic chairs around the edge, trying not to make eye contact with the three other women in the room. As though they'd made a collective agreement, all three were staring, eyes glazed, at a low table in the centre of the room that was covered with magazines. *Good Housekeeping, Woman & Home, Woman's Realm.* A vase of perky daffodils sat in the centre. Spring flowers. If she had the baby, it would be born when – October? The thought pushed its way into her head before she could stop it. Seeking a distraction, she reached forward and picked up a magazine.

Hearty meals he'll love you for! How returning to work will affect your marriage. Fabulous fashions to sew from sheets. Poll: home or career, can you have both?

She dropped it back on the table. Gilly had a subscription to *Good Housekeeping*. Perhaps she made clothes from sheets and hearty meals her husband loved. Her school friend was happy with her life, Sylvia knew that, and she admired her ability to be content with her lot. But she couldn't understand it. Humans had stood on the moon, a woman was the leader of the opposition, Ziggy Stardust and Blondie and John and Yoko were making new rules – and then breaking them again. Why choose a regular life when you could choose an exciting one?

'Mrs Tallis?'

She looked up. A nurse was standing in the doorway to the waiting room. She didn't smile.

'Ms,' she said, and the other women in the room looked up when she spoke. One of them could only have been eighteen. Her face was pale, her eyes bloodshot.

Sylvia stood up and walked towards the nurse, her stomach doing backflips.

'Come this way, please.'

The nurse led Sylvia into a private room with a hospital bed, a small wash basin and a table on wheels loaded with various medical equipment. A doctor appeared – Dr Bennett, he said – and asked her the same questions Greenham had. Why couldn't she have the baby? Was she completely sure? Did she want counselling? By the end of his interrogation her brain was spinning and she felt close to tears. Apparently convinced, Bennett handed her a clipboard, a pen and a form. She took the paperwork and sat back on the bed as he left the room.

Boxes to complete. Consent to sign. A life to abort.

She took a deep breath. She couldn't believe she was actually in the position of having to do this. She remembered a girl in her year at school who fell pregnant at sixteen. At least, that was the rumour when she left school so suddenly in the middle of term. The child must be around eight by now. What pity she'd felt towards the girl. And how determined – and arrogant, she admitted now – she'd been that it wouldn't happen to herself.

'Have you filled in the forms?' The nurse was back.

'Yes.' She handed the clipboard over and the nurse put it aside. Sylvia sat in silence as the nurse took her blood pressure, and winced as a needle went into her vein to draw blood.

'I want you to know you can change your mind at any time up until you take the first medication.' The nurse stared at her, unsmiling. Sylvia nodded again, thought how happy her mother would be to become a grandmother again. A baby niece or nephew for her sister's brood.

'I'm sure,' she mumbled. She wondered if it would be a serious, thoughtful child, like she'd been, or happy-go-lucky, like Jim.

'You'll need to come back for a second appointment tomorrow,' the nurse was saying but her words had gone fuzzy, as though she was hearing them under water. She felt dizzy, nauseous. She could do this. She had every right to do this. She could erase this accidental conception and carry on down the path she intended. That's what she should do. But sitting there on the crisp white sheets of the clinic, she understood with a flash of clarity that for reasons unfathomable to her right then and there, she wasn't going to.

PART TWO

'In prehistoric times cave-women needed cave-men with their superior muscles to move large stones, kill hairy beasts and carry heavy loads. But nowadays with the help of modern electronics a dainty manicured finger could launch a spacecraft. It's still nice to have a man in the kitchen to open a pickle jar now and again, but it isn't an absolute necessity.'

From the book Making Friends with the Opposite Sex *by Californian scientist Mrs Emily Coleman (Cressrelles, 1974), quoted in an article in the* Liverpool Echo, *1976*

APRIL 1976

London, UK

SYLVIA

It had felt natural to say yes to Jim when he'd asked her to marry him one warm summer's afternoon on a picnic blanket overlooking the Brittany coast. It was at the end of a three-week road trip around France following her year in Paris. They'd come out of the year apart unscathed; they were still together, still in love, so when he asked her – quite unexpectedly to Sylvia's mind – it felt natural to say yes. And that was it, they were engaged. But she never thought they'd end up tying the knot quite in this way.

'Don't fuss,' she said when Jim called her at the office, as he'd taken to doing daily.

'I'm not fussing, I'm just checking in.' She could hear the smile in his voice. He'd been smiling ever since she told him she was pregnant. She swore he looked taller, walked with a bounce in his stride. It was endearing and horrifying at the same time.

'You don't need to call me here. I've told you I feel perfectly fine.' She lowered her voice and turned around in her chair to face away from Max. She didn't intend to tell anyone at work about her situation just yet. Not until she had to. She needed time for it to sink in herself, to make sense of the decision she'd made at the clinic. It had been so sudden and yet so definite. An almost physical urge not to abort. As though the baby itself had prevented her from going through with it. And then she told Jim and suddenly it was completely out of her hands. Her mother's wavering voice down the phone, delighted and disapproving at the same time. *What will the neighbours think?* Her sister Susie, already planning to drive over with a drawer-load of cast-offs. And Jim, taking her hands and saying with glee, *We'd better just do it then, let's get married as soon as we can.* And then there was a registry office and a pub in Wandsworth booked for two weeks' time, so everyone could pretend it didn't happen in the wrong order and Sylvia could become a respectable married pregnant woman, just like they all wanted.

'Will I see you tonight?'

'I said I'd spend it with Maggie. We're going to go to that new Indian place at London Bridge.'

'Right.' Jim paused. 'Can you eat that sort of stuff?'

'What do you mean?'

'All those funny foreign spices, perhaps they're not good for the baby.'

Sylvia suppressed a sigh. *Sit down and put your feet up. Can I make you a cup of tea? Are you eating enough?* That was how their interactions went these days. Not office politics and Fleet Street gossip and juicy news stories. They had a new prime minister, for goodness sake, but all Jim wanted to talk about was which foods she should avoid. Maybe it was just the shock of it; maybe it wouldn't last. It couldn't, surely. She wasn't suddenly fragile and weak – and she certainly didn't intend to let him or anyone else treat her that way.

'I'm sure it's fine, Jim. Don't fuss,' she said again.

'I just want to look after you both.'

'I'm perfectly capable of doing that myself.'

They said their goodbyes and Sylvia returned the phone to the cradle. She looked back down at the papers in front of her. Letters. From Deirdre and Mary and Donna and Christine and other women from Tunbridge Wells, Gloucester, Stoke-on-Trent, Southend-on-Sea. She'd been surprised when Roger had presented her with a bundle of them a few days after her article was published.

'Most of them are about your feature, so I thought you may as well edit the damn things,' he'd said, adding, unnecessarily she thought, 'Valerie doesn't have time.'

So now she was letters' editor – well, only for those intended for the women's pages, but it was something. She wasn't being sent to interview Peter Hall, as Max was about to (because of course he who called actors 'a bunch of egotistical toffs' was best served to interview the director of the

National Theatre and not she, a regular and enthusiastic theatregoer thanks to Maggie's access to discount tickets), but it was a definite vote of confidence in her from Roger, however small.

She'd tried to keep her face calm when the paper landed on her desk without ceremony last Friday; there it was, her piece on Switzerland over nearly a full page in the women's section with several photos she'd taken at the rally.

SWISS SISTERS FIGHT FOR RIGHTS: FIVE YEARS AFTER GAINING THE VOTE, THE BATTLE CONTINUES

Her byline in bold below the headline. *Her* byline! Not only attached to a golden oldies interview (that was in there as well, of course: Fran and Percy from Golders Green, whose best piece of advice on marriage had been 'don't argue when you're hungry'), but a serious news feature on a subject she felt passionate about, a feature she'd pitched and persuaded Roger to run.

She'd read it start to finish, even though she already knew it almost by heart. She noted Sam's subbing changes – true to Valerie's word, there were few, though to her mind the ones there were seemed clumsy – and felt the piece anew, as she always did when her writing was published. Somehow, seeing it in print made it concrete and gave it a gravitas it didn't have when it rolled out of her typewriter on office A4, multiples of 'x' obscuring unwanted words.

'Strong stuff, darling,' Valerie had said when she walked past her desk, and Sylvia didn't even think she was being sarcastic.

Max's enthusiasm was less ambiguous – 'Dog's bollocks, that, Syl' – but the boost she felt on hearing her colleagues' praise quickly faded when Clive, passing through the office with a coffee in hand, looked over her shoulder at a close-up shot of Hanna, the reform school girl, and let out a low whistle.

'What a stunner. Can you get me her number?'

Max had laughed. 'I doubt she's that desperate, old man.'

'I don't know.' Ellis looked up from his typewriter, a grin on his face. 'Offer her some cash for her life story and even a fat old bugger like you might get lucky.'

Sylvia had sighed and closed the paper. She thought of Evelyne and her friends.

Switzerland must seem like the most backwards place to you.

Hardly. But the men's comments only propelled her onwards. Now she had one big feature in the bag, she needed to capitalise on her success by pitching some more. She'd stayed late every night this week searching for ideas, reading news-in-briefs, telephoning contacts, scouring the cuttings library.

Ever since the clinic, it had become a compulsion because all she saw now was an egg-timer, the sand flowing fast, running down, urging her to do more, work harder, get those features in before it was too late. It felt like she was playing a game of snakes and ladders and, if she wasn't careful, in around six months' time she'd have no choice but to slide down the longest ladder in the game and end up right back at the bottom again.

JUNE 2016

Montreux, Switzerland

JESS

From <maggie.hartwell@gmail.com>

Darling Jess,

My heart just about burst to see the photo
you messaged me. I'm so glad that woman,
Nina, let you have it. How young your mum
looks – and how fashionable, with her Afghan
coat and flares! I suppose we were all that
young, once. It's so long ago I can hardly
remember looking that fresh-faced. Although,
I always think you don't change much on
the inside. Sometimes I still think I'm 25, and
then what an awful shock I get when I look in
the mirror!

I'm so delighted you've started to do some investigating. I know you're still unsure about it, but I really do think it's the right course of action. You've been so brave about it all, Jess, even though you might not feel it. I know it's been so hard, but you're at the beginning of the end of the tough times now, I know it. You're going to get through this and come out the other side.

Keep me updated with your next steps and know that I'm here whenever you want to talk.

Lots of love,

Maggie xx

It's a good few days before I can find the time to do anything about searching for Daniel Buchs. But one late afternoon, with the kids wiped out after a day at the outdoor pool and collapsed in front of *Finding Dory* (they've been speaking English all day, so I've let them watch the French language version, and I feel a pleasing sense of defiance to imagine what Julia might say about that), I sit outside on the terrace with my mobile. First I search the online phone book and find an incredible eighty-nine listings under the name Daniel Buchs.

My heart sinks. I don't think I can bear to call eighty-nine numbers, most of them in German-speaking Switzerland, and try to explain what I want over the phone.

I try Google instead and get 133,000 results. I scan down

the webpage: LinkedIn profiles, Facebook profiles, various websites in French and German that I don't understand. Though the number of results is overwhelming, excitement prickles my skin. Daniel Buchs could be out there, breathing, living. I just have to find him.

But how?

He could be any of these people or none of them. I need more to go on, to narrow things down a bit. I debate just messaging some of them through their social media profiles, but I don't know what to say. *Hello, you might have once had a sister who knew my mother around the time she gave birth in a Lausanne hospital in 1976 and possibly might have known what went wrong.* It's ridiculous – but maybe it's the only way.

I open a document and start copying links to the social media profiles of all the Daniel Buchs I can find. I scour Facebook, LinkedIn, Twitter, hoping my Daniel Buchs isn't so technologically inept that he doesn't use such things; he must be at least sixty now, after all. But even if he doesn't, someone else might have mentioned him online. No one is completely untouched by the internet, surely. Although Brigitte Mela seems to be, I remind myself.

After an hour's work I have a substantial list to work through. Some I can tell immediately are probably too young, but I list them anyway. Perhaps he's one of those people who names their son after themselves, so the son might lead me to the father. Others could be duplicates, it's hard to tell. Some are just a brief mention – one on a website for a sailing club in Zug, another in the caption on a group photo of hikers from a walking club in Reichenbach im Kandertal, wherever that is. I track down email addresses for the administrators of both and add them to the list.

I reopen the first on my list, a LinkedIn profile of a middle-aged executive of a software firm in the canton of Zurich. A thrill seeps into me as my fingers start to compose a message, but then they stop in their tracks when I think of Dad. *Don't do this Jess, you don't know where it could lead.* I push his voice aside, hearing Maggie instead. *Darling girl, what about you?* Don't think, just do it.

I start to type, hoping he speaks enough English to understand.

> I'm sorry to contact you out of the blue, but I'm looking for a man named Daniel Buchs who I believe is the brother of the late Evelyne Buchs, an acquaintance of my mother's. It's regarding my own personal situation . . .

I pause. Maybe it's best not to say too much right now. It probably won't be him. And I don't want to tell every Daniel Buchs in the country about my sorry life.

> If you are this Daniel Buchs, I would love to have the chance to ask you a few questions about your sister's time in Lausanne in 1976, as I believe it may shed some light on

circumstances within my own personal life. I
would be very grateful if you could message
me back . . .

I read it over. It's strange, seeing the words glowing from
the screen. During the past two years I've achieved so little
in my search. I've floundered, not knowing what to do or
where to go for help after the hospital came up with nothing
but dead ends. Unsure, even, if I wanted to pursue it. And
now I'm sitting here doing something active, something that
could lead me to them.

I remember how Dad and I left things, the day I went
to his house to tell him I'd got the job over here, after I'd
convinced myself – with Maggie's encouragement – to do
something proactive instead of 'wallowing in misery', as
Patrick had so kindly put it before he moved out.

'I don't see why you can't just carry on as before,' Dad
had said. 'Let's just forget those stupid tests and put it behind
us.' He'd been making tea in the kitchen and didn't even
look at me.

'I don't think I can, Dad.'

'If you go out there, you might not like what you find, it
might just upset you further. Please just leave it, Jess. You're
still the person your mother and I brought you up to be.
You're still you.'

When he finally looked up, the pain on his face was so raw
that I nearly gave in to the guilt. But I couldn't let myself.
Everything had fallen apart, and I didn't know how to put

it back together again until I had the answer to the question that hung over me.

'Dad, you're a journalist, you must understand that I need to know the truth. I can't explain why, I just do. I can't move on otherwise.'

'Well, *I* don't want to know, Jess. I just don't want to know.'

I stare at the screen on my tablet. Was he afraid? Afraid that our relationship might change? It's possible. The DNA tests may have erased the foundations of my identity, but they haven't altered how much I love my parents, and I can't imagine they ever will. But maybe Dad's worried he'll feel differently about me if I find what I'm looking for.

I take a deep breath, trying to quell the fear that's held me back these past months – the fear that I'll lose him too.

I read the message again, take a breath, my finger hesitating. And then I hit send.

To distract myself from my emails, the next day I decide to take the kids to a free afternoon concert at Montreux Jazz Festival, which has just kicked off for two weeks, filling the lakeshore with laughter and music that sometimes, with the wind in the right direction, floats up to the house. Michel and Julia both warned me off, moaning of crowds and high prices, but I think they both knew I'd go. I can't pass up the opportunity to visit the most famous jazz festival in the world, right on my doorstep. And today's a beautiful day for sitting in the park watching music. I just hope the kids won't get bored.

I raid the fridge and cobble together a picnic lunch. I grab sunscreen, hats and a picnic blanket and order Léa and Luca into some semblance of ready. When we reach the festival site it's busy, but not unbearably so. The air hums with laughter, music and the hiss of hot grills from the line-up of food stalls along the waterfront promenade. I drag Luca past the ice-cream vans with a promise he can have his pick later on, after our picnic. There are already quite a few people sitting in the park where the stage is set up, waiting for the band to come on. The programme says it's a South African vocal harmony group.

'*Je veux une glace,*' Luca says for the second time. I feign ignorance, even though I know exactly what he means.

'In English, Luca,' I say.

'Ice cream,' he says.

'Later.'

He starts to cry, but stops again abruptly when the singers take to the stage. Luca's little face fixates on them, eyes wide, mouth open, as they begin to sing in rich, deep, perfectly blended harmonies. I lean back and close my eyes, trying to switch off thoughts of Daniel Buchs and Nina and Dad. I haven't slept well since I've been here, often waking in the early hours and tussling with the thoughts dancing round my head as light gradually seeps in through the slits in the shutters. But now the rhythms and sonorous voices of the singers on stage fill up my head until there's no room for anything else. Just music, and the warmth of the sun on my skin and the cool grass under my legs.

'Jess!'

I feel a tap on my shoulder and open my eyes, squinting into the sun. My head feels groggy and there's a bitter taste in my mouth.

'Jess,' Léa says again. 'Where's Luca?'

I look up and see he's not there with us. During the time we've been in the park the grass has filled up with people and I start to panic. How long was I asleep? And where the hell has Luca gone?

'You didn't see him wander off?'

Léa shakes her head.

'Promise me you'll stay right here and don't move at all.'

The tone of my voice shakes her face into a frown and she nods meekly. 'I promise.'

I leave Léa on the picnic rug and pick my way through the crowd to the edge of the park, past the portaloos and onto the waterfront promenade. My heart's hammering and nausea rolls through me. I can't lose Julia and Michel's son. I stop and look around me, trying to take deep breaths. He can't have gone far. Think logically. But my head feels thick with sleep, and my eyes are streaming from the sun because I left my sunglasses on the rug with Léa. And now I'm thinking I shouldn't have left Léa on her own and what kind of a bloody nanny am I anyway?

Maybe he's near the ice-cream stands. That must be it. My panic eases a little as I weave my way through the crowds with a purpose now, heading to the stand where Luca had stopped me and pulled on my hand, pleading for strawberry cheesecake flavour. But he's not there.

I turn around, heading back down the line of stalls, scanning the crowds. Hot tears press against the backs of my eyes. What if he's been abducted? Or fallen into the lake and drowned, or wandered onto the main road and been hit by a car? Perhaps this was why I wasn't meant to have kids of my own, because they'd come to harm under my care. That must be it. It was for their own safety because I'm a bad person who falls asleep when I'm meant to be looking after children.

I'm running through scenarios of how to break the news to Michel and Julia when my heart just about stops at the sight of him. He's standing near the lake wall eating an ice cream that's melting in the sun and dribbling all down his hand. He's looking up at someone and smiling a food-smeared grin, but the man's back is turned to me and I can't see who it is. I get closer and realise I've never seen the guy before and my stomach lurches in fear. I run the last few metres to the bench and sweep Luca into a bear hug so he squeals.

'Thank God,' I mutter into his shoulder. He starts to wail and I realise I've squashed his ice-cream cone into my hair.

The man says something in French. I turn and see him staring at me with a questioning look. He takes his sunglasses off and looks at me.

'I don't speak French.' I disentangle myself from Luca and pick my hair from his ice cream.

'I said, what are you doing?' His American twang is similar to Michel's.

'I could ask the same of you.' I stare at him, hands on hips.

'I found him wandering on his own.'

I bristle. My brain's whirring with what ifs. He clearly bought Luca the ice cream. Why would a stranger do that unless . . .

'Okay, well, I've found him now so—'

'Wait,' he says as I pull Luca away. 'Who are you?'

'His nanny.'

He nods and frowns as if in realisation of something he already knew. 'Right. Mum said they'd hired one. An English teacher, aren't you? Well, I hope you're better at teaching them than you are at looking after them.'

My mouth drops open at the gall of this stranger just as my head's processing the earlier part of his sentence. 'What are you talking about? What's your mother got to do with it?'

'Maria,' he says. 'You've met her, right? I'm her son. Jorge.' He sticks out his hand.

'Oh.' My cheeks burn, indignation crumbling into embarrassment. I look at his hand and then shake it. 'I just took my eyes off him for a second and he wandered off.' I want the lake to swallow me up so I never have to see this man again.

'It happens,' he says finally, and I dare to look at him. There's a smile struggling to impose itself on his mouth. It finally succeeds and I see his eyes crinkling at the corners as he starts to laugh. 'You should see your face!'

I want to cry. I turn away from him and drag Luca with me, causing the boy to shout back '*Salut*, Jorge,' confirmation that this man is obviously in the kids' lives and I am, there-fore, likely to see him again.

'I'm sorry for laughing,' he says. 'No harm's done. He's okay.' He starts to walk alongside us as I hurry us back to the grassy area where I pray I'll find Léa.

'Thank you,' I say quietly. 'For finding him. I mean, now I know you're not an axe murderer or child abductor or something.'

'You're welcome.' He smiles, and there's a glimmer of laughter back in his eyes. 'Have you lost Léa too?'

I feel my eyebrows arch and my voice comes out icy. 'She's waiting for us over there.'

'Woah, just asking.' He puts his hands up. 'I'll come and say hello to my buddy then.'

'Jorge!' Léa sees us walking towards her and weaves her way between the sprawled bodies to reach us. He sweeps her into a hug and she squeals, her feet dangling off the ground.

'*Salut, ma belle, ça va?*'

'*Ouais,*' she says. 'We have to speak English – for Jess.'

'Of course.' He looks at me and I realise I never told him my name. 'I just met Jess – she was getting worried about your brother.'

'Oh, you have found him?' Léa asks, and I can't help but smile at the indifference of both kids: Léa, more excited by Jorge's arrival than her brother's reappearance; and Luca, quietly eating the remains of his ice cream with a studious intensity.

Jorge joins us on the grass and my nerves settle as I listen to him tease Léa and tickle her until she begs him to stop. Luca, finally sated with ice cream, falls asleep on the picnic blanket and I lie back on my elbows as the next band comes on, a local jazz quartet Jorge assures me is fantastic. Léa settles down next to him and I sneak a sideways look at them as they both watch the stage, Jorge nodding his head along to the beat and Léa attempting to copy him. His face and arms are tanned, his mop of light brown hair slightly bleached by the sun at the front, thin white lines in the crinkles beside his eyes. There's some sort of official lanyard around his neck and I see his picture beneath the English word 'Staff' in bold letters. In my panic over Luca, I hadn't noticed that at first.

'Good, huh?' he says to me, nodding to the stage, and I nod back. I rummage around in my bag to get out my phone to take a picture of the band. I press the camera icon on my phone and hold it up to the stage, take a picture.

'Me and Jorge!' Léa says. Jorge nods and puts his arm around her. I fill the frame with the two of them. Jorge's gaze seems to bore into me. I take the snap and put the phone back in my bag.

'You work for the festival?' I ask him.

He nods. 'I'm a booker.'

'Meaning what, exactly?'

'I listen to a lot of music. Go to see live bands, talk to venues and agents, try to find up and coming bands we can book for the festival.'

'Sounds like an amazing job.'

'It is,' he says, and then hesitates. 'But it's torture at times, too.' He looks towards the stage and I see his face darken momentarily before a smile returns to his lips. 'I guess it's like being a science teacher instead of a scientist. Or a stagehand instead of an actor.'

A nanny to someone else's children instead of a mother yourself, I think. I wonder if he has kids. I glance at his hands and see he's not wearing a wedding ring. Not that that means anything, of course. Neither am I. At our age there's always baggage, even if it's not visible.

'So you play?'

'Yeah, piano. I have a band. We gig for fun around the region.'

'But you want more?'

'Who doesn't?' He shrugs. 'But I have to earn a living, and like you say, this is a pretty awesome job. Speaking of which, I should go.' He checks his watch and gets up from the grass.

'Oh, right.' I hesitate. 'Listen, you won't ... tell your mother, or the Chevalleys, will you?'

His eyes hold mine. 'About what?'

'About losing Luca.'

He cocks his head to one side and heat prickles the back of my neck. 'There's nothing to tell,' he says. 'But just look after them, okay? They're good kids, these two.' He smiles, and there's no reprimand in his voice.

'I will.'

He nods, as though convinced. '*À bientôt les enfants,*' he says to the kids, and then he turns away. I squint into the sun at

145

his retreating back as he picks his way through the crowd to the lakeshore.

'Jorge's the best.' Léa flops on her front on the grass. Then she turns her head and smiles. 'But you're second best.'

APRIL 1976

Oxfordshire/London, UK

SYLVIA

Basil was the first to greet them, his tongue lolling out of his mouth and his ears flapping as he rushed towards the car.

'Basil! Heel!' Pamela half jogged down the drive after the Jack Russell. Sylvia forced a smile. Deep breaths. 'You're here! Goodness, and only half an hour late too! Traffic must have been good?'

'Not bad, Mum,' Jim said.

They stepped out of the car and Pamela pulled them both into a hug in turn. She stepped back and threw a pointed look at Sylvia's stomach, as though she could see the pea-sized being within. 'Well, I can't say the timing is *quite* what we had in mind for you.'

'Darling, let them come into the house before the interrogation starts.' Simon slapped Jim on the back and kissed

147

Sylvia on the cheek. She was always struck by how much Jim looked like his father. This would be her soon-to-be-husband in twenty-five years' time. The thought unnerved her, not because Simon was unattractive, but because it felt like one more sign that life was already mapped out for them, however differently they attempted to live it.

Inside, Pamela summoned Sylvia to help her make tea as Jim and his father talked on the lawn, freshly mown into perfect stripes.

'I'm not going to harp on about it.' Pamela poured water into the teapot. 'All that matters is you're getting married and you'll be blessed with a child, and that's simply wonderful. Tongues will wag, but we'll just have to turn a blind eye.'

Sylvia was arranging the biscuits on a plate with methodical precision. Jammie Dodgers, Bourbons, Rich Tea.

'Thank you, Pamela,' she said with equal care. 'I'm glad you're pleased.' At least now there would be no big ceremony in a church, no manor house reception with one hundred pairs of eyes on her the whole day. Though she would never say it to Jim, part of her was relieved. *Thank you, baby.*

'Delighted. It's such an exciting time for you both! I just wish you had a little longer to sort things out. You'll be moving in with Jim straight after the wedding, I presume?'

Sylvia looked through the kitchen window to the garden where Jim and his father were sitting in the spring sun. A blue tit was flying in and out of a birdbox fixed to the side of the house. Strangely, she hadn't thought what they'd do about that, but she supposed they'd have to move in together now they'd be a married couple with a baby on the way. A pang of sadness struck her. No more sharing with Maggie. She didn't feel they'd been flatmates nearly long enough. 'I suppose I will,' she said. 'But there's time to think about that.'

'Time? You're getting married Saturday after next!' Pamela's voice was shrill. 'And your pregnancy will go very quickly you know. There's so much to do. You'll have to think about what equipment you'll need, which room you'll use as a nursery. I expect you'll want to decorate it. And don't leave it too late – I was so tired in the last trimester of both my pregnancies I could hardly lift a finger!'

Sylvia followed her into the garden carrying the biscuits, the wake of Pamela's perfume making her feel queasy. She settled into a wicker chair and watched as her future mother-in-law poured the tea. 'I'll be mother,' Pamela said.

'You *are* mother, Mother,' Jim said, and the three of them laughed at the predictable in-joke. Sylvia feigned a smile. She wished Jim's sister was here. But Jemima was probably still in India or Pakistan or wherever she'd run off to this time, as Pamela always put it. *Why can't she be more like her brother?*

'How's work, Jim?' Simon asked. 'Callaghan keeping you in headlines?'

Sylvia watched Jim as he told his father about his latest features and the lawsuit the magazine was embroiled in. He'd come a long way since his internship. Sylvia felt a flush of pride – for him, for both of them. They'd done well since leaving Oxford. They'd fulfilled the expectations their tutors had of them. But now Jim was going to continue on his upwards trajectory while she stalled. In another couple of years their careers would probably look very different. Did he realise? Would it even have occurred to him how this could affect her?

'And how about your job, Sylvia darling? Are they planning a good send off?' Pamela said.

'Oh, I haven't told work yet.'

'Yes, well I suppose it won't do to tell them until after you're married.' She fixed Sylvia with a knowing smile. 'But don't leave it too late. They'll be wanting to find a replacement, I suppose. And you may as well make the most of it. A few extra lie-ins, time off for doctor's appointments. They should be going easy on you now.'

'I don't want them to go easy on me.'

Jim threw Sylvia a warning look. 'Syl loves her job. She's going to find it tricky to give it up.'

'I'm not going to give it up. I'll have a few weeks off and then go back, if Roger agrees. It's not the fifties, you're not expected to resign when you get married.'

'That's not what I meant.' Jim's voice was light but she caught the subtext: *and you know it.*

Pamela pinched her mouth into a thin line. 'Darling, I know you're a *career girl*,' she said, waggling her head for emphasis, 'but this is more important. Who will look after the little one if you go back to work? Baby's going to need you at home now. Everything else must take second place.'

Sylvia stared at the grass. A lone trio of daisies had obviously escaped the gardener's mower and stood sentinel in the centre of the lawn. 'It doesn't have to be like that these days,' she said, trying not to think how much a nursery or a nanny would cost.

'Well, I don't know about that. I know times have changed since my day, but babies still need their mothers.'

'I think babies need their mothers to be happy.'

'I'm just saying—'

'Pam.' Simon cut her off. 'This is for Jim and Sylvia to work out. It's a quarter of a century since our day. It won't all be the same now. I'm sure the baby will be fine, whatever they decide. They are responsible adults.'

'Well, I'm sure they are.' Pamela raised one eyebrow. 'Oh! Look at those wretched things!' She got up and walked over to the three daisies, picked them one by one, went to the other end of the garden and threw them on the compost heap.

She got married in purple, much to Pamela's dismay. Sylvia had loved the dress the moment she saw it in the shop with Maggie on a pre-wedding trip to Oxford Street. Maggie, chief – and only – bridesmaid wore green, and the whole thing brightened up an otherwise grey but humid late April day. Sylvia felt a rush of affection for her new husband that he, though once eager for a full-blown traditional affair, seemed so overwhelmed they were actually getting married that he didn't seem to care that the dress wasn't white or that they were one of many couples at the registry office that day, or that his parents felt the need to apologise to hers for their son causing Sylvia's *delicate state*.

'I love you,' Jim whispered as he bent to kiss her after the ceremony, a broad smile on his face. And for a brief moment, she felt perhaps everything would be okay.

Her father gave a speech after they sat down to roast beef and Yorkshire pudding, as Susie's youngest cried, and Jemima, on a brief hiatus from her travels, chased the kids around the small pub garden. Afterwards, her father hugged her and said he was proud of her, whatever path she chose. She balked at that, wondering if it actually meant the opposite, that she'd disappointed him for accidentally veering her life off its intended course. But she didn't ask him; didn't want to hear the answer. Her mother fussed over the wrinkles in Sylvia's dress, smoothed her hair and worried about the one glass of champagne she'd had to toast her own wedding. 'They say you shouldn't have any, you know,' she said, lighting a cigarette, the smoke curling up to the ceiling.

They left in Jim's mini in a rush of goodbyes, hugs and congratulations. Sylvia drove them up the motorway, glad of the sudden silence after the noise of the pub. They checked into a country cottage near Bourton-on-the-Water for their one night of honeymoon and he insisted on carrying her over the threshold, despite her protestations. He poured himself a whisky from the minibar and she opened the doors to the little patio and walked out into night air that smelled like freshly cut grass. He joined her, put his arm around her.

'Well, here we are, Mrs Millson.'

'Tallis,' she said. 'Ms Tallis. I'm keeping my name.'

He stared at her. 'I didn't know that. You didn't say.'

'You didn't ask.'

'No, I suppose I didn't. But why on earth would you do that?'

'It's important to me. Professionally, I mean. I don't want my byline to change. You understand.' She twisted the unfamiliar second ring around her finger.

He looked at her with a sad smile. She saw the effort it was taking him not to press the matter, and she loved him for it. Finally, he nodded. 'Okay. Ms Tallis it is. As long as you're still my missus.'

She turned to him and planted a light kiss on his mouth, looked into his soft, kind eyes.

'I am,' she said.

JULY 2016

Montreux, Switzerland

JESS

Despite myself, I still feel a jolt of joy to see his name in my inbox. Patrick Faulkner. But then I open the email.

I read it once, then again, and again.

> I've found a new place to buy, Jess, and I need a deposit, so I think we should put the flat on the market. 50-50, that's what we agreed. I guess we need to move on now, sign those divorce papers.

I drop my phone on the duvet and lie back on the bed. Though I knew this would happen, it still hits me like a punch in the gut. I read it again and sense a slight question mark in his email, as though he's asking me if I really mean it, if I actually want us to go through with the divorce, and I wonder for the hundredth time if I could forgive him and move past what he did. Part of me aches to do so, but I know I can't let myself, despite what it means for my future. How could I, when he hurt me to the core when I was already so broken? He kicked me when I was down – and that feels unforgivable.

Light is streaming through the window of my bedroom, even though it's only 5am. Sleep has eluded me for the past hour. The house is silent – it's even too early for Luca to wake – and the lack of noise is oppressive, pushing me to fill it with thoughts and feelings I'd rather ignore. Like those weeks after we met in that bar on my friend Rachel's thirtieth birthday: his wide smile, the crinkles by his eyes, the touch of his hands on my skin for the first time. It's strange to think how much lighter my head was back then, not weighed down as it feels now. Only filled with love and hope and expectation. We'd get married, live in a nice house, have a couple of kids, succeed in our jobs, earn enough money. I remember how utterly sure I felt it would happen in that way, even if I never articulated it out loud. It's what I wanted, what all my friends wanted – to have it all. Thirty when we met, thirty-four when we got hitched. Perfect timing. I thought we were strong enough to handle anything, but in the following five years so much changed, so much happened to set us apart from each other, and it turned out we weren't that strong after all.

We're not us anymore.

That's what Patrick said when I confronted him about what a workmate had seen: a kiss in a doorway. Smiles and laughter. Tumbling into a cab.

You've let this situation take over your life, you're just wallowing in misery. We don't laugh anymore, and I need to laugh, Jess.

As though it was my fault, as though I pushed him into bed with her.

A knot of anger pulses in my temples. I know I can't have been easy to live with as I wrestled with the fallout from the tests, but I expected more from my husband. I expected understanding and patience as I figured out how to live in this new orbit – because that's what it felt like, as though my whole world had shifted on its axis. I knew, from the bewildering period after Mum's accident, what a cruel thing it is to have your life rocked so fundamentally and yet everything around you stay the same. And here I was again, grieving for something lost, but still having to put one foot in front of the other, go to work, buy groceries, cook dinner. How could I stand in the supermarket deciding between chicken soup and minestrone? How could I sort whites from colours as though it mattered? How could I go to St Mary's every day and teach Year 9 students about the symbolism in *Wuthering Heights*? What I've learnt is that you just do. So I just did. But it didn't mean I was okay; it didn't mean I was the same inside. And perhaps I took it out on him; perhaps he bore the brunt of it. But wasn't that marriage?

In good times and in bad, that's what Patrick and I vowed to each other. But I guess the bad times just went on too long for him to deal with. So he cheated.

It's been five days since I sent messages to thirty-one Daniel Buchs from my list. I've had six replies, three of them in German, all saying – I deduced using Google Translate – that they do not have and have never had a sister called Evelyne and I am barking up the wrong tree. Some were curt, others polite, one even made suggestions, saying I should place an advert with a newspaper. But none of them was *the* Daniel Buchs.

Time passes slowly when you're constantly checking all your available technology for new messages. I consider Daniel Buchs number five's suggestion. Of course I've thought of that before, but I couldn't bear it if a newspaper started asking questions and found out what happened to me. Granted, they might also then discover what I need to know, but the price for that would be my name all over the papers. Patrick, Maggie and Dad are the only people who have ever needed to know what I discovered two years ago, and I want to keep it that way.

What with Patrick's email and my constant anticipation of a message from another Daniel Buchs, I'm in serious need of distraction – thank goodness for Léa's birthday.

'You can't wear that yet!' I say as Léa skips into the living room in the pale pink dress I helped her pick out on our shopping trip yesterday, along with a pair of sparkly sandals I would have coveted when I was a kid.

'But I really want to!'

'You're going to play in the rope park, it'll get dirty. Save it for the party later, okay little one?'

'I'm not little. I'm going to be eight. *Huit ans.*'

'You're right. That is extremely grown up.'

'*Léa! Change ta robe, maintenant!*' Julia comes into the living room in a waft of perfume. She's wearing a pair of khaki trousers and a white V-necked T-shirt. They're nothing special but still manage to make her look chic. I remember seeing that T-shirt in her wardrobe. Little does she know. The thought takes me by surprise, and it pleases me.

'Oh *mon Dieu*, there's still so much to do,' Julia says. Léa flounces away, her long glossy mane swinging behind her. 'I haven't put up any decorations for the party. And there are the gifts to wrap. Maria is bringing most of the food, but I wanted to bake a cake and I haven't had time. What sort of a mother am I?' She gives brief laugh, perhaps expecting a protestation from me, but I don't say anything. If Léa were my daughter I'd have made time to make her a cake. And then something occurs to me.

'Listen,' I say. 'I don't need to go to the rope park with you all. Why don't I stay here and decorate the house? I can wrap the presents if you show me where they are. Sort out the living room for the party. Maybe I can even rustle up a cake. I mean I'm sure it wouldn't be as good as yours but . . . well, I can try.'

Julia lets out a long breath. 'Really? Jess, that would be *super*. Are you sure? I know Léa wants you to come with us.'

'It's fine. It's more important that you and Michel are there with her.'

'*Merci*, thank you, really. That's a huge help.' She puts her hand on my shoulder briefly and I see her gratitude and something else – relief? I smile back, shrug, as though it's nothing.

When they've gone out through the door in a clatter of laughter and shoes on wooden floorboards, I set to work, pleased to be able to do this for Léa, to give her what her mother didn't have time for. I'll draw on all my years of classroom cut-out skills to make some brilliant decorations for the party, and then I'll tackle the cake. I put some music on and help myself to a glass of wine from a bottle Michel opened last night. Then I sit down with a pile of coloured paper that Julia bought but never did anything with, fish out my trusty silver-ink pen I for some reason brought with me from the UK, and get to work. Soon I have a pile of neat multicolour bows that I intend to string together across the room. Seeing them, the weight in my head seems to lift a little. I know Léa's going to be impressed and I can't wait to see her face when she realises I did this, not Julia.

I tune the radio to a suitably naff technopop station and sing along tunelessly to whatever comes on as I tackle the serious business of making a cake – a chocolate sponge that I intend to make into something vaguely resembling a hedge-hog with the help of a packet of chocolate fingers I found in the cupboard. It's only afterwards, when the cake's in the oven and I've licked the mixing bowl clean and cleaned up the mess I've made that I realise I haven't looked at my phone for a good hour or so. I wash my hands, pick up the phone and see the email symbol.

My pulse quickens. It's another Daniel Buchs.

> Dear Mrs Faulkner. My hiking club forwarded your message to me. I was very surprised to read your email because I did have a sister called Evelyne who died in 1996 and lived in Lausanne for many years. Can you please tell me why you wanted to find her?

I read the email four or five times before I comprehend what's in front of me. I've found him. Evelyne Buchs' brother has just emailed me. My hands are shaking. I pour another glass of wine and take a gulp. This could be it. The breakthrough I need. I email back straight away, not wanting to let fear creep in and stop me.

> I know it's a long shot, but I'm actually looking for someone else who was in Lausanne at the same time as your sister and my mother – and, I imagine, you. I was hoping your sister might have known something about her. Her name is Brigitte Mela.

When the oven timer goes off, I take the cake out of the oven and slide it onto a cooling rack. I watch the steam curl into the air, as though there might be answers to be found within it. My head feels full of thoughts that I can't make sense of, and I'm impatient for Daniel Buchs to reply immediately, to tell me what I need to know.

I can't sit still, so I pick up my phone and stalk through the flat. I go outside and sit on the terrace, but I can't settle. I wander back into the living room, then my bedroom. I remove my journal from the bedside table drawer and take out the picture of Mum with Evelyne in 1976 – the one Nina pressed into my hand when I left her – searching it for answers it cannot give. Daniel must have taken the photo, Nina said. *That's right. They arrived on the same night, just before the demonstration.* What if Daniel does have the answers? Do I actually want to know, after all?

I put the photo back in my journal and leave my room, intending to head back to the kitchen, but as I reach the door to the master bedroom, I hesitate. I can feel its pull, drawing me in. I put my hand on the door handle, feel the cool metal in my hand. I know I'll be breaking their trust. Violating their privacy. But I also know I'm not going to stop. There's something magnetic about this room that compels me towards it.

I push the door open, and there it is, this reflection of their perfect lives. There's the bed where they made their perfect children. The wardrobe containing Julia's perfect clothes. The photos on the walls, testament to their perfect, untroubled lives. My life was mostly untroubled, before all this. Not perfect, but pretty good. But over the last few years it's all disintegrated. Mum's accident. The tests. The failed IVF. The all-consuming grief that Patrick could only handle for so long before seeking light relief with someone else. So standing in this doorway is like looking into a parallel universe, paraded in front of me like a sick gameshow. *Here's what you could have won . . .*

Inside, I drift around the bed, trailing my hand over the duvet cover. Several framed photos sit atop a chest of drawers. One's of a younger Léa sitting on a sofa with baby Luca in her arms. Another, slightly grainy, shows two women on a bench by the lake in the sunshine, laughing. They look happy and relaxed, and I wonder who they are. A third is a photograph of Michel and Julia on their wedding day. I pick it up. They're young, maybe twenty-five or so. Michel wears a grey suit and light pink tie, and his thick hair is gelled back in a way that's unlike how he wears it now. The self-consciousness of that gel makes me smile. Julia is stunning in a floor-length ivory dress that's nipped in at the waist and flows out into a wide skirt. She's wearing a bit too much make-up, but she looks amazing nonetheless.

They look amazing together.

I think of me and Patrick on our wedding day. We certainly didn't look like that, but we were good together, too. I remember how he looked at me like he couldn't believe his luck. I remember how happy I felt, that I was finally embarking on this adventure called marriage, emulating my parents in this, even if I'd never had the ambition to emulate the heady heights of their careers. I thought our marriage would last as long as theirs had, that we'd have kids for them to be proud of, but in the end I failed at that, too.

I put the photo back down on the chest of drawers.

Would I have failed so badly if I'd grown up out here instead?

I don't know what compels me to go from looking to touching, why I can't stop myself doing something I shouldn't. It's like I'm searching for something I can't name, some clue about Julia's life that might just provide the answer to mine, the secret to making everything okay again, to achieving what she has. I walk over to Julia's bedside table and open the top drawer beneath it. It's crammed with make-up, packets of earplugs, hairbands, lip balms. I pick up her contraceptive pill packet and see she's taken today's.

What I am doing?

There's another packet of prescription medication but it's all in French and I can't make out what it is. Sleeping pills?

A sudden sound catches my attention and I drop the packet back in the drawer, heart going double speed. I wait, listening, but there's nothing, only the radio, still on in the living room, the DJ wittering away in French. It must have been outside.

I close the drawer and open the one beneath. This one is much more organised. I sit on the bed and take out a folder and find Léa and Luca's birth certificates, and then Michel and Julia's marriage certificate. Julia Sarah Meier and Michel Jean-Pierre Chevalley, married on 24 July 2003 in Montreux's *hôtel de ville*. The town hall. Also in the folder is a bunch of handwritten letters and print-outs of emails, some between Michel and Julia, but they're all in French. One letter is in German. It's signed with only a large capital A and two kisses. A woman, clearly. And given the classic, neat script, I wonder if it's an older relative. It's dated twelve years ago. I flip it over and see it's addressed from A. Meier in a place called Thun. I wonder what it says, and why Julia's kept it so long.

Another song comes on the radio, a Britney Spears track from the late nineties that reminds me of university halls, warm beer and sticky dance floors. I should leave the bedroom, go back and ice the cake, shove in those chocolate fingers. I put the papers back in the folder and the folder in the drawer, and as I turn my head my eyes catch some movement in the mirror on the bedside table and I inhale sharply when I see that in the reflection of the doorway is Jorge.

I'm not sure who is more shocked. Heat rushes to my cheeks.

'What are you doing?' he says.

'I'm, er . . . I just . . .'

'Do Julia and Michel know you're in here looking through their things?'

I shake my head, mumble a no. *Oh God.* I feel like one of my own students being told off for nicking another kid's sandwiches, only I know it's far, far more serious than that. 'I came in here to . . . get something and then I . . .' My voice trails off as I can't even think of a good excuse – because there isn't one. I don't deserve to be excused. *This isn't me,* I want to say.

He's looking at me with a mixture of bewilderment and disgust. Perhaps he's mulling it over, debating whether to tell them or not. I know this is my fault, and yet I can't stop anger flooding my veins, shouting over the shame. Anger at what my life's become, at my own inability to deal with it, and at him, standing there where he shouldn't be and judging me.

'What the hell are you doing here anyway?' I say. 'And don't you know how to knock?'

He looks taken aback. 'Mum's not feeling well. I went to see how she was and she asked me to bring over the food for Léa's party. I didn't think anyone would be here so I let myself in with Mum's key, then I heard the radio was on so I came to see who was here.' He pauses. 'Are you stealing something or just being fucking nosy?'

'I'm—'

He holds a hand up, as though he doesn't want to hear my excuses. 'Look, can we just get out of this room?'

He leaves the doorway and I hear him walk down the corridor. I close the drawer I'd been rooting around in and see my wretched face in the mirror. Is this it? I've messed up another job already? I feel ugly sobs rising up. Pathetic. I can't even bear to look at myself.

I take a deep breath and walk down the hall into the kitchen where Jorge is leaning against the kitchen worktop, arms folded over his chest. Trays of food are laid out on the kitchen table – slices of quiche, pastries, cupcakes, fruit salad. He's turned the radio off and the silence screams at me to say something. My head feels fuzzy and I wish I hadn't had that second glass of wine.

'Listen,' I begin. 'I'm really sorry I was in there. I shouldn't have been, I know, and I can see how bad it must look. I don't even know why I did it. But I wasn't going to take anything and I didn't mean any harm.' All I get in response is a pair of arched eyebrows and a gaze that makes me squirm, and I just know that's it, he's going to tell the Chevalleys that I'm a snooping, kid-losing waste of space and I'll find myself *on a break from work* for the second time in one year. Panic grips me and I realise I'm just going to have to plead. 'Please don't tell them,' I say. 'It's not like me to do that, but I'm just going through some stuff and it's sending me a bit crazy, but I won't do it again, I really won't. I know it was wrong.'

'Are you drunk?' he says finally, eyes shifting to the empty bottle of wine on the counter.

'No.' I shake my head, although part of me wants to at least have that excuse, to be able to say it was the wine that pushed me to go through Julia's drawer, to stamp all over her trust.

He doesn't seem to believe me anyway. 'I'll make you a coffee.'

I hesitate. 'Tea please.'

He rolls his eyes and picks two mugs out of the cupboard, puts the kettle on. 'You're lucky to be working for Julia and Michel, you know. They've been so good to my parents over the years, they're like family. I don't want to see them get hurt, or ripped off, or robbed or . . . whatever the fuck you might do to them.' He's almost shouting.

'Nothing, I'm not going to do anyth—'

'So you're going to sit down and tell me exactly what kind of "stuff" you're going through and then I'll decide if I have to tell Julia and Michel or not, okay?'

I nod, gesture towards the kettle, say meekly. 'Teabag in first, please.'

I don't have any intention of telling him the whole story, but as soon as we're sat on the sofa with mugs in our hands and I open my mouth to speak, that's what comes out. Perhaps I know that only the truth is serious enough to compensate for my behaviour. Or maybe it's simply that now Jorge has presented himself as my sounding board I know, suddenly, I desperately need one. I also know he's going to regret he ever asked.

So I tell him about the coach accident that killed Mum in Turkey in 2012 – a jolly for a women's magazine that went horrifically wrong thanks to an unroadworthy coach and its overworked driver. I tell him how she bled out during the half hour it took the ambulance to turn up. I tell him about the shock and bewilderment of grief. And about what happened many months later when Dad and I, emerging from the fug of recovery, went to give blood at a mobile donation unit in London, a small, spontaneous gesture in honour of Mum.

It's strange now, to think back to that day. I remember it

so vividly. The London mizzle that fell so lightly but made everything so soggy. Rounding the corner and seeing the van and knowing, without even having to speak the words, that this was something we both wanted to do. At that time we were both still hurting, but it was a pure, uncomplicated hurt: we simply missed her. United in grief, we were swimming slowly through the recovery process, knowing that life was continuing on its path, as it always does, whether you're ready for it or not. What comforted me was that although our futures had changed fundamentally with the news of that coach crash, we would always have our shared past: our family, the three of us for thirty-five years, that couldn't be taken away from us. Or so I thought.

The nurse was round and cheerful and bespectacled. She thanked us for donating. We told her why and saw sympathy in her warm face. She gave us chocolate. And then she asked if we knew our blood types.

'Neither of us did,' I tell Jorge, 'so we asked to know, and when we got the results later on it didn't make sense. The combination of our blood types . . .' I shake my head, vaguely aware of Jorge staring at me. 'It wasn't possible, you see, that we were related.'

I feel Jorge's hesitation, his shock. 'So your mother . . .'

'No,' I almost shout. 'It wasn't that. We knew it wouldn't be that. Mum wouldn't. She just wouldn't have cheated on Dad.' I swallow back a hard lump of guilt. Because I know, though neither of us ever admitted it out loud, that it had occurred to us both. But only for a moment – at least, for me. 'I checked Mum's old medical records, but it didn't clarify anything. Her blood type could have resulted in mine – from a different father. But I knew it wasn't that, I just knew.'

I remember the feeling I had, as though memories were rushing forward and taking their place in a big jigsaw puzzle, forming a picture I'd never seen before. Maggie saying, *Such lovely blue eyes you have, they must have skipped a generation!* Aunt Jemima joking that I couldn't possibly be her brother's daughter because I was far too clever and witty. Me, wondering why Rachel looked so like her mother when I didn't look at all like either of my parents.

'Dad couldn't deal with it, didn't want to know more. But I couldn't just leave it, I had to know. So I looked up a DNA testing company and ordered a kit. I persuaded Dad to give me a saliva swab, and I took strands of hair from Mum's old hairbrush. We still hadn't got rid of her stuff, you see.' My voice cracks, but I can't stop now; I have to get it all out. 'The wait was horrific. I couldn't sleep. And then, when the letter finally came in the post, I drank half a bottle of gin before I could bear to open it.'

But then I did.

And there it was, typed in stark letters under the clinic's letterhead. *DNA testing for Jessica Faulkner, Jim Millson, Sylvia Tallis.* A paragraph of medical speak and percentages and then the final verdict, clear as anything. *Conclusion: unrelated.* A thread I'd tugged that unravelled my entire identity until I couldn't see the shape of it anymore. A letter that took away my history, that called our family a lie and left me nothing but a gaping hole where my sense of self should be.

'I came here in part to see if I could find my biological parents,' I say. 'They were most likely Swiss, or at least the woman was. Mum – the person I've always known as my mother – gave birth prematurely at the hospital in Lausanne when she was over here for a story, and somehow I must have been swapped with her baby. That's the only explanation we could think of, anyway. I contacted the hospital and they've investigated, but they don't know how it happened. Only three other women gave birth to girls that night. Two they tracked down and tested. But the third woman they just couldn't find. She'd disappeared. No paper trail.' I shake my head and stare into my cooling cup of tea.

Brigitte Mela. The only likely candidate to be my biological mother.

'It's taken me two years to pluck up the courage, but I felt I had to come here to see if I could uncover anything myself. Maybe I can find her.' Perhaps my biological father too; maybe even the other daughter – the woman who's been living the life that should have been mine. Though I'm not sure if I actually want to know who that is.

I take a breath and look at Jorge, but when I see the stricken expression in his eyes, my face prickles with embarrassment. I shouldn't have told him. *Shit,* I really shouldn't have told him. I don't even know this man.

He runs his fingers through his hair and lets out a long,

tense breath as though he's been holding it in the whole time I was speaking. '*Joder*,' he says, and I can guess from the tone of his voice what that particular Spanish word must mean. 'I wasn't expecting that.'

I put my mug on the coffee table and my head in my hands. 'I'm sorry,' I say.

I look up and he's staring at me with incredulity. 'It's completely insane, Jess. I'm just … I mean …' I almost want to laugh, he looks so shocked. 'When you said you were going through something, I thought maybe … I don't know, a break-up or something.'

'Well, now you mention it, my husband and I are getting divorced.'

'*Joder*,' he says again.

I take his mug from his hand and add it to mine on the table. 'I realise my head's not in a good place right now,' I say, my voice soft, 'but I really want this job and I think those kids are fantastic and I promise I'm not going to do anything to hurt them – or their parents. I really am sorry.'

'Have you had help with this? I mean, therapy or something?'

I shake my head. 'I think this is my therapy, being here in Switzerland. I need to find out the truth. I think that's the only thing that's going to help.'

He looks at me and his eyes make me shrivel. 'You won't find the truth in Julia's drawers.'

'I know.' My cheeks burn and I hang my head. 'I don't know what came over me.'

171

He sighs, nods, seemingly convinced. 'I won't say any-thing. But if you mess up one more—'

'I won't,' I interrupt him. 'Thank you. Thank you so much. I really appreciate it. No more snooping, I promise. And I'm going to watch Luca like a hawk.'

He gets up from the sofa and stands in front of me, his hands on his hips. 'I have to go. I'm late for something. But look, Jess, I'm concerned about your state of mind with all this to deal with.'

'I'm fine. I'll *be* fine.'

He walks over to the kitchen and scribbles something on a bit of paper and comes back and hands it to me. 'My number. If you ever feel like you're going to throw yourself off a mountain or something, call me first, okay?'

When he leaves, I sit on the sofa, waiting for my pulse to slow. I feel winded, the breath knocked out of me by all I've said, all that's taken place in the last few years. I don't know how long I sit there in the silence, and so I'm startled when my phone throws out a short, sharp message alert, drawing me out of my thoughts. I pick it up and my heart jumps to see that it's Daniel Buchs.

It's brief, terse almost. Quite unlike his previous email.

May I ask why you want to find Brigitte Mela?

I drop the phone like it's scalded me. He knows her. He knows my birth mother.

MAY 1976

London, UK

SYLVIA

They got the keys for the new flat in Kennington on a Wednesday evening after work. A two-bed garden flat in a Victorian terrace. It felt to Sylvia like a grown-up person's home, a family home, far from the scruffy place she'd shared with Maggie for the past two years. It had a large double and a smaller room that was perfect as a nursery. A kitchen diner with plenty of space, a sitting room with a fireplace, original features, a patio. When Jim put his arm around her, smiled at the estate agent – 'this is the one' – she'd suppressed an urge to turn around and run out the door.

'If you only do things when you're ready, you'll never do anything at all,' Maggie chastised her the following weekend. They were putting an end to their time as flatmates with a takeaway from their new favourite restaurant, the curry house at London Bridge. 'I mean, do you think most people in Britain are ready to experience the flavour sensation of an onion bhaji? No, I think not. But once they try it, they'll bloody love it.' She held one up. 'This, my dear, is the future.'

'Did you really just compare my newly married life to an onion bhaji?' Sylvia burst into laughter, and then tears started running down her cheeks. Maybe it was just the heat of the spices. 'I'm going to miss you, Mags.'

'It's not like you'll never see me, silly.' Maggie bit into the bhaji. 'But I can't believe you're making me get a new flatmate. It's going to feel strange to have another girl rattling around.'

'She'd better like *Columbo*.'

'That's one of my interview questions.' Maggie picked up her beer with a paint-speckled hand and Sylvia felt a pang of sadness. No longer would she find flecks of pink and white and green on her socks at the end of each day, the detritus of Maggie's absent-minded habit of picking dried paint from her clothes, her hair, her skin, something that had always driven Sylvia crazy but now only made her want to cry.

'Oh, I got you a present.' Maggie put down her beer and left the room, returning a minute later with a wrapped package, clearly a book.

Sylvia tore off the wrapping paper and laughed when she saw the title. *Superwoman* by Shirley Conran. 'How to save time and money,' she read the front cover. 'How to be a working wife and mother.'

'I thought you might need it.'

She knew Shirley Conran by reputation, of course, as the former women's editor of the *Daily Mail*. And she knew this book spent weeks and weeks on the bestseller lists after it was published last year. But she'd never got around to reading it. It didn't apply to her, she'd thought. She had no house to keep, no children to look after. She was unmarried and unencumbered. She didn't need a how-to guide about housekeeping.

'It's about shortcuts; you know, like avoiding buying clothes that need ironing.'

'Right,' Sylvia said.

'Listen.' Maggie took it from her and opened it to the first page. '*The purpose of this book is to help you do the work you don't like as fast as possible, leaving time for the work you enjoy,*' she read.

Maggie looked up and her face was so full of hope and optimism that Sylvia felt a lump rise in her throat. Maggie, lovely Maggie, she cared so much.

'Oh Syl, I'm sorry. I thought you'd like it. It's not about being just a housewife, it's about how you can have everything. You can work *and* have a child and be successful at both. Because I know you're going to be. All you need, according to this,' she said, flicking to a page in the middle of the book that she'd clearly read before, 'is a *fast and unerring sense of priority*'.

Sylvia picked up a bhaji. 'I just didn't think I'd be here yet.' She took a bite and felt the heat of the spices warm her face, prickle her eyes until she felt them fill.

Maggie put a hand on hers. 'Everything comes to an end.

But that doesn't mean the next new thing won't be just as exciting. It'll be different, that's all.'

She nodded, even though she wasn't sure she agreed. 'Onwards then.'

Maggie squeezed Sylvia's hand. 'And upwards.'

The phone call came in the afternoon but she nearly didn't pick up. Clive and Ellis were in a heated discussion about whether the scandalous rumours that had just provoked Jeremy Thorpe's resignation as leader of the Liberal Party were true or actually a conspiracy by the South African security services. No amount of swearing or balled up paper missiles from their colleagues on the floor seemed likely to get them to take their expletive-filled argument elsewhere. And what with the clatter of typewriters and numerous phones ringing, Sylvia didn't realise for a moment that this one was hers.

'You're in luck, Ms Tallis.' The female voice on the line was brusque, sharp, business-like. 'Anne Warburton will see you on the seventeenth of May at the embassy in Copenhagen, four o'clock sharp.'

Sylvia's stomach leaped. She'd got it. She'd got the damn scoop.

'That's fantastic news, thank you so much.' She lodged the receiver under her chin and reached for her diary. The secretary hadn't said it as a question and Sylvia didn't take it as one. This wasn't something you turned down. She flicked over a page to the seventeenth of May and read the single entry: Guys Hospital, 3pm. Shit. Greenham had said it was important, something about monitoring her blood pressure.

She hesitated, twirling the phone cord around her hand, knowing as she said it, that she shouldn't. 'I don't suppose by any chance Ms Warburton could do the sixteenth of May instead?'

There was a pause on the line and Sylvia could picture the pursed lips and steely gaze of a diplomatic secretary who knows her own importance. Formidable, that's how she'd heard Warburton described – clearly, her secretary was following her example.

'No, Ms Tallis, she cannot. I shouldn't have to remind you that this opportunity is not being afforded to any other journalist and you would do well to seize it when offered.'

She stared at the diary, put her hand on her stomach and felt the gentle swell. She could go to the hospital another time, surely. 'Yes, absolutely, I'll be there on the seventeenth.'

She put the phone down, picked up a pen and crossed out the hospital appointment.

'Tallis. Why the smug grin?' Max walked back to his desk with a mug of Betty's coffee in his hand, an industrial strength brew that powered most of the office through the afternoons.

'Warburton. I got her, Max.' Sylvia blew out a long breath and sat back in her chair. She couldn't take it in. The only British journalist to get an interview. An *exclusive*. This would be it. This would be the piece to give her career lift-off. And how apt that it should be about Anne

Warburton, a trailblazer in a man's world, whether she intended to be or not. Sylvia had admired the woman ever since she'd heard about her appointment by Callaghan, and last week she'd pored over the pictures of the ceremony in Copenhagen, when Warburton presented herself to Queen Margrethe, wondering what it must feel like to be in such a position.

'Well, if you can get her then she's yours, Tallis,' Roger had said when she proposed the idea in the features meeting to snorts of derision. 'I hear she isn't giving any interviews at all.'

Well, she wasn't – apart from one, now, to her.

'Fucking well done,' Max said.

'Don't talk to the lady like that, Harmer.'

Sylvia turned at Clive's voice and saw him stroll over to their desks. His argument with Ellis had clearly come to an end but the rancour was still evident in his face.

'I appreciate your concern, Clive, but the *lady* feels that swearing is entirely appropriate at this point in time,' she said, before beaming at Max. 'Thanks very fucking much.'

Clive rolled his eyes. 'Why the excitement?'

'Sylvia just pinned down Warburton for an interview.'

'The new ambassador to Denmark?'

'Britain's first female ambassador, may I remind you,' Sylvia said.

Clive pursed his lips in an expression of begrudging respect tinged with something else – jealousy, perhaps? 'She's granted an interview to *you*?'

'She has. It's an exclusive.'

'That's seriously fantastic, Sylvia. Roger might even crack a bloody smile,' Max said.

'Yes, well done, Tallis,' Clive said, and Sylvia saw how much it pained him to say it. 'I suppose she would want a woman so she'll get less of a grilling.'

'Whatever you say, Clive.' She'd learnt in the past year to become inured to Clive's little comments. Keep calm and carry on – the wartime phrase came back to her and it felt apt. This is what she did. This is how she would get ahead. Not by shouting louder than the men, but by staying focused, working hard and forging ahead with quiet determination. From what she knew of Warburton, she thought she would approve.

She nearly forgot to get off the tube at Kennington, so unused was she to their new home. Either it was that, or her daydreams about her new assignment were proving more than a little distracting. She walked slowly along the street to the flat, pausing once or twice to catch her breath. She'd been dogged by breathlessness in recent days. She still had occasional bouts of sickness, and last week she'd had an insatiable desire to drink milk. Her body was changing, responding to the new life inside her, insisting its presence as hard as she tried to forget.

At the house she fumbled with the keys, found the right one at the second attempt, walked along the musty corridor and opened the flat door.

'Jim?'

'In here!'

His words echoed in the near-empty flat. The plan was to go furniture shopping at the weekend. 'We can choose paint for the nursery, and maybe a cot – or is it too early?' Jim had said, while Sylvia wondered if she'd have time to nip to Selfridge's to get that copycat Diane von Furstenberg wrap dress she'd seen in her paper's fashion pages. Anyway, she sort of liked the flat this way for now – a blank canvas, a space to create whatever they wanted, hopefully something they both liked.

'Guess what happened today?' She shrugged off her coat and draped it over the back of their one chair, an old red velvet armchair Jim had picked up in a second-hand shop in Oxford eons ago. She had been initially dismayed to see the tatty old thing had joined them in their new place. But at least it was somewhere to sit.

'You got a pay rise?' Jim came in from the kitchen and kissed her.

'Nope. As if.'

'What, then?'

'Another foreign assignment! I'm going to Denmark to interview Anne Warburton.'

'What?'

'Warburton, she's Britain's first female ambassador.'

'I know who she is.'

'Right, well, I put in a request to interview her and the whole features desk practically laughed in my face, said it was common knowledge she wasn't granting interviews to anyone ... and then today, they called me and said yes! You should have seen Clive's face. *Well I suppose she thinks a woman will go easy on her,*' she adopted Clive's haughty tone and dropped her chin to mimic his fleshy face, expecting Jim to laugh, but he didn't. 'What? Don't you think it's exciting?'

Jim put his hands on her shoulders, kissed her forehead. 'Darling, you know I'm crazily proud of you. But—'

'There's a "but"?'

He put his hands up in a defensive gesture. '*But*, I think things are different now. I don't think you should be going away on foreign trips. There's the baby to think of.'

'The baby goes with me, obviously.' She patted her stomach.

'Well if you're going to be facetious.'

'What's the problem with me going abroad?'

'In your state, maybe it's not wise.'

'I'm pregnant, not ill. And I'm only a few months gone.'

'Foreign travel can be tiring. You don't want to take any risks with your health, or the baby's. Can you just tell Roger you'd prefer domestic assignments for now?'

'No, because I wouldn't, and there's no reason to.'

'I think there is. And I'm the father, I do have a say.'

'Your *say* is wrong. I'm perfectly healthy, the midwife said so.' She swallowed her own lie. She'd rebook it – at a convenient time.

'Syl, I know your career is important to you, and it's

fantastic you're doing so well, but it's not as important as our child, is it? I mean, you're going to have to give it up anyway.'

'Am I?' Her thoughts flicked to *Superwoman*, the book Maggie had given her, and the page she'd read on the tube home. *Two requisites for a working mother are stamina and an understanding family.* Well, she had the first one.

'Yes,' said Jim. 'For a while at least. I mean, you wouldn't want to leave a tiny baby with a stranger, would you?'

'You sound like your mother.' She knew that would sting, and indeed she saw annoyance spark briefly in his eyes before his usual calmness returned.

'Maybe this time my mother has a point.'

It helps to realise that husbands can be unconsciously selfish, emotional and unreasonable about the working wife situation, Shirley Conran had written. *Therefore it may be unreasonable of you to expect him to be reasonable.* Like hell it was.

'And I suppose you'd be happy to give up your career just like that?' she said.

Jim looked confused and she felt like slapping him out of it.

'I'm not the one who's pregnant.'

'No, that's right. So don't assume to know what a pregnant woman can or cannot do. I will go to Denmark, because I want to, because our baby will be perfectly all right, and because I have no intention of giving up my career. And if you don't like that, Jim, well you're just going to have to get used to the idea.'

His face wasn't angry, just a mixture of surprise and hurt. She felt like she'd kicked a kitten. But it was for the best. He had to know now. She had to set the ground rules for their precipitated married life because there was no way she was going to let her future son or daughter stumble across a dusty scrapbook of her unfulfilled dreams stashed under the bed in twenty years' time.

JULY 2016

Montreux, Switzerland

JESS

<From: jessicafaulkner76@gmail.com>

Dear Mr Buchs,
  I would rather not say why I need to talk
to Brigitte Mela. It's a personal matter. But I
would be very grateful if you could give me her
contact details, if you have them.

Jorge's kept his word – he hasn't told Julia and Michel about
my transgressions, so I still have a job. We've exchanged several texts over the past week, his tone thawing a little with
each one, so I'm feeling – to my relief – forgiven. And though
I hardly know him, it's nice to have this person checking up
on me. It's comforting to know that someone here knows

184

my sorry tale and seems to care enough to check I'm okay, even if it is only to make sure I'm not going to take down the Chevalleys with me when I crash and burn.

I haven't heard back from Daniel Buchs since my email and the waiting is torture. I debate emailing him again, but I don't want to scare him off. Perhaps he's just busy.

On Tuesday I take Léa and Luca to a water park at Le Bouveret. On Thursday we drive to Leysin and go summer tobogganing, screaming all the way down. On Friday we take the train up the Rochers-de-Naye mountain to see the marmots. The kids watch in delight as the furry brown animals poke their whiskers out of the burrow and call to each other in a distinct, bird-like chirp. But I'm more fascinated by the view up there – a glorious panorama over what feels like the whole of Lake Geneva, framed by mountains stretching into the far distance. Little black choughs sweep overhead, playing on the thermals.

What would it have been like to have grown up here, with all this on the doorstep? Would it have been better than growing up in South London? Instead of fresh Swiss air and weekends hiking, I had Sunday strolls in Greenwich Park followed by a pub roast. I had the thrill of the city a tube ride away, school trips to exhibitions, Saturdays gawping at dinosaurs in the Natural History Museum with Dad, musicals with Mum and Maggie, gigs at Brixton Academy with friends, bargain hunting in Spitalfields, curries on Brick Lane.

So different, I presume, to the youth the other daughter had – my parents' real child.

I wonder, for the millionth time, what I'd be like if this had been my life instead. If I'd lived the life I was actually meant to. Would I be toned and fit and an expert skier? Would I speak three languages? Would I still be a teacher? Would I still be me?

After the DNA test, I'd often find myself looking in the mirror, as if my reflection could tell me something about who I was. I needed to know where my eye colour came from, whose nose I had inherited, whose propensity for indecision and procrastination, because without knowing, I simply felt rooted to nothing, as though I'd been cut loose to float in this world like driftwood bobbing on the tides.

'Jess! There is five of them,' Luca says.

'*Are* five.'

'Look!'

I stand behind Luca and Léa and put my hands on their shoulders, watching the marmots scurrying about. Bigger, fatter squirrels, basically. 'They're pretty cute,' I say.

'Can we take one home?' Léa asks.

'Afraid not.'

'*Oh mais ils sont si mignons!*'

'They'd probably have your fingers off.'

'What?'

'Never mind.'

I try not to think about her too often. The other daughter. Mainly because it messes with my head. But also because I imagine her to be better than me. Prettier, more confident, more sorted. Would *she* be a soon-to-be divorcée with a stalled career and a clock ticking in her ears as loud as Big Ben? I expect not. I presume she doesn't know – after all, *I* didn't for thirty-seven years – and sometimes I imagine being the one to tell her. Smashing her life to pieces, making her feel how I felt after the tests changed everything. But then guilt and grief and confusion catch up with me and I want to protect her.

I don't want her ever to know, because I wish I didn't.

On Sunday, after Julia's spent another long Saturday in the office, she tells me the four of them are going to the house of some family friends for an afternoon barbecue. As though she wants to remind me that I'm not actually part of the family, she doesn't invite me to go with them.

'Go and enjoy your day,' she says. 'We already take up far more of your time than we should.'

I suppose I should be pleased she's spending a day with her children and I have Sunday to do as I wish, but when I see them all get into the car and drive off, I feel like she's usurped me. A cuckoo in my nest. Jealousy catches in the back of my throat when I think of Léa's delighted face, Luca's excitement, Michel's obvious pleasure that his wife is joining them for a second outing in two weeks.

The perfect little family, all together.

I'm lying by the lake, head in the shade of a tree, legs soaking up the heat of the July sun. The grass is packed: sun-bathers, picnickers, groups of teenagers with ghettoblasters blaring identikit Euro-synth. Opposite me is a large family that seems to have brought the contents of their home to the lakeshore: long trestle tables, foldable wooden chairs, a huge portable barbecue, cool boxes from which emerge endless cans of beer and meat and salads in Tupperware. There are screaming toddlers in frilly sunhats and UV suits, and over-sized men whose fleshy behinds are wedged in deckchairs that strain under their heft. There are smooth-skinned teen-age girls trying to look older than they are in string bikinis and lashings of waterproof mascara, shrieking as rake-thin boys in baggy shorts threaten them with water balloons in a deluded attempt at flirtation.

It's hardly a peaceful place to spend a Sunday afternoon, but the fascination of people-watching has kept me here for a good couple of hours so far. Nevertheless, it's strange to be surrounded by so many and yet feel utterly alone.

There's only one person I want to speak to right now. I roll over on my back, stare up at the canopy of leaves and dial his number. He picks up on the third ring and my heart tears upon hearing his voice.

'Dad? It's me.'

He lets out a little sigh, as though in relief. 'Jessie. It's good to hear from you.'

'I'm sorry it's been so long.' I pause, fighting to keep my voice bright. 'What have you been up to?'

'Oh, you know, this and that. Lunch with Brian in the pub yesterday. Popped into town to the bookshop. I'm going round to Alice and Richard's for dinner tomorrow.' There's a pause. I know he wants to ask about Switzerland, but he also doesn't want to know. I can picture the conflict gouging lines on his forehead. 'Is everything all right, Jessie?' he says finally. 'Are you doing okay . . .' he pauses, as though he can't quite say it, 'out there?'

'Yes, everything's fine. I just called to say hi.'

'Well, I'm glad you did. I miss you.'

'I miss you too.' I remember him pleading with me. *Please don't try to find them. Leave it be. What's done is done. Just forget it.* 'Dad?'

'Yes?'

'You know I love you, don't you?'

'Yes, sweetheart,' he says, a wobble in his voice. 'And I love you too, very much.'

Now you do, I think. *But what if I find your real daughter? What then?* I've never doubted my parents' love for me, not really, but there have been times when I think I've disappointed them. Not been ambitious enough for them, not been forthright enough, not achieved enough. So what if, as I fear, the other daughter is better than me? What if she's everything my parents wanted? Might Dad end up loving her more?

He breaks the pause. 'What's happened, Jessie? Have you found anything out?'

'No. I don't know anything, not yet. I just wanted to chat, that's all.'

Another pause. 'Do you remember when you fell over roller-skating and bashed your head on the pavement? You must have been about eleven or twelve.'

I smile. 'Yeah. I was so proud of those stitches at school. Got all the attention.'

'D'you know, I'd forgotten all about it. And then I came across this photo of the three of us in an album and I noticed you had a big plaster on your forehead and then I remembered it so clearly it felt like yesterday. And yet before seeing the picture, it had gone completely out of my head!'

I remember Mum taking me to the hospital to get stitches; how annoyed she'd been at having to wait so long to be seen because she had some work thing she'd be late for. Rachel telling all the boys at school I'd been in a fight so they'd think I was cool, and her by default.

'Anyway,' Dad continues. 'I got it framed. It's a lovely picture, even with the plaster on your head. We all just look so . . .'

Happy?

'Anyway. Just thought I'd say.'

I swallow down the lump in my throat. 'I'm glad you framed it. I'd like to see it when I'm back.'

'When is that again?'

'Another month. I'll come and see you as soon as I'm home.'

'Good,' he says. 'I'll invite Maggie down. We can all have a good catch-up.'

'I'd like that.'

'Good,' he says again. 'Jessie?'

'Yes?' I can hear he wants to say something, and I hope he'll tell me what I need to hear, that everything's okay, that he doesn't think of me any differently, that he'll always love me, whatever I find out.

'Take care of yourself, okay?' he says.

I nod, keep my voice steady. 'I will, Dad, I will.'

I hang up. My arm drops to my side and I lie there, looking up at the sunlight filtering through the leaves, remembering being eleven, when the only thing I had to worry about was staying upright on roller-skates. I long to go back to that time, when I was still me, when my parents were still mine, when I knew my place in the world. Dad has lots of photos in his house – I've seen them so many times I can picture them in my head now. There's one of me and Mum sitting on a wall eating ice cream, in France, I think it was – she'd taken us along on a press freebie for the travel pages. Another of the three of us, me a teenager, at Aunt Jemima's wedding in Italy. And one of Patrick and me in my parents' garden in Greenwich not so long after we met, his arm slung around me, a big grin on my face. These are the people who've shaped me, and the experiences that told me who I was. But it pains me to look at those photos now because when I do, all I see is what's gone.

They show the person I thought I was, and tell me nothing of who I actually am.

I ache to know who that is. I ache to have a place in the world once again. That's why, whatever my fears, however it may change things with Dad, I know I need to do this.

When Julia, Michel and the kids arrive home, I'm back from the lake, showered, and sitting on the terrace reading a book.

Léa rushes to me and gives me a big hug, telling me about how much fun she had, about playing ping-pong with her friends, about the sausages on the barbecue and the tiny sip of wine she had when her parents weren't looking.

'I wish you were there too,' she says, and my heart soars. I look over at Julia, standing in the doorway, and perhaps it's my imagination, but I think I see her bristle at her daughter's words.

'Tomorrow,' I say to Léa. 'Tomorrow it's just you, me and Luca again.'

'Jess needs a break from us sometimes,' Julia says. 'She must be exhausted looking after you two all week.'

I smile at Léa, bring my face close to hers. 'Never,' I whisper. 'I love it.'

'Well, we're lucky to have you,' Michel shouts from the kitchen, where he's making coffee. 'You and Maria, both. I don't know what we'd do without you, right Julia?'

He comes over to the terrace door, puts his arm around his wife's shoulders, and she nods back, mumbles agreement with a tight smile. But I feel it, nonetheless. I feel what my place in this family is – the outsider, the interloper, the temporary help – and I wonder then, how it's come to this. What am I doing here, pretending to be the mother I'll probably never be? How did my life unravel so badly, when it had the potential to be like Julia's? Why does she get to have all this, and not me?

Tears prickle my eyes, and before I can embarrass myself, I claim a headache, blaming too much sun, and head to my room. I sit on my bed and take out the photo of Mum in 1976, wondering what she was thinking then, and what she'd think of me now, if she knew what a mess my life had become. If she knew I wasn't hers.

When I crawl into bed I reach for my phone as usual and my chest lurches when I see the message symbol. I punch in my unlock pin and sit up in the bed.

> It's been a long time since I heard the name
> Brigitte Mela.

I'm holding my breath as I scroll down.

> Anna is her real name. Anna Meier. But please,
> I ask you to reply and tell me why you are
> looking for her? It's important that I know.
> Daniel Buchs

I read the message twice, three times, four. I stare at the name. *Anna Meier.* That's why the hospital couldn't find her. They didn't have the right name. Anna Meier. Such an alien name to me, and yet it could be my mother's name. I say it out loud in the quiet room.

Anna Meier. I say it again and some part of my brain kicks in, telling me it's familiar.

Meier. An image flashes across my mind of a document.

Julia Sarah Meier and Michel Jean-Pierre Chevalley . . .

Julia's maiden name. A prickle walks its way up my spine

as I remember what else I found in her drawer. A handwritten letter in German and a signature with a large, looping A. Handwritten, not typed. Old-fashioned script. Kisses after the signature. Definitely an older relative. An older relative called A. Meier.

I put down my phone and gently lie back on the pillow, as though my head's as delicate as glass and if I'm not extremely careful, it's going to shatter into tiny pieces.

MAY 1976

London, UK

Sylvia

The letter arrived in the office with the morning post, Sylvia's name in a cursive script on the envelope, a Swiss stamp in the corner. It was little over two months since she'd been to Switzerland, but it felt so much longer. She pictured the small apartment – the girls crammed around the table, steam rising from the fondue, David Bowie on the record player, Daniel drinking beer on the tatty old couch. So much had happened since then. Opening the letter was like stepping back to before: before she'd admitted what was happening to her, before the clinic, before she took a left turn off the route she thought she was on.

Dearest Sylvia,
I can't tell you how excited I was to receive a copy of the

*wonderful article you wrote. We are so incredibly grateful
to you for shining a light on our cause and helping others
understand our fight. I knew, from the moment I met you,
that you were on our side, and it means so much to us I
cannot say! And so I wanted to invite you back. We're
staging an event later in the summer, a feminist festival,
where we hope to spread the word about everything we're
passionate about. Will you come? It will be the school
holidays, you can stay with me, and I would be simply
delighted to show you a little more of my country at the same
time. Say you will?*

With my very best wishes,

Evelyne

Just the idea of it filled Sylvia with the same sense of freedom she'd felt that day on her old school's lawn. Some more time in Switzerland, in summer, when the air would be bright and clear, with people who would understand her worries about her pregnancy, her job prospects and her new husband's suffocating desire to stop her doing anything interesting. In recent days she'd felt a clawing sense of claustrophobia, which was reflected in the news making it to her paper's front page. It hadn't rained enough in recent months; the dry winter had morphed into a drier spring, there was talk of drought and empty reservoirs and water rationing, farmers harvesting early and animal feed tripling in price. And then there was the doom and gloom over the economy: inflation, spending cuts and debt. She would love a brief respite from all that, a chance to get away from it all. Yes, she had Copenhagen coming up, but why not Switzerland too? She very much doubted Roger would let her write another article on such a similar subject, but she could go anyway, just for fun. Of course, she and Jim were meant to be saving, not spending money on flights. They'd need the cash for rent and furniture for the new apartment, plus all the equipment for the baby. And then there was Jim's aversion to her travelling whilst pregnant. But the more he acted like her protector, the more she wanted to break free, because wasn't now the time? The time for her to do as much as she could, to pack it all in, because how long would it be until she could go abroad again, once they had a child in tow?

She picked up a pen to write to Evelyne straight away, to say yes, she'd definitely come, but had to put it down again as a wave of nausea socked her in the stomach. She stood up and with careful steps walked through the open plan to the ladies. She pushed the door open, went into a cubicle and sat on the toilet, waiting for her body to decide if it needed to throw up or not.

What was she, about four months gone? She'd expected this to be over by now. That's what Jim's mum had said, if she'd remembered correctly, because she had trouble concentrating on the reams of baby-related information Pamela continually spouted at her down the phone every time she called – which was often. The first trimester is the worst, after that it gets better, that's what Sylvia thought she'd said. Well it hadn't. Just her luck.

She stared at the yellow linoleum between her feet until the nausea passed. It appeared she wouldn't throw up after all, small mercies. She peed and left the cubicle, stood in front of the mirror and splashed water on her face. She looked at her reflection and saw her tiredness, as well as something else. Her hair was thicker, perhaps, her face a little plumper, her breasts fuller – and it was only a matter of time before the men in the office noticed that.

She smoothed her hand over her shirt and felt the modest curve she'd so far successfully managed to hide under shirts and jackets, but it was getting warmer, and she would get bigger; she knew she couldn't hide it for long. She'd have to tell Roger soon, but the thought made her feel sick again. She didn't want him to know. Didn't want her colleagues to know. She didn't want to be one of those women who fucked up a promising career by having a baby. Though she was confident the new employment protection law meant Roger wouldn't sack her for being pregnant, who knows if he'd agree to any maternity pay; that part of the legislation hadn't come into force yet, and there was no formal arrangement at her paper. She knew some editors agreed to paid leave if they valued their female journalists – but did Roger value her enough? She wasn't so sure.

She sighed. Just a little longer and then she'd face it.

'Sylvia, dear, are you quite all right?'

She looked up and whipped her hand away from her stomach. She hadn't heard Valerie come into the bathroom.

'Yes,' she said. 'I'm fine. Just a little hot.' She dried her face with a paper towel and reached into her pocket for her lipstick.

'It *is* rather muggy outside,' Valerie said. 'Let's hope we get that much needed rain soon.' She came to stand next to Sylvia and looked at her in the mirror as she applied a slick of lipstick. 'You look a little off-colour.'

She smiled. 'Nothing a cup of Betty's coffee won't knock out of me.'

'When's the trip?'

'Denmark? Next week.'

'Quite a coup.'

'Thanks. I'm pleased.'

'You should be.' Valerie plumped her hair in the mirror and turned to look at Sylvia directly. Her eyes flicked up and down her body, and there was something about her gaze that unnerved her. 'You'll be having my job if I'm not careful.'

Sylvia forced a laugh. 'Hardly. I'm sure the Queen of Fleet Street is safe on her throne for a long while yet.'

Valerie smiled. 'Ridiculous title,' she said, but Sylvia saw the glint of pride in her eyes. 'Anyway darling, must dash. Look after yourselves in Denmark.'

And she was gone.

The sickness eased after her spell in the toilet and she passed the afternoon researching Warburton's life and career from cuttings and library books. She'd spent several years working for the UK's mission to the United Nations in Geneva, and

Sylvia wondered what she thought of Switzerland and its record on women's rights. What it felt like to have risen so high in a predominantly male profession, and to have made such an impact at the Foreign Office that the prime minister made you an ambassador, the first British woman to take up such a prestigious post. How she felt about working for an organisation that, until just a few years ago, would demand she resign if she married. Is that why she never had? There was so much she wanted to ask her that she almost didn't know where to begin.

Roger stalked over to her desk in the early afternoon. 'Tallis, a word.' He retreated to his glass lair, clearly expecting her to follow.

She threw a glance at Max, who pulled a face she couldn't interpret.

'Denmark. Change of plan. I'm going to send Max Harmer instead,' he said when she closed his office door after her.

'I'm sorry?' Sylvia's eyebrows shot up. 'Why is that?'

'Because I can't send a pregnant woman on a foreign assignment.'

Her stomach plummeted and she felt heat rise up her neck. 'I was going to tell you.'

'Well, someone else did first,' he said, reprimand in his tone. 'And congratulations on tying the knot, by the way.'

Her brain raced through the people who knew about her pregnancy and precipitated wedding and she only came up with one who would also have the means to slip a quiet word to her boss over a drink in the pub: Jim. But surely not; surely reliable, kind Jim wouldn't do that to her.

She thought back to the morning after their argument. He'd said little as they got up, showered, rummaged in overflowing suitcases for their least creased clothes and tried not to set the bread on fire under a grill they weren't yet used to. He'd kissed her as he went out the door before her, affection on his face, and she'd thought he was over it. After all, Jim was a calm, rational person. It was one of the things she sometimes found infuriating about him — a fire could be raging inside her over some issue or other, but he could always douse it with his *calmness*. So she'd figured he'd think it through and see she was right, and she would go to Copenhagen as planned.

'Who told you?'

Roger waved his hand. 'That's hardly the issue. Look, Tallis, your personal life is none of my business, though of course we'll have certain considerations to discuss. I suppose you'll be wanting leave, so we'll have to think about getting in a replacement ...' he rubbed his eyes, as though the thought of it was giving him a headache already, 'but the most immediate concern is that I can't have a pregnant woman out in Denmark. We don't have the insurance.'

What? Her neck beaded with sweat. 'Roger, I can do this. My pregnancy has no bearing on my ability to do my job. I fully intend to continue working as long as I can and come back as soon as possible afterwards and—'

He held up his hand. 'I can't be responsible if something

should happen. Keith and the board would have my guts for garters.'

Sylvia thought the editor-in-chief would care less about her being pregnant and more about her bagging a sought-after interview, but she didn't say so. 'Nothing's going to happen, this is ridiculous,' she said, adding, a little more forcibly than she intended, 'This is *my* story. I got the interview. Warburton said yes to me, not Max.'

He narrowed his eyes. 'Don't get too big for your boots, Tallis. You're good, but so are plenty of others. Harmer will do a perfectly decent job.'

'Roger, please.' She worked hard to keep her voice even. 'There's no issue with this,' she gestured towards her stomach. 'I'm willing and able to go and do my job.'

'Look, just take a step back this time and then after all this,' he waved his hand, 'we'll see about getting you back on track, if you're not too distracted by motherhood.'

He said it as though she should be grateful, but indignation made her head swim. 'I don't have to be *off* track.'

'Tallis, I'm not changing my bloody mind. Now fuck off out of here.'

As she took the few steps to the door, she felt her legs shaking – from fury or shock she wasn't sure.

'Oh, and get down to personnel,' Roger shouted after her. 'We can't have a pregnant reporter going by her maiden name – you're Sylvia Millson now.'

She couldn't concentrate for the rest of the day. She stared at her notebook, pretending to work, though she could barely see the words on the page. She wanted to run out of the office and head straight down to Jim's place and have it out with him.

'He didn't tell me why. No hard feelings, I hope?' Max put a cup of coffee on her desk and she looked up, shook her head. The smell of the coffee made her want to retch.

'Not your fault. But you may as well know, I'm going to have a baby. Roger seems to think that's incompatible with doing an interview in Denmark.'

'Fucking hell,' he said, and then caught himself. 'I mean, congratulations to you and your er ... Jim.'

His slight smile and raised eyebrows induced a flush of embarrassment, before anger flooded through her. Why should she feel embarrassed to have a child? Why had other people's embarrassment pushed her into a shotgun wedding? Why on earth should she stop doing a job she loved months before the baby had even arrived?

'Thanks, my husband's delighted,' she said. She wanted to just end this, to let him go back to his desk so they could both pretend to work in peace. 'Enjoy Copenhagen. I hear it's beautiful at this time of year.'

It was all around the office within the hour.

She left the building on the dot of 6pm, turning down Max's invitation for *a quick snifter* with the boys at the Old Bell, and was home before Jim this time. She sat on the hard floorboards, avoiding that damn armchair out of principle. The wait felt interminable, the flat so silent she could hear the tick of her watch, counting down the seconds until he arrived.

'Please tell me you didn't do it?' she said when he walked in the door.

'Hello to you too, darling.'

'Because you had absolutely no right.'

He took off his coat and hung it on the back of the door and turned back to her. Calm, steady. She felt her heart pulsing hard in her chest.

'I don't know what you're talking about,' he said.

'Did you tell Roger I was pregnant?'

'What?' he said. 'Well, no. Hadn't you?'

'No, Jim, no I hadn't. But someone did, *today*, and as a result I am no longer going to Denmark to interview Anne Warburton because Roger says they haven't got the bloody insurance, although I'm sure that's a pathetic made up excuse simply to punish me for getting pregnant. So if it was you, Jim, if it was you who took this away from me then please be honest and admit to what you've done.'

He rubbed his hand over his eyes and looked at her, hurt carving creases into his features. He came over and crouched down in front of her, took her hand in his and looked her right in the eyes. 'No, I didn't. I promise you.'

She stared right back and saw he was telling the truth and something eased inside her. 'Okay,' she said. Then who the hell else did?

Jim sat down beside her, his back resting against the bare wall. 'I'm sorry, Syl, I know you were excited about the trip.' He squeezed her hand. 'But I can't say I'm not a little relieved.

204

You should be taking care of yourself now, not rushing around like a mad thing to foreign countries.'

He smiled and nudged her as he said it, but his words reignited something in her and she turned to face him. 'Jim, don't be ridiculous, I'm perfectly capable of going abroad. I'm fine, the baby is fine. Roger's decision is completely unfair and I'm going to try to fight it. I just don't know how yet.'

'You're four months gone.' He turned to her. 'And yet you don't seem to be accepting that this is happening. You say the baby's fine, but how do you know? You're not going to your midwife appointments, are you?'

She started to protest and then pulled herself up short. 'Have you been snooping on me?'

'Hardly. You left your diary lying around, I happened to glance at it and I saw you'd crossed out an appointment at Guys.'

'Look, work's been busy. Anyway, I can *un*cancel it now I'm not going to Denmark.'

'Please do.' He sighed and rubbed his eyes, the resignation of a parent trying to talk sense into a child. 'Syl,' he said slowly, 'you have to accept that things have to change. We're going to be parents – our priorities will be different.'

'*Our* priorities?'

'Yes!'

His confused expression sparked a hot rage in her and she fought back the angry tears that threatened to undermine her.

'As far as I can tell, everything you're doing and saying is about me changing *my* priorities. Well, what about you? Are *you* going to be forced to give up your job, to throw away the position you've worked so hard to get and let someone who isn't as good as you step into your shoes? Are you? Because if not, Jim, then *your* priorities aren't changing – not really. You know nothing about how it feels to have a . . . *situation* you didn't want impose itself on you and alter everything.'

He looked down at his shoes and then back at her. 'You don't want this?'

'Honestly?' Her voice wavered. 'No. I don't want to be pregnant. I didn't want to get married in a rush, as though I should be embarrassed by my predicament. And I don't want to give up the job I've always wanted and am just starting to make a success of – not even for a minute, let alone months or years or however long you are expecting me to *change my priorities* for.'

'I didn't know you felt this way. We always said we'd have kids.'

'Yes, but later. Not now, not at twenty-three.' *Perhaps not ever*, she stopped herself saying. 'We talked about this.'

'I know, but I didn't think you were so firm about it that you wouldn't want a baby if an accident happened. I mean, it's a *happy* accident, isn't it?'

She stood up, walked over to the window, looked out at the row of terraced houses opposite. The spring sunlight was fading and lights were already on in some. A cosy living room. A woman washing up at a kitchen sink. Kids opening a front door, stepping into an illuminated hallway.

Happy accident.

'I nearly had an abortion,' she said, her back to him. Her watch ticked on. She turned around and saw hurt and confusion on his face. 'Before I even told you. I was debating not having the baby.'

'You would have done that?'

'Well, clearly not. I couldn't go through with it.'

'But you thought about it? I can't believe it, Syl.'

'I had the signed forms. I went to the clinic. I was about to take the pills. So, yes, I could have done it.' She saw his sadness, his hurt, and part of her wanted to hug him tight and say, *I'm sorry, I shouldn't have even thought about it, I should have told you, everything will be okay now.*

But she wouldn't. Because she didn't believe any of those things. She wasn't sorry. She didn't think everything would be okay. And she needed him to know that.

'I was scared, Jim. And I still am. This isn't what I wanted and I'm scared I've ruined my life, scared my career's been nipped in the bud before it's even got going; that I'll be stuck at home, bored and unfulfilled, looking jealously on as you climb the ladder. I'm scared I'll be a terrible mother. I'm scared I'll resent the baby. I'm scared of . . . everything, it seems. And all because the stupid pill failed. Not because we chose it, rationally, by talking together and deciding, but because a contraceptive that's meant to liberate women has ended up doing the complete opposite to me . . .'

He looked up at her and she hoped he understood. That's all she wanted: for him to understand how this felt for her.

But then he stood up, came over to her, put his hands on her arms and looked her in the eyes, and she knew, even before he said it, that he hadn't.

'Syl, darling, you're overreacting. It's a baby, not a life sentence.'

She smiled, shook her head, shrugged his hands off her arms. She picked up her jacket from the back of the armchair, walked out the door and slammed it behind her.

JULY 2016

Montreux, Switzerland

JESS

I always wondered why Mum and Dad never had another child. I remember asking them once, separately. Mum said I was all she needed. Dad said Mum didn't want to go through it all again. I knew I wasn't exactly a planned baby, and sometimes – usually when I'd had a row with Mum over homework or chores or how late I could stay out – I wondered if perhaps she'd have preferred not to have had me. Once, in a fit of rage, I slung that accusation at her like an uppercut. I remember how she flinched like I had physically hit her, how she put her hands on my arms and looked me right in the eye and said, *No, never, not for one second.*

Growing up, it didn't really matter to me not to have a sibling. I had plenty of friends, a conveyor belt of piano lessons and netball games and drawing classes to keep me entertained, sporadic but thrilling excursions with Maggie, and the undivided attention of my parents when they were home. But now I yearn for a brother or sister, someone who could really understand what it might feel like to be told your parents aren't your own.

<From: jessicafaulkner76@gmail.com>

Dear Mr Buchs,
   I can't really explain on email why I need to find Brigitte/Anna – it's a long story. In short, something happened to my mother in 1976, and I think Anna may know what that was. Please, are you able to give me her number or email address?

I sit back in the garden chair and survey what I've written. *And does she have a daughter living in Montreux?* That's what I want to ask. The thought of her name – my probable biological mother's name – on the letter in Julia's drawer makes the skin on the back of my neck prickle.

Admittedly, my internet search for Anna Meier turned up millions of page results, so there's clearly more than one out there. But can it really just be a coincidence that Julia knows an A. Meier, that her own maiden name is Meier? I stare at her through the window, pottering about the kitchen, going to the fridge, grabbing glasses from the cupboard. I can't face the idea that she could be . . .

'Here.' She emerges onto the veranda and puts a bottle of wine and two glasses down on the table. She's changed out of her work clothes into a pair of yoga pants and a vest top. Her dark hair is swept up into a loose bun that looks effortlessly stylish in a way my own dirty blond mop never quite manages. Her skin looks flawless in the dusky light. She sits down opposite me and I force a smile, trying to silence the constant questioning in my head. Does she look like either of them? Can I see a hint of Dad's nose? The shape of Mum's eyebrows?

I shake the voice away. It's incomprehensible. It's ridiculous. This perfect woman cannot be *her*; she cannot be my parents' child instead of me.

She hands me a glass. '*Santé.*'

'Cheers.' I tap hers and look her in the eyes, as is the Swiss way.

Not Dad's. A shade darker than Mum's.

'This must seem strange to you, to have me here in the evening instead of Michel,' she says.

I shake my head, smile. 'Well, maybe a little.' The kids went to bed half an hour ago and it does seem odd to be sitting here with her while Michel's in a bar helping to drown the sorrows of some workmate going through a break-up. I don't know how to *be* around Julia, so little time do I spend with her. And now, sitting next to her, I feel her presence cast a shadow over mine, as though her beauty and poise and confidence are erasing me to a faint blur.

'I'm glad we finally have this time to chat. I can't believe how crazy it's been at work, and then with Léa's birthday and everything, I feel I haven't had the chance to catch up with you, to see how it's going.'

I take a sip, swallow. 'It's going well, I think.'

'The children just love you! Léa doesn't stop talking about you.' She puts her glass to her lips and I wonder if it's to mask the forced smile she can't quite make real.

'I'm glad. They're great kids.' If Julia *is* their daughter, that would make Léa and Luca Dad's grandchildren. He'd have what I know he always wanted. The thought curls into a hard knot of pain in my chest. They'd be his blood – but not mine, never mine.

Julia takes a sip of wine and puts the glass back on the table. 'You're halfway through already! How have you found Switzerland so far?'

'It's wonderful,' I say. 'Another life.'

'Will you stay? I mean, I'm sorry we can't offer you longer. Once the kids are at school there won't be any need, since we can put them in after-school club. But if you want to stay and find another job as an English teacher, at an international school perhaps, I could help you look.' She pauses. 'Or maybe you'd want another position in a family, like this. Less stressful than in a school, I imagine.' She smiles, and I catch the condescending undertone to her words: *you obviously have no career ambition, unlike me.* But I won't rise to it.

'I haven't decided yet,' I say.

She's not on Facebook. So I either need to think of an excuse to ask when her birthday is or find out another way.

I think her age was stated on her marriage certificate, but I can't remember what it said. Maybe I'll have to go in there again and look.

I think of Jorge's anger, the platitudes I gave him. *No more snooping, I promise.* But things are different now.

'Things have been a little tricky for me lately. I need to make a fresh start, but I'm still figuring out what that should be.'

'Oh,' she frowns. 'I'm sorry to hear that.' She takes a sip of her drink and then cocks her head, smiles. 'It's never too late to start over, though, is it?'

I smile, thinking of the several failed rounds of IVF, the years of trying and failing, another rod on the back of our marriage when it clearly wasn't strong enough. I think of Patrick's email and my approaching fortieth birthday in the autumn, and I think that, yes, for some things it is too late. But she doesn't know how that feels since everything's been so easy for her.

'Well,' I say. 'Here would be a good place to try. I can see it's wonderful to live here. You're very lucky.'

'Yes, we are,' she says. 'But in a way you make your own luck, don't you?'

Sometimes, I think. And other times things just happen to you that you have absolutely no control over. I wonder what it would feel like to tell her. To tell her she isn't who she thinks she is, that her parents aren't her own, that she wasn't meant to have this lucky, lucky life. But if I inflicted that pain on her, then I'd be inflicting far worse on myself, because if she was the other daughter then I'd have another question, a question I don't think I'd want to know the answer to: would Mum and Dad have preferred her – this ambitious, beautiful, *sorted* woman who's managed to have it all – instead of me?

I have to wait for a quiet moment one sunny mid-week morning to sneak back into Julia and Michel's bedroom. Maria won't be round until 2pm. Léa and Luca are outside in the garden. I know I don't have long before I'll have to be out there breaking up a squabble or tending to a mild injury. But that's okay, because I don't intend to be long. I know what I want.

September eighteenth. That's when Léa said Julia's birthday was when I asked her. Couldn't remember how old she was though. Part of me feels relieved. But the other part feels an ominous sense of foreboding. Okay, so we don't share a birthday, but we're only two weeks apart – or could be, if Julia's my age.

I go straight for the drawer and slide it open. I riffle through the contents until I get to the folder I saw before. I open it, flick through the papers and take out the marriage certificate. Their ages are written next to their names: Julia Sarah Meier, 26; Michel Jean-Pierre Chevalley, 29. I quickly do the maths and my stomach plunges to realise that yes, she's my age. Julia will be forty in September – just two weeks after me. I put the marriage certificate back and take out the letter from A. Meier that I found last time. Could this be Julia's mother? I unfold the paper and run my hand

214

over the ink. I can't understand a word but the handwriting is beautiful. I copy the address into my journal. Hopfenweg 31, Thun. It's dated 2004. She's probably long gone.

My phone pings and I jump like a rabbit at a gun, my elbow knocking into the dressing table. One of Julia's necklaces falls off the side of the mirror onto the wooden top. A bead smashes. *Shit.* My heart races as I wait, listening, hoping no footsteps are coming down the hall. But there's nothing. I take my phone out of my back pocket and open the message.

> Hola guapa. Hope you're dealing ok with all your crazy shit. I'm playing with my band at a jazz club in Lausanne on Thursday night. If you can get away, come?

Bloody Jorge. Is he psychic? Can he sense I'm in here? My shame rises as though he's caught me all over again.

I return the phone to my pocket and examine the damage. Just one of the beads is broken, but it seems a clean break – fixable, I hope. I pick up the pieces and put them in my pocket along with the rest of the necklace. I fold up the letter, return it to where it was in the folder and slot the folder back into the drawer. I want to root around further, see if there's any evidence of Julia's parentage, but Jorge's text has unnerved me, as though he's watching me, and I've already done enough damage. So I stand up from the bed, smooth away the indent on the duvet cover, and slip out of the room.

I dish out ice lollies to the kids and the three of us sit on the grass in silence, the sun on our faces and sticky orange sliding down our fingers. With my other hand I take out my phone and open maps, type in Thun. It could be her. Julia's A. Meier could be *my* Anna Meier. My birth mother. Perhaps she's still there, or perhaps she left years ago.

The only way to know is to go and find out.

I fix Julia's necklace late at night when the rest of the house is in bed. There's an uncommon stillness that's slightly eerie in a home usually so full of noise. I sit cocooned in the low glow of my bedroom and wallow in the welcome quiet.

I piece the fragments of the broken bead back together and glue them with a fixative I found in the kitchen drawer. I don't understand what it says on the tube, but it looks like the sturdy kind of stuff I've used at home. I wonder what my tenant is doing now. Lying in the bed I once shared with Patrick, perhaps. Or maybe watching a film, making herself a cup of tea with my kettle.

I take my time, carefully pushing the pieces together and scraping the excess glue away when it oozes out. I don't want the cracks to show; I don't want Julia to know I've been in there, snooping.

I won't do it again. I'll just pop in briefly one day when everyone's out so I can put the necklace back, hopefully before Julia's missed it. There were so many necklaces hanging from the mirror that I somehow doubt she'll notice.

I lie back on my bed waiting for the glue to dry. My hand goes to my neck, touches the delicate silver chain I wear every day, the one Mum gave me on my wedding day. I remember how her eyes filled up and how that shocked me, because forthright, confident, stoic Mum never cried. Took her back to her own, she said. Stirred up memories.

You were there too, even though you weren't meant to be. That's what Dad always used to say to me, before the DNA tests proved that I wasn't actually there at all.

We used to laugh about it. A shotgun wedding, the family scandal. It gives me cold shivers now, because who *was* there? Could it possibly, unfathomably, have been Julia?

My breath starts to come faster and I feel my pulse speed up. Sweat breaks out on the back of my neck and I'm suddenly shaking. I focus hard to control the panic. A long breath in, hold, slowly out.

When my hands stop shaking, I pick up Julia's necklace again and inspect it, examining the tiny trails across the surface of the once-broken bead. Hardly noticeable. Particularly if you didn't know it was ever broken. And only I know that.

JUNE 1976

London, UK

SYLVIA

Heat draped itself across her shoulders. It whispered hot breath on her neck, ran clammy fingers between her breasts, dribbled down her forehead. Strands of hair stuck to her temples and sweat trickled under her arms beneath the light cream shirt that today felt as heavy as sheepskin. It was only ten in the morning and yet they were all simmering like rabbits in stew.

'Don't these fans work?' Sylvia shook a cold carton of chocolate milk she'd picked up on the way in after an unbearable tube journey. She punched in the straw and sucked down the cool sweet liquid in greedy gulps.

Max shrugged. 'Too hot for them to work properly, according to maintenance.'

Sylvia sighed. 'Well, I know the feeling.'

'D'you know what?' Max grinned. 'Yesterday the umpires at Wimbledon were actually allowed to take their bloody jackets off.'

She laughed. 'I know, I saw it on the news. First time ever, apparently.' She loved Wimbledon, with its sense of history, its manicured lawns and its quirky traditions. Despite everything else that was happening – the drought, the economy in meltdown, scandals rocking the political establishment – Wimbledon would carry on, upholding Britishness for two weeks in a small pocket of SW19.

Jim always laughed at her obsession with it. 'You pride yourself on striving to be different, and yet you're addicted to this British institution that's allergic to change.'

He was right, of course. It should have riled her, this fusty institution that was refusing to give women equal prize money despite a threatened boycott, but there was something about the bright white outfits, the almost-whisper of the commentator's voice and the silence between points that calmed her. It was a hiatus from real life, a pocket of serenity in a tumultuous world.

'They're talking about fucking weeks of this ahead, apparently,' Max said.

'Surely not?'

'We're leading with "Hotter than Honolulu" in tonight's edition.'

Sylvia rolled her eyes. 'Only in Britain is the weather news.'

But she had to admit, this felt newsworthy. At first it had been a novelty, the papers full of photos of swimmers in the

Serpentine, city workers cooling their feet in Trafalgar Square's fountains and Brighton's beaches packed with weekenders escaping the city. But as the heatwave continued, day after day, touching ninety degrees, it was as though London was caught in a pressure cooker. She saw its effects in the office workers flaked out in St Paul's churchyard every lunchtime, in the sluggish steps of pedestrians on Fleet Street, walking as though carrying the heat on their backs, and in the general irritation that seemed to have infected the office. Sharp voices down the telephone, arguments in the corridors, more expletives than usual, a constant hum of exasperation. It was surely the heat that had Roger stalking the newsroom like an injured bear, the heat that changed his demeanour from merely wearily gruff to downright angry, the heat that made him dismiss any feature idea she proposed in the weekly meetings without a hint of discussion. The progress she felt she'd made with her Switzerland feature had melted away like an ice lolly in the sun.

But of course it wasn't just the heat. She was being punished, she knew, not only for letting the side down by being such a stereotypical woman as to put babies before career, but for losing the paper the Warburton interview. It turned out that Britain's first female ambassador hadn't taken kindly to being told the journalist who was gifted the UK media's only interview with her wouldn't be taking up the opportunity after all. Initially, after first Max and then Roger got off the phone to Warburton's secretary, clearly bruised by the experience, Sylvia had allowed herself just the briefest moment of self-satisfaction.

See! she wanted to say, *Warburton wanted me, not Max, so you should have let me go.*

She even wondered, for a minute, if Roger would change his mind and send her after all, but he didn't, and the opportunity was lost. It felt as if he'd been taking it out on her ever since.

Sylvia chucked the empty carton of chocolate milk in the bin and turned back to the blank piece of paper in her typewriter. She had an hour to write some scintillating lifestyle tips for the 'at home' feature. How to keep the flowers in your garden hydrated during a hosepipe ban. A recipe for potato salad to go with barbecued meats. Tips on how to keep cool making love during a heatwave (Valerie's idea). A tried-and-tested way of giving dry, brittle fingernails a DIY moisture boost. *Twice a week for two months, soak your fingers in a bowl of warm olive oil for five minutes . . .* Frankly, her heart wasn't in it. She wanted to just get up and leave. She yearned to escape London's suffocating grip and head for the mountain air of Switzerland; away from the heat, from Roger, from her unwanted future. Thankfully, in a few days that's exactly what she would do.

He rang, as he had every day, in the early afternoon.

'If you come back, I'll get rid of that armchair you hate.'

Sylvia smiled down the line despite herself. 'That's hardly the point, Jim.'

'I know, I know. But I don't know what else to do, Syl. I've said I'm sorry for not . . . understanding. I'm trying, okay? I'm trying to understand why you're so mad about having our baby. But I need you here. You're my wife, my *pregnant* wife, we should be living together.'

'I can't talk about this now.' She stared down the room, watched Valerie standing behind Ellis's shoulder, leaning over him as she looked at something on his desk. She laughed, put a hand lightly on his arm.

Sylvia knew Jim had nothing to do with Roger finding out about the baby. *Take care of yourselves*, Valerie had said.

Of course it could only be a woman, a woman with two of her own, who would recognise the signs. And Sylvia couldn't help but think that Valerie had not only told Roger about her pregnancy, but also encouraged him to take the Warburton interview off her. *You'll be having my job if I'm not careful . . .*

'You always say that. So when, then?'

'I don't know.'

'Meet me after work?'

'No. I have to pack.'

She could picture him shaking his head, biting his tongue. She knew he wouldn't dare try and stop her going.

'My parents are meant to be coming down on Saturday. What do I say?'

'Just tell the truth. I had to go to Switzerland.'

'Syl . . .'

She sighed, twirled the phone cord around her finger, studied Max mumbling to himself as he jabbed at his typewriter, trying to conjure the right words. She wondered if Jim did that too. She'd never seen him at work, nor had he her – apart from those early days on their student paper. They

222

each had their own daytime world when they existed outside of coupledom, and she loved that. If she didn't have her job, what would she have to tell him at the end of each day? She couldn't imagine hearing about his day at work and only being able to offer up talk of children's parties and nappies in return. But Maggie was right, this couldn't go on.

'I'm not punishing him,' she'd said to Maggie, repeatedly, after one post-argument night back at her old flat turned into a few days, and then a few weeks.

'You just need some space, yes, I know.' Maggie rolled her eyes. 'Well, you haven't exactly got it here.'

That was certainly true. Maggie's bedroom seemed so much smaller and more cluttered than Sylvia had ever noticed when she actually lived in the flat. She'd never quite realised what a hoarder Maggie was. Every surface in her room was covered with trinkets from her travels, stuffed toys, funny postcards sent by friends years ago, pictures in dusty old frames. And then there were the sketches, and paint swatches on paper with scribbled notes next to them – *one of these colours for the emperor's palace walls? Ask John which he prefers* – and the cardboard models of sets, evidence of Maggie's job, of her future, marching on, exactly in the way she'd worked so hard to have it.

As Sylvia lay in the single bed that first morning – 'You're pregnant, I can hardly make you sleep on the floor,' Maggie had said, forming the sofa cushions into a makeshift mattress on the bedroom carpet for herself – she heard Maggie's new flatmate Rose come out of her old room and head for the shower, and a pang of regret socked her in the stomach like a physical blow. Things were moving on without her, continuing in their intended direction as she moved off on a tangent.

This wasn't how it was meant to be.

'Life isn't a straight line, Syl darling. Haven't you figured that out by now?' Maggie had said.

'I want it to be.'

Maggie laughed. 'What, and give up spontaneity, the excitement of the unknown? Don't be silly.'

Sylvia propped herself up on her elbow and looked at her friend. 'I've fought hard to be on this path and I want to stay on it.'

'I know you have. So have I. But things happen – or don't happen – that aren't always of your making and you just have to deal with them. I didn't want to be a bank teller, but I dealt with it. And I'm sure there'll be more things thrown at me in the future that I don't necessarily want. But that's what life is about. It happens to everyone.' Maggie flopped down on her pillow. 'Plenty of women would kill to be in your situation, you know.' Her voice was soft. 'It may not be where you imagined you'd be right now, but that doesn't make it bad. You've just got to accept it and do your best to make it a success. And I know you can, because you're you, and that's what you do.'

Maybe she could. But that wasn't the point. Her argument with Jim had wounded something deep inside her. It was the first time she had truly recognised that the man she loved, the man who had always supported her career ambitions as much as his own, didn't really understand the gulf that existed between their respective experiences. Because the barriers she faced – barriers created and sustained by members of his own sex – weren't real for him, they were only abstract. Of course he thought it unfair she was paid less than Max despite the existence of the Equal Pay Act; of course he applauded the progress when, last year, it was finally made illegal to discriminate against women. He would say these things and he would mean them. But he'd never had to actually fight those battles himself. He'd never had a tutor who marked him up or down depending on the length of his skirt. He'd never been told he shouldn't be ambitious because it's not attractive. He'd never had an editor refuse to sign off his expenses because he'd turned down his sexual advances, as she knew had happened to Marnie in her previous job. He'd never found out that a fellow journalist with the same level of experience earned more because they pissed standing up. She wanted him to know how it felt. She needed him to feel how she did, or she didn't know where they could go from here.

'When I'm back,' she said to him now, over the phone. 'We'll talk when I'm back.'

Though she hadn't needed a reminder of how quickly time was passing, she was given one as the train rattled along the shore of Lake Geneva. It was nearly four months since she'd last taken this journey and she was struck by how different the landscape looked now. The mountains were no longer dip-dyed in white – only slivers of snow remained on their summits, topping green and brown and black. The sky was a hazy blue, and the train rushed past sailboats and rowers, their blades slicing through the calm surface like knives through warm butter.

At Lausanne station she boarded a bus up the hill to St François, the cobbled square with the church and the cafe where she'd had a coffee and a croissant before leaving last time. As she stepped off into the square, her brain skidded momentarily into déjà vu, except it felt more like a snippet of another time, another life – a future life, perhaps. The sensation of having lived here, of sitting in that cafe every day, of knowing this town like it were her own. She stood still for a minute trying to hang onto the feeling, but it slipped away as quickly as it had arrived.

She remembered the way to Rue Haldimand. Down the steep cobbled street with its intricate wrought-iron signs, across Rue Centrale and up into Place de la Palud, where the mechanical clock whirred into life every hour. Past the fountain and right into Rue Haldimand, number eight on the left.

She pressed the intercom and waited.

'*Oui?*'

'Evelyne, it's Sylvia.'

'Oh *mon Dieu!*'

She pressed herself on the door when it buzzed open and made her way up the four flights of stairs, feeling considerably more breathless than she had the last time she was here. The door to flat four was ajar and she knocked and pushed it open. '*Allô?*'

The door opened wide and Evelyne stood in front of her in shorts and a loose white blouse, a pink patterned scarf barely keeping her hair in check. As Sylvia kissed her and was welcomed in, she saw Evelyne wasn't alone. Behind her, standing on the tatty old rug in the centre of the room was another girl, a very young-looking girl, with straight brown hair that fell below her shoulders, arms like matchsticks and a vulnerability that made Sylvia want to reach out and pull her into a protective hug.

'Sylvia, this is Anna,' Evelyne said. 'We're going to have a full house.'

JULY 2016

Lausanne/Montreux, Switzerland

JESS

From <maggie.hartwell@gmail.com>

Darling Jess,

For the first time since I persuaded you to go over there, I'm wondering if I did the right thing. I was so distraught to read your email and see how upset you are about the whole Julia thing. But are you sure, darling? Because I can't contemplate what an extraordinary coincidence it would be if I'd pushed you into a job with someone so connected to your history. And I wonder, Jess, without wanting to dismiss what you've discovered, whether you're reading a little too much into this? If

there's one thing I learnt from having your
mother, the tenacious journalist, as a friend, it's
that fact is sacred. Don't torture yourself with
this unless you know it's true. I'm so sorry this
Daniel Buchs fellow has gone silent; I can tell
how much you wanted him to help you. I wish
with all my heart that I could help you, darling,
but I'm afraid I'm a rather useless detective.
But what you must know is that I am here for
you, and that regardless of what happens out
there, you'll always have me, and your dad, by
your side.

He's coming to London next week to see
my new show, by the way. I can't tell you what
an utter nightmare it's been working with such
an upstart young director. Positively dictatorial!
I shall never do it again. But I have to say I'm
proud of my sets – particularly under such
challenging circumstances. Fingers crossed I'll
make it a hat-trick at the Olivier Awards next
year (but don't tell anyone I said so!).

Call me/text me any time, and take EXTRA
good care of yourself.

Lots of love,

Maggie xx

It feels strange to be in a dark room watching jazz when
it's still light outside. The audience is a dim mass of heads

bobbing to the music, while the stage is lit up in soft yellow and purple, illuminating the band and causing sweat to bead on Jorge's forehead. He's sitting at the piano, pounding the keys with a practised fluidity, pumping the pedals so vigorously he occasionally unseats himself. He's rocking his head to the music, eyes closed, feeling what he's playing rather than seeing it.

I've been drinking my wine far too quickly, as I tend to when sat in a bar on my own, so my head's spinning a little when the lights go up for the interval and I see Jorge making his way over to my table. He grins and greets me with the obligatory three kisses.

'Glad you could make it, Jess.'

'That was really incredible,' I say.

'*Merci.*' He smiles, sits down at the table and signals to the waitress to bring him a beer. His face is glowing, and not just with sweat from the lights and his exertion at the piano. His pupils are huge and I can see he's buzzing from a natural high. This is Jorge, I think. His other job's just for money; this is what makes him *him*.

'How have you been? Are you doing okay with … everything?' He looks anxious, as though he has to tread carefully lest I disintegrate in front of his eyes. But I've had two years to absorb the fact my entire life has been a lie; he's only recently learnt it.

I nod, give a dismissive wave of my hand.

'Fine,' I say. I don't tell him that my mind is constantly whirring, creating scenarios, that I've had trouble thinking

230

of anything but Daniel Buchs and Julia and Anna and Thun, that I can't shut my brain off at night so I spend each day dizzy with tiredness, that it feels like I'm going mad.

Fact is sacred, Maggie had said.

But I haven't got any facts, and I don't know how to find them. All I can do is work with what I've got – and, right now, I've got Jorge. I don't feel brave enough to tell him what I might have discovered, though. I may have blurted out my life story to him, but there's no way I'm going to tell him I was snooping in Julia's private documents again. I'm so ashamed of my behaviour that I haven't even told Maggie, and I suppose I could tell him what I told her – that Julia mentioned her maiden name and left a letter from A. Meier lying around in the kitchen – but it's one thing to put that in an email, another to be able to say it out loud and not have my face betray my lie.

'Have the Chevalleys ever seen you play?' I ask Jorge. Even if I don't tell him my suspicions, I can pump him for information.

He looks surprised at the question. 'I don't know. I don't think so, no. Why?'

'No reason. I just thought your parents might have talked to them about your playing. They must be proud of you.'

He takes a swig of his beer. 'Yeah, Mom's my biggest cheerleader, as all moms are, right?' I see his eyes widen as he realises what he's said. *'Joder.* I'm so sorry, Jess, I didn't think.'

'It's okay.' Other people still having their mothers is a fact of life I've learnt to get used to. 'So you don't see the Chevalleys that much?'

He sinks back in his chair. 'I guess not. Sometimes.'

'Your mum's worked for them a long time?'

'About ten years.'

'Do you know much about their background? Is Julia from the area? Do her parents live around here?'

He looks at me, cocks his head. 'I don't remember. Why do you want to know?'

'Oh, just curious.' I look down at the table and swirl my wine in the glass. I wish he'd give me something. I was hoping he'd be a mine of information. 'So you've never met either of her parents?'

'No, I haven't.' He shifts in his seat, looks uncomfortable, and I wonder if he knows something he doesn't want to share.

'Or Michel's?'

He shakes his head. 'Er, no.' He puts his hands on the table. 'Can we talk about something else please?'

'Oh. Okay.' Perhaps when I go to Thun this Sunday, I'll find another connection between Anna and Julia. Even if Anna's no longer there, perhaps someone will know her and be able to put me in contact. I wonder if I need to prepare anything in Swiss German, a message I can show people to read just in case they don't speak English.

'Do you speak Swiss German?'

'What? No. Why?'

'I might need someone to translate a short text for me. Do you have any friends who speak it?'

'No, and it's not a written language anyway.' He shakes

his head and lets out a short laugh, adding, 'You're a strange one, Jess.'

I don't know what to say, but my surprise obviously shows on my face.

'I invite you here because I wanted to see you again, because I thought – despite first impression, oh and second impression – that you might actually be a fun person to hang out with. And perhaps you might have wanted to hang out with me too, being a newcomer in a foreign city. But all you can do is ask me about the Chevalleys and if I can translate something into Swiss German? Sorry, I've got better things to do.' He gets up from the chair and grabs his beer from the table.

I feel heat rising in my face as I play back the conversation in my head and hear myself. 'Wait!' I stand up too. 'God, I'm sorry. I'm really sorry. I did – *do* – want to hang out with you. I wanted to see you play and I'm really glad I have because you're just incredible. I'm sorry that I'm a little distracted. I've got a lot on my mind at the moment, but I know I need to try to think about other things. Can we start again?'

He looks at me. 'We're playing in five minutes.'

'Then I have five minutes to attempt to be more scintillating company than before. *Please,*' I plead.

His face softens into a smile and he sits back down again. 'Well,' he says, 'I'd like to see you try.'

So I drop the ball in my teeth and we actually have a proper conversation. I ask about him, and he asks about me, and I realise I've become so obsessed with my quest that I haven't appreciated all the experiences I've collected during my stay in Switzerland so far. I wish I was here with no agenda other than to enjoy living in a foreign country with all its surprises.

'You have to do your laundry on a certain day?' I say, when he tells me about the quirks of Swiss living that foreigners don't understand.

'Yep, there's a rota up in my apartment block for the communal machine in the basement. If you don't keep to it people start getting passive–aggressive. Notes on the machine, a knock on the door and a polite telling off.'

'That's hilarious. Why don't you just have your own machine?'

He looks at me in mock horror. 'What? Have a noisy machine right there in my flat?' I laugh and he takes a swig of his beer and smiles back. 'You get used to this stuff when you've been here a while.'

'How long is that?'

'Since I was fourteen.'

'So you're a Swiss citizen now, right?' I calculate that, if Jorge's about my age, he's been living here for around twenty-five years. Surely that makes him Swiss.

He shakes his head. 'No. You can apply after a decade or so, less if you grew up here, but it's expensive and you have to jump through so many hoops I just haven't bothered.'

'But do you feel Swiss?'

He shrugs. 'I guess. I mean, sort of. I don't feel more Spanish than Swiss in any case – apart from when I mess with the washing rota.'

'I wish I had the opportunity to have dual citizenship. I'm just boringly one-dimensional,' I say, and then my stomach jolts as I realise what I've said. Biologically, I'm presumably at least half Swiss. But for a twist of fate, I'd be more Swiss than Jorge. I might have a Swiss life like Julia's, with her kids and husband and high-powered job and posh house above the lake.

I don't know what happens to my face just then but he must see it cloud.

'I can find someone to translate what you need into German,' he says, and his gaze is so direct I want to look away.

It's late by the time the gig's over and I really should be getting back to Montreux. But part of me doesn't want to leave because I feel a weight's been lifted. Somehow, during the course of the second half, I actually managed to switch off from my worries, stop thoughts of Julia and Anna swirling round my head and enjoy the here and now. Perhaps the feeling of lightness that came over me while talking to Jorge in the interval – I mean, *really* talking – helped.

I'm nevertheless thinking of slipping away when he comes over, ignores my protestations and grabs my arm to steer me in the direction of another table where his bandmates and friends are congregating. The audience is gradually trickling out the door and the waitress is clearing up.

'The bar manager usually lets us stay for a bit, so we can have a drink and wind down,' he says to me before addressing the group. 'This is my friend Jess, she's going to join us.

Jess, this is everyone.' He proceeds to introduce me to them individually and I undergo a lengthy round of three-kisses before sitting down next to Jorge. His friends are all talking in French and I can't understand a word. A man with long hair and tattoos asks Jorge something and they laugh and chat for a minute, until he turns to me. 'Sorry, is this okay?'

'Yes.' I smile. It really is. Just being in this atmosphere, with people my own age who are relaxed, having fun, enjoying life, is good for me. It's been so long since I've done that. *Too* long.

'Sam, the saxophonist over there,' Jorge nods to a slim guy in a black shirt currently pouring wine for someone else, 'has just been invited to play at a music festival in Bucharest. It's a big deal.'

'Wow, that's great.'

'And Elliot – he's our drummer – recently won a prestigious jazz drum competition.'

I nod, eyebrows raised. 'And you?'

He laughs. 'Oh, I haven't done anything particularly impressive lately.'

I look at him. 'Well, you impressed me,' I say, and then feel my chest lurch. 'With your playing, I mean.'

He looks at me and smiles. 'Thanks, Jess,' he says, and then we're quiet, and I don't know what else to say to break the slight embarrassment I feel. I look away from his brown eyes and think of Patrick, and the wedding ring I still carry in my purse, and the way we spiralled from such a good thing into hurt and frustration and mutual incomprehension; the way I couldn't even look at him the day he left, the way his betrayal lingers like a bad odour I can't wash off. The air in the club feels hot and oppressive and I feel my throat constrict, my palms start to sweat.

'Sorry, I've got to go now,' I say, and I stand up and run out of the club.

The feeling of lightness I briefly achieved in the jazz club trickles away throughout Friday, and by the time evening comes around I'm so impatient to get to Thun at the weekend that I can barely sit still. It's 9pm. Maria's been and gone. Dinner's cooked and eaten. The kids are in bed. I'm trying to watch a film with Michel, but I feel jittery, like I've had too much coffee, and I keep checking my phone every two seconds in case Daniel emails me, though I'd have thought if he was going to, he would have by now. He clearly knows Anna – why not just give me her contact details? Perhaps I should write to him again, ask him to at least pass my email on to her.

I know I've been fidgeting the whole way through the film because Michel keeps staring at me sideways, a brief – but ever so brief – flash of annoyance shadowing his eyes.

'Are you okay, Jess?' he says when I change position on the sofa for the umpteenth time.

'Yes, fine.' I smile, put my phone down, and try to stop fidgeting.

The news has come on. The anchor introduces a segment and then I see a reporter standing outside what I think is the

Swiss parliament. The camera trains on a group of people celebrating something. My eyes fix on a particular woman in the group. She's a dignified figure, maybe late sixties or seventies, dressed in a smart navy trouser suit, grey hair in a neat shoulder-length bob, a string of pearls around her neck. She's embracing a man and there's such emotion in her face. There are people all around her, but I can't take my eyes off that one woman.

'What's this about, Michel?'

He breathes out, shakes his head. 'Oh, something quite important has happened. The *enfants placés* are finally going to be given compensation.'

'Sorry, the what?'

He hesitates. 'It's not something Switzerland talks about very much.' He pauses and frowns. 'It concerns children who were taken away from their families by the government.'

I raise my eyebrows. 'What do you mean?'

'It was government policy for decades, right up until the late seventies, early eighties. If the authorities decided a child wasn't being brought up properly then they would take them away and either put them in an institution or place them with another family, often on a farm.'

'Like in foster care, you mean.'

'I guess so, but some of them didn't end up being very cared for. They were considered more like unpaid workers and sometimes treated very badly. Beaten, not fed properly, not allowed to go to school. Some were sexually abused. Others were sterilised against their will.'

'Wow.' I sit forward, my eyes on the woman on the screen. I thought Switzerland was cows and chocolate and bankers, not this. 'I've never heard of this before.'

'I'm not surprised. The country is only recently talking about it properly. It's been a . . . shameful secret, I guess.'

The woman in the report is now standing next to a man – her lawyer, I presume – who is reading a statement to camera. The thought of what she may have been through when she was a child, and how that may have affected her life ever since, makes me shiver.

'The government apologised a few years ago. Now all the surviving victims will get compensation and I think there will be some study into why it happened,' Michel says. 'It's about time.'

I don't understand what the reporter is saying, but I can see how much it means to the woman on the screen, and the other people around her. A chill slithers down the back of my neck. I may have been through hell in the last few years, but my childhood was safe, secure and loving. How many of these children had that?

'How many were there?'

Michel shrugs, shakes his head. 'I don't know exactly. Thousands, I think.' His phone begins to ring and he fishes it out of his pocket. 'Excuse me,' he says to me with an apologetic smile. He gets up from his chair and walks into the kitchen area, phone to his ear. '*Chérie, ça va?*' I hear, and that's the extent of my understanding as he rattles off something in French.

239

A moment later he comes back to the sofa. 'That was Julia. There are major delays on the trains and she can't get back from the office so I'm going to drive to get her now. Are you okay to stay here?'

It's late, and I'd almost forgotten Julia was meant to be here too, so infrequently do I see her. I don't really want her to come back, to spoil the easy camaraderie that exists between Michel and I when she's not here. But I shrug and smile my agreement. I'm not going anywhere. 'Of course.'

He taps my arm in thanks, just lightly. 'You're a star,' he says, and I beam back, warmth sliding into my cheeks. He grabs his keys from the kitchen work surface and I hear him walk down the corridor and shut the front door. Moments later the engine of his Mercedes fades up the road and all I'm left with is silence, and the dignified smile of the woman on the television.

JUNE 1976

Lausanne, Switzerland

SYLVIA

When she was eight, Sylvia walked home from primary school to Maggie's house one day to find Maggie's mother sitting in the kitchen drinking tea with two other women. All three were pregnant, their bellies in various degrees of expansion, but all, to Sylvia's eyes, weirdly, grotesquely bloated. One was balancing a mug on her belly, the steam rising into the kitchen. Another was so big she couldn't sit right up against the table because her bump was in the way. As for Maggie's mother, when she saw them she stood up and her large stomach momentarily threw her off balance so she swayed backwards and steadied herself against the kitchen worktop. *Whoopsadaisy!* she'd said and laughed, because it was funny, or at least Sylvia could see now, looking back, that it was. But back then, aged eight, she didn't think so.

The women's overblown bellies shocked her, bewildered her, their laughter was confusing. Soon they descended into hysterics, tears rolling down their faces, and Sylvia remembered being appalled. It wasn't funny, this strange inflation act that had somehow been performed on all three of them. It wasn't funny at all.

The memory came back to her as she stood in the apartment, listening to Evelyne explain how Daniel and Anna had arrived that morning and needed to stay with her for a while. Something about having run away, left the family farm. She remembered what Evelyne had told her when she'd first met her brother: *He's had a falling out with our father. Again. It happens a couple of times a year at least.* She guessed it was just a repeat performance – only this time he had his pregnant girlfriend in tow.

'I'm so sorry,' Evelyne said in a quiet voice, though Sylvia was sure from Anna's blank expression that the girl couldn't understand French in any case. 'I didn't know they were coming, it's all a bit of a shock ...' she trailed off, her eyes flicking to Anna's belly, as though she couldn't quite believe what she saw. 'Monique will put you up. She's just around the corner. Would you mind? We'll still spend the weekend together, go to the festival. I can't throw them out and there's no space for another guest.'

'No problem at all,' Sylvia said. She put her hand on Evelyne's arm, keen to quell her obvious stress at these unexpected guests. 'I don't mind where I stay.'

She looked over at Anna, sitting neatly on the sofa.

They were clearly at a similar stage of pregnancy, their bellies swelled not to the extent of the three women in the kitchen so many years ago but enough to be obvious, unless you were trying to hide it. But that's where the physical resemblance ended. Anna was so thin, so young, all spindly arms and big eyes. Sixteen and pregnant? Sylvia couldn't contemplate it – it was daunting enough at her age. She thought back to when she met Daniel, how surly he was, how preoccupied, and his words at the march: *I just think everyone should be free to do what they want in life.* Is this what he wanted – a baby, at just nineteen himself? Somehow, Sylvia doubted it.

For some reason the girl's face stayed with her all night, as she slept in a corner of Monique's living room, partitioned off with a tie-dyed sarong. And it was still with her in the morning, when Evelyne picked her up in her van to drive to the festival, which she explained was being held in a disused warehouse on the edge of town. Evelyne seemed less anxious than the night before, back to being the garrulous, energetic woman Sylvia remembered from her last visit, and she was clearly excited about the event she'd spent many weeks helping to organise. They were expecting hundreds of women from all over the area, she said. There would be small group sessions devoted to divorce, to sex, to marriage issues and family life, debates on abortion and contraception and homosexuality, as well as food and music and dancing. They'd even invited a 'self-help' guru from California to lead a session on getting to know your body's intimate parts and reclaiming pleasure.

'Nothing's taboo!' Evelyne said breezily, and Sylvia couldn't help but laugh at what Jim's mother would say if she knew what her daughter-in-law was doing instead of playing the dutiful wife as Jim showed them around the new flat. The thought reminded her of everything that had changed in her life since she was last in Switzerland and she wondered if she had inadvertently let the side down by becoming a married pregnant woman, if this radical young Swiss feminist would disapprove of her slide into convention.

Evelyne seemed to read her mind. 'Congratulations, by the way,' she said, nodding at Sylvia's stomach. 'It suits you.' To Sylvia's relief, there was no judgement in her tone.

'Thanks,' she replied. 'It wasn't exactly planned.'

'But at least you had a choice.'

'Yes,' Sylvia said, thinking of the teary-eyed young girls in the clinic and the doctor's stern voice and her inability to go through with it. 'I did.'

'And you're not sixteen.' Evelyne sighed, and Sylvia heard the stress come back into her tone. She didn't need another opportunity to ask more.

'So, who is Anna exactly?'

'Daniel's girlfriend, apparently.' Evelyne laughed, shook her head. 'I can't quite get my head around that.'

'You didn't know he had a girlfriend?'

'No. But it's not even that ...' She kept her gaze on the road. 'Anna lived with us, at the farm. When I left four years ago she was only twelve, just a child. Still is, really. Only now she's sixteen and pregnant by my brother.'

'Why did she live with you? She's a distant relative or something?'

Evelyne raised her eyebrows. 'No, no. That would be even weirder. She was placed with us.'

'What do you mean?'

'She's from a poor family. Her father walked out and her mum couldn't take care of her, I seem to remember. So Anna was placed with us by the authorities. They paid us to have her.'

Sylvia looked at Evelyne, but she kept her eyes ahead. 'A foster placement?'

Evelyne shrugged, then laughed. 'Another pair of hands for Dad to push around, more like.'

'What do you mean?'

'Oh, she had work to do, like the rest of us. Milking cows, raking hay, mucking out, that kind of stuff. Daniel and I did that too, but I know Anna had it harder than us. Dad was a bit of a taskmaster.'

'How old was she?' Sylvia asked, aware this was becoming something of an interview, but she just couldn't quite understand it.

'When she arrived? About eight or nine I think.'

'Didn't she go to school?'

Evelyne nodded. 'Initially, but soon after she got to high school my father said there was too much work so she'd have to stay home. I mean, Dad would rather I'd stayed home from school too – he never saw the value of *education for girls*,' she said, rolling her eyes and lowering the tone of her voice in what Sylvia took to be a caricature of her father, 'but I was never going to let that happen. I even threatened to call the authorities on him,' she laughs. 'But Anna, well, I guess she couldn't fight him on it like I did, and no one ever came to check up on her, so she just stayed home. I'd come back after school and she'd look like she was about to fall asleep on her feet. Poor kid. She always looked so damned miserable.'

'She never saw her own family?'

Evelyne shrugged. 'I don't know. She never went any-where, so I guess not. I know she has a sister, but I think she was placed with some other family.'

Sylvia couldn't picture that thin, pale girl doing manual labour from the age of eight, far away from any kind of family. The most Sylvia had been away from her folks at that age was for one week, on a school camp in Wales. She'd cried herself to sleep three nights in a row she'd missed her mother so much.

'So what happens now? They won't go back to Betten?'

Evelyne laughed. 'No way – well, not unless they're caught and she's forced back. They ran away – and about time too, judging by the size of Anna's belly. I'm surprised no one's noticed already. If my father had found out, I hate to think what he'd have done. There are institutions where they put young unmarried mothers and force them to give up their babies.' She shook her head. 'Just another way the patriarchy is trying to keep women in check, punishing us for having sex before marriage just like men do.'

Sylvia stared at the road. Kids of eight being sent to work on a stranger's farm? A tyrant of a boss who wouldn't let her go to school? Running away in fear of the consequences of her pregnancy? It didn't sound like a decent foster care system to her. 'She must be pretty scared right now,' she said.

Evelyne shrugged. 'Apparently they're in love, and Anna thinks that solves everything,' she laughed. 'Daniel's slightly less naive, but still. He hasn't got a job, Anna didn't even finish school, and things aren't exactly economically rosy in Switzerland at the moment. How are they going to cope? They came here because they knew I wouldn't send them back, and they can stay with me for now, but it can't be a permanent arrangement. It's a tiny one-bed flat and I can't afford to feed all three of us.' She shook her head. 'They've got a hard road ahead, that's for sure.'

Sylvia nodded. No doubt. But it sounded like Anna had had a pretty hard road to get here, too.

The festival was like nothing Sylvia had ever been to before. The large warehouse was loosely divided into different areas by makeshift walls made of cardboard boxes. Each one was dedicated to a certain issue, with participating women sitting cross-legged on the floor in a 'circle of trust'. As Evelyne had promised, nothing was taboo, and it wasn't long before the passionate women from the MFL had their visitors opening up about the things that were important to them:

domineering husbands, medical issues that male doctors dismissed as unimportant, boredom and frustration over endless housework and child-rearing, or their inability to find a nursery place so they could get a job. Sylvia saw women break down in tears because they were pregnant and didn't want to be, others picking up leaflets about divorce, contraception and commune living. Outside, in the car park of the warehouse, a folk band was playing while people sang and danced and laughed in the sun, and a group of young men stood talking under a tree, toddlers at their feet. Sylvia was struck by the atmosphere: one of warmth and understanding and solidarity, one where women could simply be themselves, unimpeded by society's constraints or expectations.

If only real life was like this, she thought, her head conjuring a picture of Roger's face when he took the Warburton interview off her; Jim's voice when he said *you're going to have to give up your job anyway*. If only everything wasn't such a fight all the time.

The festival over, Evelyne wanted to relax the next day, so they didn't go far in her van that Sunday. Lutry was a pretty medieval village just a short drive from Lausanne, and by mid-morning it was already full of people strolling along the lakeside, swimming, eating ice cream, making the most of the good weather. It was probably as hot as London – Evelyne had told her the drought was proving as damaging to Swiss farming as it was in the UK – but it felt different out here, without the airless smog and the bitter tang of exhaust fumes, with the breeze from the lake and the clear, clean water to dip toes into.

After everything Evelyne had told her about Anna, Sylvia yearned to talk to the girl directly – but she couldn't. Anna didn't speak English or much French, and Sylvia's very basic school German wasn't going to get her very far. So, with the two of them sitting together on the grass, while Daniel and Evelyne walked along the lakeshore, deep in serious con-versation, Sylvia felt stymied – and she was sure Anna was feeling the same. The girl was looking at her, a shy smile on her face. She put her hand on her stomach, then pointed to Sylvia before making a thumbs up. Sylvia laughed, nodded, gestured back. 'Okay?'

Anna nodded and held up five fingers, pointing to her stomach. Judging by the similar size of their bellies, Sylvia supposed that meant five months gone, just like her. She repeated the gesture, holding up five fingers, and Anna smiled so her whole face lit up.

She looked *so* young. Sylvia felt a sudden pang of sympathy for her – what must she be feeling, to have a baby coming and no job, no home, no parents in the picture and such a tough upbringing? And there was she, with a husband, a nice flat she'd currently deserted, a job with a regular salary and the right to return to it after maternity leave.

What would Anna think of her, if she knew? Would she think Sylvia ungrateful not to be as delighted with her pregnancy as Anna clearly was with hers? She wished she could tell her that she was rooting for her, that she hoped everything would go well for her, that her future would be better than her past. But she couldn't, so instead she fished around in her bag and found a packet of English sweets she'd picked up at Heathrow.

She held it out to Anna and the girl took one with a smile. *Merci.*

Sylvia took one too and they both sat back on the grass, the sun on their faces, their mouths full of caramel sweetness.

Down by the lakeshore, Evelyne and Daniel were standing ankle deep in the water, facing each other, their conversation clearly heated. Sylvia glanced at Anna and saw she was looking at them too, her eyes shiny. Spontaneously, Sylvia reached out and squeezed her hand. Anna turned to her and smiled, a smile full of fear and sadness and uncertainty and hope, and in that moment Sylvia knew they understood each other perfectly, despite the language barrier. However dissimilar their backgrounds and however big the gulf between their futures was likely to be, here, in this moment, on the lakeshore at Lutry, they weren't so different after all.

JULY 2016

Thun/Reichenbach, Switzerland

JESS

On Sunday morning I get on a train heading for Visp, where I'll change for a second one bound for Thun. In my phone's maps I've pinned Hopfenweg 31, the place that could prove the key to everything. The usual guilt about Dad unfurls in my chest as I watch the houses and fields and orchards go by, but I push it away. I won't feel guilty about something that's not my fault. I won't feel guilty for needing to know who I am. Perhaps, later today, I'll find that out. My stomach plunges at the thought. I don't know if I'm ready.

According to my phone it's only a ten-minute walk from the station to the address on Julia's letter. I dither for a minute and then walk under the railway bridge. Soon I'm in what appears to be the town centre. A river of milky turquoise water rushes between two streets, the railings sporting flowerboxes spilling yellow and pink and orange. I lean over the rail, watching the torrent below. Glacial meltwater probably, travelling who knows where on its long journey from the mountains I see in the distance far above. I wonder what it would be like to jump in and be carried along, unable to go anywhere but where the water takes me. No decisions, no responsibility, entirely in the hands of the current transporting me on its inevitable path.

My eyes start to blur from the movement of the water and I pull back from the railing. I know I don't have that luxury. I have to actually make a decision and I suppose I know what that decision is going to be. I've come this far, after all.

Hopfenweg is a quiet residential street flanked by large detached houses with red tiles on the roofs and coloured wooden shutters. There's no traffic and I walk in the middle of the road, scouring the letterboxes for house numbers. I find thirty-one easily. It's a large cream house with red shutters and a wooden front door below a porch with a little pointed roof. I switch off my brain before it can start an argument in my head, step up to the door and ring the bell.

The woman who opens it looks to be in her fifties. She's wearing jeans and a green T-shirt, with clearly dyed dark brown hair and red-framed glasses. She says a word in German that I couldn't possibly replicate and smiles, her face open, curious.

I suddenly haven't a clue what to say. 'Hello,' I start, and she cocks her head, waits. 'Do you speak English?'

The woman hesitates. 'A little.'

'I, um . . .' I feel heat creeping into my cheeks. 'Are you Frau Meier?'

She shakes her head. 'No, perhaps you have the wrong house.' She starts to shut the door.

'Oh, er, wait, please,' I say. 'Do you know if someone called Anna Meier used to live here?'

She looks at me blankly and shrugs. 'We have lived here for ten years. I do not remember who lived here before us.'

'Right.' All the anticipation of potentially finding something out falls away and I feel the tension in my chest dissolve into disappointment.

The woman looks at me. 'Are you okay?'

I want to go inside, look around, see if I can find something, anything, that might point me towards Anna Meier, or Julia, or both. But I know there won't be anything left a decade after anyone called Meier moved away. 'Yes, I'm fine. I'm sorry to have disturbed you.'

Frustration overwhelms me as I walk back into town. Every tiny lead I have turns out to be nothing. I knew it was a long shot, coming to Thun, but I didn't expect my fledgling mission to be over so quickly.

At the station I scour the board for train times back to Montreux, but my eye is caught by another name. Reichenbach im Kandertal. It takes me a few seconds, and then I remember that's the place where Daniel Buchs' hiking club was. I take out my phone and search the online map and realise it's not that far from here. The train leaves in ten minutes.

I wonder, for the hundredth time, why he hasn't responded to my last email. Maybe, seeing as I'm so close, I should go and find out why.

Reichenbach feels different to Thun. Smaller, more rural, more like the Switzerland I imagined when I thought about coming here. It smells of flowers and manure and summer. I walk from the station into the village and pass houses that look like the sort of thing I saw on chocolate boxes at the airport – wooden chalets with weathered shutters and balconies bedecked with flowerpots. Some are clearly very old, their facades decorated with carved patterns, animals depicted in faded paint, words drawn in an elegant calligraphy. Chopped firewood is stacked up in piles under overhanging balconies. Some houses have shopfronts on the ground floor, one's a bank, another is labelled *Gemeindeverwaltung,* whatever the hell that is. I stop outside a bakery – that's clearly what *Bäckerei* means, even without the visual clue of edible treats in the window.

'*Grüessech,*' says the lady behind the counter after the bell over the door signals my arrival. Given it sounds similar to what the other woman in Thun said to me, I imagine that's Swiss German for hello.

I point to a macaroon and hold up one finger. She nods, wraps one in paper and hands it to me, saying what I assume is a price.

'Er, sorry, I don't speak German.' I hold out my hand with some change in it and she smiles, takes a few coins.

'Um, can I ask you something?'

She nods.

'I'm looking for someone who might live here. His name is Daniel Buchs.'

'In Reichenbach?' she frowns. 'I don't know, but I only live here recently,' she says. 'You ask Linda Keller in the Gasthaus Hirschen. She is here a long time.'

I thank her and leave, finding a wall to sit on and eat my macaroon. I don't have Daniel Buchs' address because he wasn't among the eighty-nine listed in the online phone book. I debate just emailing him and asking him to meet me, but something's holding me back. I'd rather just find out a bit about him, and then see.

The guesthouse is a large old chalet half a minute's walk from the bakery. I push open the door and love it immediately for its Swissness. There are hearts carved into the backs of wooden chairs, gingham tablecloths and etchings of mountain scenery on the walls. Though I hardly saw any people outside, in here it's busy with diners finishing Sunday lunch, the air pungent with the rich smell of hot cheese.

'*Grüessech.*' A youngish woman with an apron around her waist approaches me.

I mumble my best approximation of the word back. 'Is it possible to speak to Linda Keller, please?'

'She is in the kitchen. It's lunchtime. Busy.' She gestures around the restaurant as though I might not have noticed.

'I can wait,' I say. 'Can I sit over there?'

'You want to order something?'

I ask for a beer and take a seat at the bar. I feel momentarily self-conscious to be sitting here on my own, but no one else in the restaurant seems to give me a second glance. Soon I relax into the comforting hum of their laughter and chatter, which, though I don't understand a word, seems universal – the sound of friendship, happiness, home. It's familiar, and yet it's odd to find this familiarity when I'm waiting for a stranger in a small village in rural Switzerland, so far away from everything I call home – or used to, at least.

I don't know where home is anymore.

Not the Greenwich house – that couldn't be home without Mum in it, and now Dad's sold up anyway and moved to Chichester. And not the Peckham flat, the place Patrick and I fashioned for ourselves, a place so full of hope for the future when we moved in. That stopped being home after Patrick left. Now, home isn't a place, but a collection of small things: the smell of flowers in Maggie's garden, the passenger seat of Dad's car, an old stuffed toy donkey Mum bought me as a baby, currently locked away from my tenant in a wardrobe with my most precious things back in the flat in Peckham. Familiar things that cumulatively bring me some comfort, but don't quite make a whole.

Half an hour later there's still no Linda Keller and I've started a second beer. I signal to the waitress and ask if Linda has time to see me now. She nods. 'I will ask.'

A few minutes later a short, round woman with dark red hair emerges from double doors at the back of the room. She's wearing an apron and her cheeks are ruddy, as though the lunch service has been particularly strenuous.

'*Grüessech,*' she says. 'You wanted to speak with me?'

'Yes, thank you. I'm looking for someone who might live here and the lady in the bakery said you would know.'

'I know everyone in Reichenbach.' I swear I see her already ample chest puff out even more.

'Great. Well, I'm looking for a man named Daniel Buchs.'

She smiles. 'Oh yes, I know him very well.'

My heart dances. 'You do?'

'He comes here at least twice a week for lunch. One of my best customers.'

I look around me, as though he might be here right now, though of course I don't have a clue what he looks like – the grainy photo on the hiking website gave no more than a rough idea.

'You're from England?' She's looking at me as though I'm a curiosity.

I nod.

'I adore Cambridge!' she says. 'I love the . . . what do you say . . . ponts?'

'Punts?'

'Yes, punts! They are *tip top*!'

'They are,' I agree, though I've never been on one, or indeed to Cambridge. 'So, Daniel Buchs. Could you tell me where he lives?'

She cocks her head. 'Why do you want to know?'

'It's okay,' I say. 'I'm not a complete stranger. He's an . . .

acquaintance. We've been in contact on email. I was just passing near the village and thought I'd surprise him, but I don't know where he lives.'

She looks at me and appears to come to the conclusion that I'm not a criminal casing the joint. 'Kientalstrasse,' she says.

'Could you …?' I pass her a beer mat and fish a pen out of my bag and she takes it, scribbles the address on the back. 'Thank you,' I say when she passes it back. 'Thanks for your—'

'Such a shame he's been on his own so long. I don't know why he never met anyone else. One of our most eligible bachelors!' She laughs and I smile politely, seeing in her expression a badly veiled longing for someone who, I suspect, has never shown more than a friendly interest in her. 'I think she put him off for life!' she adds. 'I always thought there was something not … *correct* about her. He's a very friendly man, but she was … colder. Always something troubling her. Always sad.'

'Who?' I drop the pen back into my bag.

'His former wife,' she says. 'Anna.'

I've spent so long thinking that finding my mother was the key to the mystery of my life that I hadn't considered I might find my father first.

Then again, perhaps he isn't. He could have been married to her later on, after 1976. But it's certainly possible that he is the person Anna had a child with back then. And that child could well be me.

It's probably only a two-minute walk but it takes me a dozen. I sit on a bench by the church – a beautiful white chapel with a tall spire covered in slate tiles – and stare at a field where brown horned cows are grazing, heavy bells around their necks. Part of me wants to head right back to the train station and get as far away as possible, take a plane from Geneva and go back to the UK to see Dad and Maggie and forget I was ever here. But another part is drawing me towards Daniel Buchs' house, where perhaps, finally, I'll understand something of who I am.

I take my phone out of my bag and read the last text message I got from Dad.

> Nice evening with Bob and Ken in the pub.
> I won the pool. Going to London to see
> Maggie's show tomorrow. I'll report back.
> Love Dad x

Nothing could replace the years of Dad being Dad. Nothing could change the memories we share, the interests we have in common, the way we see eye to eye on politics but rarely like the same movies. Our shared eye-rolling at Aunt Jemima's latest hare-brained project. The way I always tease him about his outdated dress sense and his penchant for kippers. But would *something* change if I met my biological father?

What, I'm not sure, but it feels like Pandora's box and I don't know if I want to take the risk of opening it, just as I couldn't bear the memory of Mum to be in any way altered by meeting Anna.

It's not like I have anyone else to ask because it's not as if there are many of us. I know, having spent a considerable amount of time searching online, that there are other, similarly bizarre cases: twin boys adopted at birth who grew up in different families, neither knowing about the existence of the other; a British girl who only found out at thirty that she had been adopted as a baby, and then traced her birth mother to Argentina. Maybe they would understand. But what am I meant to do? Call them up? It's hardly feasible, and even if I could, the idea makes me feel slightly sick.

It's like being part of a strange club that no one actually wants to be in. The 'What If?' Club. The Alternative Lives Club. I don't want that membership card.

I get up from the bench. I've made no decision in my head, but my legs seem to be carrying me there. I turn the corner by the hotel and walk fifty metres down the road until I come to the address Linda Keller wrote down. It's a large wooden house in a similar style to others in the village. There's a gate with a trellis of bright red flowers growing over it in an arch. Beyond is a garden that seems to extend from the front around the right-hand side where I hear some noise.

I walk a bit further and stop when I see a man bending over a patch of soil. He's planting something in the flowerbeds, and the clatter of the trowel on the stone path he's kneeling on is the noise I heard.

I retreat a few paces so he doesn't see me, and watch.

He picks up the trowel, digs a hole, drops the tool on the path, picks up a plant from a polystyrene container and puts it in the hole, scoops in soil, drops the trowel again, pushes the soil into the hole with his hands. Repeat. I can only see the side of his face but he looks about the right age. His hair is short and almost completely white. He's wearing jeans, a faded T-shirt and sunglasses.

I want to ask him so much: *Who are you to me? Are you my father? Is Julia your daughter, the person who lived my life? Do you know what happened back then to give me my life in the UK and Julia hers out here?* But I feel paralysed. Transfixed by this man who as yet is oblivious to my presence. All the grief and searching and wondering and heartache of the past few years are concentrated in this point in time right here. I can open the box, or I can tape it up and leave it be.

I'm still debating which path to choose when he stands up, wipes his brow with his gloved hand, turns his head and looks right at me.

JULY 1976

London, UK

SYLVIA

Rosemary and Bob's story wasn't an unusual one: they met at a dance in June 1926. By July they were engaged, married in August and their first child, George, named after the King, was born nine months later. 'You want to know the key to a successful marriage?' Bob had whispered when Rosemary was in the kitchen making tea. 'Just say "Yes, dear" and do whatever the hell you want.' Sylvia had smiled back at his beaming face, ignoring the squeeze of her knee he delivered as he said it. It pleased her greatly, towards the end of the interview when Rosemary was showing her out, to hear the seventy-two-year-old woman's own marriage tip: 'If you want him to do something, just make him think it's his idea.'

It was the fiftieth golden oldies column she'd written and

it felt like a milestone – and a millstone around her neck. She could ask the questions in her sleep. She could practically predict the answers. She dreamt of Dennis and Gladys and Trevor and Ivy, their experiences merging with hers and Jim's so she woke up feeling she was seventy years old, with deep folds under her eyes and her wedding ring so entrenched on her finger she couldn't get it off. She'd type up her interviews diligently, wanting to do justice to the time and respect – mostly – her interviewees had given her, wanting to convey the energy, love and wisdom she saw in their weathered faces.

But she couldn't help but feel dismay when Valerie came back to the office after interviewing Glenda Jackson, or Ellis was roundly applauded for his feature about the social and economic drivers behind the emergence of punk rock, or Max was sent off to America to report on the 200th anniversary of the declaration of independence.

After Roger told Sylvia her *replacement* had been appointed and she would be expected to show her the ropes when she started in late August, she stared at the blank page in her typewriter as though her fingers were paralysed. She'd only earned her place in the thick of things so recently, and yet already she was relegated back to the periphery, with someone else poised to erase her from the paper altogether.

But whenever she felt such despair, a wave of guilt crested inside her and washed it away. She kept picturing Anna's shy smile and twig-like arms, kept thinking about what Evelyne said: *Dad was a bit of a taskmaster. She always looked so damned miserable.* Despite what the girl had been through, despite the

situation she now found herself in, that smile was so hopeful
it had clamped shame down on Sylvia like an iron fist around
her throat. Anna had practically nothing. No money, no job,
no home, no family in the picture – but she had hope for the
future and a fierce love for her unborn child. Sylvia hadn't
needed to speak the girl's language to understand that. Is that
why she'd agreed to meet Jim after work?

He was wearing shorts – he never wore shorts – and the
sight of his bare knees, the comically pale and bony knees of
a desk-bound fitness-phobic, made her smile. She'd missed
those knees – and, for that matter, those arms, that face.

Jim shrugged at her quizzical look. 'What? It's bloody
hot.' He grabbed her left arm and pulled her to him, and
she let him plant a kiss on her lips. 'God, Sylvia, I've missed
you. And you.' He looked down at her belly, her light shirt
skimming the curve. 'Wow, he's really growing.'

'He?'

'Or she. I don't mind.'

She smiled but felt the familiar thread of panic needling
her insides.

'You look beautiful. Blooming, isn't that what people say?
Well, you really are. Everyone else is a sweaty mess but you
look radiant.'

She looked down at her feet. 'Let's walk a bit,' she said.

They strolled towards the Serpentine, past couples loung-
ing on the grass, girls in bikinis, men with their tops off, as
though it was Sunday on a beach in Spain, not a London

park on an early Wednesday evening. Usually by now the British summer was preparing to pack its bags and head off for hibernation, but this year was different. It was interminable. The worst drought in 300 years, said her paper – and it wasn't simply Max's hyperbole, it was true.

'Work okay?' she asked.

'Oh fine. I'm doing a piece on the EEC. Running next week.' He paused. 'But I don't give a flying fuck about that. I just want you back, Syl. The flat's so empty without you.'

'Haven't you bought any furniture?' She said it as a joke, but he didn't take it as such.

'Not a thing. I'm waiting for you. It's as empty as when you left it. Just my bed – *our* bed – and your favourite armchair.'

She thought of Maggie's crowded bedroom. She ached for space. And she feared for the end of her friendship. *It may not be where you imagined you'd be right now but that doesn't make it bad.* Maggie's words came back to her. And how the hell else was she going to manage work and a baby if she didn't go back to Jim? But that couldn't be the reason she did.

They reached a shady spot near a cafe and she stopped, sat down under a tree and looked out at the Serpentine where a few rowing boats were meandering over the water. She thought of sitting with Anna next to the lake in Lausanne. The expression of delight on her face when Sylvia copied her own tentative sign language to indicate her due date. The obvious pride and excitement in Anna's face as she put her hand on her belly. Was she, Sylvia, simply an ungrateful wretch? But then she thought of Jim's words. *You're overreacting.*

'Jim,' she started, 'I need you to—'

'I *do* understand,' he interrupted. He sat down beside her and took her hand in his. 'You think I don't, but I do – now. I admit I didn't before, but I've had a lot of time to think these past few weeks – and a few choice words from Maggie.' Sylvia's eyebrows shot up at this. When had Maggie met with Jim? She hadn't said anything. 'So I've sat in that damn armchair and thought about what it must have been like for you, to find out you were carrying a baby you didn't want.' He faltered on the last word, as though he could hardly bring himself to say it. 'And I can appreciate, now, how awful that must have been for you, even if I can't fathom what you ... contemplated.' She opened her mouth to say, *I'm sorry, I should have told you beforehand,* but he held up his hand in a gentle gesture that seemed to say, *just let me say this, let me get this out.* 'And I can see how horrible it must feel to have to give up the job you love – even for a short while. I know you love it, Syl, because I love mine too. But we're in this together, aren't we? I see that now, I really do. So while I can't turn the clock back and stop it happening, and I can't exactly give birth to the baby for you, I want you to know that I'm completely in this with you. I'll do everything else I can to make the raising of this child as equal a task as possible. So I've been thinking, if you want me to, after the baby is born I'll give up work and stay home and look after him – or her – so you can go back to work as quickly as you want.'

She couldn't help the surprise shooting into her eyebrows. 'You would do that?'

'Yes. I mean, I could maybe try and go freelance, do a bit of work at the same time.'

'I don't think it would be so easy to—'

'Okay, then I won't freelance.' A brief flash of annoyance shadowed his face. 'I'll just look after our child. Someone has to, and I'm saying it can be me.'

'Your mother probably wouldn't agree.' Oh how she'd love to see Pamela's face if Jim became a stay-at-home father!

'Well, sod my mother. And I'll get some jip from the boys, but I don't care. It's 1976. We can do whatever we want. And I want you. So this is what I'll do.'

She shifted on the grass, unpeeling her skirt from the back of her legs.

'I appreciate it, Jim, I really do. But it wouldn't make financial sense, at least initially. Roger's agreed to give me paid leave, so it would be stupid not to take it.' She felt painfully confused when she thought of last week's conversation with her boss, when they'd discussed the terms of her maternity leave: grateful she wouldn't lose her job, but furious at his obvious disdain. *Just make sure your mind's on the job when you come back.*

'Only you could twist that into a bad thing,' Jim said.

'I'm not saying it's a bad thing,' she whipped back. 'At least I know I'll still have a job to go back to. But it doesn't change the fact it's the woman who has to press pause on her career. And maternity leave won't change attitudes, I know that for certain. Not unless men get leave too.'

She'd seen how Ellis and the other men in the office looked at her now. Even Max, a little. It wasn't a lack of respect, exactly, but a sort of assumption that she was no longer the ambitious young journalist she once was, because she must now have other things on her mind, other priorities – the inevitable priorities of a twenty-something woman.

She didn't want to be inevitable. She wanted to surprise and impress. But it felt like you couldn't do that and be pregnant. Instead, you were expected to spend your time chatting about names and nursery colours with the secretaries in the office, and since she didn't want to do that, she seemed to have disappointed them too.

Jim sighed. 'I'd love to smash the patriarchy for you, Syl, but that's a rather big ask for one man to accomplish within a three-month deadline.'

She laughed, and it felt good.

'Okay,' he continued with a smile that looked so grateful, so relieved. 'So down the line, after your maternity leave, when you're ready to go back, I'll quit and take over the childcare. Either that or I'll work like a demon while you're off, pick up some extra freelance, and maybe we'll be able to afford some kind of nanny or nursery, at least part time. Whatever it takes to make this work.' He squeezed her hand. 'We can make this okay, Syl. We can make this a wonderful thing.'

Music started playing from the cafe. That Elton John number that seemed to be on the radio every time Sylvia switched it on.

'That bloody song!' Jim shook his head, his mouth turning up in a wry smile. 'It's like the mantra to my summer.'

She looked at him, at his kind eyes. She touched the gold band on his wedding finger. None of this was perfect. None of this was as she'd planned. But she had so much more than some. So much more than Anna.

Don't go breaking my heart, Jim mouthed Elton's words.

And when she heard the next line, Sylvia knew Kiki Dee was right. She just couldn't.

AUGUST 2016

Montreux, Switzerland

JESS

From <maggie.hartwell@gmail.com>

Darling Jess,

I've read your last email several times now
and tried to make sense of everything you've
discovered. I can't fathom why Daniel didn't
tell you he was married to Anna, and what
that means. I know you feel very frustrated
and confused, maybe angry with him too.
Remember you're allowed to be all those
things, Jess. I know how you beat yourself
up about everything, but this is such an
extraordinary situation, so just let yourself
be whatever you need to be. It's perfectly

understandable that you couldn't just confront Daniel when you saw him there. Wait until things settle in your head a little, and then maybe email him again? I think he owes you answers now.

I saw your father at the show the other night. I don't think it was his cup of tea, to be honest, but he was tactful, as always, and effusive about my sets and that's the main thing! He's doing okay, getting through things in his own way. I know he'll be glad when you're back – as will I. And don't worry, I haven't said a thing to him about what you've discovered – that's for you to do, if you wish.

Hang on in there darling, you're making such good progress. Call me anytime.

All my love,

Maggie xx

'Where's *maman*?'

'She's gone to work already. So has your dad.'

'But I want to give her this.' Léa holds out a letter and I take it, knowing as I attempt to read it that I haven't absorbed fluent French by osmosis over the last few weeks, much to my disappointment.

'What does it say?'

'I will play on Saturday and people can come.'

I see the signature is Madame Jeanneret and I know

that's the lady who runs the tennis course, a lithe woman in her fifties with short blond hair and rather severe black-framed glasses.

'Like a tournament? Wow! Can I come?'

'*Oui.*' Lea nods. 'And *maman* and *papa*. I want you all to come.'

'And Luca?'

She frowns for a second and then nods. 'If he wants.'

'Good. We'll all be there, I'm sure. I'll put this in the kitchen and make sure your parents read it when they're home from work, okay?'

'Okay.' She nods. 'I'm going to beat Céline.'

'Is she your arch rival?'

'What is that?'

'The person you want to beat the most.'

'Yes,' she says. 'I hate her.'

'That's a bit harsh.' Poor Céline, whoever she is. Knowing Léa as I now do, I certainly wouldn't want to face her over a net. 'Now go get your swimming stuff ready. We're meeting Jorge at the pool, remember?'

She skips off towards her bedroom and I walk to mine. I gather my towel and swimsuit into a beach bag and check my phone, relieved to see there's no message from him cancelling on me. My stomach does a little hop at the thought of seeing him again, at having a day by the pool with some adult company.

Despite the low regard he's entitled to hold me in after my behaviour so far, it seems he isn't averse to spending some more time with me too, and the thought is a pleasant surprise. I just hope he doesn't ask too many questions. Part of me wants to explain my obsession with the Chevalleys that night in the jazz club, and to tell him about my trip to Reichenbach, about seeing Daniel in the garden, a question in his eyes as he looked up and I turned and fled. I want to ask Jorge why I did that; I want him to solve this whole mess for me and stop the jitters that ripple through me when I think of Daniel potentially being my father, and of Julia possibly being the woman who's living my life. But I don't want to admit to the extent of my snooping in Julia's things, of finding the letter from Anna Meier, because I don't want to see dislike or pity or anger in his face. I want to see the smile he gave me as we sat around a table with his friends in the jazz club, the crinkles around his eyes as we laughed about Swiss washing rotas.

He's not there when we arrive and I busy myself sorting the children out. I apply sunscreen to Luca as he tries to wriggle from my grasp, set out the towels on our chosen patch of grass and pile discarded clothes into a vaguely neat heap by my beach bag. I'm content to sit at the edge of the pool as Luca and Léa take it in turns to throw themselves in – Luca, curling himself up in a ball to create as much splash as possible; Léa holding her nose with one hand and jumping arrow-straight into the water. It's warm and the cloudless sky is a delicious shade of blue. A slight breeze in the air keeps it from getting too hot. It should be sublimely relaxing, but my blood can't settle. My mind's on a treadmill.

Suddenly I feel hands on my back and my brain is purged of thoughts for a few, empty moments when all I can feel is the unpleasant, bristling sensation of water up my nose and in the back of my throat. It can only be two or three seconds until I emerge spluttering to the surface to see the kids laughing at me and a sheepish Jorge standing on the edge of the pool where I'd been sitting.

'What the . . .' A choke in my throat ends my sentence and it's just as well. I cough and breathe deeply as my heart rate begins to slow again.

'Sorry,' Jorge says, but I see from the smile twitching at his mouth that he isn't at all. 'I couldn't resist.'

I glare at him, wanting to both punch him for nearly drowning me and hug him for turning up. 'Right,' I say when I can speak again. I struggle to stop my mouth twisting into a smile. 'Come on, kids!' I lunge at the water and spray an arc of it onto his legs. He jumps back, but not quickly enough to avoid his shorts being soaked. He stands there laughing as Léa and Luca take my lead and soon he's so drenched he may as well be in the pool.

'Okay, you asked for it.' He strips off his sodden T-shirt and it lands on the ground with a heavy thwack. He jumps in the water, sending a tidal wave over our heads, and then all four of us are having a water fight, flinging our hands through the pool so spray hits our faces and we can hardly see. Léa leaps on Jorge's back to try and push him under, Luca's tugging at his arm, I'm splashing his face and he's gasping for air, begging us for mercy. And then I'm laughing, unable to stop, my stomach

274

aching with the effort, and it feels so good, so familiar, like revisiting an old friend I haven't seen in years and years. I need this. I've so needed this. Maybe Patrick was right: laughter is one of the most important things of all.

After five minutes I'm exhausted. I haul myself out of the pool and sit on the edge again, the sun prickling my skin as it dries.

'You wound them up nicely, they'll be knackered later,' I say to Jorge when he joins me on the edge. He's tanned and lean, and I'm aware of my own less-than-toned belly and the ugly tan lines from my first trip to the pool when I underestimated the strength of the Swiss sun.

'You're welcome.' He grins.

'No work today?'

He shakes his head. 'Now the festival's over I have a couple of weeks off. I'm staying here this week, then I'll head into the mountains with a few friends next week.'

'Hiking?'

He nods. 'We'll spend some time in the Valais, hike, camp, sleep under the stars.'

'Sounds amazing.'

'Maybe another time you can come. But not with these two.' He nods to the pool.

'I don't know, I think they'd both be faster than me. When I went hiking with them and Michel a few weeks ago I was definitely the slowcoach.'

'Slowcoach,' he repeats it, savouring the word. 'I like that.'

I forget he's not a native English speaker, he's so good at it.

275

And French, obviously. And Spanish, naturally. But not Swiss German, I think, remembering my behaviour at the club.

'I'm sorry about last week.' I stare into the pool, avoiding his eyes. 'I had a lot on my mind and I guess I wasn't able to focus on much else.'

He looks at me and shrugs, smiles. 'Forget it. Want to talk about it?'

'Jorge, Jorge, *regarde-moi!*' shouts Léa and she takes a breath, leans over, head down in the water, until she's doing an ungainly handstand, legs akimbo.

'*Très bien. Encore une fois!*' he calls back when she emerges.

I think of him catching me snooping. Of the private letters I riffled through. I shake my head. 'There's nothing much to say.' But I want to tell him, I *need* to tell someone. I look at him. I can be selective, I suppose. 'Actually, I think I might have found my biological father.'

His eyebrows shoot up. 'How?'

'It's a long story.' I think of the letter, the elaborate script of A. Meier that led me to Thun and then Reichenbach. 'This man . . . he's the brother of someone who used to know Mum. I found someone here in Lausanne who once knew them both.'

'So are you going to contact him?'

'I already have, but I didn't know then that he might be my father. And now I think that's likely, I don't know if I should contact him again. I don't know if I want to actually meet him.' For so long I've thought I needed to know who my biological parents are. But now I don't know if I can stand in front of them, face to face, and talk to them. I don't know if I can make them real. Because if Anna and Daniel are my real parents, what does that make Mum and Dad?

Jorge's silent for a minute, and I don't expect him to understand, so it's a surprise when he says 'Your parents will still be your parents, you know.'

I feel pressure behind my eyes and concentrate to keep the tears from forming. 'Will they?' I look at him. 'What if I start something I can't stop? I'm scared of changing my life, rewriting my history. Scared of what it means for my relationship with Dad, and for other people, for ...' I trail off, thinking of Julia, the kids. If she's *her* and she doesn't know it, then I have the power to ruin her perfect life, to turn everything she knows on her head. Bitterness bubbles up inside me. My life was smashed apart, so why not hers too?

'When I was a teenager, Dad and I didn't get along too well,' Jorge says. 'I spent all my time playing music, I didn't want to study, I failed exams.' He pauses. 'I think it was partly because we'd just moved here and I wasn't fitting in too well at school. Music was my refuge.'

I look at him; wait for him to go on.

'Mum was supportive of my music, but Dad thought I should study hard and go to university so I could get a *proper* job. The more he went on about it, the more I wanted to play. I think I enjoyed provoking him, it was like a game. I couldn't see that, actually, he was scared. He wanted me to get qualifications so if the music didn't work out, I wouldn't end up as a janitor like him. He was angry because he thought I was throwing away a chance that he didn't have. But I couldn't see any of that, I thought he was just being an asshole. We fell out for a long time.'

'What happened?'

'I failed my final year of high school and my music teacher, who I worshipped, finally said exactly the same thing to me as Dad had: that I needed to graduate high school, I needed a fallback in case the music didn't work out. When he said it, I realised Dad was right. I repeated my final year, studied hard and got back on track. If I hadn't, I don't think I'd have the job I do now at the festival. And believe me, playing the occasional gig doesn't pay enough to live in Switzerland.'

'So you and your dad made up?'

He shrugs. 'Yeah. I mean, I was too much of an idiot to apologise at the time, but he forgave me anyway and we're good now. But my point in saying all this is that even when we fell out, I knew he loved me. He didn't like what I was doing, but he was always going to be there for me, whatever mess I made of things.'

I look at him and he looks down at the water.

'You only have one dad, that's what I mean. He'll never love you any less and you'll never replace him with anyone else. That's just the way it is.'

I nod, taken aback by his words, by the perception and understanding Patrick seemed so unable to give me, but before I can say anything he gets up from the edge of the pool. 'Toilet,' he says, and walks off.

*

Julia's actually home when we get back from the pool. Léa and Luca rush into the sitting room and start wittering away to her in French so I leave them to it and retreat to my bedroom to send the email that's been brewing in my head all afternoon. I hope Jorge's right, that Dad will stick by me even if he doesn't want me to do this. I know I have to do it because I'll never get any kind of peace within myself unless I find out who I am and what happened. But still, I intend to protect myself by being evasive. If Daniel knows what happened back then, he'll understand what I'm saying. If he doesn't, then he'll just dismiss me as a nutcase and I'll have time to consider whether to enlighten him or not.

Dear Mr Buchs,

The words sound strange in my head as I type them on the screen. Daniel Buchs, my probable biological father.

> Please excuse me for disturbing you again,
> but it's very necessary. Something happened
> to me a long time ago. I don't know why, or
> how, but it's become very important to me to
> find out what actually happened. I now know
> you were married to Brigitte – Anna – and I
> think you and your former wife may be able to
> provide me with some answers. If you really
> have no idea what I'm talking about then I

apologise and hope you'll forgive the intrusion. But I can't help but think that you might know something about what happened to me in a hospital in Lausanne in September 1976. So I beg you, please reply with any information you may have.

　With very best wishes,

　Jessica Faulkner (daughter of Sylvia Tallis and Jim Millson)

I hit send before I can change my mind and feel my stomach plunge. It's done. I'll soon know, one way or another, whether Daniel and Anna have any clue that the woman they call their daughter was somehow swapped at birth with their real child – me.

As I shut the lid of my laptop, I hear crying in the other room. Léa, screaming in French and wailing in a babyish tone I haven't heard from her before. I walk into the room to find out what's going on and see Julia sitting on the sofa with an exasperated expression on her face, her arms around Luca, who sits on her lap. Léa's leaning over one arm of the sofa, her face red and streaked with tears.

'What's going on?' I say. When Léa sees me, she runs to me and flings her arms around my waist. She says something else in French and I hear my name in there, and though I don't have a clue what she's saying, from the stony look on her mother's face I gather it's not a compliment about her.

'I can't go to Léa's tennis competition next Saturday, but she doesn't understand how important work is at the moment,' Julia says. Her expression tells me she clearly expects me to side with her. 'Much as I'd love to see her play, I just can't get away.'

'But it's a Saturday.' It comes out of my mouth like a reflex and Julia frowns, purses her lips.

'Right now, Saturday is a working day for me. There's an event at the stadium, all the sponsors will be there and I must be too,' she says, then to Léa, '*C'est la vie, chérie.* That's life.'

I feel Léa's tears dampening my shorts and I stroke her hair, wanting to bundle her into a hug and tell her it's okay, I have time for her, even if her mother doesn't. But I don't say that. I nod at Julia, a brusque recognition of what she's said, an acknowledgement that she's my employer and I won't contradict her, even if I think she's crazy to put her work ahead of her family. She meets my eyes as her daughter clings to me and I see disapproval in her face – as though *I'm* the one who's in the wrong – and I feel fury rise up in me. How dare she be critical of me when I'm the only one of us putting a smile on her kids' faces these days? How can she be so cavalier with her family, this precious, precious thing, when some people aren't lucky enough to have one?

'Come on,' I say to Léa. 'I want you to show me what you've done in that new drawing pad we picked up last week.'

I take her hand and lead her into her bedroom where she flings herself down on the bed.

She doesn't speak. I sit there and turn the pages,

complimenting her on her drawings as my heart bursts for this eight-year-old girl who I didn't know six weeks ago, but who right now feels more my own than Julia's.

Is this how Mum felt? Is this what it feels like to have a daughter? Even if it turns out she's not your own after all.

I'm still fuming about Julia's behaviour the next day when the doorbell goes. I get up from the table, where I've been helping Luca complete a jigsaw puzzle, and go to the door. Léa lifts her head from her book and I shoot her a smile, but she doesn't return it and looks down again. I've been trying to think of things that might lift her spirits, but as yet nothing has succeeded. She's got as much on her mind as I have, it seems.

A delivery driver is holding out a package. He nods at me. *'Bonjour, Madame.'*

'Bonjour,' I offer, hoping that's all I'll have to say.

He rattles off something that I don't understand but I don't need to; the box is addressed to Mme J. Chevalley and the electronic signature pad he hands me is all the explanation I need. I take it, scribble something that vaguely resembles my signature and hand it back. He gives me the package.

'Bonne journée.' He turns away, walks to his van and opens the door.

I take the package inside. The kids don't even look up as I walk through the sitting room and take the box into my bedroom. I sit on my bed and stare at it.

It's branded Coca-Cola so I know it must be something

to do with Julia's work. I've heard her talk about Coke, say what an important sponsor they are of the events she organises. Why it's arrived here, instead of her office, I really don't know. Neither do I know why I've brought it into my bedroom or why I feel an urge to open it.

All I know is I don't want Julia to have it.

My heart quickens. The house feels quiet. Léa's too subdued to be antagonising her younger brother. I think of her face, her tears, and the flash of anger in Julia's eyes when I said, *But it's a Saturday.* And I suddenly realise I don't care what's in the box. I don't want to snoop anymore. I don't give a shit. But I do want to upset Julia, just as she upset her daughter. I want to mess up the job that's so important to her, punish her in whatever small way I can.

I get up from my bed and open the wardrobe door, unzip my empty suitcase and put the box inside.

I'll dispose of it later.

PART THREE

FLEET STREET MANHUNT

The new six-part series *Forget-me-Not* (ITV, 10.00) takes a career girl's view of newspapers and the men in them. Pat Powell (Patricia Brake) is an ambitious and attractive young journalist who wants to get to the top and enjoy an old-fashioned manhunt for 'Mr Right' at the same time. Aiding and abetting her in the chase is Avril Phelps (Cyd Hayman). Avril is the women's editor of the paper they both work for and is a sophisticated divorcee who enjoys romantic adventures. [...] Let's hope the kissing stops for long enough to leave them time to do some work.

TV preview in the Daily Mirror, *1976*

AUGUST 1976

London, UK

SYLVIA

Sylvia hadn't wanted to act like Valerie. She'd wanted to be encouraging, the older mentor nourishing the journalistic dreams of a young woman in a man's world. But it was taking all of her effort not to adopt Valerie's unassailable gaze, frosty demeanour and unfailing rejection of sisterhood, and she wasn't entirely succeeding. When it came down to it, Diane was bright, ambitious and would clearly make the most of this rare opportunity to get into Fleet Street. Sylvia attempted to screw her internal rage into a ball and throw it in the wastepaper bin – but she missed.

'We get plenty of requests to feature,' she said, nodding to the page in last Saturday's paper, where Ethel and William stared back at her. 'We put a call out at the end of each week's column and there's a backlog of couples who've written in,

287

so you won't run out. You just have to select who you want to feature when and call them up to arrange the interview.'

'And hope they don't pop their clogs in the meantime,' Diane said.

'It happened once, sadly.'

'You're kidding!'

'Doris, I think her name was.' A smile tugged at Sylvia's mouth. It wasn't funny. But the conversation only added to the surreal nature of the day. Here she was, sitting at her desk with a considerable baby bump and increasingly swollen feet, mere weeks from leaving the job she'd always wanted, explaining to her *replacement* that one of the perils of writing a feature about elderly married couples is that they might die before you get to interview them. 'We sent her husband a bunch of flowers and lined up the next one.'

'Crikey,' Diane said.

'One out of fifty-four isn't bad.'

Diane snorted. 'No, I suppose not.'

Sylvia explained how the letters page worked, and where she got her ideas for the 'at home' section; she went through the process for pitching ideas to Roger, the politics of the features meetings, and the necessity of going to the pub at least once a week. She explained all this with a pang of longing for what she was about to temporarily lose and a simultaneous realisation of how much she'd learnt in this job. When she started here not so long ago she'd been just like Diane: a puppy with a new bone, desperately excited at the opportunity and determined to retain it at all costs. But somehow, despite all her best efforts, life had made her drop that bone, only for it to be quickly snaffled up by the next young terrier in the park.

She still had several weeks to go at the paper, and it felt as though Roger was rubbing her nose in it by getting Diane in for training so early. She was to shadow Sylvia in the next few weeks, go where she went, listen to her interviews, be there in her meetings, get friendly with her contacts, until – or so it felt to Sylvia – they would merge into the same person and when she left on maternity leave Roger wouldn't even notice she'd gone. The only thing keeping her even slightly positive about the whole affair was Jim.

Since she'd moved back into the Kennington flat, he'd been different – he wasn't fussing over her so much, he talked less about impending parenthood and more about their work, their friends, their lives in London, like he used to, before everything changed. She told him about Diane, about the fear she felt in handing over her job to a newcomer, the panic that she'd never get it back in quite the same way. And instead of dismissing her worries with meaningless platitudes or positive-thinking mantras, he listened, he sympathised and he tried to offer ways to cope. His empathy finally allowed her to breathe out and know it for the genuine support it was.

As part of Diane's essential training she took her to El Vino's on a late Thursday afternoon. Sylvia sipped a lime and soda while Janice and Marnie shared a bottle of white with

Diane as they filled her in on Fleet Street's sexual liaisons, indiscreetly pointing out the main protagonists if they were present in the bar – as many were, on a Thursday in the height of silly season, when the heat was so enduring that even Big Ben had packed up.

'Valerie and Roger, really?' Diane asked.

Janice leant forward. 'Rumour has it, his wife just found out and kicked him out.'

'Rumour has it? You mean you saw something in his office,' Marnie said.

'Not exactly. But I may have overheard a phone call. Something about custody. He's getting them every other weekend.'

Sylvia felt a guilty twinge of relief. Perhaps Roger's grumpiness towards her wasn't personal but simply a reflection of the circumstances in his own life.

'Well,' Diane said, when Janice and Marnie had sailed off into the throng and they were left alone on the table, 'this has been fascinating.'

Sylvia smiled. 'Fleet Street gossip. Par for the course.'

Diane finished her glass. Her pupils were wide, her skin slightly flushed. 'I just love it,' she said. 'All this. The buzz, the gossip, the energy. I don't know how you can bear to give it up.'

'I don't have a lot of choice.' Sylvia gestured to her belly. Sometimes the baby elbowed her in the bladder so hard it made her gasp. 'But it won't be for long.'

Diane nodded, and that could have been the end of it. But

then the younger girl's lips formed into a thin line, her eyes creased at the corners and her head leant to one side in what was, Sylvia realised with a jolt of shock, an unmistakable gesture of pity. A gesture that said Diane was sorry for her, but that she thought her a fool, and she would make the most of her foolishness by stepping smoothly into her shoes. At least that's what it felt like.

And that was when Sylvia knew she had to do something. She couldn't just slope off on maternity leave with her job in the clutches of an eager Cambridge graduate without making some sort of grand parting gesture. She had to find a final story. A story that would make an impact and leave a lasting impression so forceful that Roger would be begging to have her back.

And she knew what it had to be.

A story that had been brewing in her head ever since returning from Switzerland. A story that would highlight a cause and potentially bring some justice to a vulnerable young woman.

When Roger came back from a meeting the next morning, she knocked on his office door.

'Can we talk?' She poked her head into the office and instantly regretted it. The combined pong of body odour and cigarettes nearly made her retch. She wondered if he'd spent the night here.

'It's not the best bloody time right now, Tallis, but go on then, be quick.'

She sat down, tried to breathe through her mouth and told

him about meeting Anna, how she was sent to work on a farm as unpaid labour at the age of eight, how her host family later deprived her of school. She told him about what she'd found scouring the British Library: a private foundation set up in Switzerland in the forties to help kids on 'forced place-ment' after a magazine reported mistreatment in the foster care system, and a report about a 1970 court case involving two children subjected to abuse in an institution. Clearly there was something amiss in the Swiss care system.

'I think this *needs* to be written. I want to interview her – and maybe others. Evelyne mentioned Anna had a sister who was also taken, maybe I can find her and get her story too. But I'll need some research time and resources. And a trip back to Switzerland.'

'Tallis, I told you—'

'Insurance. I know, I know.' She brushed a damp piece of hair behind her ear. 'Look, I'll do the trip in my own time and fund it myself,' she said, suppressing the little voice that said *you're meant to be saving.* 'I'll sign a waiver if you want me to. Keith and the board need never know I went – until I get the story no other paper has and then I'm sure they wouldn't mind a jot. But I want to know if you approve of the idea, if you'll publish it.' She leaned forward. A trickle of sweat ran down her boss's temple. 'Roger, I really, really want to do this. I think it's important. Will you back me?'

He sat back in his chair and sighed. 'You know something, Tallis? You remind me of my younger self.'

She hesitated, smiled. 'Is that a yes?'

AUGUST 2016

Lausanne, Switzerland

JESS

The ball thwacks against Léa's racket and whistles past the girl at the other end of the court.

'She's got a mean passing shot.'

Michel nods. 'You play?'

'No, but I've watched a lot of Wimbledon,' I say. 'Agassi was always my favourite. Loved the fact he eventually married Steffi Graf. Tennis fairy tale.'

'You're showing your age,' he says.

'I know.'

He laughs and we clap enthusiastically as Léa thumps another groundstroke down the line, leaving her opponent standing. A slight, blonde girl with ruddy cheeks, she looks like she's about to cry, and I feel sorry for Céline. She's on the receiving end of an eight-year-old in a seriously bad mood – but to give Léa credit, she's channelling her grumpiness usefully and is likely to win the match if she carries on like this. I never knew pre-teen tennis could be so competitive.

I sit back on the bench and feel my body relax beneath the August sun. It's nice to be here, finally, after such a stressful morning. Léa screaming that she didn't want to go. Refusing to put on her tennis outfit until Julia threatened to take away her new Harry Potter book. And then Julia rushing around, harried, because an important package for her event that day hadn't turned up in the post. She'd had it sent to the house specifically, she'd told me, because time was tight and she didn't want to have to drive to the office before the event if it arrived on the Saturday morning.

Are you sure nothing came in the week, Jess?

I shook my head, unable to even mutter a response. Sickness grew in my stomach as I pictured myself putting the packet in the recycling bin near the pool. The deviousness of it. The pointless stupidity. But I know I can't go back on it now.

Léa and Céline get up from their chairs and throw each other evil glares as they prowl to their respective ends of the court. It's Léa's serve. She throws the ball high in the air and pummels it down, but it's slightly long.

'Maybe she could be the next Graf.'

Michel laughs. He takes off his baseball cap and wipes the sweat off his forehead. I think of Jorge by the pool, water droplets on his tanned skin. 'I don't know, I don't want to push her too hard. She's only eight,' he says.

'Got to start them young. She's got less than a decade if she's going to beat Martina Hingis' record as the youngest Grand Slam singles winner in the modern era.'

He laughs. 'You really know your stuff.'

'Like I say, I've watched *a lot* of tennis.' A memory drifts into my head of a brown box television set in the mid-eighties, the vivid green swatch of the grass, the thick-thock of the ball, the polite applause, Mum coming to sit on the shag pile carpet beside me, a bowl of strawberries in her hand for us to share. Me teasing her for shouting at the telly when her favourite player was losing, her smiling in self-awareness at her rampant competitiveness. The memory settles on me like a warm blanket.

'*Je veux faire pipi,*' Luca says, and the scene evaporates and I'm back on the bench on the side of the arid red clay court.

'*Zero-trente,*' the umpire says after one of Léa's serves sails out.

'*Attends, chéri,*' Michel says to Luca, not taking his eyes off his daughter as she prepares to serve again.

'This is an important game,' I say to Luca. I don't want to miss Léa's impending triumph because I'm helping a small boy go to the toilet.

She serves to the forehand and Céline whacks it back, Léa chases it down and returns it well – or so I thought until the linesman calls it out.

'*Zero-quarante.*'

Léa's mouth falls open and she drops her racket. I feel indignant on her behalf. That was clearly in, and now she's got three break points against her. But she'll pull it back, I know. So I'm surprised when she yells, *'C'était sur la ligne!'* with considerably more venom than you'd expect from such a small person. The umpire shakes his head. He has grey hair and an authoritarian air. I wouldn't mess with him.

Give it up, Léa. But I should know by now that's not in her nature.

'C'était sur la ligne!' she cries again in a tone of voice that would make McEnroe proud. She picks up her racket and smashes it on the ground in fury. Picking it up again she sees the frame is broken and lets out a wail of anguish before dumping it on the court and storming off.

'Merde.' Michel gets up to chase after her.

I stand up to go with him and realise Luca has peed all over the bench.

'Léa?'

No answer. I look at Michel and he nods me on. He's spent ten minutes trying to get his daughter to unlock the cubicle door, and now I've seen to it that Luca is relatively dry and not about to wet himself again, it's my turn.

'You were really good out there. Really, really good. I was just saying that to your *papa*.'

I hear a sniff, and then nothing.

'You know, these things happen sometimes. You and I know the umpire made a mistake, but it's important to carry on. And it didn't really matter because you were about to win anyway.'

A small voice. 'I don't care about the match.'

I glance at Michel. He frowns, gestures for me to continue.

'Okay. Well . . .' I don't know what else to say. 'That's okay if you don't want to play anymore today. But you should really come out and shake your partner's hand because that's what people do at the end of a match. It's a rule. I saw it on Wimbledon. And you're so good that one day maybe you'll get to play at Wimbledon for real, and then you'll be glad you know little rules like that. What do you think?'

'I don't care,' she says again, and then, more quietly, something in French. I catch the word *maman*.

Michel blows out a breath, shakes his head, mouths *She wants Julia* at me. '*Bientôt, chérie*,' he says. 'She'll be home tonight.'

'But I wanted her to see me play.'

'I know you did,' he says. 'But you had me and Jess and Luca watching you and we all thought you were so good! You can tell *maman* all about it when you get home.' A pause, no reply. 'Will you come out now, *chérie*? Will you unlock the door and then we can all go home?'

I think we're going to be there forever until I finally hear the click of the lock and Léa's standing there in front of us, her face blotchy from crying.

'I will shake Céline's hand,' she says in a small but firm voice that makes me want to hug her. 'And then I want to go home.'

*

As soon as we're back at the house it's as though the afternoon never happened. I get the paddling pool out for the kids and use the garden hose to fill it with water. They're soon splashing about with abandon, as though the tantrum and the pants-wetting incident are ancient history.

'Don't judge her.' Michel sits down opposite me on a garden chair.

'Of course not, she's eight.'

Michel makes a strange snorting noise. 'Not Léa. Julia.'

I don't know what to say. Of course I'm judging her. For never being around for her kids. For missing important events. But mainly for having so much that I want but can't have, and not bloody appreciating it.

'I don't—'

He waves his hand to dismiss it, as though he doesn't want to hear my protestations. 'She loves her job, and she's so good at it. Her manager is always telling her she's indispensable.'

I remember being called into Peacock's office at St Mary's. Years of impeccable teaching, a marked improvement in exam results, an outstanding Ofsted inspection and yet I'm forced onto sabbatical, just like that, because of one tiny lapse in judgement during a difficult time. No one's indispensable.

'But . . .' I start, and then I don't quite know how to finish. 'Léa clearly needs her mum around a bit more.' I look at the pool, watch Léa splashing her brother as though she hadn't a care in the world, and my heart aches for my own mother, for her quick wit and fierce support and her hugs, her wonderful, enveloping hugs. I know I can't ever get that back, but I wish with all my heart I had the chance to be the other side of the equation, to give a mother's love to a child just as Mum gave hers to me. I can't fathom how Julia can treat her good fortune with such disregard.

'She will,' he says. 'This is temporary. In the autumn, Julia will have her weekends back. Léa will be fine.'

I think that's the end of the conversation until he says, 'It's hard for her, you know. Julia didn't have the best childhood herself.'

'No?' I assumed Julia had been born with a silver spoon in her mouth.

Michel shakes his head. 'She wasn't from a well-off family. They struggled.'

I look at him, will him to carry on. Julia's family. The Meiers.

'Julia's mother had her very young and then her father left, so Julia was pretty much brought up by her grandparents. There was never much money to go around. Julia works so hard because she doesn't want to be like her mother.'

I nod, trying not to let shock take over my features. Could that have been my background? Would that upbringing have given me the drive to achieve what Julia clearly has? Sometimes I think I rebelled against Mum's ambition; I chose a safe, secure profession because she didn't. Or maybe I just wasn't cut out to be a trailblazer. Maybe I would have sunk without the safety net of my parents – unlike Julia.

I think of this house. The posh designer sofa, the fridge with its fancy ice-making facility. The giant television and the iMac. The million-franc view of the lake. I thought Julia was all this, through and through. But instead she hasn't had it all on a plate. She's worked, fought, risen up. I feel something curl up into a hard fist inside me. She's even more damn perfect than I thought.

'Gosh,' I say, because Michel's looking at me, clearly expecting some kind of response. My throat is dry and it comes out as a croak. I badly need a glass of water. 'Well, good on her.' I nod to the house. 'You guys have done well.'

He smiles. '*Merci*,' he says. 'We wouldn't swap it for anything.'

Léa calls out to her father and I use the interruption to get up and go into the house. My stomach is churning and I walk to the toilet, feeling bile rise up my throat.

I can't do this anymore. I need to get rid of all the toxic feelings inside me. I need to stop being jealous and insecure and confused and guilty and in the dark about my entire existence. I need to hear from Daniel.

I need to finally know who I am.

It's predictably late when Julia finally makes it home. The kids are in bed, I'm reading on the sofa and Michel is doing something on his laptop at the dining table. It's peaceful after the drama of the day, but the calm is broken the minute she brings her bad mood through the front door. Tension emanates off her; it's in the way she throws her car keys on the table by the door, in her footsteps down the hall, in the deep line between her eyes when she comes into the room. Michel and I look up simultaneously, but her eyes go first to me.

'Ça va, chérie?' Michel gets up to greet her. He kisses her and puts his hands on her arms, looks into her face as she says something in French and lets out a long sigh. He goes to the fridge and pours her a glass of wine, passes it to her as she sits down at the table. She looks at me again, smiles, but it doesn't reach her eyes.

'Long day?' I venture.

'Yes, it was.' She takes a sip of wine, but doesn't take her eyes off me. 'It didn't go as expected with the sponsor, especially because that important package I needed didn't arrive. My manager was not pleased.'

I feel a tremor ripple through my body as I look at her, but then I remember Léa's anger on the court, her small voice in the toilet cubicle, and it fortifies me. 'I'm sorry to hear that,' I say. 'Léa's competition didn't go too well either.'

'I know, Michel messaged me.'

She holds my gaze and it's as though we're in a schoolyard stare-out, each waiting for the other to look away first. But this is more than a childish game. I think of the package, languishing in a recycling bin, and it feels as though someone else did that, not me. The same person who riffled through her drawers, whose flashes of anger and envy and pain make her act irrationally. And then I blink and look down at my book, because although I know I didn't say any of that out loud, Julia's gaze is so direct that it's like she's reading my thoughts.

'It's been a stressful day all round,' Michel says. He looks from me to Julia, a perplexed appeaser in a mental punch-up. 'Thank God it's Sunday tomorrow. Let's hope the kids have a lie-in.'

She turns to him and smiles, and the tension lifts like mist evaporating in the sun. And yet it feels like something has changed. Something was said in that moment we held each other's gaze. Unspoken, but communicated none the less.

Don't judge her, Michel had said. Yet now it feels like she's judging me.

SEPTEMBER 1976

Lausanne, Switzerland

SYLVIA

Sylvia had tried her hardest to get Evelyne to explain everything to Anna: why she wanted to see her, what she would be writing about, what newspaper she worked for. Evelyne swore she had, but when they turned up at Anna and Daniel's pokey sixth-floor flat in a suburb of Lausanne, Sylvia wasn't convinced Anna had given a single thought to having her story in a newspaper – she simply seemed excited to see Sylvia again, and it occurred to her that perhaps she was the only pregnant woman Anna knew, the only person she could get some much needed reassurance from.

With Evelyne as translator, Sylvia answered the many questions Anna flung at her when she was hardly through the door: had Sylvia had breathlessness (yes), heartburn (no), and insomnia (yes, most nights, out of worry, mainly), like

Anna had? Was she excited to meet her baby (of course, she said, *I wish*, she thought), was she scared about the birth (not really, but only because she'd hardly dared give it a thought)?

Anna ushered them into the battered wooden chairs she said the previous tenant had left behind, and served them glasses of tap water. They didn't yet have a table; the only other furniture in the studio flat was a bed, neatly made up by the window. Evelyne had given them a few pots and pans for the kitchenette, and that was it. The place was tiny and dark without the main light, which was just a bare bulb hanging from the ceiling. Sylvia thought of her and Jim's airy sitting room with its bay window and polished wooden floorboards, their spacious kitchen, and the spare room that would be the baby's, Jim having diligently painted the walls pale yellow.

After two stressful months crammed into Evelyne's flat, Anna and Daniel had finally managed to move out, Evelyne had told her with relief (brother and sister, it transpired, were not designed to live together as adults), after Daniel took on two jobs. So in addition to working on a building site in the daytime, he was also making croissants in a bakery in the early hours of each morning. How he found time to sleep, Sylvia didn't know. And how lonely Anna must be, holed up in this tiny flat on her own, in a new city where she didn't know anyone. Sylvia had wondered if Anna could get a job herself, but Evelyne had said no. She was sixteen, pregnant and unmarried – even if someone would take her on, it would be risky to make herself 'seen'; she and Daniel couldn't get married until they both came of age, and until then she was at risk of being sent back to the farm, or some awful women's detention centre, if the authorities found her – and then her child might be taken from her and given up for adoption.

So it was best to stay off the radar.

They hadn't even told the landlord Anna was living here – as far as he knew, Daniel occupied the flat alone. The cheap metal ring Anna was currently twisting around her wedding finger was just a small attempt to stop any prying neighbours from asking too many questions.

Still, the apartment was progress, Daniel's two jobs were progress, and maybe, just maybe, they could get through these next few years until easier times arrived. Sylvia hoped so with all her heart.

'What was it like, growing up where you did?' she said, to start the interview. She and Evelyne were sitting on the two chairs, while Anna sat on a cushion on the floor, her back to the wall, an arrangement Anna had insisted on.

'It was home,' Anna said.

Sylvia looked at Evelyne as she translated, and then frowned. She looked back at Anna. 'Were you happy?'

'Until Father left. But after that we didn't really have any money, and then Mother lost her job.' She paused. 'I think she was very unhappy. She cried a lot.' Anna looked down, picked at the edge of her skirt. 'She loved us though, our mother. She loved us and she didn't want us to go away. I don't know why she let them take us.'

'Tell me about what happened when the authorities came for you,' Sylvia said gently.

Through Evelyne's translation, Sylvia heard about the day Anna last saw her mother and older sister. The despair on her mother's face, tinged with something else – resignation, Anna had decided after years of thinking about it. Her own confusion as the men came to the house and grabbed her and Cornelia by the arms. Cornelia spitting at them, screaming. *Get your hands off me!* The car ride for what felt like hours and hours until her mouth was dry and she desperately needed to pee. The road sign – Ferden – where Cornelia was pulled from her seat. The door slamming shut and the car pulling away again, going she didn't know where without her sister.

Anna spoke about arriving at the farm where Franziska, Evelyne's mother, showed her to a cot bed in the corner of the kitchen where she would sleep, how she'd been asked to serve the dinner to the four of them that very same night, and how Franziska had chided her when she spilt a drop of sauce on the tablecloth, and ordered her to go and wash it as soon as she'd eaten. She spoke about having to get up at 5am to milk the cows before school, and then coming home and going straight to work again, mucking out the cow shit or washing the family's sheets.

'Did you mind it?' Sylvia asked, aware, as she did so, that Anna was having to relate this tale in front of Evelyne, the daughter of the people she was speaking about. But at least Anna knew that Evelyne had left too, that she understood something of what Anna had gone through.

Anna shrugged. 'I'd done chores before, at home, although not as many. I was always tired, but that meant I slept well. And at least the work filled my day. It stopped me having too much time to think – about Mum and Cornelia mainly. I missed them so much.'

Sylvia looked at her, willing Anna to meet her eyes. 'Did they ever hurt you at the farm?'

Evelyne glanced at her momentarily, and Sylvia wondered for a second if she was going to refuse to translate. So she was relieved when Evelyne conveyed the question, adding something else that Sylvia didn't understand, but from the softening in Anna's face she knew it was encouragement, not a warning.

'Herr Buchs shouted a lot,' Anna said. 'He hit me sometimes. Franziska told me off all the time; I could never do anything right. But I suppose I got used to it.'

Sylvia looked at her. There was something else, she knew it. 'And?' she prompted.

Anna raised her head and looked Evelyne right in the eyes as she spoke. 'It wasn't what they did, but what they didn't,' she said. 'They didn't love me. I was never part of their family, even though I lived there for years and years. I was just a farmhand. No, worse – a dog. They were never kind to me, they never cared if I was hungry, or tired, or cold, or ill. They only took me to the doctor when I was sick because they needed me well enough to work – and then they resented me for how much it cost them and made me work even harder. They took me out of school, even though that was the only thing I liked in my life, and when I pleaded to go back, Herr Buchs hit me.' She paused. 'Actually, I wasn't even a dog, I was lower than that. They liked their dogs far more than they liked me.'

As Evelyne translated, Sylvia heard her voice waver, and she knew Anna heard it too.

'For the first year I hoped it was all a mistake, that Mum would come and get me back. But she never did.'

'You weren't allowed to see her?'

She shook her head. 'I haven't seen her since I was eight years old. And the people who took me never came to see me, to tell me how she was. I couldn't even send a letter. I once asked Franziska for a stamp, but she told me it was best if I didn't write. I don't know why. But I never gave up hope that I would see her again, some day. I just needed to get out of there – and now I have. As soon as I'm married, I'll go back and find her.'

'Did you think about running away before?'

'Every day,' Anna replied. 'But I couldn't go back home, the authorities would just take me again. I had no money, I was underage. I thought if they caught me then I might be sent somewhere worse. I'd heard stuff at school about places where they sent disobedient kids – horrible places. I couldn't risk it.'

'And then you got pregnant.'

Anna nodded, smiling. 'The baby saved me. It's the best thing that's ever happened to me.'

Sylvia exchanged a glance with Evelyne. She knew her

friend didn't share that view, that she felt Daniel's life had been curbed by this pregnant girlfriend, that Anna's would also be curbed, when she had a baby to care for. *This is why there should be easier access to contraception,* Evelyne had railed before they arrived at the flat.

'Daniel hardly even spoke to me until I was fifteen,' Anna said. 'Then one day he defended me when Herr Buchs was telling me off about something – I forget what, he told me off so often I stopped listening. But this time Daniel stood up for me, and he took a beating for it. That's when we became friends, and everything was so much better after that. I wanted us to run away together, but he wouldn't, even though he hated his father. He couldn't bear to leave his mother there alone, he said. But when I discovered I was pregnant we both knew he had no choice. We'd have to leave.' Anna put her hand on her stomach. 'So the baby saved me, you see. It saved both of us.'

Sylvia took a deep breath. It pained her, what the girl had been through. How little love she'd had in her life, how little help. And she knew, after hearing her story, how much Anna wanted the new being growing inside of her. She thought of her own baby and hoped she would somehow manage to feel the same.

'*Danke,*' Sylvia said, when the questions came to an end, and they both smiled at her attempt at German. She would send Anna a copy of the article when it was published.

'Brigitte,' Anna said suddenly, as though the thought had only just occurred to her.

'What?' Evelyne said.

'You can't use my real name. Please call me Brigitte. It's my mother's middle name. Just in case the authorities read it. They can't know it's me.'

Sylvia nodded and wrote the name down to show her the spelling. 'Okay?'

Anna nodded. 'When are you due?' she asked.

'October tenth.' Sylvia didn't match Anna's smile. 'You?'

'October sixteenth.' She beamed, and Sylvia saw how excited Anna was at the prospect of having a baby. She didn't have much to provide, but she would give it the most important thing of all, the thing she hadn't had nearly enough of herself – love.

They left Anna and Daniel's flat and caught the bus back into Lausanne city centre.

'I want to do something for her,' Sylvia said, when they were installed in a cafe. Perhaps it was just her stupid hormones, but her time with Anna made her want to weep.

'You are. You're writing that article.'

'Something more. Something concrete. They have nothing. How are they going to cope with a baby in that tiny flat?'

Sylvia sat back in her chair on the cafe terrace and rested a hand on her belly. Listening to Anna had been emotionally hard, but for some reason she felt physically drained, too, with a headache pounding at her temples. Guilt-induced, probably. Guilt that she had so much in comparison, and yet had been so ungrateful for it.

'They'll just have to, there's no other choice,' Evelyne said. The waitress came and they ordered drinks – coffee for Evelyne and lemonade for Sylvia. The air had the metallic smell of fresh rain on hot tarmac. Back home, summer had finally broken over the bank holiday weekend with a downpour almost as intense as the drought that preceded it, and here it felt like autumn was finally around the corner, too. It was the end of the long, hot summer – and the beginning of a new phase of life.

'Thank you for translating,' Sylvia said. 'It must have been strange for you, hearing all that about your parents.'

'A little.' Evelyne paused. 'A lot.' She looked down at her coffee. 'It wasn't a surprise, any of that. I mean, I was there. I know what my father is like, how he treated her. But I suppose I never really thought about it beyond the physical. I never thought about what she'd lost. I just accepted it. I was a teenager when she came to the farm and I was so caught up in my own battles with my father that I didn't consider how hard it must have been for Anna to be away from her own family.'

'Do you know anything about them?'

'Not really. I never asked.' Evelyne picked up her coffee cup and Sylvia saw her eyes were shining.

'You were a child too. You couldn't be expected to do anything.'

'Maybe not. But perhaps I could have been her friend. I just thought she was this skinny, morose kid who never smiled, but in my arrogant youth I never really thought to do anything about that. It's ironic, you know. The other day I was in Geneva protesting the bulldozing of a centre set up to help women, and yet I was too wrapped up in myself back then to help a young girl in my own home.'

'Well, you can be her friend now. She's going to need one, that's for sure.'

'I know, and I will.' Evelyne shifted in her seat, took a sip of coffee. 'We needed the money, you know, and the extra help. It's not an easy life, farming.' She paused. 'But I know that's not an excuse for how we treated Anna.'

Sylvia said nothing, sensing that Evelyne had more to say.

'Mother has been writing me letters.' She laughed, but there was bitterness in it. 'That's pretty brave of her really. I can just imagine her waiting until Father has gone down to the cows, and then whipping out her notepad. Scurrying furtively to the post office.' She shook her head and her smile dropped. 'Breaking contact with my mother was like collateral damage. She wouldn't stand up to him, so I had to leave her too. I didn't want to.'

'She's a product of her generation. And so are you – breaking free of all that.'

'I suppose so.' Evelyne shrugged. 'I'll never forget the moment I understood that things didn't have to be as I'd been brought up to believe. It was 1969, I was about Anna's age, or a little older. I heard a report on the radio about a women's march in Bern, protesting that the government was intending to ratify the European Convention on Human Rights, even though women didn't yet have the vote! It was unbelievable, as though they didn't even consider women to be humans with rights.' She shook her head. 'The march was led by a woman called Emilie Lieberherr. God, she was a powerful speaker. Equality. Women's rights. The vote. These weren't notions I'd heard too often before then, but everything she was saying just made complete sense to me. It was like someone had provided the answer before I even knew I was allowed to ask the question.

'That was the beginning of the end for my relationship with Dad. And then he didn't even vote for women's suffrage in '71,' Evelyne laughed. 'He told me, threw it in my face like a boast. I knew after that, I couldn't stay. There was simply no middle ground.'

'Will you ever see them again?'

'I hope so, one day. I may not like him much right now, but he's still my father. And I still have good memories from when I was little, before farming ground him down, before I woke up to the path he was sending me on. I suppose it's like Anna implied: however tough it was for me, at least they were my family, at least there was love, even if my father buried it well.'

As Sylvia raised her glass, a sharp, sudden pain stabbed her in the abdomen, taking her breath away. She dropped the glass on the table, spilling its contents.

'Are you okay?'

'Yes, I think so. Just a strange pain for a second.'

Evelyne pushed a paper napkin to her and Sylvia mopped up the lemonade. She could feel the baby move almost constantly now. Just five weeks to go. Almost fully baked. How strange it felt to think back to a year previously, when this was the furthest thing from her mind.

'How does it feel, to be having a baby?'

'Bizarre. Surreal. Bloody uncomfortable.'

Evelyne gave a wry smile. 'Perhaps I'll change my mind one day, but I just can't see that I'll ever have a child. And I know I'll never get married. It feels like social conditioning, a way for society to cast me in a mould and keep me in check. I want a career that earns me enough money to eat expensive dinners and travel to Paris for the weekend and drink cocktails.' She laughed. 'I want to have steamy affairs at music festivals and sleep on the beach in India and drink beer at Oktoberfest. I want to sleep with a man half my age when I'm fifty. I want to be free to do as I please, for as long as I please.'

Sylvia smiled. 'I wanted all that too,' she said, before amending her sentence at Evelyne's raised eyebrows. She twisted her wedding ring around her finger. 'Okay, I know I'm not as radical as you, but I wanted the career and expensive dinners and the freedom to do as I pleased.'

'No steamy affairs?'

'Well . . .'

Evelyne laughed.

'Getting pregnant at this age was the last thing I wanted. I feel like I've veered off down a path I never intended.' She and Jim now had a taupe-coloured sofa, a coffee machine and a crib in the spare room. Had she lost her aim in life like a coin down that sofa?

'Then fight.' Evelyne grabbed Sylvia's hand across the table. 'Fight to make things different. Fight to have a career and be a mother too. If we all fight in our own small way then maybe things will change.'

Sylvia smiled, hearing Maggie in Evelyne's words. If those two brilliant women thought she could do it, maybe she just could. 'I suppose we'll just have to see what happens,' she said. 'To the both of us.'

Evelyne picked up her cup of coffee. 'To women. *Santé.*'

'*Santé.*'

It was just after they'd toasted the future that Sylvia looked down to see a circle of blood growing steadily outwards across her skirt.

AUGUST 2016

Montreux, Switzerland

JESS

I'm sitting next to Julia in the car and I don't know why I'm here.

'Let me drive you. We haven't had much time to chat recently and I'm going that way anyway,' she said this morning. Daniel Buchs still hasn't replied, and I can't bear to spend all day refreshing my email. I'm hoping the art exhibition will be a distraction, and I was quite looking forward to taking the train to the gallery in Martigny on my own, spending the half-hour journey contemplating my crazy mixed-up life while watching the mountains go by. It's Sunday, Julia's only day at home, and I want to scream at her to actually spend this time with her family, not with me. But she insisted, so here I am, snapping my seatbelt on and watching her pull into the traffic. I wonder, with a growing sense of unease, why she insisted quite so much.

She doesn't say anything for the first few minutes and the silence goads me. I want to ask her about how she grew up, about her home life, the absent father and single mother that Michel talked about, the parents who could possibly be mine. I open my mouth, and then close it again.

We're on the high motorway above the lake when she finally says it.

'I know what you did, Jess.'

My stomach plunges. I look at her. Her eyes are fixed on the road ahead and she's smiling in a serene way that freaks me out.

'I know you signed for the package from Coca-Cola. I called the delivery company. They emailed me a scan of your signature. So I know you received it, but what I don't understand is why you didn't give it to me.'

I look away, out at the lake. Sweat beads on the back of my neck. 'I don't know,' I admit.

Julia sighs, and I understand she knows it isn't really about the package.

'It wasn't a deliberate thing. I mean, I didn't intend to keep it from you, I just ... did.' I pause. I know now why I'm here, why I'm sitting next to her in this car. It's like the clouds have parted after rain, and I suddenly see what's going to happen. I know we won't leave the car until the truth has been spilled, and the thought is almost a relief. I take a breath. 'Okay, I was cross with you.'

She glances at me, and then back at the road. 'Why?'

I hesitate, then rip off the plaster. 'Because you were choosing to go to your work event rather than Léa's tennis competition.'

She nods, as though I've confirmed her suspicions. She indicates and pulls out to overtake a car ahead. I glance at the speedo; we're going significantly over the limit. I want to tell her to slow down, but I don't.

'*D'accord.*' She gives a short laugh. 'I understand. You think I'm a terrible mother and I should stay at home with my kids like a good Swiss *Hausfrau* and not go to work?'

'No.' I shake my head. 'Unless you want to, of course.' *I* want to. I'd have given up my job in an instant to stay home with my children if I was lucky enough to have them and could afford to. But I know it's not fashionable to say so. It's like my guilty secret, something you're not allowed to admit to these days. 'But I think you should tuck your children into bed occasionally, and be there on the weekends when your daughter has an event that's important to her.'

I think of Mum, always on the go, but still there – usually – to kiss me goodnight and watch me fail at three-legged races. A memory tugs at my brain: a row with Dad, angry whispers that stopped when I approached, a cancelled work trip, Mum's smile a little too bright.

Julia gives a brusque laugh of exasperation. 'You think I don't know that? Of course I do. Of course I'd rather be with my family than at work. But these things happen. It's a busy time and I can't avoid it if I want to get ahead in my career. And I do, Jess. I don't want to be aimless, achieving nothing, floating through life without focus. That's not an example I want to give my children.'

I feel the dig as though she's stuck her flawless painted fingernail into my arm.

'And anyway,' she continues, her voice strained. 'I don't know why you want me around more. It's clear you think you can do a better job at being their mother than me.'

I look at her and she glances at me simultaneously and it's the first time we've made eye contact since we started this conversation. We both look away instantly, as though we've been burned, but before I do I'm surprised to see hurt behind the anger.

'No,' I say, keeping my voice steady. 'I don't.'

The car enters a tunnel and the sound of the traffic bounces off the concrete walls and roars in my ears. I feel like screaming into the noise, letting everything out until I'm purged of all emotion, stripped back to the bare truth in my bones. The truth that says I've wanted my own kids for so long and I can hardly bear to face the fact I may not get to have them. I'm breathless as I watch the pinprick of light expanding, bigger and bigger, until it envelops us and we're out the other side.

'You do,' she says. 'You've been undermining me the whole time. You think I haven't noticed? Of course I have! You want the children to think you're better than me. So you bake special cakes and make sure you give them endless bedtime stories and come up with these amazing party decorations and let them watch television when you know I'd say no. I've seen you, and I've put up with it because I have to, because we can't find anyone else to replace you at such short notice. But don't think I haven't noticed. Don't think I'm happy about it.'

'I haven't,' I say. 'I didn't do that to—'

She cuts me off. 'Yes, you did.' We're driving past Villeneuve now, entering the Rhône Valley with its apricot orchards on the plains and vineyards creeping up the slopes. Aren't there any cameras along here? Or maybe she's so rich she doesn't care about getting a speeding ticket.

'And another thing.' She looks at me again. I look ahead, willing her to keep her eyes on the road. 'I know that you've been ... what's the word ...' She makes a winding motion with one hand as she searches for it, then slams it down on the steering wheel. 'Spying. You've been spying in our bedroom. I found the necklace, Jess, and I know it was you. Neither Maria nor Michel would break it and not tell me. And the kids don't have the skills to glue it back together so well. So it must have been you. *Putain,* Jess, what were you doing in there?'

I'm tempted to deny everything, to make out she's crazy, she's accusing me unfairly. But I realise, with a shock, that it's a relief she knows. I've been holding my breath for weeks, and now I can breathe out.

'Okay,' I say. 'I did snoop. I shouldn't have, but I did. The necklace was an accident. I'm sorry.'

'But why? Just because you could? Why were you looking in our bedroom?'

And with that release of breath comes six weeks of confusion and anger and heartache and love for Léa and sadness at my impending divorce and despair at my own fucked-up life that's turning out nothing like I expected. It rises up in me like a hairball in my throat that I have to cough out.

'Because you're so lucky,' I say, my voice strangled. 'You're so bloody lucky and you don't seem to appreciate it. You have a great husband, two adorable children who love you and want to be with you, an amazing career, and you're living in this idyllic place. You have everything I want, and yet you're never there. You're never bloody there. And I couldn't help it, maybe at first I wanted to ... find something out that would make you not so fucking perfect.' I laugh. 'But the thing is, I couldn't find anything. You've got perfect clothes and perfect hair and perfect wedding photos and a perfectly clean bloody house. Your life is amazing and mine ...' My voice breaks and I gulp back a knot in my throat. My eyes are blurred and I can't see the road clearly anymore. 'My life is an utter mess right now,' I eventually manage, 'and I guess I just wanted some of your perfection to rub off on me.'

I wipe my eyes, feeling humiliation wash over me. I've fucked all this up. My new start, my Swiss cure, I've ruined it.

She indicates and pulls into a service station that has a big picture of a St Bernard dog smiling out at us. I glare at it. She turns off the engine and faces me. 'I'm not perfect,' she says, and I hear her voice waver. 'You *have* found that out. I'm terrible at motherhood. I can't bear children's parties, even if it's for my own kids. I get bored reading them stories for longer than five minutes. I can't bake a cake even from ready mix. The house is only so clean because we have Maria. There's no way I could do all the housework on top of my job and Michel doesn't even try.' She shakes her head. 'And Michel and I fight all the time at the moment. Not helped by the fact he thinks you're so amazing.' She laughs. 'I'm jealous of *you*.'

I look at her in surprise. 'What?'

'I'm jealous because you're so good with the kids. Léa adores you. Michel keeps telling me how you've got your priorities right by having a career break and some time abroad. He wants us to do that, keeps telling me we should travel with the kids, while they're young. But I can't think of anything worse. I think it would drive me crazy to be with them 24/7. Yes, it's a busy time at work but it's not just that. I *need* it, Jess. I need to work. I need to be out of the house during the day, because being a mother is not enough. I had children because Michel wanted them, because my friends were having them, because it's what you do. But motherhood bores me, I think. And believe me, I've tried. After Luca was born it didn't make sense for me to continue to work and pay a huge sum for both kids to go to *la garderie*, so after maternity leave – which is only fourteen weeks here – I left my job to stay home with them.' She sighs, gives a small shake of her head. 'I really tried. But I was so bored and frustrated. It made me so miserable to spend my day at playgroups and the park, while my former co-workers were working on such exciting events. I couldn't do it, so after a year, when a similar position at my old company came up, I went back.'

She looks at me.

'Don't misunderstand me, Jess, I love my kids. I love them so much. But I can't do what you do. So yes, I've been jealous.'

I'm so shocked I don't know what to say. All this time I felt so inferior, so small, compared to her. But she was envious of me? My brain flits back to an argument I once heard between Maggie and Mum when I was a teenager: *You don't know how lucky you are to have her.* And Mum, replying, *I do, I do, but that doesn't make it easy.*

Do we always want what we don't have?

'Michel . . .' I pause, not sure if I should say it. 'Michel said you work so hard because you had a tough upbringing,' I say. 'Because your mother struggled.'

Julia shakes her head and lets out a laugh laced with cynicism. 'Did he? Well, Michel likes his theories. But it's simpler than that, Jess. I want to work because I enjoy it, because I want a fulfilling career, just as Michel does. Am I not allowed to want that because I'm the mother?'

I open my mouth to say something, but she cuts me off.

'You know, Michel wouldn't have liked to stay home with the kids full time either, but we never even discussed that because it clearly couldn't be him, financially. And yet when

I want to go back to work, when I *need* to go back to work, to have some sense of purpose in life, just as he does, I'm the one left feeling guilty.'

She shakes her head and I see the stress drawing lines on her face.

'I would have gone back part time, but that wasn't an option. And it's been so hard since then, to earn back the respect I used to have. A co-worker got the promotion that should have been mine, and I've had to work twice as hard as anyone else to prove to my manager that I'm dedicated to this job, that I'm not going to leave the office to rescue my sick child from nursery at an important moment, or worse, become pregnant again.'

We're quiet for a moment and I feel an unfamiliar surge of sympathy for this woman, whose life may be so different to my own but isn't, as I've long assumed, so perfect after all.

'I'm sorry,' I say. 'I'm sorry for snooping and for breaking the necklace and throwing away the package. I've acted terribly. It's not like me. It's no excuse, but I haven't been myself because of ...'

She pinches the bridge of her nose, rubs her eyes, says in a tired voice, 'Because of what?'

And so I tell her why I came to Switzerland. About what happened to Mum and going to give blood with Dad and the subsequent DNA tests and the conversations with the hospital in Lausanne and Maggie telling me that I really needed to just go to Switzerland and figure it out for myself.

'I'm sorry I didn't tell you before. I just couldn't. I could barely believe it myself. And it just all sounds so crazy, you would have probably turfed me out or called a psychiatrist.'

Julia looks utterly shocked. The skin on her forehead is clammy and a piece of hair is stuck to her temple. She shakes her head. 'That's terrible.'

I acknowledge her words with a nod. I feel lightheaded. A bit like I did that day, after donating blood. The tears come fast down my face and I don't wipe them away. I shake with emotion but I don't try and stop; I can't. I just sit there, purging myself of everything I've held on to for so long, until I feel her hand on my shoulder. She reaches over and pulls me into a hug and I cry some more, breathing in her familiar floral scent as she holds me tight.

'I'm so sorry,' she says. 'I'm so sorry for what you've gone through.'

I don't know how long we sit there. But eventually my tears turn into ugly heaving shudders and then subside, and all I'm left with is embarrassment. I've been a madwoman. But she doesn't tell me so. Instead she smiles and says, 'Come on, let's go and get a coffee.'

We get out of the car and walk past the giant beaming dog into the service station. It has red chairs and white plastic tables and Swiss flags strung across the ceiling. I sit down at a table and Julia goes to the self-service area and brings back two coffees.

'I want to help you,' she says. 'Perhaps I can do something. Help you look.'

I pause. She's being so nice to me, after I was so awful.

Where once I wanted to throw my discovery at her, to shatter her life as mine was, now my instinct is to keep it from her, to protect her. But I know I can't. There have been enough lies in the past six weeks.

'I have to tell you something else,' I say. 'When I was in your room, snooping . . .' I don't know how to say it. 'I found a letter.'

Her face hardens but I keep going. I have to get this out now.

'I'm sorry I looked, I really am. But this letter, it was from someone called Anna Meier.' I pause. She looks confused. 'And that's the name of my probable mother. Well, the hospital told me her name was Brigitte Mela, but then someone else told me she'd changed it to Anna Meier, I don't know why. And so I've been thinking . . . I've been wondering . . . I've been *obsessed* with the idea quite frankly, that she is your . . . and you might be . . .'

Julia sits back in her chair. She shakes her head, stares at me. 'I don't know anyone called Anna Meier.'

'You don't? But your maiden name was Meier.'

She shakes her head again, says in a voice you might use to a small child, 'Jess, Meier is one of the most common surnames in Switzerland.'

'Oh.'

'Angela,' Julia says suddenly. 'Could you have misread it? I don't remember any particular letter, but it could be that I kept one from Angela Meier, my aunt.'

I think back. I picture myself in the bedroom sitting on

the duvet, pulling the folder out of the drawer. Did it actually say Anna Meier? No, of course it didn't. Nowhere on that letter did it say Anna. Only A. I knew that, I always knew that, but somewhere in the mess of my injured, hurting head, I'd forgotten I did.

SEPTEMBER 1976

Lausanne, Switzerland

SYLVIA

Sylvia had thought her French was good enough to cope in most situations, but not, as it turned out, in this one. Never had she had the need for medical vocabulary before, and giving birth in a French-speaking city wasn't exactly something she'd anticipated.

'What the hell are they talking about?'

'Something's broken, I think. But I don't really understand medical stuff,' Evelyne said. 'I'm so sorry. I've asked them to go and find someone who speaks English. I know they have some people here who do.'

Sylvia nodded. She was trying to keep calm, despite the shock of the warm blood that had soaked her dress and the pain in her abdomen. She thought of Jim, back home in London, without a clue of what was happening to her here. She saw his face when she told him she was going to Switzerland again, would sneak it in before she turned thirty-six weeks and couldn't fly; how he bit his lip and tried so hard not to say anything. Guilt travelled through her body to the pit of her stomach. She'd call him when she knew more.

'Madame Tallis.' The doctor – she presumed he was a doctor – approached the bed. He looked at her from over the top of his glasses and she was reminded of the haughty glance of her own doctor, Greenham, back in London when she'd asked for an abortion. So long ago. 'Your placenta has likely suffered an abruption. I don't think it's severe, but it may worsen so we should deliver right away, by caesarean section.'

Sylvia shook her head. 'But it's too early.'

'You're thirty-five weeks? Yes, it's a bit early, but the baby is viable and I don't want to risk him going into distress.'

She nodded. 'My husband, he's in England. Can we wait until he gets here?'

'I'm afraid not. We want to prepare you straight away. Nurse Marty will get your husband's number and make a call, but we mustn't delay.'

He asked her to sign something and then left her bedside.

She blew out a long breath. 'This is my fault,' she said to Evelyne.

'What are you talking about? Of course it's not.'

'I haven't taken care of myself, or the baby. I've been too bloody selfish.' She thought of the missed midwife appointments. The travelling. The insatiable desire to pack in everything while she could. 'Maybe this wouldn't have happened if I'd done what I was meant to. If I'd listened to Jim and calmed down a bit.'

'Don't you think like that. These things happen, however careful you are. You don't have to treat yourself with kid gloves just because you're pregnant. My friend Fabienne was working right up until the day her child was born and the baby was just fine.'

Sylvia smiled, squeezed Evelyne's hand. 'Thank you.'

She looked down at her belly. Soon, the baby would be here. A living, breathing little person. She wasn't ready. She still had her regulars to write and the golden oldies column to do for next week's paper and this big feature to get in the bag before Diane stepped so competently into her shoes. This wasn't meant to be happening yet, it wasn't meant to be happening at all, and she didn't know how in hell she was going to cope when it did. But she knew she couldn't pretend any longer.

The time had come. She was going to be a mother.

Sylvia was being wheeled down the corridor in a bed, Evelyne at her side, when they saw her.

'Anna?' Evelyne said.

She was lying on a bed in a large ward, one hand on her stomach, her face wet with tears.

'Please stop,' Sylvia asked the nurse pushing her. 'What's she doing here?' she said to Evelyne.

'I don't know.' She left Sylvia's side and went to Anna.

'She said her name was Brigitte,' the nurse said, and Sylvia felt her stomach lurch. Brigitte. Anna's pseudonym, to avoid the authorities knowing who she was. Sylvia realised then, that whatever had happened to bring Anna to the hospital, it wasn't her intention. Evelyne had told her she planned to have the baby at home in that tiny flat, on her own, despite she and Daniel imploring her not to. But it was true they had no health insurance, no money to pay hospital bills, and Anna was so scared of being found that she'd refused to countenance hospital. So to be here now, Sylvia realised, something serious must have happened – and Anna must be petrified.

'Yes, her name is Brigitte,' Sylvia said to the nurse. 'But her friends call her by her middle name.'

Evelyne walked back over to Sylvia, tension in her face. 'After we left her flat, she went out to get some groceries and was knocked down by a car – on a pedestrian crossing, for God's sake.'

Sylvia felt the colour drain from her face. 'What? Is she okay?'

'The car wasn't going fast but she fell – and some passer-by called an ambulance. Apparently she's okay, but the accident has triggered labour.'

Sylvia looked over at Anna and the younger girl met her eyes, fear evident in her expression. Sylvia smiled, trying to convey her sympathy. She hoped that seeing her here too would bring her some comfort. It suddenly seemed right that they'd be going through this together, on the same day. Ever since they'd met, she'd felt some connection to the girl,

331

despite their vastly different experiences, so perhaps Sylvia was meant to be here today, giving birth in Switzerland. She was almost glad, if it could bring some reassurance to Anna.

'Does Daniel know?'

Evelyne shook her head. 'I'll call him, but he's working – and they need the money, I doubt he can leave his shift.'

'Stay with her,' Sylvia said. 'I'll be okay. Just stay with her – she needs someone.'

Evelyne nodded, squeezed her hand. 'Okay. Good luck.'

'Do you want some music?'

'I'm sorry?'

'Music. You can choose from what we have.' The obstetrician pointed to a record player in the corner of the operating theatre. 'It's nice to have some music playing while we operate, and we like to ask the mothers to choose. What do we have today, Amélie?'

The nurse flicked through the stack of records and read out names. 'Jacques Brel, Johnny Hallyday. Or how about Abba – *Mamma Mia*!' She laughed and Sylvia couldn't help but respond in kind. This was surreal. How did she come to be giving birth to her child in a Swiss hospital? Her baby wouldn't be Swiss – she knew the country's citizenship laws didn't provide for that – but it would be born on Swiss soil. Because she persuaded Roger to send her here. Because she met Anna. Because – she'd finally worked out – the pill must have failed when she'd had food poisoning after a meal at a Chinese restaurant in January.

'Do you have any Elton John?' she said, thinking of that hot summer's day in Hyde Park, Jim's smile, his eagerness to have her back.

Whatever it takes to make this work, he'd said. *We can make this okay, Syl. We can make this a wonderful thing.*

She hoped he was right.

'Lie on your left side please,' said the anaesthetist, and she winced in pain as the sharp jab of a needle in her spine took her breath away. A rush of fear flooded her veins along with the anaesthetic, worst-case scenarios running through her head.

What if it wasn't okay? As she lay back on the bed and a screen was placed in front of her face, her thoughts drifted back to Anna. She wished she was here beside her, that she could reach out and take the girl's hand, tell her that she was scared too.

She heard the angry cry just before the baby was held aloft by the surgeon.

'Congratulations, you have a baby daughter.'

The nurse wrapped the child in a white towel and placed her in an incubator and wheeled it to Sylvia. She gasped when she saw this creature, this miniature person she had grown inside her, and reached over and touched the child's tiny red fingers.

'Hello you,' she said, and then, more to make herself realise it than for the baby's sake: 'I'm your mother.'

AUGUST 2016

Montreux, Switzerland

JESS

I never made it to the exhibition.

Michel's questioning eyebrows don't get a response when we get back to the house. Julia says something to him quietly before taking my arm and leading me into the garden.

'*On y va, les enfants!*' Michel claps his hands, and I figure she's told him to take them out somewhere.

I sit down on a garden chair and Julia stands looking at me, hands on her hips. She's always appeared so sorted, so composed, it's strange to see her looking confused and lost. It makes her seem more human somehow, more like me.

'I don't know what to do now,' she says.

'Me neither.'

'We need a drink.'

She disappears into the house and returns with a bottle of

wine and two glasses and a photo in a frame that, I remember with a jolt to my stomach, I'd seen sitting on the chest of drawers in her bedroom during one of my snooping episodes. It's a photo of two women, probably not a lot older than I am now, sitting on a park bench by a lake eating ice cream. Looking at the clothes and hairstyles, I'd put it at mid-nineties.

'This is Karin, my mother,' she points to the woman on the left, in a long red skirt, gold hoop earrings visible beneath her voluminous mass of curly brown hair. 'And this,' she moves her finger, 'is Angela, my aunt.'

I take the photo from her and stare at their faces. What strikes me most is the joy they exude. Both women are smiling, relaxed, happy, their natural closeness obvious.

'You've never mentioned your family.'

'Mum died ten years ago. She didn't have a very easy life. And I never really knew my father. He left when I was little.' She takes the photo from me and looks at it. 'So I like this photo, because it reminds me that she did have some happiness, some good times.'

'I'm sorry she's gone.'

She nods, gives me a small smile. 'I know you are.'

I look at her with new eyes. All the assumptions I've made about her have dissolved into nothing and I realise I've never known her at all. And while she may not be my parents' child, the other daughter, we have more in common than I took the time to see.

'You know, when I first arrived here, Léa told me you'd said to her she could achieve anything she wanted in life if she put her mind to it. It's stuck with me because that's exactly what my mother always said to me.'

Julia smiles. 'She sounds like a wise woman.'

'But it's not always true, though, is it? I thought it was, growing up. I saw Mum, a successful journalist, just as Dad was, and I thought I could make whatever life I wanted, like she had. I thought I'd become a respected teacher, find a lovely husband, have a couple of kids. But here I am, with none of that right now, and it's been painful to realise that life doesn't always work out as Mum made me believe it could. Sometimes circumstances just work against you.'

I think back to my lowest point, a couple of weeks after Patrick and I split up, the shame and despair of standing in Peacock's office, crying.

If things were different, I could have been going on maternity leave.

If the IVF had worked the first time.

If I hadn't been so overwhelmed by the DNA results that I'd been unable to continue the draining cycle of hormone injections and scans and disappointment.

If Patrick hadn't cheated.

If I hadn't lost my sense of self by walking into that blood donation van.

'I still believe what your mother told you is true,' Julia says. 'Of course, it isn't always easy – and you've been through some hard times. But you can pick yourself up and try again.'

I shrug. 'I don't know where to go from here.'

'You have more than you think. You have your health, and

that's so important. It sounds like you're close to your father, which is something I never had. And you *are* a respected teacher – you've made a huge impact on my children and for that I'm very grateful, however ... *envious* I may have been of that.'

I blink to fight back the emotion prickling my eyes. Maybe she's right; I can forge a new future, a good future, even if it isn't the one I always thought I'd have. But first I need to get past what's holding me back. 'If you'd found out what I have, would you want to meet them?' I say.

Julia sighs. 'I can't imagine what it must feel like, Jess. So I don't know. I think you can only do what feels right to you. But I do think meeting them might be the first step in your new start, don't you agree?'

My phone pings but I leave it in my bag.

'I felt paralysed, you know, when I went to Reichenbach. I felt paralysed when I saw him. I was staring at the person who might be my real father and I couldn't do it.'

'Maybe it wasn't the right time. But it doesn't mean you'll always feel like that. I can come with you, if you want. Or I could talk to him beforehand, be your mediator.'

'You'd do that?'

'Yes.' She reaches forward and puts her hand on my arm. 'We have to help each other now, not be jealous. We've both had everything all wrong.'

And just like that I know she's on my side.

'Back in a minute.' She gets up and heads inside, presumably for the toilet. I look out towards the lake where a boat is sliding into port. It reminds me of when I first arrived here, of my mission to discover the truth and my need for a Swiss cure. So far I've failed on the first count, but perhaps, now, after today's cathartic unburdening, I might be able to succeed on the second.

I remember my phone and fish it out of my bag to read whatever message was sent. My heart lurches when I see the email.

<From: d.buchs99@swisscom.ch>

Dear Jessica,

    I'm sorry for my long silence. I knew that one day this could happen, but for many years I haven't decided how I would deal with it. I would like to meet you. I think that, perhaps, you have already seen me, one day in Reichenbach. Something made me think it was you there, outside my house. But first you have to meet someone else. Anna must explain what happened in Lausanne in 1976. It is her story to tell. I hope, after that, you will still want to meet me. She lives in Germany now with her husband. Her number is . . .

'Jess? What's wrong?' Julia's face is creased in concern when she comes back into the garden. I hand her my phone. She reads the message and looks at me.

'You've found her.'

I nod. My body is shaking, like I'm low on blood sugar. I raise my glass, feel the dry, cold wine slip down my throat.

'Are you going to call her?'

'I can't.'

'Then I will. If you want me to, I'll call her right now.'

I breathe out a long breath. Do I want that? She takes my hand, squeezes it. 'That's what you came here for, *n'est-ce pas?*'

I nod. Julia takes a last, hard look at me, punches the number into her mobile and goes into the living room. There's a pause, and then I hear her voice, speaking German. I fixate on a sailboat on the lake and try not to think about what she might be saying, what Anna might be telling her in response. I just look at the sailboat as it moves slowly through a dark patch on the water, blown by the light wind, and wonder where life's going to take me now. It's ten minutes before Julia finally comes back into the garden. She stands in the doorway and I see tears in her eyes.

'Does she want to meet me?' I say.

She nods.

SEPTEMBER 1976

Lausanne, Switzerland

SYLVIA

They looked so similar. That's what struck her. Both hairless, wrinkled, red-faced bundles. Both with several days in an incubator ahead of them. Both so tiny; little hands curled into small fists, as though they were spoiling for a fight. She supposed they were. Fighting to get out of there.

'She'll be okay, you know,' Sylvia said, even though she knew Anna couldn't understand. A nurse had brought her to the nursery in a wheelchair, just hours after the operation that had made her feel like she'd been run over by a truck, and there she found Anna, staring at her daughter. Sylvia's own baby – as yet unnamed, she was waiting for Jim – was in the incubator next to Anna's, and the two little girls could have been twins, so alike they looked. They even lay in the same pose – tiny arms flung above their heads. She supposed all babies looked the same at this age. Only the ankle tags said whose baby was whose. *Bébé Mela, Bébé Tallis.*

Sylvia squeezed Anna's hand and the girl looked at her, tears filling her eyes. She seemed traumatised, perhaps by the natural birth that Sylvia felt quietly lucky to have escaped, despite the pain she bore now, perhaps overwhelmed by the reality of having a baby, of the task ahead of her. Sylvia thought back to the day they met, of the hope and excitement she'd seen in Anna's face, and her words during the interview, the love she was ready to give – but that all seemed to have vanished. Instead she saw simply a very young, very scared 16-year-old, daunted by what she'd done.

It felt like their roles had reversed, because for the first time since she'd found out she was pregnant, Sylvia felt calm, contented. She'd never much cared for other people's babies. Didn't know how to handle them. Didn't know what to do when they cried. Didn't understand their wordless communication. But when she'd seen her daughter for the first time a few hours earlier, and when she looked now at this little being, fresh out of the box, she didn't feel fear; she felt, to her considerable relief, only love.

How? That, she didn't know. Had it been there all along, waiting for this child to arrive, or was it a chemical reaction born of the fact that she shared her genes with this little body, that an invisible line connected them?

After months of anxiety and fear, a calmness had descended upon her. She loved her child. Maybe that meant she wouldn't be a terrible mother, maybe she wouldn't turn bitter with resentment. Maybe, in fact, there was a chance things wouldn't turn out as badly as she'd feared.

Neither Daniel nor Jim was here. Jim was on his way, Sylvia knew, the nurse having spoken to him on the phone just after the surgery. Upset to have missed the birth, worried about both of them, he was on the next plane out. Daniel, Evelyne had told her, had turned up briefly after his shift at the construction site, when Anna was in labour, but had to leave again for the bakery and wasn't there for the birth. Sylvia couldn't help but worry for them. Would they have enough? Would Daniel handle his heavy workload? Would Anna cope with motherhood, all alone in that dingy flat? She wondered what was going through the girl's mind now – whether thinking about all that was the reason she looked so miserable.

She supposed she wouldn't see Anna again, once she'd taken her baby home to London, and the thought pained her. She'd write regularly to Evelyne, find out how she was doing. She and Anna had shared a profound experience in their lives that had led to a new beginning for both of them, but what directions would their lives take now – and the lives of these small beings in front of them? Two babies, born in the same place, at nearly the same time, but in all likelihood with such different experiences ahead. She hoped life would work out well for both girls, whatever it threw at them.

She squeezed Anna's hand again, took a last look at her child and asked the nurse to wheel her back to her bed, leaving Anna alone in the room, quiet but for the beeps of the monitors and the occasional little sigh or almost-cry from the two newly minted bodies in the incubators.

When Jim finally arrived, bursting through the door to the ward like a building was on fire, Sylvia was half asleep, drifting in and out of vivid dreams the nurse said were probably caused by the painkillers. She forced herself awake to greet his anxious face and the million questions he'd clearly accumulated in his head during the hours he'd spent getting there. He wheeled her down the corridor to the nursery, and her heart swelled with pride on witnessing the look on his face when he saw his daughter for the first time. She felt teary then and fought back her emotion, not yet ready to admit to Jim how fiercely important it now felt to have this child in their lives, this child she hadn't even thought she wanted.

'Did you call Roger?'

Jim nodded, but didn't take his eyes off the baby in the incubator. Jessica, that's what they would call her. Jessica Tallis-Millson. A rather grand name, Sylvia thought. A name with prospects. A name suitable for a CEO or an editor or a professor or whatever heady heights her daughter wanted to reach in life.

'I did, and I gave him a piece of my mind while I was at it, for agreeing to your crazy idea to come out here again, at your stage.'

'I didn't exactly give him a lot of choice.'

'That's what he said.' He dragged his gaze away from Jessica and smiled, kissing her on the top of her head. 'Well, it's done now, and you're okay. You're both okay. My girls.' He grinned. 'Just look at her – she's gorgeous!'

Sylvia had to agree, though she wondered if all parents thought that, in awe as they surely were at this magic trick they had performed, conjuring new life like a rabbit out of a hat. She couldn't yet say whether the baby looked anything like her or Jim. She seemed too small, too delicate, too young for any characteristics to be evident on her face. Sylvia supposed that would come later.

'I'll go to the embassy in Bern tomorrow and try to get the paperwork sorted. Then whenever she's ready to be discharged, we can head home.'

Sylvia nodded. Jessica was healthy, the doctors said, despite her tiny size. If all went well, by the end of the week she should be able to come out of the incubator and they could take her home. Sylvia couldn't wait to be back in London, to introduce Jessica to her city, to settle her into the flat, for their lives as a trio to start properly. Nerves fluttered in her chest. Would this initial euphoria last? Would it compensate for missing out on the adrenaline highs her work gave her? Shell-shocked from the operation, woozy with tiredness and painkillers, flooded with love for this little person, she'd hardly thought about work these last few hours. Yet Jim's arrival had reminded her of home, of London, of their life together, and she felt growing frustration at the way in which her workflow had been so abruptly interrupted. Anna's interview notes were still in her handbag. She'd had to abandon her plans to search for Anna's sister and do more research about the Swiss care system – she didn't even know if she had enough to write a decent piece. But when she looked at that little face, at her daughter's flawless skin and tiny fingers, the frustration eased a little.

'Look at that,' Jim said. 'She's got a tiny freckle on her left foot, third toe in.'

Sylvia peered at her daughter's squirming foot, poking out of the blanket she had just kicked off, and saw the little brown mark, as small as a pinprick. She hadn't noticed it before, and it momentarily surprised her that she didn't already know every inch of the body she had herself created. But then Jessica was so new to this world, so freshly made, and Sylvia so overwhelmed, that she supposed it wasn't surprising at all. She'd only held her daughter once, briefly, before the nurse said she had to go back in the incubator and presented her with a breast pump in exchange.

'We've got so much to discover about her,' Jim said. 'What colour will her hair be? How tall will she be? Will she have a good singing voice?'

'That's doubtful, judging by the two of us.'

'Will she be good at sports? Will she want to follow us into journalism? Will she like Marmite? I want to know everything.'

Sylvia took his hand and leaned into him, gazing at the incubator. 'You will. We have a lifetime to find out.'

He smiled at her. 'I can't wait.'

They kissed her, Jessica Tallis-Millson, and headed out of the room, past the other babies in their cribs, their tiny warm breaths mingling in the air as one.

AUGUST 2016

Montreux/Lutry, Switzerland

JESS

From <maggie.hartwell@gmail.com>

Jess, you've found her! After all this time, after
everything that's happened. I'm so pleased
for you, darling. Will you meet her? I hope so. I
think you need to.

   You know, this whole journey of yours
has brought back a lot of memories for me. I
remember so clearly when I first saw you as a
baby. You were so beautiful, so tiny, and I felt
such love for you right from the moment I met
you. And you know, I can't imagine you not
being part of my life all these years. It makes
me feel quite ill to think that, if the hospital

hadn't got things so wrong, I wouldn't have had you in my life. It's brought me such joy to see you grow up as you have, I've felt so proud to have you as my goddaughter.

I can't imagine what you must be feeling right now, at the prospect of finally meeting Anna. From what Daniel said in his email, I presume she must already know you're hers. Why? For how long? How did she find out? Did she try to find you? I'm sure you have all these questions churning around in your head – and you deserve the answers, Jess, you really do. I hope you get them – and that it brings you the peace you need.

If you decide to meet her, just remember that we are all there with you in spirit – me, your dad, and your mum – we're there holding your hand in this. We're your family, darling, whatever happens.

Now, tell me more about this Jorge chap . . .

'Are you going to meet her?'

We're sitting on rocks on the lakeshore, holding drinks from a pop-up bar that seems way too cool for elegant, posh Montreux.

I nod. 'Julia said Anna will come to Switzerland next week, wants to meet me in Lutry, where she says she used to go sometimes, back when she lived around here.' I still don't know if I want to. I don't know how I feel about any of this anymore. But I know I have to go through with it. I have to end this somehow. I need to know how, and why, I came to live someone else's life. Tears prick the backs of my eyes and, to my embarrassment, I can't suppress a loud, ugly sniffle.

Jorge looks at me. 'Come here.' He puts his arm around my shoulders and pulls me in to him. I smell a mixture of sweat and suncream and musky man-ness. It's comforting. Warm. Lovely. If only I could just stay like this, and not have to face up to everything I've done, everything that's been done to me.

'It feels like a betrayal.'

'What do you mean?'

'Of my parents. Of Mum, especially. She didn't know. She thought I was her daughter, through and through. And now it's like I'm looking to replace her with this new mother. I can't bear to think that she might think . . . I can't . . .'

He squeezes my shoulder. 'You know it's not like that. You're never going to feel any differently about your mum. Nothing that comes in the future can take away what happened in the years you had with her.'

I sniff, nod. I know that's true. But what I can't ever know is how *she* would feel if she knew what I now know: that I wasn't her real daughter. Would she love *me* less? And does Dad, now? Can he, in his heart of hearts, think of me in the same way as he did before?

'I haven't told Dad I've found them,' I say. 'But I have to meet her, don't I? I can't just walk away from this now.'

He nods. 'Even if you just meet her once. Then you can move on, knowing what happened. Closure, that's what they say in America, right?'

'Closure.' I ponder the word. A few years ago there was nothing to close. I knew who I was – or at least, I thought I did. It feels so long ago now. So much has changed. I take my head off his shoulder and sit up, looking out at two paddleboarders drifting past us on the placid lake. 'I wonder where I'd be now, if Dad and I hadn't stumbled across that blood donation van. I wouldn't be here, that's for sure. Still in London, I guess. Still married. Still in my job.'

Jorge looks at me, a smile tugging at his lips. 'Sounds fucking boring to me.'

I smile back, meeting his eyes with my own. I see that he cares, he really cares, and it feels good. 'I guess it does,' I say.

I arrive early in Lutry on the day I'm due to meet her and I don't know what to do with myself. I walk down the curve of the lake wall towards a bench in the shade, a short distance from the spot where Anna told Julia she wanted to meet me. It's a baking hot day, but I think I'm sweating more from nerves than from the heat. I can feel the damp under my arms, even in this sundress, which is the lightest thing I own. It's white with tiny red flowers and I got it on a shopping trip with Mum, five or six years ago.

Go on, I'll treat you.

I want to look nice today. I want Anna to think well of

me. I don't want her to be disappointed in how I've turned out. But I also need to subliminally state my connection to Mum, to show, in some small, unspoken, sartorial way, that she's still with me, she's still my mother and I'm still her daughter. Wearing this dress satisfies both of those needs.

I look at my watch. Ten to midday. I glance down the promenade. It's fairly busy. It's a Saturday lunchtime, so the restaurant terraces are full. Couples and their kids are strolling by the lake, ice creams in hands; some people are swimming in the water, or sunbathing on the grass down the end of the promenade, under willow trees. It's like any other day, for them. But for me it's a threshold, a turning point. However, unlike the other one, back in London with Dad when we went to give blood, this one I'm walking into with my eyes open. I know what I'm doing – even though I don't know if I want to do it.

I didn't think I'd recognise her. But when I see her, I know her instantly. She's standing by the wall near the cafe. She's wearing a mid-length navy skirt and a white sleeveless shirt, with flat red sandals. Her eyes are covered by large tortoise-shell sunglasses and she's carrying a small red leather handbag over one shoulder that she keeps hoisting up, as though it's heavy, but it's so small that I doubt it. She's nervous, that's what it is. The realisation relieves my own nerves a little.

I stand up. Smooth down my dress. Take a sip of water from the bottle I'm carrying, hoping it will settle my troubled stomach. I think of Mum, the last time I saw her, just before her trip to Turkey.

See you soon, darling. Don't do anything I wouldn't do!

Would you do this, Mum? I think now. Are you okay with me doing this? I wish I had her blessing. I wish she could tell me that it's okay to meet the woman who gave birth to me. I debate turning around and walking to the train station and going back to Julia's. I could pack my things and be out of there that afternoon. A short flight and I could be with Dad, back trying to pretend this whole thing didn't happen. I take another sip of water and it's while I'm tightening the cap on the bottle that she looks directly at me and then I know the decision has been made for me.

She takes a step forward, then stops. Takes her sunglasses off. I stand up and walk towards her, my legs shaking so much I don't know if I can actually cover the thirty metres to where she's standing. I stop in front of her and then I don't know what to say.

'Jessica?'

I nod. Her hand goes to her mouth and I see her eyes crease. 'Hello,' she says in English. 'Hello, Jessica.'

I don't know what to do. Whether to hug her, or kiss her three times in the Swiss way. In the end I stick out my hand in what seems like an absurdly formal manner given our relationship. But then again, she's a complete stranger to me. 'Hello,' I say, and she takes my proffered hand in both of hers and squeezes it. I pull it away after a moment.

'*Sehr schön,*' she says, as though to herself. Her eyes look watery. They're my eyes, I realise. My colour. Or mine are her colour. Her face shape is mine, too. An oval, with a sweetheart hairline. Her hair is darker than mine, but it's surely dyed.

This is my mother.

I'd always just dismissed the fact I didn't look especially like either of my parents. Shrugged it off. It was what it was. But now, here, is evidence that in fact I do.

'Did you have a good journey?' I say it only to say something, and once it's out there it seems ridiculous. I'm meeting my long-lost mother for the very first time and I'm spouting small talk. She smiles, doesn't take her eyes off me and I think perhaps she hasn't understood. 'I'm sorry, I don't speak German,' I add. 'Uh, I mean, Julia said you can speak English?'

My words seem to snap her out of her thoughts. 'Yes, yes, I have learnt it for you,' she says, her accent a singsong.

I cock my head, confused. 'We only just met.'

'I mean, I've been learning it for forty years because I knew you were growing up in England and I hoped ... I wished ... I would meet you one day.'

My stomach twists. She knew. She knew where I was the whole time. I feel hot, too hot, as though I might faint. She takes my arm and leads me to the lake wall and nods for me to sit. I can't keep my eyes off her face.

'I used to come here all the time,' she says. 'I'd bring the pram and walk along the lake and sit at the end on a picnic blanket.' She turns to me, takes my hand again. 'I don't know where to start.'

I take a long breath, trying to calm my racing pulse. 'How

about with how you knew? How did you find out I'd been swapped with another child? I mean, that must be what happened, right? When did you find out? And if you knew the hospital had made such a terrible mistake, why didn't you do something about it?'

She looks down at her lap and I see her hands are shaking. A family walks past us with a toddler pushing a plastic buggy, which she rams into my foot. The mother apologises and ushers her child away with stern words, but I barely look at her. My eyes are on Anna, willing her to speak. I need to know, right now. I need this story out.

'You have to understand, I was only sixteen when I had you.' She looks up at me. 'I should never have been pregnant at that age. We had no money. I rarely saw Daniel in those first few months when we arrived in Lausanne because he was working all the time to support us. I was so alone, and after being so happy I'd left the farm I was living on, I became very scared.'

'Of what?'

'Everything. Scared the authorities would find out I was an unmarried sixteen-year-old and take the baby away from me, put it in some horrible institution or with some family that wouldn't love her. And I was scared that, even if they didn't, I wouldn't be able to give you a good life. I didn't want you to end up like me.'

My head feels light, fuzzy. My brain is trying to grasp something, but it's just out of reach, languishing in the fuzz.

'And then there was Sylvia. She was older than me, and

354

I thought she was so chic and sophisticated and intelligent, with a career and prospects and a husband with the same. I was completely in awe of her. And when she interviewed me—'

'Wait, you actually met Mum? She interviewed you?' I'm struggling to keep up with this succession of facts that are revelatory to me.

Anna nodded. 'Yes, for an article about my time at the farm. Daniel's parents' farm. I'd lived there since I was eight, when the authorities took me away from my mother and sister and sent me to live there. I worked like a dog, and they gave me no love, little kindness.' She shakes her head and something pricks at the back of my mind.

The television news. A lawyer and a distinguished older woman with tears in her eyes. What had Michel said? Something about children taken from their families and sent to work on farms. Abuse. Neglect. Government apologies.

'Sylvia seemed very interested in what had happened to me. I didn't know why, back then,' Anna continues. 'I thought I was just unlucky in the life I'd had. I didn't know it had happened to thousands of other children, too, that it was a systematic failure. I didn't know the government would later apologise for a system that took us from our homes and deemed my mother and others like her to be unsuitable parents.' She breathes out a short, sharp breath and looks down at her feet. 'What a thing to say! My mother loved me and my sister, even if she couldn't always provide for us. She wasn't unsuitable, she was just alone, and poor, and unhappy. It wasn't acceptable to be divorced in a small community in the 1960s, so everyone looked down on her. Mum had no family in the area, no one to support her, so she got a job, but people said she was neglecting Cornelia and me for going to work – there weren't many childcare options in those days – and then rumours started about Mum and a local man. They said she was living a "loose life", and that's why she lost her job – and then us. Instead of trying to help her, the authorities took her children from her and left us in a place far, far worse than the home we'd left. And they never came to check we were okay, they never seemed to care what happened to us.' She shakes her head. 'Society was completely against women like my mother, women who didn't behave as they wanted.' She sighs. 'But then people are good at making bad decisions, I certainly know that.'

'What do you mean?' I'm completely lost, desperate for clarity and trying to process everything she's said, like my brain's two steps behind her, struggling to catch up.

She waves her hand as if to brush away my question, and I see she's going to have to do this in her own time. 'Sylvia – your mother,' she says, faltering on the last word, 'heard about my background from Evelyne, Daniel's sister, and she wanted to write an article for her newspaper. I think she saw it as a . . . what do you say?'

'A scoop.' I've always known the story of my birth. That Mum was in Switzerland on a commission for her paper and gave birth prematurely in a hospital in Lausanne. But I never knew – or at least, I never thought to ask – what the article was about. I just assumed it was a follow- up to her first piece, the one I retrieved from the paper's online archive, and that it never actually got written. It blows my mind to think it was about Anna, about my biological mother. They actually met. They spoke. And they parted with the wrong babies.

'And then when we happened to give birth at the same time, in the same hospital, it felt like fate, I suppose.'

'Fate?'

She looks at me and I see tears running down her face. 'I've been so worried,' she says.

'About what?' I don't think I want to know. Dread is thumping in my chest.

'Worried that you'll hate me when you find out . . .'

I take a breath. 'Find out what?

'That it was me. That I swapped you with Sylvia's baby.'

SEPTEMBER 1976

Lausanne, Switzerland

SYLVIA

She heard the cries before she saw they were coming from Anna. The sound she was making was animalistic, as though generated by her very soul. Sylvia walked as quickly as her day-old wound would allow and turned the corner to see Anna, hands on the glass wall of the nursery, Evelyne by her side.

Sylvia reached them and put her hand on Anna's shoulder as the girl's legs seemed to give way and she collapsed to the floor. Sylvia looked through the glass into the nursery and saw only one baby instead of two in the row both their daughters had been in, and her stomach dropped.

'What's happened? Where's Anna's baby?' she said to Evelyne.

Evelyne put a hand out, a steadying gesture. 'It's okay. It's not what you think. She's been transferred to intensive care because she's got a mild respiratory infection, but it's just a precaution because she's premature. The doctors have assured me the baby's going to be just fine. I keep telling her, but she won't listen.' She looked at Anna, as though she didn't know what to do with her.

Sylvia crouched down and put a hand on Anna's arm. The girl looked up and the expression Sylvia saw there was desperate. 'She's going to be fine,' Sylvia said. 'I know it. They'll both be okay, these babies of ours.' She squeezed Anna's arm, as though to impart some of the strength she felt, some of the faith she had in their futures, such a new feeling she almost didn't know what to do with it.

Uncomprehending, Anna looked into her face as if she was searching for something, but Sylvia didn't know what. Help? Reassurance? Anna put her hand on hers and said something in German. It was a rare word Sylvia recognised, but she thought she'd misheard because she didn't understand why Anna would say it.

'What did she say?' She looked up at Evelyne, who shrugged, bewildered.

'She said "I'm sorry". But I have no idea what for.'

Evelyne said something to Anna, but she only shook her head, crying like her heart was breaking.

It took three nurses to persuade her back to her bed.

AUGUST 2016

Lutry, Switzerland

JESS

I don't say anything for a while. It was the last thing I'd been expecting.

'You gave me away.' I can hardly comprehend it. Though I haven't experienced motherhood, I find it hard to believe any mother could do that. But then again, it was forty years ago, when times were different; Anna was sixteen, scared and traumatised.

She nods, puts her hand to her mouth.

'And you took Mum's baby.'

She nods again, looks at me with watery eyes. 'I swapped the ankle tags when you were both in the nursery, just a few hours after you were born. It wasn't planned. I just did it spontaneously, when the nurse stepped out of the room for a moment, and then she came back and it was done, it was

360

too late to change it.' I see tears on her cheeks but I feel my heart harden. I can't go easy on her. I need to understand this. I need to push right to the very end, until I have every tiny detail out of her.

'I get, maybe, that you might have felt unable to care for a child. But you did, anyway. You just cared for the wrong one. Why didn't you just give me up for adoption? Why did you have to steal Mum's baby?'

I wonder, briefly, if passers-by are wondering what I'm doing to make this woman cry, but I don't care. I'm owed this explanation and I will have it.

'I wanted *Sylvia* to have you, only Sylvia. I didn't want to give you up to a stranger who wouldn't care about you, the way my foster parents didn't care about me.'

I'm hearing the words, but my brain is having trouble grasping them.

'I knew Sylvia could give you a better life than anything I could offer you. I know it sounds crazy but somehow, in my young head, it made sense. I would still have a child – and I *so* wanted a child to care for, to stop me feeling alone – but I would know that my own baby, *you*, would be brought up with so many more opportunities, with the privileges that money could offer. I just wanted you to have the best life possible, everything I didn't have. And perhaps also . . .'

'What?' I say. 'What?'

'Perhaps a small part of me thought if the authorities found out I was sixteen and unmarried and took Sylvia's baby away from me it wouldn't hurt as much as if they took you.'

361

She hangs her head and I hear her almost whisper, 'I can't believe I felt that about her.'

I shake my head. I can't process this. 'So you loved me, but you gave me away anyway?'

Her face crumples. 'Yes,' she whispers. 'Yes. I gave you away *because* I loved you. Everything I did was done out of love. I loved you so much I thought my heart would break. And I regretted my decision almost as soon as I did it. I even went to try and swap you back, but Sylvia's baby had been transferred to another ward and you weren't next to her anymore so I couldn't, it was too late. I will never forget that feeling; I have never felt such despair.'

She pauses, but I wait for her to go on. She knows I need to know every little detail of this.

'And I couldn't just confess what I'd done. I was scared I'd lose both babies and end up with nothing. I thought I'd go to jail, and my baby would be put in some institution, or with a family that didn't love her, and then history would repeat itself. I couldn't, I just couldn't.'

She breaks off and wipes her eyes. She opens her handbag with shaking fingers and takes out a tissue. I watch her blow her nose, I see how her eyes – her eyes like mine – are red from crying and her face is blotchy.

'I'm sorry you went through all that,' I say finally, and she looks up.

'You don't hate me?'

Part of me wants to hate her. More for my parents than for me. She stole their child. But I can't. For whatever reason,

I've had the life I've had. And, I realise, with sudden clarity, that despite everything I've been through, I'm glad I've lived this life. All the pain and heartbreak and grief and sense of failure of the past few years don't cancel out the most important thing I've always had, the thing Anna lost – a loving family.

'I can't hate you,' I say, 'because I've had a good life. I had a great childhood and I love my parents more than I can say. And these past four years, losing Mum and then finding out she and Dad weren't my biological parents, they've been gut-wrenchingly painful. But they wouldn't have been so painful if there wasn't so much love to start with. I can't fully understand why you did what you did, but I can't hate you for it, because to hate you would be to hate my whole life, and I can't do that. I won't betray what I've had by wishing you'd never made that decision.'

As I say it, I feel relief rushing through me, lightening the pressure on my chest. I've spent so long feeling sorry for myself, grieving, obsessing over Julia's life and what might have been mine, that I didn't stop to think that I wouldn't want a different life because I wouldn't want to change one iota of my time with my parents. Not Dad's suffocating worry about my studies and my finances. Not Mum's ambition and support and sometimes overbearing drive for me to achieve. Not their fierce arguments about politics and history and household chores that always dissolved into wry smiles and stupid jokes and exasperated laughter. Not our dinner table banter, not Dad's delicious Sunday roasts and Mum's bizarre, but oddly tasty, chicken curries. It was never perfect. But it was mine, and it's made me who I am. And perhaps that's okay. Perhaps being me is just fine.

'I've always loved you,' Anna says. 'I've always thought of you, and I've always loved you.'

'Well then I'm extra lucky,' I say, 'because I've had two mothers loving me.'

SEPTEMBER 1976

Lausanne, Switzerland

SYLVIA

'Anna?'

She and Jim were about to go home. After five days in hospital, Jessica had been given the all clear, so later that day they would start the long journey back to London by train and ferry, given Sylvia couldn't fly so soon after the C-section. Her bags were packed, she'd said goodbye to Evelyne, thanked the nurses. But now here was Anna, crying on her own in front of the mirror in the ladies' room – not the animal cry of a few days ago, but a desperately sad, resigned weeping that tore Sylvia's heart out. She'd thought Anna would be feeling happier now since her baby was due to come out of intensive care later that day. Evelyne had told her she'd be able to go home soon too.

Sylvia walked up to Anna and pulled her into a hug,

absorbing the girl's sobs into her dress, feeling her body shudder. They stood like that for several minutes, Anna's face buried in Sylvia's shoulder, Sylvia regarding them both in the mirror, wondering how someone so clueless as she about motherhood could bring any comfort to someone else.

Gradually, Anna's sobs became less frequent, her shudders eased. She stepped back, and Sylvia wiped the remaining tears from her face. 'It's going to be all right,' she said. 'Daniel and Evelyne will help you. And I know you can do this. You've coped with so much already; you can cope with this too.'

She didn't know if that was true, and she knew Anna hadn't understood a word she was saying, but she hoped something came across in her tone of voice, something that would help her feel brave enough to tackle the road ahead.

'Hedi,' Anna said suddenly, pulling out of Sylvia's arms.

Sylvia cocked her head. 'Your baby?' She made a rocking motion with her arms.

'*Ja.* Hedi. *Meine Tochter.*' My daughter.

They left later that day, Jessica in a painfully expensive new baby carrier Jim had picked up in a Lausanne department store. Sylvia went over to Anna and kissed her goodbye, leaving her with a carrier bag filled with muslin cloths and bottles and nappies.

'Some things I can't carry on the train,' she said. '*Für dich.*'

They walked towards the door, Jim carrying their daughter in a basket. Sylvia turned back and waved, her heart aching to see tears once again streaming down the girl's face. And just like that, they were gone.

AUGUST 2016

Lutry, Switzerland

JESS

We walk in silence towards the other end of the promenade. From time to time Anna glances at me, a tentative smile on her face. Part of me wants to smile back, to pull her into a hug and tell her it's okay, I understand. But the other part of me isn't sure I can, just yet. It's all too much to take in. I'm still trying to process the fact that this is my birth mother, in the flesh, walking beside me. I try to imagine her back then, so young, so scared, so neglected by those who should have cared.

We pass the ice-cream stall at the end of the promenade and walk on past the sailboats in the harbour to the children's playground, where two toddlers are fighting over a swing. I could have played here, with her. She could have pushed me on that swing, while Mum and Dad pushed another little girl in another life that I had instead of her.

'Who is she?' I ask, surprised I haven't already. But then again, there are so many things I need to ask I think it's going to take a lifetime. 'My parents' biological daughter, the baby you brought up?'

Anna pauses, looks at me. 'Hedi,' she says.

Hedi. I swill the name around in my mouth. The name that should have been mine. It's alien to me. I'm not a Hedi.

'She doesn't know,' she says.

I stop on the path.

'We never told her. We decided it was for the best. We didn't want to disrupt her life, didn't want to cause her pain.'

My head spins. '*We?*' I say. 'You mean Daniel knew all along, too?'

'He's known for a long time, but not at first.' She gestures to a bench and we sit down next to each other, looking, I imagine, like any other mother and daughter out for a walk on a sunny late summer afternoon. But I'm aware how young she is to have a thirty-nine-year-old daughter. Her face is plump, with only a few lines around her eyes; her hair is still thick. Sixteen, she was. And here I am pushing forty, having not yet managed to have children. How different our lives have been.

'He didn't know until Hedi was – you *both* were – about twelve.' She shakes her head. 'He loved Hedi – adored her – but as she grew up, things deteriorated between us because he suspected Hedi wasn't his.' She pauses. A hard line has formed between her eyes. 'She didn't look like either of us, you see. And though he wouldn't even have considered she

368

wasn't mine, he thought that I . . . He thought I'd been with another man, perhaps with a seasonal worker at the farm. He even asked if someone had forced himself on me. I wondered if he thought . . .'

'What?'

'It doesn't matter.' She waves her hand briefly, as if brushing away a bad memory. 'You know, it wasn't easy, our life together, back then. We had so much to deal with. For the first few years I was constantly scared the authorities would catch up with me, especially after those unpaid hospital bills, and I was very . . . upset about everything. Now they'd probably give it a name.'

'Depression?'

She nods. 'I think the only thing that got me through that was Hedi, my darling girl. I had to be okay for her.' She looks at me. 'I know what I said, that I thought it wouldn't hurt as much if they took her from me – but I soon realised that wasn't true. I've always loved her as my own and tried to do the very best for her.'

I meet her eyes and see that's true.

'But we did make progress,' she continues. 'Evelyne did what she could to help us financially, and Marta, the widow next door who became my friend, helped us fend off questions from other neighbours. When I was old enough, we got married, and I became a nanny, looking after another woman's child as well as Hedi. Daniel was able to give up the bakery and start veterinary studies at night school. I finally went back to visit the village I grew up in and an old family friend helped me find my sister, Cornelia, who'd returned there after she got out of the terrible detention centre they'd put her in because she'd refused to obey her foster parents. Seeing her again was so wonderful, so healing, even though I never got the chance to see our mother again. She'd died, you see, several years previously.'

She pauses, looks down at the path, and I wait for her to go on.

'But things were okay, I felt I'd got my life on a good path, and I had some hope for the future. Maybe we would have made it through the hard years, Daniel and I, but he kept pressuring me about Hedi, kept pushing and pushing. I always wondered if it was because he regretted it all, regretted breaking contact with his parents and taking on a pregnant girlfriend at such a young age. I don't know,' she sighs. 'But the secret weighed so heavily on me all that time, that in the end I gave in and told him what I did. And then he left.'

I see the tears rolling down her face but I don't go to comfort her. I can't tell her it's all okay, because it isn't, and now I know things haven't been all right for her for a very long time. She's paid for that crazy decision in the hospital.

'But you didn't tell Hedi?'

She shakes her head. 'We agreed it would be best not to – for her, and for us. I was scared of messing up her life – I'd done that once already; I didn't want to do it again. And we were both frightened that if she wanted to find Sylvia, we'd lose her. So we told her we were splitting up because we didn't love each other anymore. Hedi stayed with me, but she's always had a good relationship with her father. He never loved her any less for knowing.'

I remember Daniel's long radio silence, and my intuition that he knew more than he was saying. 'When I contacted him initially, he didn't admit he even knew you. He didn't tell me he knew what I was talking about, even though he must have guessed who I was.'

'He called me,' she said. 'After you emailed him the first time. He called me and said he thought it was you, even though we didn't recognise your surname. Faul-ken-er, is that right?' She stumbles over my surname – Patrick's surname – and I suddenly think how much I now want to change it back, to be Tallis-Millson again, the name my parents gave me.

'My married name,' I say, and she nods.

'But because you asked for Brigitte Mela, we knew it must be you because that's the name I gave to the hospital back then, when I was petrified of bills and social services and the government.' She shakes her head, breathes out a long breath. 'It was the first time we'd spoken about what happened in more than twenty-five years, since we divorced. You can't imagine how it felt to know you were looking for me. I couldn't believe it. But Daniel was scared of opening up all that history, of what it would mean for Hedi.'

'So you won't tell her now? Now I've found you?'

'I don't know. Should we?'

She looks at me as though I can solve her dilemma, but I know I can't. I think of the heartbreak of receiving the DNA test results. The devastation it has wreaked on my life since. It sends shivers through me to think that Hedi still doesn't know. She's the other daughter – and right now she's like me before this all happened. She likely has a boss, possibly a lover, probably friends and colleagues and gym buddies, all of whom help create her sense of self. And there is no reason for her to doubt that self. There's no reason for her to think that everything she has known is not how it was meant to be.

'I can't decide for you,' I say. 'But I won't track her down and tell her, you don't have to worry about that. I won't be the one to inflict that pain on her. That's for you to do, if anyone.'

She nods, takes my hand and smiles though the tears are streaming down her face. '*Merci*,' she says. 'Thank you.'

'Where is she?' I ask suddenly. 'Is she here in Switzerland? Or in Germany?'

Anna shakes her head. 'No,' she says quietly, anxiety in her expression. 'She lives in London.'

My stomach leaps. 'How long?'

'Five years now. She married an Englishman she met at work in Zurich.'

I let out a long breath and look out across the lake towards the mountains sketched lightly against the late summer sky. To think she's been there, all that time. She was breathing the same London air as me when I found out Mum had died, when I went to give blood with Dad eighteen months later, and when I got the DNA results. She was there, shopping on Oxford Street, seeing a show in the West End, commuting to work on the tube. Have I stood next to her? Have I seen her face and not known her?

'She's happy?'

'Yes. She's done well. She has a good job, a nice husband. Their son is three years old now.'

I watch her face as she says it and see she's proud, and a gentle swell of jealousy rolls over me like the wake from a paddle steamer on the lake. But it's not because of the perfect picture of her life that I've just built in my head. It's because Hedi still has her mother here to be proud of her. A mother who clearly loves her so much, even though she's not her biological daughter.

'I'm glad,' I say, and I realise I mean it. I'm glad Hedi has a happy life, that she has parents who love her, just as I've had. I think of Dad, at home, not knowing I'm doing this today. Did he ever suspect, just as Daniel did?

'You said Daniel didn't love Hedi any less when he found out,' I start. I'm scared of what I'm asking.

Anna shakes her head, wipes her eyes.

'Are you sure?' I turn to look at her as tears burn at the back of my skull. 'Because I've been so worried, since I found out, that maybe Dad would . . . love me less now. That maybe Mum wouldn't have . . . if she'd known.' My voice breaks.

Anna squeezes my hand tight and stares at the ground below the bench. I suddenly realise she hasn't told me everything yet, that's there's more to know. 'What?' I say. 'What is it?'

She looks up at me. 'She did,' she says, and my stomach

plunges. 'She still loved you just as much, and so I know your father will too.'

'How do you know?' I whisper.

'Because she knew. I told Sylvia twenty years ago.'

OCTOBER 1976

London, UK

SYLVIA

Sylvia leapt at the sound of the doorbell and then cast a glance at the Moses basket where her daughter lay sleeping – finally, finally. But Jessica hadn't woken. She lay still, her hands flung above her head, her face turned slightly to one side, her breath coming in whispered snores. Sylvia let out a long breath and tiptoed to the doorway, stepping over a play mat, a stack of nappies and a pile of unopened cards and presents. She must open them and reply. And she must clear up. Must do the washing. But most of all she must sleep. Yes, she must sleep.

'How's the little angel?' Maggie whispered when she opened the door.

'Sleeping like a log – for now.'

Maggie followed Sylvia into the front room. 'Oh my

goodness, I love her more each time I see her. Look at those teeny fingernails!'

'She's less angelic at three in the morning.'

Maggie laughed. 'I bet. But still, just *look* at her!'

Sylvia did, and smiled. The first few weeks had been hard – and they still were, despite the fact she had Jessica in some semblance of a routine now. Her daughter was occupying practically every minute of her day, what with feeding her constantly and changing nappies and attempting to keep up with the pile of dirty washing that grew at an alarming rate, so she at least had something clean to put her in each day. Frankly, she felt being a mother was in some ways as horrific as she had feared. When she did have a moment to herself, all she wanted to do was crawl into bed. The skin under her eyes had turned a surprising shade of purple, her hair was usually unwashed and most of her wardrobe seemed to be stained with baby sick. It was fair to say she wasn't dealing with motherhood like those well-turned-out mothers she used to see strolling round Hyde Park with state-of-the-art prams. But that didn't surprise her. None of the practicalities surprised her either – apart from the fact they were possibly even more time-consuming and cumbersome than she had feared. But what *did* surprise her was how little all of that mattered to her when she looked at Jessica. Perhaps, she considered, she'd focused so much on her fears that she'd never thought about the good things a baby could bring. The joy of her first smiles – 'Just wind,' Pamela said, the first time she visited – the shrieks and gurgles that Sylvia found surprisingly delightful, that tiny fist tight around her finger.

'I'm so sorry I missed the opening,' Sylvia said.

Maggie followed her into the kitchen. Her hands were covered in dried paint spots, as per usual. She dismissed Sylvia's apology with a wave. 'Don't be silly. You could hardly help it! But you must come and see it when you're able. The new theatre is amazing, you'd love it. Just tell me when and I'll babysit.'

'I'd love that,' Sylvia said. 'I need to see your sets – I bet they're fantastic.'

'The *Guardian* actually mentioned them in their review!' Maggie beamed. 'I mean, not me personally of course, I'm only an assistant, but I was excited anyway.'

'Oh Maggie, that's brilliant. And one day they *will* mention your name, I know it. You are going places.'

She shrugged. 'Maybe. Anyway, it's a good start. And now the show's opened I have more time on my hands – until we gear up for the next one. So I thought I'd take the opportunity to nip out and visit my favourite new mum and her beautiful bub.'

Sylvia smiled as she poured water into a teapot. 'We want to ask you something, Jim and I.' She carried the tea into the sitting room and they sat down on the sofa, the baby's Moses basket at their feet. 'Will you be Jessica's godmother?'

Maggie put her hands to her mouth. 'Oh Sylvia, I would love to be! I would be utterly honoured.' She drew back, and Sylvia saw her eyes were shining. 'Really, I'm touched.

Gosh, me, a godmother. It's the most important job I've ever had, Syl.'

'You'll be great at it. Everyone needs a fun godmother to lead them astray when they decide they hate their parents.'

Maggie laughed. 'And that's me? The eccentric *faux* aunty?' She nodded, resolved. 'I think I can live up to that stereotype. All I need to do is introduce a teenage Jessica to some of the people at the theatre and I'll obtain instant legendary status.'

'You'll have to stay there a while then.'

She shrugged. 'It's the National Theatre, darling! I've got the job I always wanted. I'm not going anywhere for a long while, I can tell you that. They'll probably have to throw me out when I'm so ancient I can't paint straight anymore.'

Jessica gave a little gurgle in her sleep and Maggie gasped, putting her hands to her mouth. 'Oh just look at her, she's so delicious I could eat her up! How have you and Jim produced such an amazingly beautiful baby?'

'Oh, thanks very much!' Sylvia said, a mock hurt expression on her face.

'You know I don't mean it like that. I just can't fathom how anyone can create such a perfect thing!'

Neither could Sylvia. She still had trouble comprehending this baby was hers. Something that ate and slept and peed and cried. A tiny little human, made from hers and Jim's genes. She and Maggie watched as Jessica stirred in her sleep, flinging her tiny arm sideways to rest against a soft toy Sylvia had bought her on their first tentative trip outside the flat: a brown donkey with a red ribbon and a jaunty look in his marble eyes. Spontaneously, she'd bought the same for Anna's baby, Hedi, and had posted it to Evelyne's flat for her to pass on. She'd had the impression Anna wouldn't be able to give very many toys to Hedi. Plus, she liked the idea that the two of them, born on the same day in the same hospital, would have the same furry body to cuddle in their beds as they grew up. Something to link them to their common beginnings, whatever happened in their futures.

It wasn't the first time Sylvia's thoughts had drifted back to Anna and her baby; they'd occupied her mind frequently since she'd left Switzerland three weeks ago. She remembered finding Anna crying in the hospital, the look of utter desolation in her face. Though Sylvia couldn't tell her so, she'd recognised how daunted Anna must have felt to have a baby to care for, at the age of sixteen, with little money and no family to help her. Though she had Daniel, there was an ingrained sadness about her that Sylvia guessed came from being without close family for so long.

An aloneness.

She hoped it wouldn't always be so. She hoped having Hedi would give her back the sense of family life she lost when she was ripped away from her mother and sister.

'Speaking of beautiful things,' Maggie said. 'Where did that come from?' She nodded to the shiny new electric typewriter sitting on the desk in the bay window.

'Jim,' Sylvia said.

Maggie ran her hands over the keys. 'Must have cost a packet.'

'An investment, that's what he said.'

She'd blamed it on the hormones when she cried after Jim came home with it one day, but actually she was knocked off kilter by his generosity and the message behind it – that he was offering her this beautiful new machine so she could keep writing, freelancing, if she wanted to.

'Any extra cash would come in handy, after all,' he'd joked. But she knew it wasn't about that. She knew he finally understood that, while motherhood had turned out to be far more enriching than she could have imagined, writing was just as intrinsic to her happiness, to her sense of self.

Though right now she couldn't imagine being away from Jessica for one second, she remained resolved to go back to work after her maternity leave was up, to wrestle her job back from Diane. It felt more important than ever to show her daughter that women could pursue the career they wanted.

So she would be a mother *and* work. She would work *and* be a mother.

She would damn well have her cake and eat it too.

It wouldn't be easy, but she would try. And with Jim's support, she would do it. That's just the way it would be.

When Maggie had gone, she sat down at the desk in front of the typewriter and looked out of the window. The trees were moulting, and the heat of the summer felt a long time ago. She put her fingers on the keys, feeling their smoothness, their weight. She looked down at her daughter, still sleeping. There was a pile of washing that needed doing, but she supposed that could wait. She needed to go to the shop before it closed to get groceries, but perhaps they could order take-away tonight. She should sleep, but what difference would half an hour really make? Perhaps, instead, she could use the time to start writing what she needed to, what she felt she owed to another mother in another country.

She didn't know if the material she'd gathered before her trip was interrupted by Jessica's arrival was enough, if the article would pass muster with Roger. But she would try.

She picked up her notebook, covered in shorthand, and flipped back to the beginning.

She inserted a sheet of paper in her wonderful new type-writer and punched a letter: B.

Brigitte.

AUGUST 2016

Vevey, Switzerland

JESS

It's funny how everything can change in a moment. Yesterday my life was a set of memories, experiences and supposed facts that made up my personal timeline. But now I know that another life was running simultaneously in the background all along. A parallel life with different memories and experiences that, but for one snap decision, would have been mine.

I check into a hotel in Vevey. I can't go back to Julia and Michel's place right now. I have too much to think about. I need to be on my own. Plus I have something vital to do. Something I am desperate to do and yet, at the same time, can't quite bring myself to. So for now I lie on the bed at the ridiculously expensive hotel and think, trying to let it all sink in. Somehow, my spinning brain plucks out the

singular, uncomplicated thought that I don't have my tooth-
brush with me.

I turn my head and see the letter Anna gave me, visible
in my open handbag. I can't believe it's there, this physical
evidence of a past I didn't know I had.

A few days ago Anna was a phantom, a mystery who may
or may not exist. Someone rooted in a time so long ago that
I couldn't fathom she could also exist now.

But she does.

I've looked into her eyes that are so like my own. I've felt
her hand on mine. I've got her mobile number saved in my
phone. And now I know Anna made contact with Mum,
that before Evelyne died she insisted Anna tell Mum what
she did – or *she* would. And there it is in my handbag, the
proof that Mum knew, that she kept Anna's secret to herself
for nearly twenty years.

A wave of nausea washes through me to think what that
must have cost her, what burden she must have carried to
know, without telling Dad or me, for so many years.

I can't eat, though it's eight in the evening now. And I
know I won't sleep, though I'm exhausted from the emotion
of it all. So I stand up from the bed, put my handbag over
my shoulder and walk down to the lakeside. It's getting dark,
but the promenade is still buzzing with people strolling in
the mild air. I sit on the wall, sling my legs over so I'm facing
the mountains.

Something about their constancy calms me; these peaks
have been there long before I was born in a hospital down

the road, and they'll be there long after Anna's gone and I'm gone and my convoluted life is remembered by no one. The mountains that have been the backdrop to my mission out here now seem a metaphor for my life. Anna's decision sent two tectonic plates crashing together, altering the shape of our lives forever. One tiny but seismic moment, and so many lives were changed.

I take the letter out of my bag. Despite what Anna said, I'm scared of opening it.

But I do.

It's dated March 1996. I would have been at university then. Mum and Dad, newly on their own after nineteen years bringing up a child. Me, glugging watered-down lager in dingy clubs and going to rowing club socials, not because I rowed but because of the above-average quota of attractive men in attendance. I can't believe this was happening in parallel, while I remained in both such innocence and such certainty about the foundations of my life.

Dear Anna,

I read, and my heart clenches at the familiar sight of my mother's handwriting.

*It has taken me several months to write back to you because
I didn't want to give you a knee-jerk reaction. I am a writer,
you know that, and I don't like to write without thought.
But my God, the thoughts have come tumbling out these last*

months. *I have felt shock, rage, heartache, pity, more rage. I can't understand what you did. But my conclusion now, after all these months of knowing this secret you told me, is that it's done, and the main thing now is to deal with it in the best way we possibly can.*

I want to tell you something. When we first met, all those years ago, I saw how differently we viewed our pregnancies. I saw how full of hope and love you were. But I didn't feel like that. I was scared I'd ruined my life, that I might resent my baby, that I wouldn't love her. But, as we both know, motherhood is a funny thing. Whatever fears and worries you may have, there's always love. It settles upon you the day your child is born and I can't imagine it would ever disappear, whatever happens in our lives.

When you told me what you'd done, one of the many thoughts running through my head was that my biological child had grown up without that intrinsic mother's love. But I've read and reread your letter and I know you love her – the girl you named Hedi – because I feel it in your words. I'm glad she is well, and happy, and loved. My heart breaks that I haven't known her. You've taken that away from me, Anna, and you can't ever know how sad I am. Or perhaps you can, because you've done the same to yourself, haven't you? And perhaps that's worse, if that's at all possible, to have been the instigator of your own pain. I don't know yet if I can say I forgive you; perhaps that will come in time. I promise I will try.

I want to ask something of you that you must agree

to. I hope you'll think this is the least you can do for me: never look for Jessica. When you made that decision in the hospital, you made her mine. Mine she has always been and mine she will always remain. I have never felt such love as the love I feel for my daughter, and I will never give her up, or share her with the person who did. I believe it is best for both girls if neither of them ever knows what you did. So I will never try to meet Hedi — for her sake, for Jessica's sake. And if either of them finds out one day, for whatever reason, then we will deal with that together, as best we can.

I'm sorry for you, Anna. I have never forgotten the lost look on your face at the hospital, nor the things you told me about your childhood. I don't believe that excuses what you did, but it does go some way to explain it. You had no right to act as you did. But the fact remains that I can't be sorry for it, because if you hadn't made that awful decision, I wouldn't have Jessica.

I wish you luck, love and good health, Anna. I wish everything in the world for Hedi. I will always think of her. I will always be willing her to succeed, to be healthy and happy. But I don't want to hear any more. This is the end of it. Our lives touched briefly all those years ago in Switzerland and were altered forever. It's madness to think about it. But it's done, so we will leave it there.

Love your daughter, as I love mine. Be well, be happy.
Yours,
Sylvia

I put the letter down and look out at the mountains, fat tears streaming down my face. She still loved me, despite knowing the truth. She didn't want a different daughter, a better daughter, a more ambitious, sorted, successful daughter, she wanted *me* – and so, I now know, does Dad. It feels like a cloud has lifted and I'm suddenly seeing what's been there all along. I think of how much I adore Léa, how sometimes she feels like mine; I think of Maggie, who has always been like a second mother to me; and I see Anna, who gave me up out of love, but who clearly loves Hedi just as much. Biology isn't everything, after all.

I feel like I've got my life back, and all the history embodied by those family photos is mine to cherish once again. It may not have been the life I was meant to have, but it was mine. However unusual, this has been my place in the world since the beginning. I breathe out a long, shaky breath and feel the tension in my shoulders release, the pressure in my head ease, as relief floods through my veins. And I realise this relief is not only for what's gone before, but for what my future could bring, too.

Biology isn't everything.

What possibilities could be open to me, if only I remember that?

My phone pings and I reach into my bag and fish it out.

How did it go, guapa? Are you ok?

I wipe my tears away and smile. I picture Jorge's face – his unbrushed mop of hair, the amused look in his eyes after he pushed me in the pool – and I think how, during this mission into my past, he's been the only thing that's made me look forward and think about what happens after. About the future.

I text back:

> Can we meet up this week? Because I need to
> go home. I'm okay, but I need to go home.

The cake was a little uneven where Julia had cut off a burnt bit, but it tasted surprisingly good.

'You know I didn't mean you should stay at home and make cakes, don't you?' I say to her, testing our new-found *entente cordiale*.

She laughs, runs her fingers through her hair. 'Actually, Léa made it. She's far better at it than me. But I supervised, and it was fun.' She gives me a wry smile and I know she means it.

'Jess! We got you something!' Léa comes barrelling into the lounge, closely followed by Luca and Michel, a grin on his face. Léa's holding her hands behind her back and when they reach us, Michel whispers something to his daughter and she brings out a pink box with a big white bow and hands it to me. 'For you,' she says.

I look at Julia and she smiles. 'Something to help you remember your time here.'

I tug at the bow and open the box and pull out a large

silver photo frame with three separate photos in it. In one, Léa and Luca are having a water fight in the paddling pool in the garden, me in the background looking on and laughing. I remember that day well. It was in my first week here, one afternoon when Maria was home. I hadn't realised she'd taken it. The second photo is of me and the kids in the mountains; it must have been taken by Michel, just before Luca fell. We're sitting on the grass eating bread and cheese, the lake spread out far below us. I'm red-faced but smiling. Léa is snuggled up to me, her head on my arm. The third is of the two kids alone; they're standing by the pool at Pully getting ready to jump in, both pulling faces and trying not to laugh. I took it myself and Whatsapped it to Julia one day because I thought it was funny – and because I wanted to show her what she was missing out on, I recall with a flash of guilt.

'You've given them some good times this summer,' Julia says. 'They're going to miss you. We all will.'

I look at the photos and feel a lump rise up in my throat. There *have* been some good times, but I've been so wrapped up in my own dramas that I almost didn't notice. I came to Switzerland not only to find out about my past, but for a break from my messed-up life in London, for my Swiss cure. And I know that, somewhere along the way, that's what I've had. As well as mourning my broken marriage, obsessing over Julia's imagined perfection, tracking down Daniel and Anna, I've sunned myself on the most wonderful lakeshore, hiked up mountains to see views I'd never even thought could exist, watched music in the park at the world's most famous jazz festival and laughed with two little kids who got me smiling even when I didn't feel I had anything to smile for.

'I'm going to miss you all too,' I say, 'I really will.'

Léa starts to cry and buries her face in my stomach. 'Don't go, Jess. Can't you stay?'

I shake my head. 'You're going back to school next week. And I have to go home,' I say. 'I have some things I need to do.'

'But you must come back,' Michel says. 'You're welcome any time.'

'Maybe next summer?' Julia suggests. A wave of shame floods through me. After the way I've been with her, after my terrible behaviour and my even worse thoughts, she would still have me back.

'That means a lot,' I say. 'Maybe I will. But we'll see. A year is a long time, and right now I have no idea what I'm going to do to fill it. But I promise I'll come and visit sometime. And you must keep in touch. Send me emails,' I say to the kids, 'to show me how your English is progressing.'

'It's a deal!' Léa grins and gives me a high five, and I'm pleased to see I've clearly taught her something.

Michel carries my suitcase out to the waiting taxi and after hugs and kisses and tears from the kids, I'm in the car and going back to the station, eight weeks after I arrived on their doorstep in the same fashion. I board the train for the airport and make sure to sit on the left-hand side for the best view

of the lake and mountains. I take out my phone and start a
new email. There's still something I have to do.

Dear Daniel,

I'm writing to say goodbye. I have decided
we shouldn't meet, for now. I've thought long
and hard about this, but I think it's the right
thing to do. I met with Anna and she told me
everything. So many revelations. I'm glad I
finally know the truth. I needed answers. But
part of me wishes I had never found out. I'm
left wondering what sort of person I would
be if Anna hadn't made that decision. I'm
wondering what impact a Swiss upbringing
would have made on me, how you and Anna
would have shaped me. I'll never know. But
what I do know is that I am who I am, now,
and that's okay. It's taken me too long to figure
that out, but I got there in the end.

I read the letter my mother sent to Anna.
She didn't want us to ever meet, and I think
I understand why. Mum died four years ago,
but I still have Dad. He didn't want me to
come here to try and find you. I thought he
was worried he might love me less, if I found
you. But now I know he was just scared of
losing me to another father, another family.
And so I've decided I would rather not meet

you, for his sake. We all have to live with the
consequences of what happened back then,
and make the best of it. And the best of it is
that we have love in our lives. I have Dad, the
only father I've ever known. You have Hedi,
and Anna told me how much you love her.
Let's be grateful for that, and move on.

I hope you understand.

Jessica

PS. I really think Linda Keller in the
Gasthaus Hirschen would say yes if you
wanted to ask her out for a drink.

The train pulls into the station at Geneva Airport and I lug
my case off the carriage and up the escalator. At the top, I
look up and my stomach jolts. I can't help a grin spreading
across my face as I understand he's been waiting for me.

'Time for a coffee?'

I check my watch and nod. Jorge takes my case from me
and wheels it towards a cafe clearly designed for tourists, with
its red and white motifs and cowprint armchairs.

'What have you got in there, rocks?'

I shrug. 'Yes, actually. I took some pebbles from the beach
at Lutry the other day.' I know I'm going to put them in a
vase when I get home, a physical reminder of the day I met
Anna – and said goodbye to her again.

He shakes his head at me and rolls his eyes. I laugh. It

doesn't matter that he doesn't understand. Who could? This crazy life of mine isn't something anyone else has. It's mine. Unique. I'm going to have to deal with it on my own. But that's okay, I know now. For the past two years, this search has occupied my every thought. It's infected my life, destroyed my marriage, suspended my career, sent me half-crazy with fear and worry and jealousy and obsession. But now it's over. I have that magical thing – closure – and I'm glad. I don't want to talk about it anymore.

'How was your latest hike?'

'Fantastic,' he says. 'We went over a mountain pass and it was so beautiful up there. I'll send you some pictures, if you give me your email address.'

'Oh, sure.' I fish in my handbag for a pen and scribble my email address on the back of the bill.

He nods, takes the bill and folds it carefully, puts it in his pocket. 'So, is this it?'

'Is what it?'

'I don't know. Switzerland . . .' He waves his hand, gesturing vaguely in my direction. 'This.'

I keep my eyes on him, seeing his awkwardness and enjoying it. 'I don't know. Should it be?' I say finally.

'Well . . .' He looks down, fiddles with a plastic capsule of coffee creamer. 'I just want you to do what makes you happy, Jess.'

I take a sip of my cappuccino and feel my heart race as I formulate what I want to say. Part of me wants to kiss him, right here and now. I don't think he'd turn me down. But the rest of me knows I need some time on my own, to digest the last two months, and that it wouldn't be right to make promises I can't keep.

'This has been a bizarre summer for me,' I say. 'But I've really appreciated having you around to talk to. I really have. You're the only thing that's kept me even slightly sane.' He waggles his head and mock-frowns, clearly disagreeing with my judgement of my sanity. 'Okay, well, you've *tried* to keep me sane. Anyway,' I wave my hand. 'Right now I haven't got a clue what I'm going to do. I have to go home. I have to see Dad, I have to sign divorce papers. I need to spend some time thinking about what to do next. But I hope we can keep in touch and, you know, if you ever come to London, let me know. I have a sofabed.'

He grins. 'A sofabed. I'll bear it in mind.'

I hug him goodbye and resist the urge to look back as I walk away through the station concourse, following families, businesspeople and couples towards the airport check-in lounge.

I walk through the automatic doors and head for departures. But before I join the long queue, filled with people clutching their boarding passes, full of hope and expectation for the journey that awaits, I read my email to Daniel once more and press send.

SEPTEMBER 2016

London, UK

JESS

As soon as I get in the door, I know Patrick was right. It's not like I have the money to buy him out, anyway. But now, standing at the window looking at the rain pouring down outside, for the first time I feel that I want to sell the flat. I'm moving on.

It feels strange to be back in London. The air smells different, and it's damper somehow. Not just when it's raining, like now, but always. My skin has a sweaty sheen, even though it's not that hot outside. My hair, which fell relatively straight during my summer in Switzerland, is back to drying in waves that I would flatten into submission with straightening irons each morning if I could be bothered – eight weeks with Julia hasn't exactly rubbed off. It's the humidity that comes with living on an island, I guess. Funny how I'd never really noticed before.

I open my laptop and click on the internet icon. I navigate to National Rail Enquiries and buy a train ticket to Chichester for the next day. It's too late to reserve a seat, so I know I'll spend the ninety-minute journey standing by the toilets, trying to close my nose to the smell of urine as I eat my sandwich, and for that joy I have to pay more than a plane ticket back to Geneva. Still, Dad's worth it.

I start to shut the lid of my laptop but then stop. I browse to Facebook, hesitate, and then type in the name. There's only one result – it's a pretty unusual name after all. I squint. Her profile picture shows her in some sort of fancy dress, wearing a wig and a mask, and when I click into her profile most of it is set to private.

I feel an impatience rise up in me. I'm not going to go back on my promise to Anna. I'm not going to tell her. But I need to see her. I need to complete my closure by seeing the woman who's the other side of my unique life story, the heads to my tails.

I open another tab, search for 'Hedi Buchs-Wilson London'. I scroll down the page, not sure what I'm looking for, and one link stands out. I click on it. It goes to a charity website, some sort of foundation helping communities overseas. And there's her name. Hedi Buchs-Wilson: Communications Manager, Europe. There's a phone number, an email and a physical address for the office in Covent Garden. I drum my fingers on the table.

I can't just call her or rock up at her office. I want to see her from afar, not confront her. I change tack and log on to

Twitter. If she works in communications then she's bound to have a Twitter account. I put her name in the search box and push away the niggle of jealousy that she's working in a field so similar to Mum's while I was always so rubbish at writing. Still, she is on the dark side of the industry, as Mum used to call PR.

I scroll through the results, discarding a @Hedi_BW in Germany and @HediBuchs83 in Austria. The third profile is hers.

@HediBuchsWil
Communications Manager for
@StapenhillFoundation. Swiss girl in London.
Don't call me Heidi. Views my own.

Again, her profile picture doesn't show her face clearly and I swallow back my frustration. I just want to see her. I read through her latest tweets and suddenly I know what I must do. A colleague leaving. A reference to after-work drinks.

@freddiej are you coming to Henry's Bar?

I know the place.

I check my watch. 5pm. I shut my laptop, put my phone in my handbag. I go to the toilet, pat some concealer on the dark circles under my eyes, brush my hair, apply a slick of lip gloss, take deep breaths. My stomach is fluttering, but I ignore it and walk out the door.

I take the train from Peckham Rye to London Bridge, change for Charing Cross, and walk to the bar. Should I be doing this? Nervous energy propels me forward. My mission has come so far, I have to finish the task I set myself two years ago. I can't not, now.

Henry's Bar is heaving with people and straight away I realise how ridiculous this is. How do I find her when I don't even know what she looks like? I take off my jacket and head to the bar, waiting my turn to order a virgin mojito – I want a clear head for this.

It's 6pm, the start of happy hour. I'm surrounded by office workers letting off steam on a Thursday night and I feel conspicuous in my solitude. Who goes to a place like this by themselves unless they want to get picked up?

I walk around the large, low-lit space, pretending I'm searching for someone, but I don't see her. Then again, I don't know what I'm looking for. I head back to the bar, sit on an empty swivel stool at the end near the entrance and sip my drink. I take out my phone and check Hedi's Twitter feed again.

No more updates.

I wonder if they've changed their minds, if they're going somewhere else. But then I realise that if it's a planned event they'll likely have reserved a space.

'Excuse me,' I shout to the barman. He nods back. 'Is there a table reserved for . . .' I check the webpage, 'Stapenhill Foundation?'

He moves over to the reservations book behind the

counter and looks at it while shaking a cocktail. 'Yes,' he says. '6.45pm, at the back. It's marked on the table.'

'Thanks.' I slip off the stool, pick up my near-empty glass and walk towards the back of the room.

They arrive on time and fill the table with their coats, bags and laughter, clearly on a post-work high.

'Get the drinks in, Danny!' one woman says to a bloke with a ginger beard. He rolls his eyes.

'Gotta make sure he gets his round in, stingy bastard,' says another with a laugh.

I'm only about five metres away, sitting at an empty table, but they don't give me a second glance. I scrutinise their faces, but I don't know, I don't know. I need them to say their names, as they did for ginger-bearded Danny, and I wonder how close I can get without it being obvious I'm eavesdropping. But something tells me she's not here. I just can't see it. I can't imagine any of the women around the table being her.

'Sorry I'm late, I had to go to the bank.'

My stomach turns over as I hear her singsong accent.

'Danny's getting a round in. Put your order in while you can, he's not likely to offer twice!'

'He didn't offer once.' A peal of laughter.

My eyes follow the new arrival to the bar and back again. She takes a seat. Smiles.

'Christ, what a day,' says an older woman with voluminous hair.

'Forget about it. It's nearly the weekend.'

'Oh, I love this song!' A blonde woman in a pink

blouse stands up and starts dancing on the spot, singing along.

'Bloody hell, it's only seven o'clock.'

'Wait 'til you hear her at midnight – her singing doesn't get better.'

'It can't be much worse.'

'Oi!'

The table erupts into laughter and then bearded Danny is back with the drinks on a tray and a round of applause goes up at the sight of him.

I see Hedi – because it must be her – take a glass of white wine from the tray and then she's saying cheers, and I see her trying to look her colleagues in the eyes as she does so, though most of them seem oblivious to her attempts. I know it's her. Not because of her distinctive accent, not because of her Swiss method of toasting, but because of the colour of her hair, the shape of her nose, the slight air about her that reminds me of someone else. Of Mum.

'Are you using the rest of this table?'

I shake my head at the man in the lilac shirt and he gestures to his friends and soon the other end of my table is full and they're talking loudly and I can't hear what Hedi's group is saying anymore.

I go to stand up but my legs feel weak. My stomach is churning and I'm fighting to stop tears filling my eyes because the resemblance is so clear it takes my breath away. A piece of Mum, right in front of me, still walking this earth.

I walk past their table towards the bar and as I do so, Hedi looks up and for the briefest of moments our eyes meet. It's over within a second and she turns away to say something to the blonde who can't sing. But in that moment I see our lives running in parallel. I see her in Mum's arms at the hospital right after her birth. I see her lying in the incubator next to mine, our lives about to be so profoundly altered. I see her with Anna, being pushed along the lakefront in Lutry in a buggy. I see Anna and Daniel telling a twelve-year-old Hedi they don't love each other anymore. I see Mum, a letter in her lap, wondering what her nineteen-year-old biological daughter looks like, what she's doing, how she is. I see all this and I see Hedi now, a successful young professional with fun colleagues and a life she's made for herself in London, and I know I'm glad for her.

I don't feel jealous. I don't want to smash her life apart. And I don't wish I had her life. I only feel sad for her that she didn't know the mother I did, the mother I still love so much, who surely loved us both, just as Anna does.

I think of Mum, Dad and me sitting around at the dinner table in Greenwich. I remember the laughter we shared, the way she hugged me, the way they teased each other, the way the three of us just worked. Perhaps I should have had Hedi's life. Or perhaps I was always meant to have the life I've had. Or maybe that's irrelevant. Maybe life is simply what you make of the hand you're dealt.

I step out of the door into the September evening chill, my ears ringing from the music. I take out my phone and write a message.

Caroline Bishop

Dad, I'm coming down tomorrow, can't wait
to see you x

I stand there for a minute, laughter and music floating out
of the bar, then I turn and walk away.

Author's Note

When I moved to Switzerland in 2013 I didn't really know what to expect, beyond the clichés. Over the years since then I've discovered a country that is as quirky as it is beautiful, with a fascinating history, diverse culture and a unique political system. Just like anywhere, there are great things about it and some not so great things. I decided to write about two contentious aspects of Swiss history – women's rights and child placements – firstly because they interested me, and secondly because I felt they were important issues that perhaps weren't so well known outside the country. While the historical context in this novel is, to the best of my knowledge, accurate, the characters and plot are entirely fictitious. Evelyne's *Mouvement des Femmes Lausannoises* is my creation, though it reflects the aims of real women's liberation groups in Switzerland at the time. The character of Anna is also invented, but her childhood is informed by the documented experiences of the many thousands of children who, until as late as 1981, were subjected to compulsory welfare measures by a government attempting to control people it considered to be living morally unacceptable lives. However, I do not intend to reflect any particular individual experience. There were women who preferred not to have the vote, just as there were many who fought hard for further rights; there were children who had positive experiences of being placed away from their families, just as there were those who suffered far more hardship than my character Anna did. I have also fictionalised certain events, and occasionally changed the name of a place or building for narrative purposes.

Acknowledgements

Researching the historical context of this story was a fascinating task. Particularly helpful regarding the women's liberation movement in French-speaking Switzerland was Julie de Dardel's book *Révolution sexuelle et Mouvement de libération des femmes à Genève (1970–1977)* and the documentary *Debout!* by Carole Roussopoulos. My research into the history of child placements in Switzerland was informed by an exhibition in Le Locle in 2017 and the book *Enfants placés, enfances perdues* by Marco Leuenberger and Loretta Seglias. Thank you to Loretta for meeting with me and answering the many extra questions I had. For the book's UK narrative, Liz Hodgkinson's *Ladies of the Street: The Women who Transformed Journalism* helped me understand the experience of women in Fleet Street before, during and after the 1970s. Thanks also to Shirley Conran for allowing me to use quotes from her era-defining book *Superwoman*.

Acknowledgements

When I first started writing this novel it felt a complete pipe dream for it to be published. This wouldn't have happened without my brilliant agent Hayley Steed, who plucked my submission out of her inbox and was so passionate about the story right from the beginning. Thank you so much to Hayley for making this happen, and to the whole team at Madeleine Milburn Literary Agency for their support. Huge thanks to my editor, Bec Farrell, whose advice has been so insightful, and everyone at Simon & Schuster UK for their enthusiasm and hard work. Thanks also to Julia Weber, whose magical tips on cover letters made all the difference.

I am so grateful to my first readers and wonderful friends Emma Hartwell and Mari 'rhymes with Barry' Campbell, for their support, encouragement and reassurance, especially Emma for managing to remain enthusiastic after reading three different drafts. Thank you to Michaela Dignard and Sylvia Koller for understanding where I'm coming from, to Pat Hartwell, Michèle Laird, Rachel Bender, Heather Radmore, Sarah Radmore Seiler, Anne Delaney and Diccon Bewes for their thoughtful feedback at different points in the process, and to everyone else who has encouraged me along the way, particularly Clare Nicholls, without whom I wouldn't be living in Switzerland today, and Claire Doble, for all those lonely writer catch-ups.

Thank you to Matt Radmore for always encouraging me to do what I want and believing in my ability to do it, even when I'm not sure of it myself. And, of course, for persuading me to move to Switzerland – I'm very glad I did. To my dad, Graham, for inspiring me to write fiction and demonstrating how to engineer the work-life balance that makes it possible – you are the best example to follow. To my sister, Steph, who can always be relied upon to tell me the absolute honest truth about my writing (and everything else, come to think of it), and to my niece Melina, for putting a smile on all our faces. Lastly, thank you to my mum, Joan, for being my fiercest champion. I was so lucky to have you and I miss you every day.

The Other Daughter

CAROLINE BISHOP

A READING GROUP GUIDE

Topics & Questions for Discussion

1. What were the social expectations of women during the 1970s? What barriers do the women in the novel face in their work and personal lives? How do they surrender to or fight against these barriers?

2. Consider the ways female friendship is portrayed. How do women support each other throughout the novel? What happens when they don't help one another?

3. Compare and contrast Jess and Sylvia, particularly in terms of their careers, partners, and journeys to become mothers. How do they feel about their respective situations?

4. Motherhood, especially the right to choose to become a mother, is a central theme of the novel. What does motherhood mean for different characters? Discuss the various ways that motherhood is portrayed.

5. Although Sylvia fears that she will have to sacrifice her career after becoming pregnant, she ultimately decides to have the baby. What do you think led her to that decision? Were you surprised?

6. Describe Sylvia and Jim's relationship. In which ways does Jim support Sylvia and what is the significance of this? How does their relationship change once he learns Sylvia is pregnant?

7. Although Sylvia initially goes to Switzerland to write a story on the women's liberation movement, she discovers so much more during her time there. What does she uncover about the fight for women's rights, the treatment of women, and herself?

8. Consider the assumptions that Jess and Julia make about each other. What is the cause of the increasing friction between them? What do the two women learn from one another?

9. Discuss the secrets Sylvia keeps from her loved ones. Why does she keep these hidden for as long as she does? What do you think might have happened if she told Jess the truth?

10. Reread the epigraphs on pages 3, 125, and 285. What do they tell us about the attitudes of the era? How do they echo the themes and characters of the novel?

11. In the author's note, she says that she wanted to write about the child placements because it is an important issue that people outside Switzerland may not know about. Had you heard of the *verdingkinder* before? What did you learn through Anna's experiences?

12. While the novel is set in England and Switzerland, consider the fight for women to obtain suffrage and equal rights in North America. What is your understanding of that history? In which ways do women's rights still need to advance?

13. What is the significance of the title *The Other Daughter*?

Enhance Your Book Club

1. If you're interested in learning more about the *verding-kinder*, read the BBC article "Switzerland's Shame." It includes several interviews with former contract children, detailing the devastating conditions and exploitation they faced. You can find the article at bbc.com/news/magazine-29765623

2. In the novel, Swiss women have already received the right to vote. Consider watching *The Divine Order*, a Swiss film that follows a group of women as they advocate for women's suffrage ahead of Switzerland's 1971 referendum.

About the Author

Caroline Bishop is a journalist, an editor, and the author of two novels, *The Other Daughter* and *The Lost Chapter*. For the past fifteen years, she has written about travel, food, and theatre for many publications, including *The Guardian*, *The Telegraph*, *The Independent*, and *BBC Travel*. A British-Canadian, she currently lives in Switzerland. Visit her at CarolineBishop.co.uk or connect with her on Twitter @CalBish.

Also by
CAROLINE BISHOP

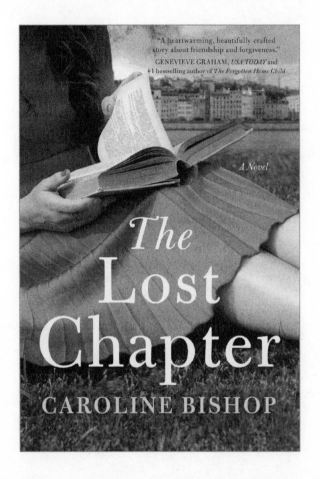

"A heartwarming story of selfless friendship,
and of women who dare to pursue the
road less travelled."

HEATHER MARSHALL,
#1 bestselling author of *Looking for Jane*

SIMON &
SCHUSTER